A MURDER OF CROWS

A

MURDER

OF

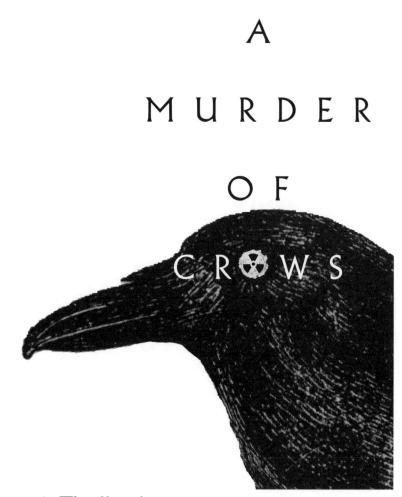

CROWS

A Thriller by
STEVE SHEPARD

LYFORD
Books

LYFORD Books
Published by Presidio Press
505 B San Marin Drive, Suite 300
Novato, CA 94945-1340

Library of Congress Cataloging-in-Publication Data

Shepard, Steve, 1946–
    A murder of crows : a thriller / by Steve Shepard.
        p.   cm.
    ISBN 0-89141-598-X
    I. Title.
    PS3569.H395M8   1996
    813'.54—DC20   96-34808
                                            CIP

Printed in the United States of America

For Martine, of course

Acknowledgments

Many friends and colleagues were kind enough to read the original draft of this book and offer their constructive comments and suggestions. They know who they are, and I thank them all. Special thanks go to my agent Wayne Kabak of International Creative Management in New York and my editor E. J. McCarthy of Presidio Press. Wayne's enthusiam and persistence made this book possible. E. J.'s insights made it better. My deepest gratitude to both of them.

A MURDER OF CROWS

Monday, September 6

George Duval stepped into the sun-dappled driveway and hesitated briefly before pulling on the brown leather jacket he wore on most rides. While the late September heat showed signs of breaking, the skies were cloudless and the warm, early morning temperatures meant a hot day. Duval knew his ancient jacket would be uncomfortable by eleven and unbearable by noon, but he had treated the victims of more than fifty motorcycle accidents and he knew the value of protective clothing. He would suffer the heat.

To his neighbors, Duval looked like the kind of man they would expect to see on a motorcycle. His black hair, pulled back into a short ponytail and his thick, close-cropped beard may have been acceptable in Los Angeles, but here in northwestern Nebraska they spoke of something not quite respectable, something even threatening. Eventually, over time, as the thirty-two-year-old orthopedic surgeon became established, local suspicions had simmered down. Much to his own amusement, Duval was now—two years after setting up practice in Chadron—a thoroughly recognized member of Dawes County's upper bourgeoisie—what little there was of it.

Duval retrieved his helmet from his motorcycle seat and leaned over to kiss the woman who was complicating his life. He no longer denied that he loved her, that she often aroused in him a kind of pleasurable ache he'd not known before. What Duval didn't know was what to do about it. As office manager and nurse, Michelle Falk had become an indispensable part of Duval's practice. His worry now was that she was becoming an indispensable part of his life.

"George, be careful. I mean it."

Duval nodded twice, trying to hide his irritation. "I will, you know I will." Duval recognized Michelle's quiet anger and knew that without opening her mouth that she was sternly rebuking him for getting on a motorcycle. To Michelle, motorcycles were death machines, pure and simple, and people who rode them were fools. Duval tried to ignore the retribution in her eyes as she handed him a black leather carry-on bag that his mother had sent him for his last birthday. It was the size of a small suitcase and came complete with a shoulder strap, a series of exterior pockets too small to be practical, and the nameplate of an outrageously expensive French designer. It had been purchased in Scottsdale, Arizona. Ordinarily, Duval would have found the gift extravagant. It did, however, make an excellent, oversized medical bag.

Duval pulled back the top flap and inspected the bag's contents. In addition to a stethoscope and blood pressure cuff, there were tongue depressors; vials of assorted ointments, salves, and solutions; a 35mm camera; a roll of film; a handful of loose business cards; and a cardboard box that had once contained a ream of bonded typing paper. Duval removed the box, shook it, then faced Michelle. "Are these the x-ray plates?"

"Yes. I put in five eight-by-tens, the last of the plates from the x-ray bin. I didn't think you wanted me to open a new box of fifty."

"No, this will do, thanks. See you Wednesday." He gave her a mischievous wink (which she answered with a short, hurt smile) before turning to walk the twenty yards up the spruce-lined gravel driveway to the secluded house they now shared.

Duval slipped his six-foot frame over the motorcycle seat, secured his medical bag behind him, and with a slight backward twist of his right hand pulled the big Kawasaki out onto the highway. He was tempted to pull the throttle wide open, but the heat shimmering off the blacktop persuaded him to go easy. He had seventy-five heat-soaked miles before him and no desire to break down on any one of them.

By his own reckoning, he had driven the route more than a hundred times. Every Monday for more than two years, Duval left the seclusion of his house tucked inside ten acres of forest-land near the old cavalry post at Fort Robinson, and followed U.S. 20 east along the banks of the White River. The route paralleled the long, vertical face of Pine Ridge, a stark wall of albuminous limestone topped by stands of scrub pine that had once shielded Crazy Horse and other desperate Sioux from the cavalry troops of Fort Robinson. Duval would pass through the city of Chadron where he maintained his main office and continue east toward Hay Springs and Rushville, watching scarred ridges and forest slowly give way to rolling, treeless, timeless open prairie. From Rushville, it was a straight-shot, twenty-two miles north to the small satellite office he maintained in the tiny settlement of Whiteclay on the border of the Pine Ridge Reservation.

Duval, like most who bothered to think about it, found the prairie landscape severe, lonely, and acutely beautiful. While medicine had lured him East, a two-year residency at Cook County in Chicago had given him a stomachful of city life. The rugged land along the Nebraska–South Dakota border had lured him back home.

He swiped at a grasshopper that had smeared his visor and contemplated the day before him. Barring mishap, he would arrive by mid-morning at the old gas station that now served as his Whiteclay office. He would open the doors and wait to see who came by. For a wood-framed building built in 1923, it made a surprisingly good rural clinic. It had a waiting room, two lavatories, a small surgical suite, a consultation room, and a private sitting room that served as the residence of Juanita Muñoz, the elderly Mexican who kept her eye on the place. There wasn't much to watch. Duval didn't like to keep a large inventory of tempting drugs and medicines in such a vulnerable location, but there were some valuable pieces of equipment, especially an old Raytheon x-ray machine that had been donated by the University of Nebraska.

Each Monday, Duval would tend to an assortment of Sioux and others who had fallen from horses, been kicked by bulls, or hit their heads in the dark. Normally, he would close up at six and race home, but tonight he would be staying at the office. Roofers were scheduled to replace the clinic's ancient shingles the next day, and a new water heater was going in Wednesday morning. He wanted to be on hand for both operations. When the heater was in place, he would ride back to Rushville, head south on State Highway 250, then east at Twin Lakes, to see John Left Hand Bull at his trailer house near Big Hill. He would then return home for dinner.

A Russian Typhoon-class missile submarine attached to the Northern Fleet breached the pale green surface of the Norwegian Sea and steamed west at a leisurely six knots. In the brilliant arctic sunlight, the vessel's powerful screws churned the waters into a seething, phosphorescent wake and startled schools of herring and haddock into darting flight.

Six thousand yards astern, the commanding officer of the USS *Oklahoma City* eyed the Russian "boomer" through a periscope. Captain Roland Vandergrift had been tailing Russian missile submarines for the better part of ten years, but he'd never seen one maneuvered so crudely. Since making first contact off Murmansk three days before, Vandergrift had watched with increasing wonder as the big Typhoon did everything possible to draw attention to itself. At odd intervals it had powered up to flank speed, broadcasting a cacophony of machinery noise and propeller cavitation. Three times it had activated its sonar, sending out powerful pings that had screamed its position. Twice it had surfaced in daylight. Whatever the Typhoon was doing, Vandergrift had thought, it didn't mind if anyone else had known about it.

"Surface contact. Bearing three one five, range twenty-thousand yards. Contact designated Bravo." The youthful voice on the intercom was excited.

Vandergrift rotated his periscope forty-five degrees to his right. Even on zoom he could see nothing. Ten miles was stretching it for a periscope gliding just a few feet above the waves. Vandergrift backed away from his eyepiece. "Sonar, this is the captain. What's it look like?"

The sonar operator's response was crisp and succinct.

"Big, sir. Good echo. Motionless. Appears to be drifting."

"A rendezvous, skipper? Tender perhaps?"

Vandergrift turned to face his executive officer. Commander Morton Hackel was only days away from getting his own command, a nuclear attack sub operating out of Pearl Harbor. Vandergrift thought his second in command had all the instincts for being one of the really good ones. "Mort, I haven't the slightest idea what that sub intends. But get videotape rolling and record off the periscope. This whole thing is getting curiouser and curiouser."

At a range of four miles, the gray silhouette of sonar contact Bravo finally resolved itself on the horizon, confirming Commander Hackel's guess. A huge Russian submarine tender rocked gently in the low swells of the smooth sea, its bow pointed northeast. Vandergrift watched the Typhoon come to within three hundred yards of the hulking mother ship, then slow to a stop.

"Sonar shows Alpha contact dead in the water," called the sonar man on duty. "No screw sounds. Sub's drifting with the tender."

Vandergrift eased *Oklahoma City* to a position 4,000 yards southeast of the two vessels and shut down to drift with his prey.

Commander Hackel appeared uneasy with the range. "You want to stay this close, skipper?"

Vandergrift tried to reassure his colleague. "Hell, Mort, he knows we're here. He's been begging us to follow him for seventy-two hours now."

Hackel nodded and turned to look at a video monitor displaying the input from the periscope camera. The tender and the submarine were practically motionless. Except for the large air-search radar rotating from the tender's mast, the television picture might have been a still. Hackel was considering the illusion when something began to stir on the submarine's long, hump-backed deck. His mouth fell open when the immense clamshell doors covering the Typhoon's twenty missile silos began to swing upward.

Vandergrift, too, was startled.

"What the hell are these guys doing?" he asked of no one in particular. He studied the image in the periscope closely, hoping that something in the picture would explain what was happening. Nothing came to mind. He turned to Commander Hackel. "This is too weird, Mort. We can't see squat from this angle. I can't tell if he's got missiles in those silos or corncobs." He turned back to his periscope. "Get a message to Atlantic Fleet and the other regulars. Tell them what we're seeing and see if we've got a bird anywhere overhead. A satellite would get us a lot better view."

Vandergrift studied the seascape in his periscope for several more minutes. He was about to give his eyes a break when he saw a handful of men climb through hatches and stand upright on the submarine's forward deck. Like submariners on deck everywhere, each was wearing a bright orange life jacket. Other than standing around looking to the northwest, they didn't appear to be doing anything. Vandergrift swung his periscope left in the direction of the sailors' gaze and spotted four motor launches heading in a line from the tender to the sub.

Over the next forty minutes, *Oklahoma City*'s Combat Information Center counted 106 men as they disembarked from the submarine and motored to the tender. No American could be sure of the exact crew size of a Typhoon-class sub, but Vandergrift was certain there couldn't be too many men left onboard. It was possible, he thought, that there were none.

"Skipper, we've got an answer from Fleet."

Vandergrift turned to see his executive officer approaching with an aluminum message board in his hand. He grabbed the board, read the message, and nodded. "So, they're giving us an *Aurora*."

"Looks like," answered Hackel, "overhead in about one hour. Amazing."

Vandergrift had never seen an actual SR92 *Aurora*. The plane, developed by the famous Skunkworks of Lockheed Aircraft in the late 1980s, was one of several projects undertaken by the Pentagon during the Reagan years. Although its name had once been accidentally revealed in a congressional appropriations document, the Defense Department had never officially admitted the *Aurora*'s existence and few people, even in Congress, knew much about its capabilities. The *Aurora* could cruise at a speed of Mach 8 and an altitude of 130,000 feet. With a fleet of twenty planes operating from secret bases in Nevada, Scotland, and western Australia, the Pentagon could position an *Aurora* and its surveillance equipment over any point on the globe in three hours or less. Unlike orbiting satellites, the *Aurora* could go anywhere, anytime.

At periscope depth, *Oklahoma City* was incapable of tracking the high flying machine. Vandergrift and his men could only assume that the plane was somewhere overhead when the clock ticked two o'clock local time.

Vandergrift studied his watch and returned his eyes to the periscope. "Well, I hope he's up there getting some nice pictures," he told Hackel.

Hackel started to laugh when Vandergrift, still peering into the periscope, suddenly grabbed his arm.

"Jesus, what in the hell is THAT?"

Hackel turned toward the TV monitor. Geysers of thick, black smoke were rocketing skywards from the open silos of the submarine.

"Detonations! Detonations in the water, bearing three three five, four thousand yards!" shouted the sonar operator.

"My God, Mort. They're blowing it. They're scuttling that son of a bitch! You getting this on video?" Vandergrift asked on the intercom.

"Videos rolling good, Captain," came the response.

"Jesus, Mort. This is fantastic!" Vandergrift watched silently for a few moments, slewing the periscope left and right to take in the scene. He turned to Hackel. "Here, take a look in the scope. I'll follow on the video monitor."

Hackel pressed his face to the eyepiece and whistled.

Vandergrift, calmer now, shook his head gently from side to side. "Damn it, Mort. Where's Jacques Cousteau when you need him?"

Hackel didn't follow and said nothing.

"Greenpeace is definitely going to be pissed about this!" continued Vandergrift, his tone somewhere between shock and amusement. "That's not to mention Friends of the Earth." The captain let out a long, low whistle. "You know how much enriched uranium is going to the ocean floor with that thing?"

Hackel kept his eyes on the periscope. "You think he's still got weapons onboard?" he asked in disbelief.

"No way. They must have unloaded the warheads before they left Murmansk. I'm just talking about the reactor fuel, the rods. That's bad enough."

Hackel backed away from the scope and looked down at a chart of the Norwegian Sea. "It's more than ten thousand feet deep here, skipper. I doubt that stuff's going to bother anyone. Probably safer here than if they tried to store it on land. We'd probably have another Chernobyl."

Vandergrift considered. "Yeah, and no terrorists are going to retrieve that stuff either."

The submarine was settling at the stern, its immense, bulbous bow now angled thirty degrees above the sea surface. The glistening black vessel seemed to vibrate deeply in some final convulsion of death and then slid stern-first beneath the waves. Vandergrift put on a headset and turned a switch to a sonar channel. He listened to the groans of twisting and fracturing metal as the sub raced to the bottom. "Man, what a waste of money," he said.

"Captain?" said Hackel asked.

Vandergrift replied with a puzzled expression. "How can a country where the principal currency is a pack of Marlboro cigarettes send a state-of-the-art, billion-dollar submarine to the bottom?"

Hackel thought for a moment. He hadn't the foggiest idea why the Russians did anything.

Smolensk weighed anchor at noon and began the slow run up Boston inner harbor to the Moran docks. Even in clear weather, movement in the constricted harbor required care, and *Smolensk* would be underway an hour before mooring securely in Charlestown.

Customs officer David McGannon poured another shot of dark coffee into a styrofoam cup and left his dockside shack to wait for the ship. A deep chill permeated the September afternoon air, and McGannon felt slightly uncomfortable as he followed the progress of *Smolensk* on a hand-held radio tuned to Harbor Control. When he finally boarded the vessel with a young assistant, he was relieved to be out of the cold.

As usual with the Russians, the container ship's papers were in perfect order and contained little of real interest. While the vessel had a capacity of 300 containers, fewer than 30 were now aboard. The new Russia didn't have much more to trade with the West than the old Soviet Union, McGannon thought. Russian ships came to America to load containers—not drop them off.

McGannon ran his finger down the manifest pages, noting a thousand cases of vodka and smaller supplies of tinned caviar and smoked herring. There were no fresh fruits or vegetables to inspect, and *Smolensk* hadn't visited any ports where diseases were a problem. That didn't leave much to look at. There were six containers carrying *Sukhoi* SU26 acrobatic aircraft destined for a dealer in Florida, and two containers of Belarus tractor parts en route to a man in Oklahoma who sold Russian farm implements as a kind of curious sideline. Another container, destined for Wyoming, was carrying what was described as a thirty horsepower, light oil and gas fired, packaged firetube boiler. It was built at a factory in Yaroslavl, and so far as McGannon could make out, had been loaded aboard *Smolensk* at Kaliningrad. He was taken aback by its weight. The unit was about seven feet long and three feet across, but weighed in at a hefty 2,800 pounds. He showed the manifest entry to his young assistant. "You ever inspect one of these?"

The inexperienced officer smiled sheepishly. "Sir, I don't even know what this thing is, let alone how to inspect it."

"It's a boiler," said McGannon. "They make hot water to heat buildings and provide steam for industry. Dry cleaners use them; so do dairies, metal foundries, and hospitals. We've had a couple of 'em come through Boston in the last few months."

The assistant seemed unsure. "How come you know so much about them?" he asked.

McGannon sounded reflective. "Because my dad was a janitor at a school. He had two of these things, real giants, in the school's basement. Heating, y' know. They fascinated me, sitting there roaring with fire and steam, giving off these incredible hisses."

"Why are we importing 'em from Russia?"

McGannon considered a moment. "They need the money. They haven't got a pot to piss in, and, if they did have one, it wouldn't work. They'll export anything they can."

"But why boilers? Don't we make boilers in our country?"

"Look, John," answered McGannon in an indulgent voice, "what do you expect them to export—high-definition TV sets? Microwave ovens? Boilers are real low-tech items. It's perfect for the Russians. They've got the technology to make these things and the low wages to make them competitive. Come on, let's take a look at one."

"But Mr. McGannon. Shouldn't we be looking for drugs?"

McGannon almost laughed. Cocaine didn't often enter the United States on Russian or other eastern European ships. The Russians had too much at stake to blow it all on a couple of drug shipments gone sour. McGannon also knew that United States Customs had nowhere near the manpower to perform a drug search on every container or other large object that came into the country. Less than one in a hundred containers coming ashore in America was opened by a customs officer, and that happened only when there was a tip.

Unlike most of *Smolensk*'s cargo, the boiler was not in a container. The heavy cylinder was attached to a wooden pallet and protected from the elements by a canvas tarpaulin. McGannon watched as the machine was lowered onto a decrepit flatbed truck at dockside, and then he instructed the Russian manufacturer's shipping agent to help him inspect it. The agent was joined by a driver, who was on hand to transport the boiler west.

The driver's name was Lazlo Pazardzik—at least according to his trucker's license—and he had documents to show that he had immigrated to the United States from Bulgaria in 1987. In his right jacket pocket, he carried a small VHF transmitter, which resembled a TV remote control handset. It was tuned to a palm-sized receiver that Pazardzik had earlier attached to the underside of a 500-hundred gallon tank of diesel fuel some 200 yards down the pier. The receiver was wired to one pound of C4 plastic explosive.

It took nearly five minutes to pull back the tarpaulin and expose the flat-faced end of a gray, three-foot diameter cylinder manufactured of cast steel. The boiler face included an engraved metal nameplate about the size of an index card and a foot-wide circular door, festooned with various lengths of tubes and wiring.

"That tubing leads to the burner nozzle," McGannon told his new assistant while pointing to the door, "and behind that would be a diffuser and a blower. If you take off that access plate, there," said McGannon, pointing to a small hatch above the door, "you can see that this thing is really just a bundle of tubes."

He took a large wrench from his equipment bag and placed it around one of the five hexagonal bolts holding the inspection plate in place. Moments later the plate was off, and McGannon shined a flashlight inside. "See," he said to his young colleague, "just a bunch of stainless steel tubes. I suppose you could hide drugs in there, but it would take an acetylene torch to get them out."

Dutifully, the assistant peered inside the machine at a large bundle of stainless steel tubes running the length of the cylinder. What he couldn't see were the assemblies of intricately shaped and precisely machined uranium 235, uranium 238, and plutonium 239, ingeniously packed among the tubes and other components. Neither could he see nor would he have understood the carefully packaged containers of a white powder called lithium deuteride or the dull metal latticework of beryllium enclosing molded chunks of polystyrene. With detonation provided by shaped plastic explosives, the hidden ingredients would first undergo nuclear fission and then, milliseconds later, fusion. The fusion would manifest itself as an explosion with the power of 1.2 megatons of TNT.

The assistant found the inspection pretty dull, but, just to sound interested, he asked about the bundle of electrical wiring attached to a harness to the left side of the tubes.

McGannon looked puzzled. Electrical wiring in contact with the firetubes? Inside the boiler? When he leaned forward for a closer look, Pazardzik depressed a thumb switch on his remote unit.

The concussion from the blast ripped through the yard, knocking open wooden crates and shattering windows. Flames immediately erupted from the ripped diesel-fuel tank, shooting thirty feet into the cool afternoon air. Fuel not yet consumed by the fire spread across the deck of the concrete pier and began licking at the bottom of nearby containers stacked four levels high.

McGannon stood frozen, momentarily stunned by erupting flames. The last thing he wanted before retiring next year was trouble. When he finally began running toward the customs shack to summon fire units, Pazardzik ran beside him. "Hey, officer, how about my truck? Can I get it out of here? Am I cleared?"

McGannon didn't understand for a second, then he realized what the man running beside him was asking. "Yeah," McGannon said in a breathless voice, "take it, get it out of here before this fire spreads. You passed, you passed."

Twenty minutes later, Pazardzik pulled his flatbed into a truck stop on U.S. 1 near an oil tank farm. Parking next to another ancient truck transporting a medium-sized forklift, he watched as one of three men in the front seat got out, then approached him. When Paul Gabrovo climbed in beside him, Pazardzik was shaking.

Gabrovo spoke in Bulgarian. "Trouble?"

"Yes. Very close call," said Pazardzik in English.

"What happened?"

"I'll explain later. I think we're okay, but I'll have to contact Ilium Control—and soon." Pazardzik took a deep breath to calm himself down and looked at the large *Rand-McNally Atlas* that Gabrovo held in his hands. "Where to this time?"

"Halfway across the country, I'm afraid." Gabrovo opened the atlas to a section showing the Nebraska–South Dakota border. "We're going here," he continued, pointing at the map, "some kind of base near Rapid City. The route's marked. Back roads as usual."

Pazardzik cleared his throat and switched to Bulgarian. "It's the middle of the damn boondocks for God's sake. Who chooses these locations?"

Gabrovo shrugged his shoulders. He just did what he was told. As Pazardzik pulled away from the truck stop, Gabrovo looked over his right shoulder at the occupants of the second flatbed. One of the men in the cab gave a "victory" sign with his fingers.

In a heavily guarded four-story building near the center of Magnitogorsk in the southern Ural Mountains, a Russian Army Lieutenant Colonel paced nervously back and forth smoking a cigarette. He was located in a dimly lit, soundproof conference room that was electronically swept twice each day to ensure against hidden microphones or other eavesdropping devices.

The room had no windows to the outside world, but a wall of double-paned glass afforded a view of the military officers manning the computer consoles of Ilium Control, located a floor below. The officer's pacing was interrupted by the arrival of Col. Gen. Uri Saratov, director of the State Bureau for Advanced Strategic Research. "General!" barked Colonel Andrei Kachuga while coming to attention.

"At ease, Kachuga," responded Saratov. "Just show me the message."

Kachuga handed Saratov the decoded cable and noted his superior's unbuttoned tunic and stubbly beard. Saratov had apparently been preparing to turn in for the evening when the message came. The message had not been detailed. A complete description and analysis of the *Smolensk* event was not due until midnight. Saratov read the preliminary report, then removing his glasses, folded the message and slipped it into his pocket. "Have the others been notified?"

"Yes. We contacted General Bransk at his office in Moscow, and got hold of Admiral Belovo at his dacha outside St. Petersburg. Neither plans to return here unless you think they need to. The other two generals should be here any minute."

"Excellent. Now show me where this happened, Kachuga."

His aide typed an entry into a keyboard, and an electronic map of the United States appeared on a five-foot square screen at one end of the room. Kachuga made another entry and the map became a blow-up of Boston with an inset depicting the Moran docks. "It was here, about one in the afternoon, local time. About an hour ago."

"They are certain the diversion was absolutely necessary?"

"Yes, sir. Customs officers were nosing around the weapon pretty carefully. They had even removed the inspection plate."

"So what? That would reveal nothing."

"Apparently one of the inspectors had some familiarity with boilers. He was getting very curious."

Saratov walked to the head of a large conference table and took a seat. He removed a pack of Marlboros from a breast pocket inside his tunic and lit it with a Bic lighter. "Anybody killed?"

"No sir. No deaths."

"There will be an investigation, of course. They'll figure out that the diesel tank was deliberately sabotaged."

"Yes. But they'll learn nothing. Fortunately, there's a labor dispute going on. A local union will be suspected."

"Excellent." Colonel-General Saratov scratched his chin. "Anything new on radiation detectors?"

Kachuga almost smiled. The U.S. Customs Service had installed a variety of radiation detectors at a handful of ports in January 1996 as part of a pilot project. The detectors were hand-me-downs from the Department of Energy, not specifically designed for use in a busy port. "We don't know if the Americans are being cheap or stupid, but, amazingly, they have made no effort to expand their pilot program," said Kachuga. "They've got no detectors at any ports we're using. Anyway, their devices might be useful in detecting nuclear material in a briefcase or a packing crate, but they're not likely to be effective against anything that is well shielded. Our weapons are very well shielded. That's one reason they're so heavy. Our informants at U.S. Customs will keep us advised of any changes."

"Good." Colonel-General Saratov stubbed out his cigarette and turned to his aide. "Colonel Kachuga, it was bound to happen sometime. Actually, I think we've been damn lucky so far. How many weapons are now operational in the United States?" He paused to consider. "What is it now, sixty-one, sixty-two?"

Kachuga had already double-checked the count. "Sixty-one, sir. Number sixty-two goes on-line in Chicago in two days. The weapon that arrived in Boston today is sixty-three. It would have been operational by the end of the week."

"Good. Just in time for Pechora, Colonel."

Kachuga seemed surprised. He folded his arms across his chest, trying to appear at ease. "So soon, General?"

"Yes, my friend," answered Saratov with a broad smile. "Pechora gets its first test run a week from Wednesday." Saratov rose to his feet and turned to leave the room. "Colonel, luck has been with us. Operation Ilium has been underway for nearly six months, and this is our first serious incident. We're already almost halfway home."

Kachuga wasn't so sure but wanted to sound positive. "Yes, sir."

"Fax the detailed report on Boston to my home tonight as soon as it comes in. And tell Bransk and Belovo to stay put. Tell the other two to go home if they ever get here." As Saratov reached the door, he turned on his heels and let a serious look cross his face. "And don't look so worried. Soon it won't make any difference what the Americans know."

Wednesday, September 8

The wind blew harder as Pazardzik and Gabrovo passed Twin Lakes. Irregular gusts, some topping forty miles an hour, were hammering against the side of the ancient flatbed truck. The vehicle should not have been on the road. Its springs had lost their recoil, and its balding tires were pounding the chassis through hopelessly weak shocks. An experienced driver, keeping his speed down, might have kept the vehicle under reasonable control as it climbed and descended from one immense sand hill to the next.

But Pazardzik wasn't experienced; worse, he liked to drive fast. As the overloaded truck sped north on Nebraska 250 toward Rushville, it swayed and zigzagged across both lanes of the road, but Pazardzik didn't seem to care. He was more concerned with the man seated to his right.

Paul Gabrovo had been roaring a constant stream of abuse for the last twenty miles, but for every "Look out, you idiot," and "Slow down, you fool," Pazardzik responded with greater recklessness. They'd been driving together for two days and nights, trundling half the back roads and farm lanes from Boston to the Rockies.

The intense dislike they'd nurtured for one another over the past six months had deepened with each passing mile. Both welcomed the thought of reaching their destination by nightfall and leaving each other for good. They were tired of the rough-riding truck, tired of the bad food, tired of the sleepless nights and scorching days and emptiness of the Great Plains. In the last hour, they had not passed a single car or seen another human being.

One mile to the north, cresting a hill, George Duval also struggled with the gusts. At the crest of a hill, he was tempted to turn back, but resisted. For John Left Hand Bull needed attention, and his trailer was only a few miles farther. The doctor continued south.

Going northbound, Gabrovo was becoming terrified.

"Watch out! Watch out!" he yelled as a violent gust briefly lifted the truck's left wheels. Pazardzik stomped down on the brakes, hoping to regain control, but the heavy boiler made steering awkward. The truck lurched, speeding downhill toward a dry riverbed.

Before Pazardzik knew it, he was fighting for his life. The truck tilted right. Some enormous, unseen hand seemed to have lifted the left wheels. This time they didn't come down. Pazardzik jammed the brakes to the floor and turned his steering wheel—to no avail. He watched the yellow centerline snake back and forth aimlessly, and then was struck by the sight of a motorcycle.

They were going to collide head-on. He watched the motorcycle twist sideways, slip over on its right side, then begin sliding along the highway toward him.

Gabrovo was attempting to scream, pushing with all his strength to force one final cry from his lungs, but if he succeeded, Pazardzik didn't hear him. Instead, he recorded the sounds of splintering wood as the truck broke through a weak guardrail of restraining-wires and nosed down a steep, twelve-foot embankment toward the dry river bottom. Pazardzik and Gabrovo both instinctively braced themselves for the inevitable crash.

"Arschloch!" shouted Gabrovo in his rudimentary German.

President Franklin Hobbs Moran pushed aside the pictures taken through the periscope and examined the second batch. To Moran, they looked no different than hundreds of others he had seen: a series of eight-by-ten photographs, some in color, others in black and white, all marked by a grid of evenly spaced, equilateral crosses. He supposed the meanest amateur would recognize them as some kind of aerial reconnaissance, but guessed only experts could see much more. For his part, a move from the amateur to the professional ranks hadn't meant much. He could distinguish aircraft shots from satellite views, could see the difference between real and false color, and might occasionally pick out a highway or some distinct geographical feature. All else was fog. He pushed the photos aside and looked at his National Security Advisor. "Are you sure about this, Rubio?"

Juan-Ramon "Rubio" Pinzon paused briefly before replying. "I don't know, Frank. I *do* know what Owen Caulfield says it is."

Moran's looked irritated. He swivelled his chair in a half circle, faced a large window at the rear of the Oval Office, and conjured up the image of the Director of the CIA. Moran thought the CIA's Owen Caulfield was a dead ringer for Harry Truman, but without the former president's forceful personality. "Why didn't Caulfield come to me Monday when we first got wind of this?"

Pinzon's tone was apologetic. "There were a couple of sentences about it on your daily intelligence summary yesterday, sir. You initialed it."

The president swung his chair away from the window and back toward his desk. The irritation remained in his voice. "Rubio, I initial a thousand things a day."

Pinzon raised his eyes from the notes in his lap and met the president's gaze squarely. "Frank, Caulfield and his CIA buddies didn't want to come to you directly on this until they had some time to study it. And let's face it, the two of you aren't exactly close."

Moran answered sharply, enunciating his words distinctly in a rising tone. "The Director of Central Intelligence spots the Russians scrapping their nukes like a junk dealer and he's worried that he and I aren't pals?" He stared at his desk blotter and crisply shook his head.

Pinzon was defensive. "It's not that at all, Frank. It's just that he thought this information would have more impact if I did the talking first."

Moran pursed his lips and let his breath out slowly, a familiar sign that he was switching from his touchy to his thoughtful mode. The fact was, Caulfield was right. Frank Moran and Rubio Pinzon had been close since their graduate school days at Harvard more than thirty years before. The brawny Kansas farm boy and the aristocratic Spaniard shared a passion for history and politics that had grown into trust and lasting friendship. Moran had sponsored Pinzon's naturalization and was the godfather of his two children. Pinzon had been Moran's Best Man and was one of a handful of people who could comfortably address the president by his first name.

The president rose from his chair and approached a small mirror resting on a bookcase to his left. If some men liked to whittle while thinking, Moran liked to fiddle with his tie. He tightened the knot of the tie his twenty-three-year-old daughter, Sarah, had given him for his last birthday and decided that Sarah's mother would have approved. Ruth Moran had been taken by melanoma ten years before at the age of forty-one, but her image and her taste lived on in her daughter.

Moran brushed back his hair with his hands and briefly surveyed the damage nearly two years in the presidency had done to his face. While the public, even his adversaries, still regarded him as handsome, the mirror told Moran that he was rapidly slipping into old age. At fifty-three, he was still athletic; he carried his 220 pounds well on his six-foot, three-inch frame. His graying hair remained thick, and his green eyes were still sharp and lively, but his skin was weakening and displayed lines and clefts where the muscles sagged. "Like as the waves make toward the pebbled shore/So do our minutes hasten to their end," he said aloud, surprised that the snippet of a sonnet came back to him. He turned to Pinzon.

"Okay, Rubio, I take your point."

Moran returned to his desk, and without sitting, cleared his throat, as if what he was about to say needed to be set apart from normal conversation.

"As I understand it, these photos are supposed to show the Russians deliberately sabotaging one of their ballistic missile submarines, a sub with no missiles onboard. For no reason that we can figure, two days ago they abandoned ship in the middle of the ocean and blew it up. Correct?"

"Yes."

"And they did it right before our very eyes?"

"Yes. They had to know one of our subs was watching them, and they probably knew we had an Aurora overhead. That's why they opened the missile hatches."

"Maybe they're short of cash," offered the president.

Pinzon didn't follow.

The president scratched his chin as if it would stimulate his thinking. "Didn't one of those reports you're always asking me to initial say the Russian navy was in a cash squeeze? Maybe it's just a cheap way to mothball a sub. Send it to the bottom."

Pinzon grimaced.

"Okay, it sounds ridiculous to me too," Moran said. He considered the matter again. "Maybe they're doing it for safety," he added. "From what I understand, their reactor designs are so bad that their nuclear submarines are a greater danger to their own crews than to us."

Pinzon smirked. "We thought of that too. But that big sub wasn't showing any signs of trouble when it steamed out of Murmansk. And it doesn't explain the pictures from yesterday."

Moran paused briefly to look again at the photos. "Okay. Explain these other pictures to me again."

"These are satellite shots," said Pinzon, his slight Spanish accent just audible to a trained ear. "They were taken over the last two days above the Kulunda Steppe in central Asia. They clearly show another batch of SS-18 multiple-warhead ICBMs being taken from their silos. They're being trucked to dismantling facilities near Novosibirsk and broken up, just like we broke up Saddam's Scuds after the Gulf War."

The president turned his hands palms up. "So? Under the terms of the START II Treaty, they're going to have to get rid of these things anyway. What's the big deal?"

Pinzon let a tinge of sarcasm creep into his speech.

"Well, for one thing, Bush and Yeltsin may have signed on to START II, but we're not exactly breaking our necks trying to carry out the terms. Hell, Frank, with the number of Republicans now on the Hill, complying with that treaty will take us years, if we don't renege first."

The president sat back in his chair and again ran his fingers through his hair. He nodded for Pinzon to continue.

"This is not like the Russians, Frank. They're going too fast." Pinzon reached into a leather satchel at his feet and retrieved a notebook-sized laminated card. Printed on both sides in shades of red and blue were silhouettes of generic missiles accompanied by various bar graphs and numbers. The card was a miniature version of a large chart that had been used in numerous Pentagon briefings to explain the details of the two START nuclear arms reduction agreements to reporters.

"Frank," continued Pinzon, "our missile reductions under the START I Treaty won't be complete for a couple of years. At the rate they're going, the Russians will be done with their START II reductions in a couple of months!"

"That's bad?" asked the president in exasperation.

Pinzon pointed to the satellite photos of the missile fields in central Asia. "In a few weeks or so, if they continue at this rate, the Russians will be down to three thousand warheads, maybe fewer. We've still got more than eight thousand. Doesn't it make you wonder a bit? Not to mention ABM."

Moran picked up a pencil and tapped it on the edge of his desk.

"The Anti-Ballistic-Missile Treaty?"

"The same. Frank, if some of those Republicans in the Senate get their way, the ABM treaty will be abrogated and we'll start building phase one of Star Wars, a missile defense system. We're threatening to deploy missile defense systems, and the Russians are destroying their ballistic arsenal? Does that make sense?"

The president fingered his tie before responding.

"All right, so this is all very mysterious. But what really bothers me is the fact that the Russians are being so quiet about it. Why are they doing all this without so much as a peep?"

Pinzon stood up and put his hands behind his back, an old habit from his teaching days.

"Frank, they're not saying anything and they're not asking for anything in return. It's not like them. Hell, it's not even human."

"Are we getting rumblings from the Russian military?"

"Nada. Zilch. And that's also a surprise. When President Turgenev took over for Yeltsin, the military had big hopes he'd slow down some of Yeltsin's disarmament moves. When he didn't, there was hell to pay from the generals and their friends in the Russian Congress. There was talk of impeachment again. Now there's not a word of protest."

Moran rose from his chair and turned back toward the window overlooking the south lawn. He watched a White House gardener digging in a flower bed and was tempted to go help him. He turned back to Pinzon.

"Let's get an informal working group together on this, a little group separate from the National Security Council and its turf-fighting staffers. Call it the Typhoon group." He watched Pinzon take notes on a memo pad and continued. "Let's get the Russian experts. Chairman Greenwood at Joint Chiefs has experience in Moscow. And get Secretary of State Price. How long was she ambassador there? Four years?" Moran paused to consider others.

"Bring in Anthony Novello from the FBI. I know this isn't his normal bailiwick, but I like his mind. Keep the vice president and Caulfield, and the other National Security types up-to-date on everything, but keep them off my back unless I say otherwise. The members of the working group can report directly to me anytime."

"And the Defense Secretary?" asked Pinzon.

"Recovery from a quadruple bypass is work enough. Keep him informed, but let him rest." The president looked at the pictures of the sinking submarine. "It's hard to believe that a country as poor as Russia can afford to send a billion-dollar submarine to the bottom, no matter what the reason."

"Well, it's not a sub any longer," answered Pinzon. "It's just a twenty-thousand-ton pile of radioactive titanium polluting the ocean floor."

Duval heard the crackling and popping first, then became conscious of the low rumbling behind him. For some moments he lay still, numb to all but the bonfire-like sounds and the searing pain across his forehead. He raised his bug-spattered visor with his left hand, touched the ridge above his eyebrows, and felt the stickiness of blood oozing from a deep gash. Further exploration proved more reassuring. He was relieved to see that he could wiggle his fingers. Now for the big test. Straining against the stiffness in his neck, he lifted his head and surveyed his lower body. No obvious damage. Both feet splayed skyward in normal fashion. He tried to extend his toes and to his immense satisfaction saw the tips of his cowboy boots move away from his body. He was not paralyzed.

He heard the crackling again, and it stirred his reawakening memory. A truck. A big flatbed truck. It had come careening out of nowhere straight for him. He had deliberately dumped his motorcycle on its right side, counting on its crash bars to keep his right leg from being crushed. He remembered sliding directly for the truck's left front wheel and watching in fascination as somehow the oversized tire lifted off the roadway and passed directly over him without contact. Amazing, he thought. Absolutely, fantastically, fucking amazing that he was still alive.

Duval eased off his helmet and looked at his watch. He'd been unconscious a couple of minutes at most, maybe less.

He rolled to his stomach to search for the source of the popping sounds. Fifty yards before him, at the bottom of a dry wash on the far side of the highway, scampering flames licked up both sides of the crumpled flatbed truck that had nearly killed him. The truck was pitched downward at a forty-five degree angle, its cab smashed flat against the narrow dry wash's north bank. The driver's door had sprung free and a large, cylindrical tank on the cargo bed was now smashed up against the cab. Duval didn't think anyone could have survived the crash. But if they had, they'd need trauma care.

He scanned the roadway for his bike. It had somehow come to rest on its left side a few feet down the highway's west embankment. He walked toward it as quickly as he could, realizing after a few steps that he was limping badly on his right leg and that his right shoulder was throbbing. The motorcycle was remarkably intact. Its front light was smashed, and the brake lever on the right handlebar had been bent outward, but to Duval's surprise the machine looked driveable. His big medical bag sat in the center of the highway, fifteen yards away. The flap securing the main compartment had been ripped open and many of the smaller contents including his business cards and tongue depressors were spewed across the blacktop, but his camera, stethoscope, and blood pressure cuff remained inside. Duval slung the bag over his left shoulder and eased down the embankment toward the burning truck.

He need not have hurried. The intensity of the fire still raging over the sides of the vehicle kept him yards away, but he was close enough to see that there was nothing he could do. The charred remains of the driver were smashed back against his seat by the steering column. Both of his arms had been pinned against his face, a defensive reaction, Duval figured, to the oncoming collision. Duval hoped he'd been killed instantly by impact. Anything was better than roasting to death. Duval thought momentarily about dousing the flames, but could think of no way to do so and ultimately no reason to.

Driven as much by curiosity as by any sense of duty, Duval crawled up the dry wash's north bank and began limping in a wide clockwise arc to see what he could. To the right of the truck, Duval made out the dark shape of a strangely twisted body lying on the lip of the dry riverbed.

It was instantly clear that his neck had been broken. Strangely, the victim's face was not seriously marred. There were no gashes or obvious contusions and no blood.

Duval reached for an outstretched wrist just to be certain of his diagnosis. No pulse. He reached inside the man's woolen jacket and found a wallet in an inside pocket. Without studying it, he placed it in his own inside jacket pocket, removed his camera from his bag, and took a close-up snapshot of the victim's head.

He then circled back down into the wash toward the rear of the burning vehicle. There, at a distance of ten yards, he raised his hands to shield his eyes from the heat and squinted through the smoke.

The cylindrical object in the truck was six or seven feet long and perhaps a yard in diameter, and it reminded Duval of an oversized, home hot water tank lying on its side. He had no idea what it was. He could make out angled pipes and bundles of wire attached to what appeared to be a circular door at the bottom of the cylinder face and above the

door some kind of access plate secured by large hexagonal bolts. Whatever the object was it looked heavy.

Duval reached for his camera and snapped off two shots of the strange
tank. He stepped to his left and tried to shoot again, but couldn't advance
the frames any farther. Out of film.

He stepped back several yards, unloaded the camera and dropped the
spent film canister into his bag. He retrieved a fresh roll, reloaded, and
looked again at the truck. He thought the smoke billowing from the flam-
ing carcass was nothing more than spent hydrocarbons from the burning diesel fuel, but he couldn't be certain. Reaching in his jacket pocket,
he pulled out a disposable surgical mask that he carried in the event of
dust storms and secured it over his nose and mouth. He was lifting his
camera to shoot when a powerful explosion ripped across the bed of
the truck.

Like a Frisbee, the heavy circular door and the access plate at the end
of the cylinder were blown from their moorings, hurtling only inches
over Duval's head. They were followed instantaneously by a blast of
heated air, which knocked him to the ground. He turned on his stomach, attempting to shield his head with his hands. Debris was still falling
seconds later when he found the courage to sit up and look back. The
first thing he saw was an expanding plume of dark, oily smoke drifting
outward from the ruptured cylinder directly for him. As the smoke rolled
over him, Duval felt the grit of tiny, warm sand-like particles raining on
top of him, suffusing all about in a mist of blinding dust. Microscopic
particles buried themselves in Duval's hair and down his collar and piled
up in irregular drifts at the bottom of his open bag.

"What the fuck was that?" he said out loud, having no idea what caused
the explosion.

When the smoke finally drifted past, Duval could see a twisted mass
of thick, stainless-steel tubing protruding from the cylinder's ruptured
face. The tubes appeared to be welded together in some kind of bundle,
like a load of bamboo. Duval stood and circled to his left. From the side,
the big tank didn't appear damaged at all. The force of the explosion
had been contained by the cylinder's thick walls; only the end had ruptured. Like a cannon, thought Duval, as he took two more pictures of
the cylinder and snapped off another of the dead driver. Satisfied, he
scrambled up the bank and back to his bike. He had no desire to expose
himself to another explosion.

He strapped on his helmet, kicked the starter, and listened to the engine come to life. While the cylinders purred rhythmically, it was instantly obvious that the shift mechanism needed work. Duval could move, but couldn't get the machine out of first gear. He quickly did some math in his head. He could do maybe fifteen to twenty miles an hour without overheating. It would take him at least ninety minutes to get to Rushville, maybe longer.

As he crested the first hill on the route north, Duval momentarily caught a glimpse of headlights in his rearview mirror. They came from a truck topping the ridge line a mile behind him. The vehicle had just started down the long slope leading to the dry wash and the smashed and burning truck. He considered turning back, but decided against it. There was nothing he could do to help, and he wanted to get his damaged Kawasaki to civilization. If the people in the truck wanted to talk to him, wanted to know what happened, they would overtake him soon enough.

Three hours later, Duval eased out of a patrol car belonging to the Sheridan County Sheriff. His right arm was resting in a loosely fitting sling and a bandage covered the fresh sutures across his forehead. Except for the flames which had burned themselves out, the accident was as Duval remembered it. Duval could make out skid marks, snaking back and forth across the yellow centerline and disappearing at the edge of the highway near a torn cable barrier above the crash site. He could see shards of glass from his Kawasaki's shattered headlight and scrapings that must have been made by his skidding motorcycle. The prairie silence was broken intermittently by the hissing chatter on the patrol car's radio and by the cyclic whining of flickering Mars lights on the ambulance that had followed from Rushville.

The two ambulance attendants trotted to the back of their truck to grab a gurney and first aid equipment while Duval and Sheridan County Sheriff Dan Reiner looked on passively. "Whoa, boys, take it easy," called Reiner, "no need to rush."

As the attendants climbed down the slope toward the crumpled truck, Reiner cupped his eyes with his hands, and squinted. He looked puzzled.

"That's funny," said the sheriff, pointing to the accident scene. "I don't see nothing in the front seat."

Duval turned in the direction of the sheriff's pointing index finger and for the first time in hours, took a hard look at the destroyed cab. He was about to speak when the two ambulance attendants scrambled up the slope toward the patrol car. They were panting from the steep climb.

"Well," asked Reiner, "are they still dead?"

The shorter of the two attendants shook his head and struggled to regain his breath. "No, they're not dead, Sheriff. They're gone."

"What?" asked Duval and Reiner in unison.

"Gone. Not there. Skedaddled," came the reply. "There are no bodies down there—dead or alive."

Duval soon learned that the truck's odd cargo was also missing. The strange cylinder, the water tank or whatever it was, had vanished.

And while he would never know it, another item was not where he had lost it. It was a business card, white with gold-embossed lettering. It read in part: George Duval, M.D., Orthopedic Surgeon, Trauma Care, Chadron, Nebraska.

The Washington, D.C., flash had set hearts pounding and nerves jangling even among the steely veterans of combat who made up the core of Ilium Control in Magnitogorsk. Only Saratov and Bransk had remained calm. It required two hours for the detailed follow-up analysis to arrive and be decoded. Saratov sat at the head of the conference table at Ilium Control and read it quickly, before passing it to his colleagues. "Where is this Nebraska?"

Kachuga typed into his keyboard and an electronic map of the central United States filled a large screen on an end wall. Using a mouse on a small monitor, Kachuga pointed out Nebraska State Road 250.

"It was here, about twelve o'clock noon, local time. About seven hours ago."

"They are certain the retrieval was unobserved?"

"Yes, sir. They got everything. They will watch the man who caused the accident, but don't see how he could know anything. So far, the authorities aren't doing anything special that we know of. They will be monitored, too."

General Bransk seemed almost bored by the proceedings. This balding Air Force officer leaned back in his chair and cupped his hands behind his head.

"Why did it take the follow-up truck ten minutes to get there?"

"They had a breakdown, sir. Simple as that. And they say they couldn't contact the lead truck by radio to tell it to slow up. Either someone's radio was not operating properly, or there was some kind of interference."

Admiral Belovo got defensive. "My men did their job, General Saratov. The weapon *was* retrieved."

Saratov rubbed his eyes with his hands, a sign of his fatigue. "I understand, Admiral. I'm not blaming anyone for this. It was bound to happen sometime. So far as we can tell, there is still no security breach. Just two very close calls; one very, very close. What are the odds on that?"

No one spoke.

Saratov sat down, then pulled out a cigarette and lit it. "I assume that a full watch team has been established and a scrub team put on stand-by."

"Yes, General, the watch team is in place," said Colonel Kuchuga, his aide, turning back to the American map. "A scrub team was ordered from here—Denver—to this city in Nebraska. It's called Scottsbluff. It's about three hours from the event site."

"Can the scrub team remain inconspicuous there?"

"For a few days at any rate. The city is pretty good-sized, about forty-five thousand people."

"Good. Keep me aware of any important news from the watch team." Saratov paused, took a deep breath, and slowly exhaled. "Gentlemen, this happened in an awfully remote location. It proves the wisdom, I think, of keeping road movements as far off the beaten path as possible. With luck, we'll get through this latest incident with no problem whatsoever. In the meantime, I'm going to get some sleep. I don't think we need any change in operations for now. Comments?"

Bransk and Belovo nodded in agreement. Zhitnik and Salavat, who hadn't talked since the conference began, kept their silence.

"Carry on then, Colonel Kachuga."

The colonel saluted sharply as Saratov put out his cigarette and rose from his chair, and followed by the others strolled lazily from the room in long, easy strides, as if he'd seen it all before.

Thursday, September 9

The tractor loomed from the predawn mist, churning up clods of red mud as it approached the shelter. Leonid Ushta watched the machine enter the work yard and circle before the fueling tower, and then he walked lazily toward its dismounting driver. "How's she working, Sergei?"

The driver wiped at his mouth with an oily rag and stuffed it into his trouser pocket. "She's working fine, Leonid, too well for a break today." Sergei wagged his finger back and forth as if reprimanding a child. "You'll do your full twelve hours this Thursday, Leonid. This machine isn't going to break down for weeks. It just came back from the overhaul shop last night."

Good, thought Ushta as he gave Sergei a friendly slap on the shoulder. "No problem with the alternator? It's charging okay?"

"No problems. This damn machine is running like a Mercedes. The new mechanic actually seems to know how to fix these things. But don't worry. We'll get word to him soon enough that he's doing his job a little too well."

Ushta smirked. Secretly, it made no difference to him anymore what they told the mechanic. He'd never see him again anyway. He would miss Sergei, though, even if the man was a convicted killer. He'd strangled some smart ass junior officer in Afghanistan with his bare hands, it was said. Ushta liked him for it.

In his four years as a prisoner in various camps in Siberia, Ushta had never worked on a project wrapped in such secrecy. He had labored on an irrigation scheme on a tributary of the Yenisey River and cleared land near the Vilyuy Reservoir, but nothing could compare to Pechora, even the name was absurd. Ushta had calculated that the Pechora River was at least 2,000 miles to the northwest of the camp.

Everything at Pechora was designed to keep the prisoners ignorant. They were not to know where they were or precisely what their labor was accomplishing. There was no contact with the local population—if there were any local residents—and the guards were pure Russian; they used no dialect or accent that might give away Pechora's location. There were no major roads or rail lines, no canals or pipelines, and no maps of any kind. Even the food was furnished with secrecy in mind. If there were any local delicacies, the prisoners never saw them. Their plates were slopped with beans and sauerkraut and beets and potatoes that could have been harvested anywhere from the Baltic to the Bering Sea. Of the 4,000 prisoners at Pechora and its sub-camps spread out over 10,000 square miles, Ushta figured he was the only one who knew exactly where he was and who also had a good idea what he was doing.

Oddly, the authorities had not considered his education. Ushta sometimes wondered if race was a factor. He resembled his Mongolian mother more than his Russian father; in Moscow, as a child, he'd even been called "Chinaman" by his classmates. Whatever the reason, the authorities apparently had no concern assigning an academic with advanced degrees in both geography and geology to a top secret camp. It was their mistake.

The latitude had been easy. Within a month of his arrival, he had taken several measurements of Polaris using a protractor "borrowed" from the local shop. He calculated that the star's angle above the horizon corresponded to roughly fifty-five degrees north latitude, a line running parallel to and roughly 350 miles north of the Russia-Mongolia border. Longitude was more difficult. But a twenty-year-old, lovesick guard had saved him. The guard bragged to Ushta one day about the beauty of his girlfriend in Moscow. "She's a real beauty, huh?" Ushta had asked.

"The best. She could be a model."

Ushta glanced at the guard's watch and saw his chance. "It must be difficult not talking to her."

"I talk to her. We can use the telephone here once a month," the guard replied.

"But if you call her in the morning you must wake her from her beauty sleep. There must be a ten-hour time difference."

"It's only five hours. I call her in the afternoon and she's already up."

Ushta had already begun calculating. Five hours east of Moscow. Russia had 11 time zones and stretched 6,000 miles east to west. At fifty-five degrees latitude, each time zone would be roughly 550 miles. Five zones was 2,750 miles. Ushta closed his eyes and saw a Mercator projection of Russia. Some fifty-five degrees north latitude, 2,750 miles east of Moscow. That would put him close to Lake Baikal, probably to the northeast. For several weeks afterward Ushta studied the mountain range that marked the eastern boundary of the Pechora project. It ran southwest to northeast and was high. He estimated that many of the peaks topped 6,000 feet and one mountain to the north reached higher, maybe to 10,000. That was too high for any peak in the Baikal Mountains on the western edge of the lake and was almost certainly Mount Snezhnyy in the Yablonovy Mountains. He confirmed his theory one day while working at a remote sub-camp on Pechora's southern boundary. There, he saw clearly where the large river bisecting the project turned sharply toward its source in the southwest. Now he was certain. The Pechora project was straddling the Vitim, some 300 miles north of Chita, 400 miles from the Mongolian border.

It was a distance he could make.

Ushta watched quantity numbers rotating on the fueling tank and figured it would take another two minutes for the tractor to be ready. He walked around the machine slowly, checking the four gigantic tires for unusual tread wear that might disable the machine. He briefly studied the rebuilt alternator put in place by the new mechanic and decided it looked good. Ushta would not hazard a guess as to the tractor's horsepower, but estimated that it would compare favorably to a small railroad switch engine. It ought to, he thought to himself; it's almost as big.

The operator's seat was at least eight feet off the ground, enclosed in a heated cab that could be reached only by a series of footrests and handholds. The tops of the tires were higher than Ushta's upraised arms when he was standing on his tiptoes. Attached to the rear of the machine was a winch, driven by the tractor's diesel power plant, and an oversized hitch. The tractor's front, its "business-end" in prisoner parlance, consisted of an enormous bucket, maybe six feet wide, with a spiked blade on its lower edge. It could be raised in an arc extending fifteen feet from the ground upward.

A fellow prisoner, who had spent some time in the West, referred to the immense, olive-green tractor as a wheeled *bulldozer*, a word Ushta did not know. But even if Ushta didn't know its name, he did know how to run it and how far it would go on a tank of fuel.

Drops of frozen water began to splash on Ushta's jacket, and he instinctively searched the sky. The brightening dawn revealed dense, low clouds. Ushta expected the icy droplets to turn to light snow, cutting visibility, muffling sound, and congealing the heavy mud that often hampered work. It was early for snow, despite Pechora's elevation, but as long as it remained a light dusting, Ushta welcomed it.

"Ushta, get moving!" The voice came from a cone-shaped loudspeaker over the yard shack.

Ushta waved his hand in acknowledgment, unhooked the fueling hose, and climbed into the cab. He pulled on a pair of wool gloves with leather palms, threw two levers, and moved the tractor from the yard toward the south road. A minute later he disappeared into the frothy, gray mist.

This day, as he had every day for the past seven months, Ushta would be working alone. That had surprised him at first, but it soon didn't seem so extraordinary. His work required only one man and a tractor, and stationing a guard over him would have been a waste of manpower. Pechora's overseers knew there was little likelihood that he or any other worker would attempt to escape.

Escape to where? Except for Ushta, no one had any idea where they were.

And if they had known, they would have been even less inclined to bolt for freedom. The Pechora project formed a rough rectangle running 120 miles north to south and ninety miles across. It was bounded by the Yablonovy Mountains to the east and smaller ranges on the edge of Lake Baikal to the west. Trekking northward would have led to the Lena River and the central Siberian plateau, southward to the high ranges marking the boundary with the remote, desert regions of outer Mongolia. If the authorities worried little about prisoners fleeing, they also had no fears that lone laborers would slack-off without supervision. Their work was checked on a weekly basis, and anyone falling short of assigned goals risked being returned to the gangs.

Ushta headed the tractor along a crude dirt road connecting the central equipment yard to a section of the project he'd been working on six miles to the south. His job consisted of clearing connecting roads between various storage yards, equipment dumps, and prisoner compounds spread across the southern third of the project. The work allowed him to see more of Pechora than most prisoners, probably more than most guards. He had twice observed the large industrial buildings grouped in a thirty-acre clearing northwest of the main camp. Given the smokestacks, petroleum tanks, and forests of utility poles, the buildings were obviously elements of a power plant. As best Ushta could tell, the plant was associated with a grid of trenches that were being laboriously hand dug by most of the laborers.

The trenches were narrow slits, averaging one to two feet deep and a foot across, that ran for tens of miles in rigidly straight lines. They undulated up and down according to the roll of the terrain, but never veered a centimeter to the left or right. The first time he had seen one, he was hauling an equipment wagon along a narrow forest path and had been startled by the sight of 300 men tearing into the earth with picks and shovels along a line marked by red-tipped surveyor's stakes. For two days afterward, Ushta tried to puzzle out why human power was being employed on a job that could be done much more efficiently and rapidly by machine.

When the answer came, he slapped his forehead in self-contempt. Men could dig the trenches without first clearing wide swaths in the forest. The trenches were invisible from the air! Satellites could pick out the power plant, camp buildings, and crude roads, but it could not discern the trench pattern being stitched into the soil. From the heavens, Pechora would appear to be a reclamation project.

Understanding the meaning of the trenches was more difficult. Some of them ran north-south, others east-west. Taken together, Ushta estimated that they formed several hundred boxes, each approximately five miles on a side. When a section of trench was complete, the laborers, under the supervision of an engineer, would uncoil uninsulated, inch-thick copper wire from huge rolls and lay the wire along the bottom of the shallow slit. The freshly dug piles of earth on either side of the trench would then be shoveled by hand back into place, and the forest floor returned to the vicissitudes of nature.

Ushta's scientific training did not include electricity or electronics. He could not be absolutely certain why anyone would build a power plant to pump thousands of volts of electricity through a grid of copper wire dug into six million acres of forest. He did, however, have some ideas. He was convinced that the project was military, and its sheer size spoke to its importance. If he was right, there were those in the West who would be grateful for his information. Ushta was going to blow the lid off Pechora and he would kill anyone who got in his way. It wouldn't bring back his beloved Irena Mendeleev, but it would be partial payment for what they had done to her.

In a one-car detached garage behind a brick bungalow on North Halstead Street in Chicago, Georgi Rovno and Alexander Onega performed a service check on a large and an odd-looking piece of machinery.

The object of their attention was a large, cylindrical tank some seven feet long and three feet in diameter, lying on its side in a steel cradle bolted to the concrete floor. A bundle of insulated cables protruded from a circular door at the front of the cylinder and snaked through a wooden support to a junction box resting on a large, sturdy table. From there the cables splayed off in different directions. One was attached to a bank of three interconnected personal computers, a second ran to a circuit breaker box wired to the local electric utility grid, and a third twisted through a hole in the garage wall and connected to a rod of copper stuck three feet into the earth behind the building. Other cables attached the junction box to a bank of automobile batteries, two portable generators, two suitcase-sized radio receivers, and a telephone jack.

The men went about their duties with little conversation. When they did speak, it was not in English. Rovno busied himself at the three identical computer terminals, running a program that checked the machines' electronic health and confirmed that the software permanently loaded into their memories was functioning properly.

Onega was occupied with more mundane tasks. He ensured that the batteries were fully charged, that the generators would start automatically in the event of a power failure, and that telephone, electrical, and other connections were secure. Satisfied that all was in order, he turned his attention to security.

The garage was not an inviting target for burglars, but even if it had been, its defenses would have frustrated all but the most skillful and determined professionals. The lone window in back had been bricked up and the rickety wooden planks that once served as a door had been replaced by heavy-duty steel. A series of motion detectors, audio sensors, and other security devices were wired to a silent alarm that ran to the

31

bungalow in front of the garage (and connected via phone line to a security firm in the Loop). When Onega was certain that no one could easily break into the garage, he pulled a chair from a corner and sat down to watch his colleague finish his work.

Rovno opened the lid of a metal box the size of a loaf of bread. Inside was a segmented metal cylinder, wrapped in a series of toothed plastic rings. He removed the cylinder and separated the segments into wheels, each edged by a single ring. Referring to a pamphlet sitting on the desk before him, he manipulated the toothed rings so that various numbers and other markings lined up with counterparts engraved on the rims of the wheels. He then reassembled the cylinder, placed it back in the box, and, after closing the lid, double-checked the connection between the box and one of the computers. He repeated the process with two other, identical devices and when finished he grimaced.

"I can't believe we're still using this shit." He pointed to the boxes containing the cylinders.

"Yeah? What's wrong with it?"

"It's twenty-five years out of date, that's what. The Americans and every other country with half an electronics industry have got all this stuff digitalized, but we're still using the old electromechanical garbage. These things ought to be in some cryptography museum somewhere." Rovno's contempt was not subtle.

"They still work, don't they?" Onega sounded alarmed. "I mean, they do send and receive in code?"

"Yeah, they work. But like anything mechanical they're prone to screw up. They wear down, jam, slip, do all sorts of crazy things."

Onega wasn't sure he followed. He rubbed his finger along a thick white scar running from his hairline to the top of his left eye, then across his cheek to his chin.

"Well, the computers look pretty good."

"They ought to. They were made in Japan. Fujitsu. Our guys just modified them slightly for our purposes."

"They work in Russian or English?"

"English of course."

"Why do you need three computers?"

"In case the first two bags break."

"What?"

"A sexist joke. They're backups."

"Oh," said Onega, not quite comprehending. "So the codes are now loaded?"

"All set, if I dialed in the right numbers." Rovno ran his fingers over one of the computer keyboards, reacted to some instructions on the computer screen, and pushed "Enter." Moments later, the sounds of clicks and whirs emanated softly from the cipher boxes. Five seconds later, all three computer screens went blank. Rovno waited fretfully until at last, at the rate of one letter every two seconds, the screens began to spell out in an oversized format the eleven individual digits of an alpha-numeric sequence. When the last number appeared, all three machines blinked: "Sequence Match. Load is Correct."

"So you got it right?"

"Apparently so," said Rovno, looking at his watch and comparing it to three liquid-crystal-display digital clocks. "Now, let's see if the thing syncs up."

"How will you know?"

"We should know for sure in about a minute. This thing should start an automatic synchronization process at two minutes before the hour."

Onega looked doubtful. "I think I'll stick to batteries and generators. At least you can see what's going on. Beats trying to puzzle out what a bunch of electrons are doing."

At 9:58 AM, the computers, receiving a radioed time code broadcast by the U.S. Bureau of Standards, began to synchronize. Two minutes later, the computers and the radio receivers were in perfect electronic harmony.

"Now what?" asked Onega.

"Now nothing. There's a test scheduled for next Wednesday. We'll come by then and see if the messages got through."

"Messages? There's more than one?"

Rovno answered Onega like a slightly exasperated teacher dealing with a particularly dull-witted student. "There's three. One arms the thing. A second orders it to fire, and a third confirms the fire order. It's called an Authenticator."

Onega didn't seem to understand, but kept up with his questions. "Where's the antenna?"

"Actually there are two of them."

"I didn't see any outside."

"The first one is that rod stuck in the ground out back. The second antenna is right there." He pointed to a length of shielded cable running from the radio receivers to a drain in the floor near the front of the garage.

"That's an antenna?"

"That cable is connected to a drain, which is connected to the Chicago sewer system, which consists of thousands of miles of metal pipe, buried beneath the earth. It makes for a terrific ground wave antenna."

"I thought that radio waves went through the air."

"Radio does. But it can travel on and just below the ground too. Air waves are disturbed by lightning, buildings, changes in the ionosphere— all sorts of things. Ground waves are more reliable. They can drive through anything, and, with enough power, they're next to impossible to jam. Even so, we have a backup system."

Onega nodded again, satisfied that no answer he got would really explain anything. He returned to more familiar ground. "I ran a security test just before you got here. The electronic alarm on the garage doors worked fine. So did the other sensors. The alarm company called back instantly."

"Good. And the old man in the house?"

"Koziak? He said if anybody had been snooping around he could have run them off before the police even got here."

"Has that idiot asked any more questions about all this gear?"

"No. He seems satisfied that it really is some kind of equipment test. He's happy to be helping a couple of 'backyard inventors,' in his words."

Rovno switched to English. "Developing the ultimate widget in your garage is part of the American myth you know."

"What's a widget?

"A thingamajig, a doohickey, a whatchamacallit."

"I thought I knew English pretty well."

"They are words for 'gadget.'"

"Oh."

"In America everybody admires some joker who invents something in his garage and gets rich. Like the guy who invented the Xerox machine."

"If you say so."

"So what does he think we're working on?"

"He believes we're developing some kind of advanced heating system for office buildings."

Rovno almost laughed. "Well this thing can generate a lot of heat."

Onega smirked. "Anyway, he's happy about the monthly rent check for the garage. He should be for what we're paying him."

"Does he say anything about our accents?"

The older man smiled. "You don't have one and you know it. As for me, he thinks I'm Polish. It's not very unusual around here." He nodded in the direction of the tank. "So, this one's on-line?"

"Yeah. A little ahead of schedule by my calendar, but I just do what I'm told, my friend."

Duval declined to shake the outstretched hand of Sheridan County Sheriff Dan Reiner.

"Nice to see you again, George. How's the arm?" Reiner sat down at his desk and patted his own right arm, as if Duval would otherwise not understand the question.

"Actually, it was a shoulder sprain and it's okay," answered Duval, taking a seat to the sheriff's right. "There was no dislocation and the x-rays Michelle took last night showed no breaks or chips. I got rid of the sling because it wasn't helping."

Reiner didn't want to let go. "So, what did Michelle have to say?" The question had a whiff of mockery about it. Reiner suspected that Duval had just taken what Reiner would call a "load of female crap."

Duval said nothing, but his mind fixed on the painful shouting match of the night before. He had called her from Rushville, told her about the accident, then assured her he was all right. She met him at his Chadron office, hugged him, kissed him, and taken three x-rays. They turned out negative. When she could finally see with her own eyes that her lover was alive and reasonably well, the shrieking had begun. How could he—a doctor—get on a motorcycle? How many times had she begged him to get rid of it? What was he trying to prove? Didn't he love her?

When Michelle went into one of her tantrums, Duval's usual technique was to sit quietly and wait for the gale to blow itself out. But he hated the "Don't you love me?" line. Its meaning was obvious enough, its implications dishearteningly childish: If you really loved me, you'd do everything I say. It was one of Michelle's standard lines, but last night his arm had hurt and he hadn't been in a retreating mood. He had looked at her seriously and offered a deal: "I'll get rid of the motorcycle if you get rid of the tattoo."

The devil tattoo, or "the too" as he called it, was an inch-and-a-half high, complete with blue horns and red pitchfork. The little guy looked like a cherub. It was situated in the center of the top third of her right buttock and, in fact, Duval found it rather alluring. He knew, though, that Michelle was moderately embarrassed by the decoration and from time to time when she was harping on something, he would bring it up with a look of mature, adult disapproval. The offer to trade tattoo for motorcycle had been turned down, but at least it had extinguished their blow-up.

"George?"

Sheriff Reiner's voice brought Duval back to the present. He decided to ignore Reiner's question about Michelle's reaction to the accident and instead pose a question of his own. "Sheriff, how many murders have you seen in your time here?"

Reiner was surprised by the question. "Me?" he asked. He considered a moment. "George, I've been a sheriff and a deputy sheriff in Sheridan County for twenty-four years and I've seen maybe eleven, twelve murders. Hell, George, we got a county here twice the size of Rhode Island, but we only got nine thousand people in it. And most of 'em ain't into heavy-duty crime. Why do you ask?"

Duval smiled. "Just wondering about tattoos. Did you know, Sheriff, that most murder victims in America have tattoos? Hell, in Chicago no respectable murder victim would be caught dead without a tattoo. It's practically mandatory."

Reiner pondered the statement briefly and then handed Duval an accident report.

"Look at this, will you? Make any corrections you think are necessary, and I'll get it typed up nice and official."

Duval began reading. Somehow, the story he'd told the Sheriff appeared considerably less intriguing when reduced to police legalese in triplicate form. He read, "subject attempted to render medical assistance prior to seeking help from SCS." He assumed SCS meant Sheridan County Sheriff. It was one of a number of acronyms and coded abbreviations that would mean little to anyone outside the sheriff's or district attorney's office. To Duval, the report seemed accurate as far as it went, but its conclusion startled him. He looked at Reiner with raised eyebrows.

"You mean that's it? The investigation is over?"

"Well, not quite George," answered Reiner in an almost fatherly tone. "Our immediate investigation is complete for now, but the case will remain open. If any additional information develops, we'll follow up, of course. And the State Police will have it on file. I'll make sure Hargrove at the Dawes County Sheriff's Office over in Chadron has a copy."

Duval couldn't believe it. "But you don't know what happened to the two guys. You've got a first-class mystery on your hands and you're dropping the investigation?"

Reiner tried to be patient.

"We're not dropping anything, Doc. Like I told you, the case will remain open. I admit it's not often we get a couple of stiffs walking away from the scene of an accident. But what, George, do you want me to do? I got twenty-two guys to cover twenty-five hundred square miles. We got car crashes, occasional barroom brawls, cows stuck in culverts, and cats up in trees. We can't spend a lot of time trying to account for a couple of dead guys that don't even appear dead."

Duval got the point. "You don't believe me. You think I'm making this whole thing up?"

Reiner rose from behind his desk, draped his arm across Duval's shoulder, and resumed his fatherly voice.

"Not that at all, George, and you know it. But look at it from our point of view. You've been in an accident. You took a good hit right in the noggin'. What did that medical technician give you, 'bout sixteen stitches across the forehead? You, yourself, admitted you were knocked cold for a while and you still seemed a little dazed when I first saw you a couple of hours later. George, if you told me that you'd had an intimate conversation with Eva Braun out there, I wouldn't have been a bit surprised."

Duval uttered a low groan. He studied Reiner's huge frame, shifting his eyes upward from the sheriff's immense belly to his oversized, florid face. "Sheriff, you and I have known each other, more or less, all our lives. You know I don't kid around when it comes to medical or law enforcement matters. I saw what I reported to you."

"I know you saw it, Doc," replied the sheriff with a sympathetic voice, "but that don't mean what you saw was really there. The way we figure it, two guys lose control of their truck, force you off the road, and then slide into a dry wash. They jump out, see you lying there and figure they've killed you. Maybe they're drunk. Maybe they're on the lamb from mortgage payments. Who knows? But whoever they were, or are, they figure they don't need a manslaughter rap or any questions from the cops. Their truck is burning like mad, so it's not like they can drive away. But they can get outta there. They either hitched a ride or took off on foot or maybe were hiding there someplace while we investigated."

Duval folded his hands together and let them fall to his lap.

"Sheriff, crispy critters don't hitch rides. The guy in the cab was gristle and cinders." Duval hesitated and his faced suddenly brightened. "Anyway, even if the two men could walk away, what about the big cylinder, the thing on the cargo deck? How did they get that out of there?"

Sheriff Reiner considered a moment, and then leaned forward on his elbows. "George, who gives a rat's ass about some cylinder. You're talking goofy. Listen, I appreciate your consternation over this thing, I really do." Reiner cleared his throat as if to emphasize that this was his final word on the matter.

"But look. What we got here is an old, burned-out truck sitting at the bottom of a dry riverbed. It's got no people and no freight. We've got no reports of a stolen truck or missing people. What do you want me to do? So far, except for your testimony, about the only crime we got here is improper disposition of a motor vehicle—abandonment. We can't trace the owners, at least not quickly, because there are no serial numbers on the truck and no tags either, at least when we got there. That's another pretty good indication that whoever was in that truck didn't have much interest in talking to authorities and decided it was better to unscrew the plates and head for the hills. Still, we can't exactly make a federal case of that, now, can we?" Reiner stood to indicate the conversation was over.

Duval tried one more time. "But Sheriff, I've got pictures. I told you I photographed the whole mess, the truck, the men, the cylinder. Everything."

Reiner sounded weary. "Tell you what George. Go home and get some rest. When the photos come back from Wal-Mart, bring 'em on by. I don't give a damn about no cylinder, but you show me a picture of a dead man, an obviously dead man, then I'll consider doing more. You show me a body, and I figure we got a problem that needs more investigation."

Duval had no need for Wal-Mart. His girlfriend, Michelle Falk, had developed an interest in photography in junior high school, and, by the time she entered college, she was good enough to earn pocket money as a stringer for Associated Press. When she first met Duval, she was both accomplished with a camera and competent in a darkroom, and it hadn't taken her long to see that the office lab where she developed Duval's x-rays could easily double as a photo lab. At first, Duval had no objections to Michelle's use of the lab in her off hours, as long as she paid for her own developers, fixers, and photographic paper.

But later, when they were becoming lovers, he found himself mildly irritated by her oftentimes strenuous efforts to interest him in serious photography. The fact was that she admired the art of Stieglitz, he preferred O'Keeffe; neither was about to convert the other. She had, however, persuaded Duval to let her develop the few pictures he did take. They were black and white and (except for an occasional shot of a running buffalo or soaring Sand Hill crane) consisted of forensic subjects, usually ghastly wounds shot close-up. Duval knew that Michelle had long thought he had too much of the scientist about him and too little of the poet.

As he got into her car and began the half-hour drive from the sheriff's office in Rushville back to Chadron, Duval, for the first time, was thankful that Michelle refused to drive a stick shift. Her '86 Mercury bore the scars of its many years of service, but still had some engine life and its automatic transmission was a blessing. Duval's right shoulder was now immobilized by pain. Alternating currents of fire raced from the middle of his right collarbone, through his upper arm, into his shoulder blade, and back again. Shifting would have been excruciating. While Michelle's x-rays had shown no fractures, Duval was beginning to wonder. He decided to get a few more pictures just to be sure.

When he pushed open the door to his waiting room, he could smell her perfume. "Hello? Hello? Anybody home?"

Michelle emerged from the door leading to the examination room. "Hi, honey," she answered, as she put her arms around Duval's waist and kissed him beneath his jaw. "Sorry about last night."

He pushed her back gently and shook his head. "I was just going to apologize to you. I didn't mean to be such a jerk. It's just that the accident unnerved me. I took it out on you." He kissed her gently on the mouth.

"Speaking of the accident, how's your shoulder?"

Duval made a face. "Actually, it hurts like hell. I wonder if we missed something last night. Think I could coax you into taking another x-ray or two?"

Michelle nodded. "Sure, but I've still got to cancel some of your afternoon appointments. Luckily, you're not too heavily booked for a Thursday."

"I'll take care of that if you'll take another couple of x-rays and develop them. This pain sure feels like more than a bone bruise."

As they walked toward the x-ray room, Michelle looked back over her shoulder and asked about the meeting with Reiner.

"They think I'm imagining the whole thing."

"What?"

"They think that when I got bonked on the head I became delusional. They think the two guys in the truck saw me lying on the road, figured they had killed me, and took off. The investigation is more or less over."

"But that's ridiculous," Michelle replied.

"That's what I said. Thank goodness for the photos. They'll show two guys who definitely didn't walk away from that accident under their own power."

Michelle helped her lover remove his shirt, and turned him toward the hallway leading to the x-ray room.

"I made some prints from the roll that we developed last night, the one that was in your bag. They're sitting on your desk. I just printed the three pictures from the accident scene, the last ones on the roll. I'm developing the roll that was in your camera right now. I'll get some prints in a bit when I'm done with the x-rays."

"I knew I was right to hire you!" Duval laughed as he patted her on the rump. "Thanks for the quick work." He watched her from behind as she led him down the hallway, and again admired the slim athletic body and the long, jet-black hair. He thought of her blue eyes and wondered about her age. Was twenty-four too young for him? He decided it wasn't and followed her into the x-ray room.

Michelle loaded a cassette into the x-ray machine and positioned Duval's torso.

"You pick out the best prints from the two rolls, and I'll take them to Sheriff Hargrove at the Courthouse downtown. He can have them couriered to Sheriff Reiner over in Sheridan County," she said. "That ought to change his mind." She blew Duval a kiss, stood behind a lead shield, and snapped an x-ray. She then repositioned Duval's shoulder and repeated the procedure.

Duval walked to his office and found three eight-by-ten prints on his desk. He realized immediately that he had made a mistake.

The picture of the victim with the broken neck had been shot too tight. There was nothing in the man's face to show that he was dead. Without a picture showing the relationship between the man's head and his torso, he might just as well have been asleep as dead. The two pictures of the cylindrical tank were obscured by smoke and flames, but the outlines of the cylinder could be seen. Unfortunately, Reiner had made it clear that he didn't care about it. Duval tempered his disappointment with his certainty that the second set of pictures would offer better proof. The man in the truck's cab was definitely a corpse, and any kind of picture would show it.

Duval turned his attention to his appointment book and began making phone calls. As he was finishing with his last cancellation, Michelle entered his office with a puzzled expression on her face. "That's odd," she said.

Duval looked up and watched her scan an x-ray plate. "What's odd?"

"This x-ray is seriously marred. Look."

Duval took the plate and turned in his chair so the afternoon light shining through his office window would illuminate the image. It was covered with hundreds of randomly distributed black spots. Duval pulled a magnifying glass from his desk drawer to see more clearly. The spots were about a sixteenth of an inch in diameter, very black at their centers but noticeably lighter toward their ragged edges. He could still see enough of the x-ray to reaffirm that he had no broken bones, but the poor quality of the plate annoyed and puzzled him. "When was the machine last checked?" he asked.

"It was checked last week. It was fine."

Duval thought again, trying to be helpful even though Michelle knew x-ray technology far better than he did. "Could it be a bad batch of plates?"

"All four plates are from the same batch, the three good ones I took last night and this bad one this afternoon. I took them all off your motorcycle yesterday."

"What about the second picture you just took of me? Is it the same?"

"It's still in the developer but should be ready about now," she said, turning back to the lab. She returned almost immediately with the second plate in her hands and a concerned look on her face. "It happened again," she said, "spotted again."

Duval saw the same curious spots he had examined a few minutes earlier.

"Oh, well, we'll worry about this later," he said, holding up the second defective-looking plate. "I can see these films well enough to know that I don't have a broken clavicle or cracked scapula. I guess I'm just a crybaby. How about my camera film? That ought to come out better. The second roll will show a severely traumatized body. I can hardly wait." He rubbed his hands together, feigning morbid fascination.

Michelle hoped he was just trying to amuse her with dark humor. She was not anxious to see the crushed and charred remains of a human being slowly appear from a blank sheet of photographic paper, but she returned to the lab without comment. She returned in fewer than fifteen minutes.

"That was quick," said Duval, intending it as a compliment.

"George, you're not going to like this." Her tone was serious.

"What's wrong?"

Michelle held up a three-foot strip of unrolled 35mm photographic film. It's just like the x-rays, but worse," she said. "It's screwed up."

Duval took the strip from her and examined the first few frames. The dark spots that had been a mere nuisance on the large x-ray plates were a disaster on the smaller format of 35mm film. Duval could make out the general outlines of the shots he had taken, but meaningful details were obscured beyond recognition. "It looks like a murder of common crows," he said.

"A what of who's?"

"A murder of crows. That's like a gaggle of geese or a pride of lions." He dangled the film strip with his left hand. "If you study the splotches you can see a pattern. It looks like a group picture at a crow convention."

His photographic evidence wouldn't convince the sheriff of anything.

Friday, September 10

Ushta felt a jarring impact and realized he had run over a large rock he might have avoided if he had been willing to run with his lights on in the early morning darkness near Pechora. He stopped the tractor, inspected the tires and was relieved to find no damage. He continued moving forward and soon her image returned.

Irena Mendeleev had been twenty-six for only three days when Ushta first saw her. When she walked into the small conference room at Moscow State University, he presumed she was a secretary to the respected academic he was scheduled to meet, not the professor herself. She was used to the error. When she extended her hand and introduced herself, she burst out laughing at his surprised and embarrassed expression.

Indeed, Irena Mendeleev simply didn't look like anyone's idea of a mining engineer. She stood barely five-feet-two, and Ushta guessed she couldn't weigh more than 105 pounds. When working, she pulled her medium length, blonde hair back into a girlish ponytail, and in her movements and expressions she reminded people more of a gymnast than a specialist in mine technology with a Ph.D. Ushta had been captivated.

Because of his expertise in geology and geography, Ushta (along with a young computer software developer) had been asked to help Professor Mendeleev determine the feasibility of a computer-generated map system that could be used in the extraction industry. The idea, which was the pretty professor's, was to create a computerized information base that would allow anyone to quickly analyze major mineral deposits across the country. Ideally, a viewer sitting at a computerized workstation would load a laser disk labeled "East Siberian Uplands," punch in "coal," and see the location of major deposits on a standard map. More detailed information on mineral quantities, geologic strata, engineering diffi-culties, and other valuable information could be accessed with the punch of a button.

The three of them had formed a solid working relationship. Ushta and Irena Mendeleev had gone further. Within two months they had decided to marry.

In less than a year, the three scientists had formulated a workable de-sign using a Sun Microsystems workstation, a computer-aided design pro-gram from Dassault of France, and some off-the-shelf laser technology from Japan. It would, unfortunately, require a substantial sum of money, especially hard, foreign currency.

That was enough to torpedo the project in the minds of the aging po-litical hacks at the Ministry of Mines. But to the delight of the professor and her two colleagues, the project was appealing to the State Bureau of Strategic Research, operated by the Ministry of Defense. Defense rep-resentatives didn't care much about mineral extraction, but they could easily envision the military value of electronic map databases. The pro-ject was put under military control and transferred to the science city of Magnitogorsk.

At first things had gone well. Ushta and his two coworkers were given the expensive Western technology they had specified and the time and laboratory facilities to pursue a practical, prototype system. They did, of course, come under military authority, which meant that their work was now a state secret, subject to various national security restrictions. None of them cared much in the beginning. They were not then fully aware that it was the Defense Ministry that mattered in Magnitogorsk. Defense set the budgets, provided security, and encouraged the direction of re-search. In every field, from aerodynamics to zoology, Defense maintained its interests. It also ran most aspects of daily life, including the court sys-tem, which it manipulated to resolve everything from spats between neighbors to accusations of espionage.

At the Pechora project, Ushta thought often of those days. He would be mindlessly shoving some mound of earth when visions of his wife would involuntarily flood up from his memory, overwhelming him first with deep grief and soon after with cold rage.

It had all begun at a party.

A twenty-eight-year-old captain named Konstantin Cepka had gotten drunk and begun pestering Irena. Cepka, who served as an army liaison officer between military authorities in Magnitogorsk and representatives of Pamyat, Motherland, and the other extreme nationalist groups, was well known for his coarse and surly behavior and for interfering in scientific questions about which he knew nothing. Irena Mendeleev had attempted to be polite. She smiled, engaged in small talk, and found excuses to walk away when his advances verged on rude. Her best was not good enough. Eventually he started touching her, first a hand on an arm, then an arm around a waist, and finally a not-so-subtle pawing of her breast.

She slapped him, and the room came to an immediate silence. With everyone looking on in embarrassment, it appeared that Cepka was about to strike back before he stormed from the room.

Late one evening four days later, as Irena worked alone at the lab, Cepka burst in, obviously drunk. He beat her about the face with his fists, ripped her clothing, raped her, and left her bleeding and unconscious on the lab floor.

The victim was found by a cleaning woman a couple of hours after the attack and was taken to an emergency room. She was released into Ushta's care several hours after that, and the two of them reported the crime to the police. The police were sympathetic and promised an immediate investigation, but over the next few days it became evident that something was wrong. Cepka was not arrested; no police technicians ever visited the lab or called on the victim with follow-up questions. Ushta went back to the police to find out what was happening, only to be told that without witnesses or corroborating evidence authorities couldn't make a case against Cepka. It was Cepka's word against a mere woman and nothing more. Without much trouble, Ushta learned that Cepka was the son of a former marshal of the Russian Air Force and the nephew of one of the leaders of a growing right-wing movement. In Magnitogorsk that meant there would be no trial.

When she learned that she was pregnant with Cepka's child, Irena began a decline that neither Ushta nor anyone else could arrest. She loved children and had long wanted one. To be carrying a child fathered by Cepka was testing all of her ample spiritual strength, but she could not imagine aborting a perfectly healthy, innocent child. Each day, as her pregnancy became more obvious, she wrestled more deeply with her conflicting emotions, slowly turning inward to the dark, silent recesses growing at the core of her mind. Cepka didn't help.

When Irena would be strolling down a street, arm in arm with Ushta, Cepka would walk by in the other direction. He was polite now, always saluting or tipping his hat to the two of them and smiling broadly as if they were the best of friends. One evening, five months later, as the pair stood at a local bar, he drinking vodka, she bottled water, Cepka came up beside them. Drunk again. He began making small talk and then with a wink to Ushta reached out and patted her belly and said, "Hey, how's the baby?"

Ushta picked up a heavy glass ashtray from the bar and smacked it against the left side of Cepka's head, sending him to the floor for good. The injury was severe. Cepka lost his left eye and suffered sufficient brain damage to ensure that his right hand would shake with severe palsy for the rest of his life. Ushta was taken to jail; his fiancée was sent home to Moscow.

Ushta sat in jail for four months while authorities waited to see whether Cepka would live or die and whether to charge his assailant with aggravated assault or manslaughter. It was during that time that Ushta learned that on a warm Moscow night his fiancée had bathed, put on her best dress, applied her makeup, and jumped from the thirteenth floor of the coop owned by her parents. Death had been instantaneous. She had talked to no one of suicide. Ushta often wondered if she had jumped on her own, or if she had received a little push from certain friends of Cepka. In the end, though, it didn't matter. They had killed her one way or the other. Now, they would pay.

Ushta turned his mind back to the road and, with his headlights piercing the early morning darkness, saw the fork in the road he had been searching for. He knew he was now exactly forty-eight miles south of the main camp, near the southern extreme of the Pechora project. He had worked the location five times before, each time spending a few weeks at the site before returning to the main camp.

In the darkness, Ushta leaned outside his tractor door and surveyed his surroundings. As far as he could see he was, as expected, absolutely alone. He threw a lever and backed the tractor toward the tree line on the right side of the road. There, being careful to keep the diesel running, Ushta set the brake, dismounted from his cab, and walked toward the edge of the forest.

He disappeared among the trees and a few seconds later emerged with a wire cable over his shoulder. He attached the cable to the tractor's winch, climbed back into the cab, and began reeling in an object from the trees. The tractor's engine roared, and the winch squealed with strain as a large fuel tank, mounted on four sets of double tires, inched forward from its hiding place and slowly nestled against the tractor. Like American infantrymen, the prisoners at Pechora called the wheeled fuel tank a "buffalo." It was about a fifth the size of an ordinary highway tank trailer, and it could be hooked to any large vehicle and towed. While Ushta didn't know its proper name, he estimated that during his various stints at the site, he had filled it with more than 600 gallons of diesel fuel siphoned from various tractors. He correctly assumed the tank was just another piece of rusting equipment, forgotten or misplaced by the sloppy military bureaucrats who ran Pechora. Someday, somewhere, Ushta thought, the tank would be missed. By that time, he figured, no one would give a damn and would find it easier to doctor some paperwork than to go look for it.

Ushta hitched the buffalo to his tractor, reeled in the remaining few feet of his winch line, and turned toward the old logging road.

He had experimented on similar two-lane tracks many times before and found them unexpectedly easy going for a rubber-tired tractor. The deep ruts would have bottomed ordinary cars, and the poor traction would have mired anything but a four-wheel-drive vehicle. Neither was an obstacle for his off-road, steel-bladed, earth-mover. Ushta's major concern was the buffalo. He estimated it weighed more than two-and-a-half tons and at first worried that its top-heavy construction would make it vulnerable to tipping. Later, after a few miles of slogging, he became reasonably certain that the buffalo could travel with stability, so he relaxed.

Shortly before sunrise, the tractor came to an abrupt halt against a fallen tree. Ushta lowered his blade, shoved the denuded pine aside, and resumed moving forward. If experience was any guide, and Ushta thought it was, the first 250 miles of his route would be a forest wilderness laced with ancient and abandoned logging trails, running parallel to the valley along the course of the Vitim River. Using a crude compass he'd fashioned himself, Ushta planned to push southwest over whatever logging trails looked most promising while keeping the Yablonovy Mountains to his left. If he could maintain a speed of five miles per hour and keep sleep to a minimum, he figured he'd emerge from the forest into the open pasture and farmland northwest of Chita in two days.

President Franklin Moran swayed slightly backward as the captain of Air Force One applied power to climb an additional 5,000 feet. From the private lavatory of the Presidential Suite, 30,000 feet over Virginia, Moran listened to the steady whoosh of the slipstream beyond the window and, looking at his watch, calculated he would reach Atlanta on time for his annual address to the American Legion.

He wasn't looking forward to it. For a man who had reached the top of the political profession, he was surprisingly ambivalent about speeches. Moran had a gift for speaking in public and had long since recognized that speech-making was as elemental to politics as atoms were to physics. That didn't make him enjoy it. Somehow, every time he spoke to the National Education Association or to some bar association or at a college commencement exercise, he secretly felt like a giant windbag. He wondered how men such as FDR, Reagan, and Clinton had felt.

Moran had not planned on a political career. Growing up on a Kansas wheat farm did not leave a lot of time for daydreaming about the White House, and it was not something that his father, Jules Moran, had ever encouraged. The senior Moran had carefully instructed his only child on the two things he knew best—the demanding work of farming and the passionate pleasures of history.

The local crop dusters were responsible for Frank Moran's second life-long passion. At the age of sixteen, he had learned the joys of aerobatic flying from them. Moran still owned and tinkered with a Pitts S1S biplane. He often dreamt of his return to the world of spins and loops when his presidency ended. He hoped he'd still have the vigor for it.

As an undergraduate in history at Kansas, Moran became interested in politics, and his interest blossomed during graduate work on his doctorate at Harvard. When he accepted an assistant professorship at Kansas, it seemed natural to get involved in local democratic politics. He began with some part-time political reporting for the local newspaper. That gave him insights into journalism that would prove invaluable in the years ahead and also got him an introduction to local politicians. He eventually became a freelance speech writer for Congressman Steve Houghton, then a full-time staffer, and finally, chief of staff in Washington, D.C. When the congressman died in a skiing accident, Moran won a narrow victory in a special election to fill his seat. The Senate came four years later, and after three terms, the presidency. If his rise was not exactly meteoric, it was fast, and more than a few senior Democrats privately resented it.

Moran considered himself a moderate. On social and economic issues, he grappled with the same conundrums and uncertainties that bedevil much of the thinking mainstream. He didn't think capital punishment deterred much crime, but he did think some people deserved it. He worried about chiselers defrauding welfare, but he also knew that without government support, some children would starve. He believed firmly in a strong national defense but was pained by its cost. He admired the efficiency of capitalism but was well aware, as all farmers are, of its very rough edges. But while Moran could see the complexities, he was also a man who could make a decision and live with it. He believed that all political problems, more or less, boiled down to what he called the "Triangle": war and peace, the economy, and race relations. His vision was simple. A president's duty was to protect the country, struggle with this "Triangle," and if possible, make the nation a better place. The latter could be done with bold initiatives or in incremental steps. History had taught him that incremental is usually better. But if his actions were incremental, Frank Moran was not much given to self-absorption or self-doubt. He thought he was doing his job well, and the country seemed to agree.

The president exited the lavatory and made his way to his in-flight office. Rubio Pinzon and Admiral Richard Greenwood, chairman of the Joint Chiefs of Staff, rose from their seats to greet him.

"At ease, gentlemen." The president took a seat facing the two men. "So, Rubio. What are our thoughts on the Russians?"

Pinzon hesitated briefly. "Well, sir, the fact is we haven't come up with much. The CIA's got nothing. No rumblings at all from any of the usual sources. Same with the National Security Agency. Our embassy in Moscow is as surprised as anybody. The National Security Council is gaming scenarios in their computers, but they've drawn a blank."

Frank Moran expressed no surprise or disappointment. "And the Allies?"

"The British are flat-footed on this one. They had no idea what the Russians were doing. The French had some satellite work of their own on the SS-18 deactivations, and actually queried us before we could get to them. But they don't know what to make of it any more than we do. The Japanese are hopelessly out of it in the military espionage world. All three governments ask us to keep them abreast of things."

"Israelis?" asked the President.

"Nothing," answered Pinzon.

The President turned to Admiral Greenwood. "And how about our little working group, the Typhoon group? You or Secretary of State Price or anyone else have any notions about what's going on in Moscow?"

Greenwood was fifty years old, black, and a career submariner. He had risen in the ranks by virtue of his intelligence and a unique ability to inspire confidence in those who served with and below him. No one had been surprised when President Moran promoted him from CNO to chairman of the Joint Chiefs. He responded to the president in a deep voice. "We've met twice since you asked us to coordinate our efforts. Secretary Price has been quietly working her old contacts in Moscow for the last two days and is getting nowhere. She says the whole things is out of character for our Russian friends. I'm afraid I'm also drawing a blank. FBI Director Novello doesn't know what to make of it either. I wish I could offer more right now, but it would only be speculation."

The president poured himself a cup of coffee from a silver service and offered to fill his colleagues' cups. Both men declined. He replaced the service and eyed the chairman. "You believe in national character, Admiral?"

Greenwood seemed to hesitate. "More or less, sir."

"Me too," said the president. "It can be taken to extremes, but different nationalities act differently. I think what's happening in Russia now is out of character, an extreme deviation from the norm. *Non compos mentis.*"

Neither Greenwood nor Pinzon indicated they wanted to speak. The president continued.

"Oh, I believe they're dismantling those missiles. I can see the subs being scuttled. But I also believe it's a sign that something is seriously amiss in the 'Evil Empire.' And I don't mean the economy. The world doesn't need a nation with a couple thousand warheads going off kilter."

Pinzon looked doubtful. "At least the number is going in the right direction."

"Rubio, two thousand or twenty-five hundred or whatever the final number is, they'll still have enough warheads to destroy every city of any size in this country a couple dozen times over. It's not the numbers that concern me here, it's what's behind them."

Pinzon didn't appear persuaded. "Mr. President," he began, "if I told you in early 1989 that within the year the Berlin Wall would be down, and Russian soldiers would be selling their belt buckles in the streets for a pack of condoms, would you have believed me?"

"Probably not."

"And if I said that the Soviets were going to pull their troops out of East Germany and Poland, dissolve the Warsaw Pact, and then dissolve themselves, would you have believed that?"

"No, but there is a difference."

"Yes?"

"Those events were forced on them. They didn't have the money, the ideology, or the stomach to hang on to a collapsing empire any longer. Afghanistan took the wind out of their sails, and Reagan's military build-up was the final writing on the wall. It's not the first time the Russians have made a tactical retreat in the face of overwhelming odds. Remember Napoleon?"

Pinzon pressed on. "So why is this different?"

"Because," answered the president, "they're taking this radical disarmament step without any pressure. We're not pushing them to cut so fast and so deep." He turned back to Admiral Greenwood. "Admiral?"

"Sir," came the deep voice, "I think history has taught the Russians that it's rational to be neurotically insecure. I think it's in their bones to be cautious and steady."

The president nodded in agreement. "Admiral, if I've got my facts right, you served as naval attaché in Moscow in eighty-six and eighty-seven when President Turgenev was a senior lecturer in economics at Moscow State University?"

"Yes, Mr. President. I got to know him when I attended a few of the economic lectures he gave in English to foreign representatives. I was the first American military man he'd ever met and probably one of the few blacks."

"Were you close to him?"

"Not close exactly. But I got to know him fairly well. We talked a lot of economic theory. You know I have a degree in economics?"

The president indicated that he knew.

"We talked a lot, drank a lot. He was trying to figure out the theory behind Reaganomics."

"So were a lot of people," Moran observed.

"Were your conversations taped?" interjected Pinzon.

"Not by me, Rubio. I don't think he was taping either, but you never know who else might have been listening. But remember, this was before he became a big political player."

The president looked across several miles of farmland leading toward the Tidewater and then turned back to Greenwood. "And what is your overall impression of President Turgenev?"

Greenwood eyed his coffee cup momentarily, as if not sure where to begin. "He's smart, very smart. Well educated too, a doctorate in economics, graduate work at the USA-Canada Institute and like you, Rubio, some time at Ecole d'Administration in Paris. He's well traveled, speaks excellent English and French and fair German. He's got some highbrow tastes, especially in painting, but no apparent weakness for money. He's happily married so far as I can tell." Greenwood stopped. When he resumed he was choosing his words very carefully. "He is a very tough man."

"Do you mean ruthless?" asked the president.

"No, if you're asking would he do anything to stay in power. I mean he's a very realistic, hardball politician who can play with the best of them. He is not, however, an autocrat or a totalitarian. I should add, incidentally, that he is very much a patriot. A real Russophile."

"Is he honest?"

"Politically or personally?"

"Both."

Admiral Greenwood seemed to squirm in his seat. "Like many politicians, sir, if you'll excuse me, he's liable to stretch the truth now and then in a good cause. If you mean does he have integrity, I would answer yes, I believe he does."

Moran seemed satisfied, but Pinzon had more questions. "Admiral, what about the men around him? Know anything?"

"I don't know most of the men serving as his ministers. Many of them were plucked from the academic world. They are men of his own background."

"And the military leaders?" asked Pinzon.

"A lot of the senior brass have been bought off, Rubio. Most of the saber rattlers who were up in arms over the START II negotiations appear to have taken the cash and agreed to shut up. Turgenev retired them with generous pensions, dachas, and secure part-time positions in obscure think tanks. It's the younger flag officers, the brigadiers and the vice admirals, that I worry about."

"Anyone in particular?" asked the president.

"Yeah, a guy I've actually met once or twice although I don't really know him well. The analysts at the Defense Intelligence Agency think he's on the fast track up, a real comer. Me? I think he's a viper."

"What's his name?" Pinzon and the president asked simultaneously.

"He's Colonel-General Uri Saratov, and he's the Director of the State Bureau of Advanced Strategic Research in Magnitogorsk. It's similar to our DARPA."

"Defense Advanced Research Projects Agency?"

"Yes, Mr. President. Only bigger, more powerful in the Russian defense scheme. Saratov's pegged for the top job in the Russian military one day."

"What's his problem?"

"Saratov's intelligent, ambitious, and bitter. He thinks the world owes him a lot. I wouldn't trust him with the contents of a spittoon."

"Anyone else?"

"There are a handful of generals and admirals of like mind, sir."

"So, Admiral," said the president, "Do you have any thoughts on why Turgenev would be unilaterally disarming?"

"None, sir," replied Greenwood. "The only thing I'm certain of is that Saratov and a few other hardliners shouldn't be taking it lying down."

"But we're hearing nothing from them," insisted Pinzon.

"That's the problem, Rubio."

The president pushed back from the table and stood up, indicating the meeting was over.

"Admiral," he concluded, "I agree with you. We've got a serious problem with a dog that isn't barking."

Duval signed the last of the Medicaid forms, slipped it into a folder, and dropped it on his desk. He took a slow sip of the coffee Michelle had just brewed and looked at the late afternoon light filtering through his office blinds. For two hours, he had been concentrating on paperwork, hoping that the mind-numbing repetition of the forms would calm his agitation. It hadn't.

"All done, honey?" Michelle entered the room with a pot of coffee held before her. She leaned over Duval's left shoulder and poured him another half-cup.

"Yeah, I think so," he said, putting his left arm around her waist. "Thanks for putting up with me." He kissed the air in her direction.

Michelle sat in the chair facing Duval's desk. "It's really bugging you isn't it?"

He wouldn't deny it: the missing bodies, the spotted film, the sheriff's nonchalance. He put his hands behind his head, leaned back in his chair, and threw his legs on the desk top. "Remember the summer when I worked for my uncle in Omaha?"

"Sure. It was just after you graduated from high school. You needed some money for college and your uncle gave you a summer job at his radio station in Omaha."

"You remember all right. It was nepotism city. Every extra summer employee was related to somebody at the station."

"So?"

"You must have been about nine, Michelle, so you may not remember this. But that summer we had one of our periodic tiger crazes. Well, Omaha did. My uncle's station jumped right on the bandwagon, pop music stations never being known to miss any passing fad. We went tiger crazy. We had disk jockeys named Tiger this and that. We had this big contest to name the new tiger cub at the zoo and we even got the mayor to officially proclaim a Tiger Day.

"Anyway, as part of this insane promotion we even had a tiger truck, this big Ford pick-up painted with yellow and black stripes. My job was to dress up in a tiger suit and drive the fucking thing around town. The thing is, the tiger truck was also our news vehicle, our mobile news unit as we shamelessly called it. So one afternoon I'm cruising the north side of Omaha and I hear this police report of a car accident and a request for the rescue squad. It's down by a reservoir not too far from the Missouri River and not too far from me, so I start my green headlights—my tiger eyes—flashing, turn on the roar, and speed off toward the accident. With me so far?"

Michelle winked.

"When I get there, I see this beat-up Buick rammed against a tree with the driver still in the car. This guy's yelling, screaming his head off in pain, and it turns out that his right foot is just about totally severed at the ankle. I know because I'm the first guy there, except for some twelve-year-old kid who called nine-one-one. Can you imagine what the cops saw when they arrived? The blinking tiger truck's still roaring, and I'm in my tiger suit trying to help this poor moron who's smashed against a tree and screaming his lungs out. I can't do a thing to help. I still have my tiger head on. Anyway, the cops take over and start turning on mechanical jaws to wedge open the car. They're talking about sawing off his foot, so they can get him out of there before the car blows up, when I'm suddenly surrounded by kids and adults demanding that I give them some free tiger tails. This guy's about to undergo amputation, fully-conscious, and the crowd wants tiger tails! I got out of there damn quick and quit the radio station. I learned two things from that incident."

"Which are?"

"I could have done a lot more if I'd been a real doctor, not just some kid interested in medicine. I guess that sealed my decision to study medicine."

"And number two?"

"Always keep your eyes open. Look around you and take stock of your situation, then act on what you see. Don't let the crowd do your thinking for you."

"In other words," answered Michelle, "you don't give a bleep what Sheriff Reiner says, something stinks about your accident and you're going to be a big pain in the ass until you find out."

"Exactly."

"Reiner wants to keep me in my tiger suit, but I'm done with that."

Michelle said nothing for a moment, then changed to an upbeat tone. "So where are you going to start?"

"I dunno. The film, maybe. The spotted film and the bad x-rays. That's one part of this mystery that we ought to be able to solve."

"Okay, I'm game," answered Michelle pouring some coffee for herself.

Duval took his feet off his desk and leaned forward in his chair. "The developing chemicals aren't suspect?"

"No. As I told you, all the chemicals came from the same source. Good film, bad film, good x-rays, bad x-rays, all developed from the same chemicals."

"And there's no batch problem?"

"All five x-ray plates—the good ones and the bad ones—were from the same batch. I can't speak for the film. But honestly, George, when was the last time you got a defective roll of film that turned out spotted?"

"Touché." Duval scratched the top of his head, reminding Michelle of a monkey. "You're certain the x-ray machine is in order?"

"It's fine."

"And my camera?"

"I looked at it again this morning. There's nothing wrong with it."

Duval was stumped. For a professional diagnostician, it was embarrassing. He stroked his beard and leaned back in his seat. "Let's start from the top. Tell me what you did with the x-rays and the films from the beginning."

Michelle showed a flicker of impatience but decided to indulge her lover. "Walter Steinbach brought your motorcycle back to the office in his pick-up about five-thirty Wednesday afternoon, about an hour before you got back from the accident. I was waiting for him, so I could develop the two rolls of film like you asked me to. I retrieved your bag, which was a jumbled-up mess inside, and dropped it on the counter next to the x-ray bin in the lab." Michelle stopped to recall events exactly. She took another sip of coffee and continued. "I prepared some photochemicals and snapped off the lights. I then opened the top of the x-ray bin, figuring I'd remove your plates from the bag and replace them in the bin. That's when all hell broke loose."

"What?"

"I turned your bag over on the counter to dump everything out, and it created a dust storm. There must have been an inch of dust in the bottom of your bag. Big plumes of dust started billowing and blowing everywhere, in my hair, into the bin, all over the floor. A real mess. Okay, so far?"

"Just fine. Go on."

"Mind you, I couldn't see any of this with the lights off, but I could feel the dust swirling all over the place. To make a long story short, I took the x-ray plates out of the box, tried to wave the dust off them, and stuck them back in the x-ray bin and closed the lid. I pulled your photo film from its reel, dropped it into the developer can, and turned on the lights. I cleaned up the mess. That's it."

"What about the film in my camera?"

"Oh, I almost forgot. I was cleaning off the camera, waiting for the first roll to develop, when I realized the camera was still loaded. I flipped off the lights, unloaded the camera, and was pulling the film from its reel when I heard you come in the front door. I dropped the exposed film into the x-ray bin and came out to see how you had survived the accident. I didn't develop that roll until yesterday afternoon, as you know."

Duval closed his eyes to contemplate. "Could the dust have messed up the film?"

Michelle considered a moment. "I don't think so. Maybe it would have made the film or plates a little hazy, but I don't think it could account for the heavy spotting. It was very fine dust. Anyway, all the x-rays and both rolls of film were exposed to the same dust."

"What happened next?" Duval thought he sounded like the district attorney in a Perry Mason case.

"Wednesday? Nothing. About a half hour after you got back from the accident, I took three of the x-ray plates from the bin, loaded them into cassettes, and shot three pictures of your shoulder. They came out fine."

Duval rested his chin on his right fist. "So, if I understand you correctly, the *only* difference between the good films and x-rays and the spotted ones is that the good ones were developed Wednesday night and the spotted ones Thursday afternoon."

Michelle knitted her brows in thought. "Come to think of it, that's right."

Duval contemplated a clock on the far wall, watching its electrically powered second hand sweep from three to nine. There was something about the clock, but it eluded him for nearly a minute. When he finally spoke, it was a single word. "Time."

"Time?" responded Michelle.

"Yes. The film and x-ray plates you developed yesterday afternoon must have been exposed to something, probably the dust, a good seventeen or eighteen hours longer than the ones you processed Wednesday night. There must be some chemical in the dust that only affects film after seventeen or eighteen hours."

Michelle was tired of the whole thing and could not stifle a yawn.

Duval saw it was time to quit. "Tell you what. I'll treat you to a nice romantic dinner, then let's ride over to Sheridan County and check out the accident site."

"Tonight? It will be dark."

"Come on. Humor me. Sometimes you can see things at night that you can't see in the daytime."

"Yeah? Like what?"

"Like bats and raccoons and opossums. And the little slivers of sparkling glass in the blacktop of a highway."

It was a cloudless night, but, when they reached the accident site three hours later, the moon had not yet risen and the available starlight was sufficient only to silhouette large objects. Duval grabbed a flashlight, and taking Michelle by the hand, stepped gingerly down the bank of the dry riverbed toward the charred remains of the truck. Both noted the absolutely still air and, except for their footsteps, the silence. For some inexplicable reason, they spoke to each other in whispers, as if they were surreptitiously violating someone's private property. "When are they going to move it?" asked Michelle, looking at the truck.

"Out here? Hell, maybe never. What difference does it make? Just another burned-out wreck."

Michelle felt strangely cold and increasingly uneasy. She wanted to get back to the car. "Now, just what are we looking for, George?"

"I don't really know, honey. Anything that seems unusual, interesting. Anything that could screw up photographic emulsions."

Michelle thought Duval was starting to fixate on the film, but said nothing.

Duval, oblivious to her thoughts, shined his flashlight over the charred cargo bed of the truck when the sound of a distinct "crack" broke the silence behind them. They both turned instinctively toward the noise, and Duval panned the sagebrush with his flashlight. There was nothing there.

"What was that, George?" Michelle said sharply, in a normal voice, while clinging tightly to Duval's right arm.

"I don't know," he replied, sounding genuinely puzzled. "It sounded like someone stepping on a dry twig."

"This place is creepy, George."

Duval took a long slow breath, exhaling through pursed lips. It calmed him. "Hell, we're just scaring ourselves, honey. We're letting our imaginations work overtime. Let's look around some more now that we're here." Duval put his arm around Michelle's shoulder and turned her so they were both facing the charred bed of the wrecked truck. In the beam of the flashlight, the bed appeared to be dusted by a white film. It was a powder, fine as talcum, and was spread randomly in paper-thin swirls over the blackened floorboards. Duval looked at Michelle. "What's that stuff?"

She shook her head in ignorance. "Taste it," she suggested.

"No way. It could be curare for all I know." He pulled a credit card from his wallet and using it as a broom, swept some of the powder into a used envelope Michelle found in her jacket.

"Now what?" she asked.

"Let's walk around this hulk one time." They were again speaking in whispers. They were inching forward at the back of the truck when they realized they were treading on a thin carpet of rust-colored material the

consistency of coarse sugar. The debris fanned out from the truck in a
thirty-foot arc, as if it had been ejected from a shotgun barrel. Duval
repeated his credit card trick and was surprised at the material's weight.
It had the density of wet sand, although as far as he could tell it was
not moist.

"Crack."

The sound was the same as before, but closer. It wasn't their imagination. Duval wished he had a gun. Without a word, he turned toward
the highway and began scrambling out of the riverbed, Michelle directly
in front of him. They were relieved to get to the car.

"George, the door's locked!"

They hadn't locked the car. Duval tried the driver's door, but it
wouldn't open.

"George, somebody's been in this car!"

"Or is still in there," he whispered. He shined his flashlight inside, but
couldn't see anyone. When he forced himself to calm down he realized
he had the car keys in his pocket. He inserted them into the lock, let himself in, and unlocked Michelle's side. Seconds later the car roared to life,
and they were gone. They said nothing for several minutes.

She spoke first. "George, there *was* someone out there."

"I know, honey. I know."

The black Buick limousine sped across the dark, rain-splattered run-
way and through the open doors at the south end of the hangar at Andrews Air Force Base in suburban Maryland. Rubio Pinzon stepped out,
adjusted his eyes to the light, and stared silently at the tiny, white biplane
parked in a corner beneath the wing of an Air Force KC10 tanker. Two
men in gray coveralls were bent over the plane's open engine compartment. One of them was President Frank Moran.

"Mr. President," said Pinzon as he approached.

Frank Moran turned and smiled. In his right hand he held a spark plug
and, in his left hand, a plug puller.

"Hi, Rubio. Thanks for coming all the way out to Andrews so late. The
suburban Maryland air will do you good. Have you met Petty Officer
Reichart?" The two men shook hands. "Thanks for the help, Reichart,"
continued the president. "Why don't you get home to your family?"

Reichart saluted. He packed some tools in a box, then walked away.

Pinzon looked at the president. "I'd think you'd have had enough of
airplanes for one day. Wasn't four hours on Air Force One enough?" Pin-

zon put his hands on his hips. "I can't believe they still let you play around with these things."

The president's Pitts Special aerobatic biplane gleamed white in the hangar's lights. Moran patted it lovingly, like a jockey admiring a horse. "Well, it's not like they actually let me fly it anymore. And anyway, they can hardly keep me from fooling around with a set of wrenches."

Moran was not a great aerobatic pilot, but he was a competent one. At the age of forty-eight, while still serving in the Senate, he had actually finished in the top five in a couple of local aerobatic competitions. He'd voluntarily retired from flying when he won the White House, figuring that the stock market would have a collective heart attack every time some camera caught him doing a loop or a spin. Now he was content with maintenance. It was better than golf. He turned to his advisor.

"Here, Rubio, help me with this spark plug." The president handed the plug to Pinzon who eyed it with the suspicion and distaste of someone who doesn't like machines. "Mixture's too rich. Plugs are fouling," said the president, turning back to the engine.

"How do you know if you don't fly it, Frank?" asked Pinzon.

"I can't fly it, Rubio, but that doesn't mean I can't taxi it around Andrews. But enough of planes. You've got some news I hear?" Moran continued working while he listened.

"Turgenev wants a meeting." Pinzon said it in a matter-of-fact tone, as if such requests were routine. "And he wants it quickly—two weeks from today."

Moran raised his free right hand to signal "stop," but kept his eyes on the engine. "So, they finally want to talk. Of course, the date speaks for itself." The president turned around. "My guess is Turgenev has decided to head the Russian delegation to the opening of the General Assembly, and he wants to meet in New York right afterward."

"New York or Washington, either one."

The president put his right hand in his trouser's pocket and searched for some loose change to jingle. He didn't have any. Like most presidents, Moran had gotten out of the habit of carrying money, typically going without a wallet. It struck him as funny that he carried no more ID than the panhandlers across the street from the White House in Lafayette. "And what, exactly, is the proposed subject of this summit?"

"Subject unknown," replied Pinzon. "They're giving us the usual, diplomatic gobbledygook. They say they want to discuss the general state of U.S.-Russian relations, details to follow. But this we do know.

Turgenev's giving the Russian opening remarks at the United Nations, himself."

"Turgenev? Himself? Now that *is* something." An unexpected request for a summit on two weeks notice was not the way the Russians normally operated. It didn't allow sufficient time for preparation. Without carefully scripted plans, summits tended to get out of hand.

The president took the spark plug from Pinzon's hand and turned back to his engine. "We can assume this has to do with arms control." Moran paused, tightened something inside the engine compartment, and then, turning back toward Pinzon, set down his tool and wiped both his hands on a rag he pulled from his back pocket. "It's conceivable that Turgenev wants to get arms reductions moving again and is taking unilateral action to force our hand."

Pinzon didn't like it, but said nothing.

"Don't you see, Rubio? It's got drama. Imagine the leader of Russia standing before the General Assembly and announcing that he's sinking his own submarines! Think of the pictures he can show. It's got headline potential, that's for sure."

Pinzon wasn't persuaded. "You think that will pressure our Republican friends to resume arms cuts?"

"Who knows, Rubio? Probably not, but maybe Turgenev is naive about U.S. politics." Moran inspected the grease on his hands in the harsh hangar lights and then wiped them again on the rag from his pocket.

"Rubio, stall Turgenev. Tell him we're considering his request. In the meantime, let's get their man over to the White House on Sunday. I'd see him sooner if I could."

"The new guy, Lentov?" asked Pinzon.

"No," said Moran, "not the ambassador. His deputy, Papko. He'll be available on a Sunday afternoon, and he's the real brains at the embassy, anyway. Sometimes the best way to get some information is just to ask. Let's do it."

Saturday, September 11

Having no odometer, Ushta could only estimate his progress. He thought he was averaging about four or five miles per hour, and multiplying that by the fifty-two hours he'd been underway, he guessed he was nearing the edge of the forests north of Chita and would soon sight farm fields and settlements.

Ushta figured he'd been lucky. The old logging trails he expected to find, had in fact, been there, running haphazardly south and southwest from Pechora. Twice he had been forced to backtrack after choosing trails that dead-ended, and once he'd been forced to winch himself from a swollen stream.

But he was gradually moving forward.

Ushta knew that without the bulldozer he was as good as dead. The huge green machine meant both freedom and life. It kept him warm, transported his food, and conserved his energy. If the bulldozer broke down or became stuck, Ushta was certain to die of exposure, but the weather was also an advantage. The light snow covered his tire tracks, and the low cloud cover made aerial reconnaissance impossible.

He assumed that Pechora authorities had begun looking for him at first light Friday morning. Inevitably they would send all-terrain vehicles southward along the unmapped logging trails, but Pechora didn't have the vehicles or personnel to follow them all. Even if they did, he reasoned, half the morons hunting him would be lost in the forest in an hour. Ushta calculated that the real danger was ahead where the mountains leveled into flatland and the forests turned to farms. If they were smart, they would wait for him there.

In the early afternoon, Ushta rounded a rock outcropping and got his first view of open terrain. He stopped the bulldozer and pulled a pair of binoculars from a bag between his feet. A broad valley about two miles distant and a thousand feet below had been divided into open squares of grassland, now covered with snow. The weak light and blowing wisps of fog made visibility difficult even with field glasses, but Ushta could make out what he thought were barns or sheds and what looked like a small house.

He was slapping his knee with pleasure, silently cheering his own navigational genius, when a flash of yellow light flickered among the dense trees on the steep hillside to his left. He snapped his head in the direction of the light and trained his binoculars on the tree line. An illusion, he thought to himself, a product of his overworked and highly suspicious imagination. A second yellow flash changed his mind. This time there was no doubt. Two yellow points of light were moving in a jiggling pattern down through the trees of the hillside toward him.

For the first time in more than two days Ushta, shut down the bulldozer's engine. The throbbing diesel had been his companion, his very life.

He found the quiet eerie. He cracked open the cab door to his left and listened. He could hear a light wind blowing through the thick needles of the forest pines, but in those first few seconds could decipher no other sound. When the high pitched whine of a straining all-terrain vehicle finally reached his ears he felt his heart pounding. The engine first pitched high, then low, then high again as the vehicle bounced up and down over a deeply rutted path.

Ushta offered a silent prayer to the God he didn't believe in and, jabbing at his starter, almost cheered out loud when the diesel came back to life. He started to roll and saw immediately that the trail in front of him was blocked by yet another fallen tree. He looked left and saw the yellow lights more clearly now, lower on the slope, closer to his trail. He considered rolling backwards, but the fuel buffalo made that awkward. It looked like the military vehicle coming down the slope would emerge from the woods just about the time he was backing by. He had no good options; he took the only one that gave him hope for survival. He shut down the engine, jumped from the right door, and scurried into the woods. Ushta thought of hiking away but dismissed the idea. Once the bulldozer was discovered, the area would be flooded with troops and escape on foot would be impossible.

His only chance was to keep whoever was about to find his machine from reporting the discovery. Killing did not appeal to him, but he had long ago decided he would do it if he had to.

Ushta watched intently as a Russian military jeep finally emerged from the edge of the forest and bounced down to the trail where his bulldozer sat mutely. The jeep pulled to a stop at the side of the trail, and a Russian sergeant and corporal, both with AK47s unslung from their shoulders, got out and moved cautiously along either side of the green bulldozer. Their careful, crouching movements made Ushta want to laugh.

Over here, you dumb shits, he said to himself. Ushta wondered if the tension wasn't making him a little crazy.

The corporal finally mounted the bulldozer, opened the door to the cab, and started the engine. The two men, both in their late thirties, seemed to be career military types. They were too old to be conscripts, too military to be sympathetic to an escapee. Neither wore the unit patch of the Pechora Regiment, and Ushta guessed they were based near Chita. The sergeant walked from the back of the bulldozer, signaled to his colleague in the cab, and began to move toward his jeep. It was obvious to Ushta that he was about to be reported.

Ushta yelled at the top of his lungs: "Here! Here! I'm over here."

Both men turned in his direction and pointed their weapons.

"Come out," yelled the sergeant over the chattering bulldozer. "Come out with your hands above your head and move slowly. Talk as you walk. Keep talking until we see you."

Ushta complied, stumbling through the brush, calling out "Don't shoot, don't shoot," until he reached the trail and was exposed.

The sergeant waved Ushta closer and then called out to the corporal, still standing at the right door to the cab. "Keep him covered, corporal."

The corporal aimed his gun at Ushta's back as the sergeant lowered his rifle and began searching his captive with his free hand. When he was satisfied that Ushta was not armed, he smiled.

"So, you're alive, huh? Too bad. I think you would have been better off dead considering what they'll do to you."

The corporal standing at the cab door began yelling toward the sergeant in an incomprehensible tongue. It wasn't until the sergeant answered back that Ushta realized they were speaking a Mongolian dialect. Ushta wanted to kick himself for not seeing it in their faces. Like him, they were Russian, but with strong hints of their Mongol heritage. Chita was a Russian-speaking city and so was Ulan Ulde not far to the west, but many of the locals were partly of Mongol descent. And most had some working knowledge of the Mongolian language. He was surprised that they didn't seem to see the Mongol in him. Most likely, he thought, they knew his name and knew he was from Moscow and couldn't imagine that he could understand Mongolian well. Assuming a stranger couldn't speak your language was a mistake people made often enough. Ushta tried to look baffled as the sergeant and the corporal conferred. The corporal was excited by what he had found in the cab. He showed the sergeant the binoculars Ushta had misappropriated and the extensive tool kit carried on every bulldozer. What really excited them, however, was the buffalo.

"It must be carrying diesel fuel," said the corporal.

The sergeant gestured for Ushta to stand fast, walked back to the buffalo, and opened a valve. He sniffed, then climbing to the top of the tank, opened a cover, shined his flashlight inside, and whistled. "Must be a couple of hundred gallons in here," he said. "You know what they'd pay for this in Chita? The black market price must be ten times official."

Ushta thought they were seriously overestimating the fuel quantity and considered saying so, but the return of the sergeant silenced him.

"We could kill him, hide the buffalo, and make a deal with Zeya in Chita," said the corporal. "He could come retrieve the mule in a week or so when the place quiets down. We could get a year's pay apiece, sergeant."

"What about the bulldozer?" asked the sergeant, pointing to the machine.

"We drive it down to the valley and say we found it abandoned. Who's going to know?"

The sergeant was becoming intrigued by his corporal's brainstorm and momentarily forgot about Ushta. He turned slightly to address his colleague still standing at the cab, and Ushta took his only chance. He grabbed the sergeant's rifle with a force and speed he had known only once before, years ago, in a tavern in Magnitogorsk. Taken off guard, the sergeant had begun to raise his arms when the rifle butt caught him squarely along the left side of his head. He keeled backward stiffly like a freshly sawed tree, hitting the ground with a solid thump. Ushta took less than a second to search for cover and seeing none, jumped into the lowered jaw of his bulldozer's gaping bucket. He was completely shielded from the view and the bullets of the corporal. From his crouched position, Ushta watched the sergeant begin to stir.

He pointed his gun at the sergeant but to his own surprise found he couldn't pull the trigger. The man was unarmed and defenseless, no matter what his intentions had been. Ushta thought it was a strange time to be discovering his own morality.

Ushta's consideration of ethics was interrupted by a sudden jolt. The corporal in the cab was attempting to operate the bulldozer but didn't appear to know how. Ushta felt the machine jump forward and watched in horrified fascination as it headed directly for the sergeant on the ground. The sergeant had opened his dazed eyes and was staring blankly at the approaching machine. Ushta screamed loudly, and the sergeant feebly held out both hands. But it was too late.

The corporal rolled over his boss. Ushta could hear a distinct cracking sound over the roar of the diesel as the sergeant was crushed, and, if his own life hadn't been in mortal danger, he might have become sick. Suddenly the bulldozer came to a stop.

For more than a minute, there was no movement by either man. The corporal remained in the cab, and Ushta held fast in the bucket. Pechora had taught Ushta many things, but patience was the virtue he now valued most. He determined to let the other man move first. The corporal, now realizing what he had done to his sergeant, was more interested in action. He contemplated a way to dismount the bulldozer and get a shot off at Ushta without being blown to pieces himself. When nothing came to mind, he again began playing with the levers before him in the cab. After several fits and starts the corporal finally found the control that raised the bucket. Slowly it swung upward from the earth, carrying Ushta with it. Ushta knew it would be only seconds before the soldier discovered how to tilt the bucket forward and dump him to the ground like so much shoveled dirt.

Ushta was wrong. The corporal never discovered the dumping lever. When he raised the bucket, he was so surprised to find no one there that in a fit of panic he leapt off the machine and ran mindlessly toward the front.

From his shielded position twelve feet above the ground, Ushta watched in wonder as the corporal ran beneath him and started firing aimlessly on full-automatic at where Ushta had been. It took a ridiculously long time for the soldier to spot Ushta curled up in the bucket above. He pointed his rifle and was about to squeeze the trigger when Ushta hit him with three .762 rounds square in the chest.

The corporal was dead before his knees hit the dirty snow.

Ushta climbed down from the cab and confirmed that both men were dead. He picked up their rifles and tossed the weapons inside their jeep. Then with some difficulty he dragged both bodies from the trail into the dense brush. He felt some relief that the crushed corpse of the sergeant held together in one piece. He stripped the corporal of his uniform and, discarding his prison rags, dressed himself in the combat fatigues and greatcoat of his nation's army.

Ushta was happy to see that the coat had been open at the time the corporal was shot. There were no bullet holes in the outer garment.

He searched in various pockets until he found a battered wallet and the corporal's identification. It included a tiny, badly shot, black-and-white photo. Remarkably, thought Ushta, because of its poor photo quality and because he and the corporal were both partly Mongolian, a casual observer might actually believe the ID was his. Ushta studied the man's name, date of birth, and military serial number until he was sure he had them memorized, then looked at the sky.

Experience told him there would be more snow that day, but Ushta opted for caution. He retrieved a shovel from the side of the bulldozer, dumped a foot of fresh snow over the two bodies and did the same with the blood stains along the trail. He remounted the bulldozer and edging forward pushed aside the tree that had been blocking the trail. Two hundred yards ahead he drove the machine into a break in the tree line and traveled another fifty yards before he could go no farther.

He shut down the machine, opened a large metal box behind the cab, and pulled out two olive drab nets constructed of fine mesh. It was standard Red Army forest camouflage and had taken him some time to acquire at Pechora. It took him nearly twenty minutes to drape both the bulldozer and the buffalo with the netting and secure it to nearby trees. Satisfied he had done the best he could, he removed the bulldozer's heavy toolbox and scrambled back toward the trail. He carefully surveyed his surroundings, making a mental note of the rock outcropping on the hillsides above him, and later, back at the jeep, of the relationship of the logging trail to the buildings in the valley below. He familiarized himself with the jeep's gears and easing out the clutch, drove toward the flatlands below.

It took him nearly two hours to move down from the forest. By late afternoon, as snow began falling in big, wet flakes, Ushta drove over a low embankment and felt the jeep's wheels contact firm pavement.

"Macadam!" he shouted to the snow-muffled air. Ahead, perhaps a mile away, he could see the same house and sheds he had seen from the slopes above. Ushta lifted his field glasses and saw smoke curling from the roof of the house and some kind of farm implement moving slowly back and forth in a field nearby. To his right, and much closer, sat a dilapidated shed, its sides unpainted and its roof bowed with age.

As darkness began to descend, Ushta debated whether to approach the farmhouse. Whoever lived there would have useful information about the region—but they could also turn him in to authorities. He stifled a yawn and decided to sleep on it. Ushta jammed the sticky shift-lever into first and proceeded toward the shed. To Ushta's relief, his jeep squeezed inside. He shut off the ignition and slept hard.

Duval needed another quarter. If he could find it, Duval planned to leave his doctor's office, walk down the block to the corner gas station, and invest in a Pepsi. The unusual mid-September heat had overwhelmed his cranky old air-conditioning system, turning his office suites into a suffocating warren of dead air. He had opened every window, switched on an oversized fan, even wrapped ice-cubes in a cloth towel and applied them to his neck. Nothing worked. He needed a Pepsi. Badly.

He found a nickel and two pennies in his desk drawer, but could mine nothing more from the assorted paper clips and rubber bands. A third check of his shirt and trouser's pockets confirmed what his first two forays had found. There was no loose change there. In desperation, he walked to a closet and began fumbling through the folds of his leather motorcycle jacket. He thought he remembered emptying the jacket the night of his accident, but he couldn't be sure. He was about to give up when he felt something hard in an inside pocket. He reached in and pulled out a wallet.

"Damn," he said aloud. He had completely forgotten the wallet he'd taken from the dead man at the accident.

It was an ordinary, brown leather, American-style wallet. It was neither expensive nor cheap, but had seen many years of service. The leather was worn smooth. The corners were rounded from countless hours in a back pocket, and the embossed name of its manufacturer had been erased from the cowhide. To Duval's surprise, there were five, freshly engraved $100 bills. Whoever the dead passenger had been, thought Duval, he could never accuse him of vagrancy.

He rifled through the rest of the wallet and came up with an Exxon credit card in the name of Paul Gabrovo and a Maryland driver's license to match. It listed an address on Good Luck Road in Greenbelt, Maryland. Guess his luck ran out, thought Duval.

He picked through his Rolodex, found Sheriff Reiner's private office number, and placed a call. Duval partly expected Reiner to be off on

Saturday and was mildly startled when Reiner gruffly answered the phone with "County Sheriff here."

"Sheriff Reiner?"

"Last time I checked. Hey, is that you, Doc?"

"It's me, Sheriff."

"Where's my pictures? You get 'em back from the drugstore yet?"

Duval wasn't anxious to answer but couldn't find any option other than the truth. "They didn't come out."

"What? Speak up George, I can hardly hear you."

Duval was sure the Sheriff heard him clearly. "I said they didn't come out. Something was wrong with the film."

Reiner burst out laughing. When he could finally contain himself, there was still chuckling in his voice.

"Boy, wish that had happened to my wife's private eye." It had been rumored in Sheridan County that Dan Reiner had been forced into a brutal divorce settlement with his last wife because of certain compromising pictures involving Reiner and the wife of a local county judge. No one had ever seen the pictures, but Reiner liked to behave as if they existed.

"So, Doc. What's on your mind?"

"I've got a wallet. I took it off one of the bodies at the accident. I completely forgot about it until I found it just now. It's got five hundred dollars in crisp new bills inside."

"Yeah? You don't say." Reiner paused momentarily, then smacked his lips audibly. "Tell you what, George. I'll have Sheriff Hargrove send one of his men by to pick it up, and they'll get it to me. Make sure you get a receipt for the money. In the meantime, give me the particulars on any IDs you've found, and I'll run them through channels and see what pops up. Would that be okay?"

Duval gave Reiner the information on the driver's license and credit card and hung up. Just to make sure, he went through the wallet one more time. In a half-hidden side pocket, he found a business card with the name and phone number of a hairdresser on Wisconsin Avenue in Washington, D.C. The name and the number had a line inked across them.

On the back, handwritten in pencil, was an odd number and letter sequence: 00 1A 0A WM M PA 1 V* 00. The sequence meant nothing to Duval. Without thinking, he put the card in his own shirt pocket. More searching uncovered two small, foreign coins. One was a West German

10-Pfennig piece and the other was indecipherable except for the letters CCCP. Neither would help Duval buy a Pepsi, so he tossed them into his desk drawer in disgust and waited for Sheriff Hargrove.

The deputy from Hargrove's office showed up thirty minutes later. After getting a receipt for the wallet and its contents, Duval rechecked his appointment book to ensure there would be no more patients for the rest of Saturday afternoon.

Satisfied that office hours were over, he called Michelle at her mother's house in Denver, switched on his answering machine, and walked to La Roma for his Pepsi and a long, languid lunch. He was searching for a pen to sign his bill when he found the Washington hairdresser's business card in his shirt pocket. Duval looked at the writing on the back and slipped the card into his wallet. He'd tell Reiner about the stupid card later. He could hear Reiner's laugh as he explained he had a card with a hairdresser's name on it.

When Duval returned to his office ninety minutes later, there were two messages on his machine. The first was from Reiner, the second from Mark Loevinger at the University of Nebraska in Lincoln. He dialed Reiner's number.

"Sheriff?"

"Hey, George. I got some good news on your driver's license. It's absolutely legitimate."

"Great. That means you can positively ID the body?"

"Well, I didn't say that, George. The driver's license was issued to a Paul Gabrovo three years ago. But—"

"But what?"

"But Gabrovo has been dead for two years. Killed in a small plane crash. Somebody went to a lot of trouble to dig up his personal information and make a very good, phony Maryland driver's license based on a real one."

Duval didn't know what to think. "Where does that leave us?" he asked, knowing the answer.

"About where we were before. Look, George, half the nineteen-year-old kids in this county got fake IDs. Some are pretty good. I know whoever ran over you out there was up to no good, but I still don't have any big crime to charge them with. I'll keep my eye on this though. Just you forget about it. Thank your lucky stars you're alive. Be grateful that cops have to worry about missing license plates and such and that you don't have to."

"But Sheriff—"

"George, let this thing go. It's no big thing. Take that little gal of yours and go to San Francisco."

"Michelle's visiting her parents in Denver this weekend."

"Well, take a week off and visit your mom in Arizona. Stop worrying about this thing. If anything turns up, I promise I'll let you know. Okay?"

Duval saw it was hopeless. He thanked the sheriff and looked up Mark Loevinger's number at his university lab in Lincoln. Until the day before, they had not spoken to one another in more than a year. It was not unusual. Duval and Loevinger had met as undergraduates at Nebraska and roomed together their junior and senior years. They liked and respected each other then and had maintained an irregular correspondence in the intervening decade, but they had never been close. Loevinger had sought out Duval's advice a couple of years ago when his four-year-old daughter was about to undergo orthopedic surgery for a rotator cuff torn in a playground accident. Now a full professor of materiels science and engineering at the University of Nebraska, Loevinger had helped Duval get his x-ray machine for the clinic at Whiteclay. They exchanged Christmas cards and occasionally did each other favors. That's the way it had been for several years, and they both expected that's the way it would remain.

When Duval decided to get an analysis of the material he had collected from the accident site, Loevinger had been an obvious choice. He could get the job done quietly with no questions asked and no records taken. When he had called Loevinger the day before and explained about the accident, the explosion, the missing bodies, and the sheriff's reluctance to investigate, Duval got the expected, helpful response. Loevinger found the whole thing a little bizarre. But he readily agreed to examine any material.

Duval had put his samples in a twelve-by-fifteen inch padded envelope and given them to a patient named Harry Blucher late Friday night. Blucher was a long-time patient and rabid University of Nebraska football fan. When the Huskers were at home, Blucher would leave Chadron at the end of his shift late Friday night, and drive 430 miles to Lincoln. Blucher got the samples to Loevinger early Saturday morning, and the professor agreed to finish a preliminary analysis by late afternoon.

When Duval punched in Loevinger's number at the lab, he was startled to hear an answer on the first ring. "Mark?"

"George, I've been waiting for your call. Where the fuck did you get that stuff?"

Duval had never known Loevinger to swear. "You mean the samples I sent you?"

"Of *course* I mean what you sent me. What else? George, are you trying to kill us here?"

Duval had no idea what Loevinger was talking about and told him so.

"George, that shit you sent me is *hot*, very *hot!* I put a PAC 2T counter on it and was getting two million counts a minute. That's off the scale, it won't—"

"Whoa, Mark. Whoa," interrupted Duval. "Slow down. You're way beyond me. Put it in layman's language. What are you talking about? What do you mean, hot?"

Loevinger calmed down. "George, the material you sent me is highly radioactive. It's giving off alpha rays. I put an alpha ray counter on it and it's recording two million alpha particles a minute. That's way, way up there."

Duval could feel his stomach tighten. "You mean I've been exposed to a dangerous dose of radiation?"

This time Loevinger tried to slow the conversation down. He cleared his throat and spoke softly.

"No, George. Not necessarily." Loevinger paused to make sure he had the right words. "Alpha particles won't penetrate anything. A piece of paper will stop them. They're really only dangerous if you inhale them or get them in your bloodstream in a cut. Did you inhale them?"

Duval was almost stuttering. "I don't know. I wore a surgical mask when I was first exposed to the stuff, when it was blowing around after the explosion I told you about. Would that help?"

"A lot, George. It would help a lot."

"But I also had a hell of a gash across my forehead."

"Was it coagulated before the explosion spewed out all the debris?"

Duval tried to remember. "Mostly, I guess. The wound was cleaned when I got some sutures an hour or two later."

"That's good," replied Loevinger, "you've probably not been dangerously exposed. But the stuff you sent is not your average chemical compound. It is very rare and dangerous stuff."

"Well, what the hell is it for God's sake?"

Loevinger continued now in his calm, deliberate sentences. "George you sent me a twentieth-century witch's brew of nuclear isotopes, many of them man-made. Among other things, I found uranium 235 and 238 and plutonium 239. The 239 was that heavy, red dust. A lot of it had burned. Plutonium burns easily, but even when it oxidizes, it remains radioactive."

Duval was understanding very little. He waited for Loevinger to continue.

"I also found traces of plastic explosive. There was lithium deuteride, actually lithium-6 deuteride, which was the white powder you sent along. Finally I found tritium, beryllium, and traces of polystyrene. Nice combination, huh?"

Duval had no idea what the combination meant. "Could it mess up unexposed photographic film?"

Loevinger found the question a total non sequitur, but answered. "If this stuff came into contact with unexposed negatives and stayed in contact for a while, it would most likely spot the film."

It was the first reassuring news Duval had heard in three days. His detective work was beginning to pay off.

"But what does it add up to?" he asked. "What was this stuff doing beside a third-rate highway out in the sticks in Nebraska?"

Loevinger didn't respond. Duval could hear his breathing on the other end of the phone line, but something was shutting Loevinger up.

"Mark?"

"George, you've hit on *the* question." Loevinger sounded relieved that Duval had finally gotten to the point. "By themselves some of these things could be explained. Tritium is painted on clock hands to make them glow in the dark. You probably own a clock like that. Plutonium, in small quantities, can be used to power pacemakers and is sometimes useful in analyzing certain metals."

Duval was getting an education. "They use plutonium in pacemakers?"

"Sometimes. And depleted uranium is used to make armor-piercing ammunition, among other things. Lithium has uses, too. They put it in batteries. Polystyrene is used for everything."

"So, what's the problem?"

"The problem is, all these things were found together and in sizable quantities from what you've told me. You add these things all together with lithium deuteride and beryllium, and I can think of only one practical use."

Duval hated guessing games. "What's that?"

"A hydrogen bomb."

Duval was certain he hadn't heard correctly. He began searching his desk drawer for a Q-Tip. *"A what?"*

"An H-bomb. A fusion weapon. A thermonuclear device probably fifty hundred times more powerful than the nuke we dropped on Hiroshima."

Duval was flabbergasted. He rose from behind his desk and started pacing with the phone held tightly to his ear. "You mean to tell me that a nuclear weapon being carried around the countryside by terrorists detonated in my face, and I'm still here to talk about it."

Loevinger's voice became excited again. "George, the bomb didn't detonate, and they weren't terrorists."

"What do you mean the bomb didn't go off? I told you about the explosion."

"That was the trigger mechanism. These things have triggers containing high explosives, my guess is thirty or forty pounds of plastic. The explosion drives quantities of uranium together, they become critical and start a nuclear chain reaction, fission. That's an atomic bomb. In an H-bomb, once the fission gets going, it creates enough energy to create fusion, and that really releases some energy. That's why H-bombs are so much more powerful than A-bombs."

Duval found it very interesting but beside the point. "So how come I'm still alive?"

"The truck fire detonated the trigger; that was the explosion you saw. The casings on nuclear weapons are very thick, very tough. My guess is that the explosion blew out the front and back ends of the cylinder you described, spraying plutonium and lithium deuteride and the other stuff out one end."

"But why didn't the bomb go off?"

"Triggers are extremely complex, highly engineered items. Unless their high explosives go off in an extremely exact and intricate manner, there is no fission and no fusion and no atomic or hydrogen explosion. The triggers won't detonate in the proper manner unless they're intentionally armed. They aren't armed until just before they're going to be used. They weren't armed in this case. It's happened before; they call it a Broken Arrow incident. Appropriate name I think."

Duval sat down again, trying to take in Loevinger's analysis. "These weapons have gone off before?"

"Sure. More than once. Our Air Force dropped a couple of hydrogen bombs on a small town in Spain called Palomares about thirty years back. The trigger detonated, but no one was hurt. We also dropped an H-bomb on some guy's house in Louisiana or Arkansas. The explosives in the trigger flattened the house, but the guy inside actually emerged unharmed. Not many people can say their house was hit by an H-bomb."

Duval's mind raced with questions. "How come you say the men in the truck weren't terrorists?"

"Because a hydrogen bomb is not a terrorist's weapon, George. Hydrogen bombs require fusion, as I said. Fusion is much more difficult to achieve than fission, which is the basis of an ordinary atomic weapon. It requires incredible industrial and scientific capacity, huge amounts of money, and lots of testing to make an H-bomb. Only a handful of nations with gigantic programs have managed to build fusion weapons. The United States, and Russia, of course, and France, Britain, and China. That's it. Fission weapons—atomic bombs in everyday language—are much cheaper and simpler and for terrorist's purposes, more than a dequate. For a terrorist, a hydrogen bomb would be overkill, gilding of the lily."

Duval's mind was racing. He had so many questions he wasn't certain where to start. "Well, who else would be running around the prairie in a beat-up truck with a hydrogen bomb and no security?"

"The U.S. government," came Loevinger's calm reply, "and there *was* security. Somebody had to pick up the two men and remove the weapon."

That, at least, seemed true. For the first time in days, somebody was making sense. "But why would the government be transporting a bomb around in a decrepit old truck?"

"Just because that truck looked old and worn out, doesn't mean it was."

"True."

"Nuclear weapons age. Components wear out. They're always removing them from missiles, taking them back to the factory for refurbishment. Warheads get moved around a lot. Especially around here with all the Minuteman silos. But nowadays, every time they try to move a warhead there's somebody making a stink about it, blocking railroad tracks, or putting barriers in the road. There's Peace Now, Greenpeace, you name it. I'm sure the government finds them all a big pain in the butt. So, they decide to do things a little more subtly, on the sly. They transport the warhead in an innocent looking old truck, with the security team trailing a mile or two behind. No peaceniks, no city council trying to ban a shipment from some highway that cuts through town."

"But this shipment has been involved in an accident. You think the government would keep quiet about that?"

"George, this is the same government that exposed thousands of soldiers to radiation without telling them; the same government that trashed the Savannah River and half the land around Hanford, Washington, with radioactive waste and kept its mouth shut for decades."

Duval thought Loevinger's reasoning was solid. "But what about safety? Couldn't that stuff out on the highway be dangerous? Don't they have to clean it up?"

"George, it would be hard to think of a better place to have a Broken Arrow accident. We're not talking Manhattan or Grant Park here. We're talking a remote stretch of prairie in Nebraska; a place with a population density of maybe one person per square mile, if that. Anyway, they will clean it up, if for no other reason than to keep the thing quiet."

"Won't the clean-up be a big deal? Attract a lot of attention?"

"Not necessarily. Most likely when things have calmed down, they'll simply plow most of the nuclear debris a couple of feet under. It won't harm anybody there, and in twenty-four thousand years it won't be much of a problem."

"Very funny."

"Actually, I'm being serious. They'll monitor what they bury from time to time, to make sure it doesn't seep down into underground aquifers. If it gets to be a problem in ten or twelve years, they'll probably dig the stuff up and ship it somewhere else. But for now, burial is the quickest thing they can do.

Loevinger's explanation was clearing up a lot of mysteries.

"Mark, do you think the Sheridan County Sheriff is involved in this thing, this conspiracy?"

"George, conspiracy may be a bit hard. But if you mean do I think the Department of Defense or the Nuclear Regulatory Commission or some other agency got hold of the sheriff, told him what was happening, and ordered him to shut up, the answer is yes. I'm sure they appealed to his patriotism, said the whole thing was a matter of national security, and for good measure told him he would end up in Leavenworth Prison for the rest of his natural life if he didn't cooperate."

"That would explain a lot, Mark. Hey, what are you going to do about this?"

Loevinger didn't respond. Duval wondered if his connection had been broken.

"Mark?"

"Yes."

"What are you going to do?"

"Me? Nothing. I used university equipment to do a private favor for a friend, which is bad enough. I don't want the feds down on me too. I'm going to pretend the whole thing never happened. There are no records of anything, not even a record of your shipment of the samples since they were hand-delivered. No one helped me with the analysis. I'm going to keep my nose out of this thing. My advice is that you do the same. As far as Uncle Sam is concerned, you've already shown too much interest."

They said their good-byes and ended the conversation.

Duval found himself absolutely bewildered. What was the right thing to do? Was Loevinger's story credible? Could it really be? Had his life been saved because he had worn a surgical mask at the accident scene? He didn't like the idea of plutonium particles slowly radiating his lungs. Damn, there had been a lot of that dust blowing around. Duval suddenly felt panic. His heart began racing and the hair on the back of his neck tingled. The dust. Michelle had been sucking in the dust. God, my God, he thought. He hadn't considered Michelle.

He called her mother's number in Denver. Alice Falk wanted to gab, but Duval made it clear he needed to talk to Michelle in a hurry. When she came on the phone, she was obviously pleased he had called. It was the second time in two hours.

"Michelle, this is serious. When you cleaned off my medical bag Wednesday night, how much of that dust did you breathe in?"

"The dust? Why do you want to know?"

"Please, Michelle, it's important."

"Well, I don't know. Not much. When the dust started flying I scrounged in the dark for a mask in the pile you left on the counter and put it on."

The relief in Duval's voice was evident.

"You did?"

"Yes. I'm allergic to dust, and you know it. There was a whole box of disposable masks on the counter since you never put them away. Why do you want to know about this?"

Duval's stomach twisted again. What should he tell her? What did he really know? He had always been honest with her and decided that was his only course now. "Michelle, I heard from Mark Loevinger. That dust may have been radioactive."

"What?" There was panic in her voice. "What do you mean, *may* have been?"

"Okay, it was radioactive. Alpha particles."

"Oh, Jesus."

"Look, honey, you probably didn't get that much. You weren't exposed long. Loevinger says that alpha rays aren't so bad; they're not like x-rays or something."

"George, I don't care what Loevinger says." She was calmer now. "Basically, I won't know how much I inhaled or how my body reacts to it for ten or twenty years. It could be lung cancer, or it could be nothing. Oh, God, how did this happen?" Her tones were now expressing more anger than fear.

"Honey, I'll explain everything when you get back here. You wore a mask. You may be just fine. People have been exposed to much worse and lived forever."

"George, I had to breathe in some of that stuff. Let's face it, I've been exposed."

"Me too, honey." It seemed a trite thing to say, but it was true. Oddly, Duval thought, he was a lot more concerned about her health than his own.

There was no comment on the other end.

Duval broke the silence.

"Michelle, I love you very much." He tried to be light, but regretted it immediately. "Well, as long as we're both radioactive—" He paused.

"Yes?"

Duval became serious. "Well, no one else will want us. I guess we'll have to stick together, permanently."

Michelle didn't know whether her tears came from anxiety or joy.

Compared to his classmates at the Academy, Colonel-General Uri Saratov counted himself lucky. If his service in Afghanistan had cost him an inch of his left leg and given him a permanent limp, at least he was alive. He had both eyes, all four limbs, two testicles, and none of the visible scars that made even friends and family members shun some veterans out of guilt, sadness, or revulsion. He personally knew five classmates who had been blown-up, beheaded, shot down, eviscerated, or tortured to death in the Hindu Kush, and dozens more who were in wheelchairs from the bombs, rockets, bayonets, and bazookas wielded by Afghan tribesmen. Two classmates had survived the war only to take their own lives when faced with the bleak prospects available to hideously maimed veterans of a costly, unpopular, and—as far as the government was concerned—eminently forgettable foreign policy disaster.

In his sixteen months in Afghanistan, Saratov had slowly developed two lasting hatreds, and those hatreds had, over time, become his passions. He equally despised both the United States of America and the weak-kneed bureaucrats who dared call themselves the government in his own country. In Saratov's view, they were the agents responsible for the death, dishonor, and degradation that had befallen the once proud Red Army. The military that had turned back the Wehrmacht, had consolidated Russian power over Eastern Europe, and had sent tremors through the hearts of leaders around the globe was now a tattered remnant of its former self. It was shredded by American weapons in Afghanistan, and starved of funds by faceless bureaucrats in the Kremlin trying to curry favor with the West. The Empire that the army had maintained, stretching from the forests of Thuringia to the Sea of Japan was now gone.

And what had Mother Russia gotten for this sacrifice? Domestically, the country knew poverty, corruption, crime, and disorder; internationally, it had become a pitiful, stumbling shadow of its former self.

The Americans were now full of themselves, proclaiming victory over the "evil empire" and mastery of a "new world order," while in Moscow, political hacks competed with one another to dishonor their nation's soul.

These realizations came to Saratov with the force of an epiphany on a cold March evening in 1984, along a nameless stream branching off the Helmand River, several miles above the Kajaki Reservoir in southwestern Afghanistan.

Saratov was a lieutenant then, a young officer in charge of two river patrol boats working the Helmand. His boats had been hit by a barrage of anti-tank rounds and had disintegrated into shards of splintered fiberglass. Eight men had been killed instantly. Another survived on the riverbank much of the night, his lonely voice alternating between screams of pain and a loud, forlorn, almost childlike sobbing, until the Mujahadeen found him in the morning and slit his throat.

Even Saratov himself had been severely injured. A jagged piece of disk-shaped shrapnel had slit his left groin, leaving a deep open gash about seven inches long, and had smashed the upper femur of his left leg. Four more soldiers were killed attempting to rescue him, their Hind helicopter brought down by an American-made Stinger missile. More than anything else, the nasty little shoulder-fired missile supplied by the Americans had turned the tide of the war.

Saratov's recovery had taken nearly a year, and it had been the most unpleasant year of his life. The first surgical attempt to mend his leg had been thoroughly botched, which necessitated a second, extremely painful operation that left him permanently gimpy. Doctors and nurses had been inattentive and uncaring; the hospital dreary and unclean; and the food bad and ventilation worse.

From his bedside, Saratov tried to follow the course of the worsening war in official newspapers. He read of great Soviet victories, of the thankful praise of the Afghan people, and of international solidarity with the Soviet effort. What he never read about were military reverses, casualty figures, or the words of wounded or dying men. He saw no pictures of maimed soldiers nor read any stories about sons being buried or fathers being awarded posthumous medals. There were no reports on parades for returning veterans, or the fate of those missing in action, or the tactics or diplomacy that might be employed to end the fighting for a piece of real estate that had no obvious value.

The newspapers confirmed what he had long suspected while serving in Afghanistan. He and the other young men sent there were little more than forgettable cannon fodder in some political game that had long since lost any meaning, and continued only by virtue of political inertia. During his recuperation, Saratov's bitterness had grown with every new soldier admitted to the hospital; and in the years that followed, that bitterness was not tempered by time. It was, however, artfully submerged beneath the stern exterior of an intelligent, imaginative, and now battle-hardened, career officer.

As director of the State Bureau of Advanced Strategic Research, he had more scientists, technicians, laboratories, factories, and money at his command than anyone else in the entire Russian Federation, and he intended to take advantage of his power.

But on this particular day in September, Saratov was feeling somewhat reflective.

He stretched his hands over his head, yawned, and pushed a buzzer on his desk. Seconds later, Colonel Andrei Kachuga entered Saratov's office and saluted.

"Be seated, Andrei," said Saratov, in a not unkind voice. "I hope you don't have the watch this evening—you look very tired."

Colonel Kachuga was surprised to be addressed by his first name. It happened only rarely, usually when Saratov was about to express a kind of sad disappointment in his aide's lapse of judgment on some matter. Kachuga lowered his eyes as if he were ashamed. "It's been a very tough week, General. First the incident in Boston, then the problem in Nebraska."

"As I told you before, Andrei, there were bound to be some accidents, some missteps. Speaking of which, before I leave tonight I want to know if there is anything more on the missing man in Pechora?"

"No, General. Nothing. I've had his file telexed here in case you wanted to see it. I put it in your box."

Saratov turned the papers in his "in" box until Ushta's file came up. He looked at the name, wondering why he knew it. He put the file back. "And what do the people in Pechora say?"

"They've got everybody out looking, but frankly they're not very worried. They expect Ushta is dead—killed in an accident maybe or frozen to death. There's no place for him to run to."

"I expect they're right. All in all, I believe we have Operation Ilium under control. Do you disagree?"

The colonel took his time answering. He removed a pack of cigarettes from his tunic and, by raising his eyebrows, asked permission to light up. He slowly exhaled his first puff and continued. "I believe all is in control, General."

Saratov leaned back in his swivel chair. "Tell me, Andrei, are you having doubts about our cause?"

Kachuga took another long drag on his cigarette, exhaled, then stubbed out the half-smoked butt in an ashtray made from an emptied grenade round. He eyed Saratov intently.

"No. I have no doubts about our cause." He paused, but hearing no response, continued. "Our country is dying, General. Our people do not have enough to eat. Our money is worthless. Our streets are overflowing with the homeless, drug pushers, and prostitutes. The kiosks are controlled by the mafia, who make millions, while army officers live in tents. Our scientists are either leaving the country or selling uranium to shady Arab contacts in the underground. Our nuclear power plants explode, our planes crash, and our phones don't work. The civilian leadership has proved itself totally incapable of getting things under control."

Saratov shook his head sadly, like a father listening to a confession from a loving son.

"Andrei, I couldn't have stated it any more clearly. And internationally, it's worse. The Germans are getting stronger every day. It's only a matter of time before they acquire nuclear weapons and start pushing their weight around again. Japan and China are booming and once again putting their noses into international affairs, even military affairs. Our former allies are either on their backs or have forsaken us. Our great army, the Red Army that stood its ground at Stalingrad and pushed back the Nazis from Moscow, is now getting clobbered by a bunch of ragtag, rag-headed mafia chieftains in Chechnya. Chechnya! The time for action is almost at hand. The army must act to save the nation. And believe me, when the coup comes, it will be supported by millions. We saved the country in 1941, and we will save it again today."

Kachuga nodded silently.

"And Andrei, this time there will be no half measures, no crying ministers begging a Yeltsin for understanding, saying they really didn't mean to revolt. This coup will be short, hard, unstoppable."

"And the Americans? Do you think they'll take Turgenev's bait? Start more arms reductions?"

"Maybe. I hope so. Every sub they pull back is one hundred fifty fewer warheads to throw at us. Anyway, the whole gambit keeps that do-good traitor Turgenev occupied and confuses the Americans."

"I suppose so," said Kachuga.

General Saratov heard doubt in his aide's voice and got to his feet. "Listen, Andrei. The Americans will never willingly accept a Russia equal to them. When the coup succeeds, they may well tear up all our arms control agreements and be back in the missile building race. They'll authorize Strategic Defense, build about fifty new ballistic missile submarines, and do everything else they can to bury us again—just like the first time. We haven't the resources to compete with that, which is exactly why Operation Ilium has been organized. Russia will never be great again until the Americans are cut down to size." Saratov turned his back on his aide and walked to the glass wall overlooking Ilium Control.

"Remember, Andrei. Our purpose is *not* to use those weapons. They are a deterrent, just like the missiles they have aimed at us. Only this deterrent can't be stopped by Star Wars or missile malfunctions or submarines with reactors so leaky that their crews die. Their flight time is exactly zero seconds, and they can't be detected on launch. Think of Operation Ilium as the installation of a twenty-first century nuclear warhead delivery system."

"I understand, General."

"You seem concerned."

"I just wonder what deterrent a weapon system can have if the Americans don't know we have it."

"Andrei. The time will come when we will tell them what we have done. When they have cut back their own missile systems sufficiently, we will make their position known to them. They will know that we can blow them from the face of the earth before they can launch a single weapon. At the slightest sign that they are going to heightened alert with the remnants of their nuclear forces, we fire. It will be over."

Kachuga said nothing. Saratov shook his head softly and reaching into his breast pocket pulled out a printed card the size of a business envelope.

"I keep this with me, Kachuga, to remind myself of our objectives. You are really not authorized to see this, but I'll make an exception. This is to show you some of the thinking of my colleagues." Saratov looked at the card briefly, himself, and continued. "These are the demands we make of the Americans. They will have a choice of acceding to our demands—or dying. Not much of a choice."

Kachuga looked at the card. It was a list, a very simple one.

1. No NATO expansion.

2. Withdrawal of all U.S. troops from Europe.

3. No U.S. objection to Russian occupation of Ukraine, Belarus, Kazakhstan, Lithuania.

4. Forgiveness of *all* loans to Russia by the IMF, World Bank, and any bank headquartered in a NATO nation.

5. No reconstitution of U.S. nuclear arsenal.

Saratov took the card from Kachuga's hand and replaced it in his pocket.

"Tell me, Andrei. Are these demands so unreasonable? Faced with certain destruction or complying with these demands, what would you do? These requests do not threaten America. But they would, if accepted, allow us, the army, and other patriotic forces to rebuild our nation."

"Yes, General!" answered Kachuga, saluting and sounding genuinely enthusiastic.

"Incidentally, Andrei. Is the name Leonid Ushta familiar to you?" Saratov asked, looking Kachuga directly in the eye.

"The missing man from Pechora? Yes, I know of him."

"How?"

This time Kachuga smiled. "You see the electronic screen on the wall here, and that giant one down in Ilium Control?"

"Yes."

"He pretty much invented them. He and his girlfriend and some academic colleague."

Duval was seething. A rage deeper than George Duval had ever known was streaming from his solar plexus to the tips of his toes and fingers, generating spasms up and down his spine and flushing his face and neck a deep crimson.

Had he killed his beloved Michelle?

Would the deadly toxins that billowed from his medical bag slowly but inexorably irradiate her lungs and burst into a full-blown and fatal cancer? Would it happen in a few months, a few years, or ever? And did the U.S. government give a damn, or was its interest in keeping a low nuclear profile so great that an agonizing death here and there seemed a small price to pay? Duval had no answers. But he found the government, however culpable, an amorphous target. It was big, distant, and bureaucratically diffuse. Whoever had decided to transport warheads on rickety trucks would forever remain unknown. It was the kind of operation that involved hundreds of people over a period of years; the kind of decision that, if it ever caused embarrassment, would be regretted by everyone—but blamed on no one. Had anyone gone to jail for deliberately exposing ignorant GIs to radioactive hazards during nuclear tests in the 1950s, or taken responsibility for the nuclear debris poisoning the soil and water at Rocky Flats? Emotionally, Duval needed a more specific villain and Sheriff Dan Reiner met every qualification.

"That sonovabitch," barked Duval as he sent a half-full glass of Pepsi crashing against the far wall of his medical office. The more he thought about Reiner, the more the Sheriff seemed responsible for everything. He had to know a shipment was coming through, thought Duval. Certainly the Defense Department or the Department of Energy would keep local law officials informed about a nuclear shipment through their territory. Wouldn't they? He wondered, then decided it didn't matter. Whatever Reiner knew beforehand, the authorities would certainly have informed him minutes after the accident that they had a problem in his county and needed his cooperation.

That made Reiner responsible for Michelle. If the sheriff had told him then what had happened, it would have ended right there. But he hadn't.

Duval had known Dan Reiner vaguely since he was a boy. Reiner was a touch outlandish and certainly enjoyed his reputation for gruff bravado, for being one of the last of the old time, western, county sheriffs. But Duval also knew that behind his twang and deliberate folksiness, Reiner was an intelligent law officer with a reputation for integrity. Duval was not only sickened by what had happened to Michelle, but genuinely shocked by Reiner's part in it. It was like learning that your best friend was a child molester. The evidence might be overwhelming, but somehow you can't quite believe it. In this case, Duval thought the facts were clear, and Reiner was not going to get away free.

He dialed Reiner's private office number, and, for the second time that day, he was surprised to find the sheriff working on a Saturday afternoon.

"Reiner, this is George Duval." Reiner seemed surprised to be hearing from him again and quickly registered the hostility.

"What now, George?"

Duval was tired of games. "I know what a Broken Arrow accident is, and I know you're covering one up." There was a long silence at the other end of the line. Just when Duval was about to repeat himself Reiner spoke.

"George, what the fuck are you talking about? The last time I heard that term was on some 1960s TV show, and if there *was* a Broken Arrow accident hereabouts I wouldn't know whether to call an ambulance or get a mop and bucket."

"You're lying."

"Who the fuck you callin' a liar, boy? Are you talking about your little mishap Wednesday, or have you just gone completely out of your mind?"

Duval had to admit to himself that Reiner was good. For some reason he thought that the mere mention of a Broken Arrow would startle the sheriff into some kind of admission.

"Reiner, Michelle's been exposed to that stuff, and I hold you personally responsible."

The sheriff sounded dumbfounded. "Exposed to what stuff, George? Is Michelle okay? Has she had an accident or something? And what's this Reiner stuff? How about Sheriff or Dan?"

Now it was Duval's turn to be confounded. Despite his certainty that Reiner was holding back, Duval had to concede that Reiner sounded sincere. It made Duval question himself. Could Reiner be telling the truth? Duval decided to try his ace card.

"Sheriff, I know what's going on. I got a chemical analysis done of some samples I took from the site. I've got contaminated photos and x-rays, and I know what contaminated them and how. If I don't get some questions answered pretty damn quick, I'm going to the press. Let's see what

Uncle Sam and the Sheridan County Sheriff have to say when this hits the Denver papers."

There was another long pause. This time there was clear anger in Reiner's otherwise controlled voice. "Georgie, boy, I think you need some help. Maybe a couple of weeks in Kauai or maybe a couple of months at some hospital where they suit you up in those tight, white jackets. I repeat, I haven't the slightest goddamn idea what in the hell you're going on about. Newspapers? Go ahead."

"I will, Reiner. I've got a friend at the *Denver Post.*"

"Lovely. You go tell your friend about your mysterious hot water tank and your shitty photography and your Broken Bow—or whatever it's called. They'll think they're talking to a raving lunatic."

"You're still lying, Reiner."

Now Reiner was furious. "George, I knew your father for thirty years before he passed away. I watched him build up that little corner drugstore into a six-county chain. I still get a Christmas card from your mom in Scottsdale every year and send one in return. I watched you grow. You know me. I may spin a whopper over a drink once in a while, but I wouldn't lie to you, and you know it." Reiner's tone suddenly softened. "Come out to my house tomorrow, and we'll wash down a couple of steaks and get to the bottom of this whole thing. Best I can do, George, and considering what an insinuating and rude shit you've been, I think it's pretty generous."

Duval didn't know whether to apologize, say "Thank you," or loudly hang up. His mind was addled, and the throbbing in his temples was extending to the back of his neck and promising to develop into a full-bore migraine. He decided on a middle course. He kept his tone distant and formal but accepted Reiner's offer. "Okay, Sheriff, I'll see you tomorrow. Say two o'clock."

"Just fine, George. Maybe we can save a good friendship." Reiner hung up.

Duval got to his feet and, looking for something to occupy his hands, decided to clean up the broken glass on the floor and the cola stains on the far wall.

The task reminded him of what Loevinger had said about cleaning up the accident site. The government would move when things quieted down. The accident had been a couple days ago and things were now quiet. Hell, they'd been quiet from the beginning, he thought. He realized that he needed to get to the site for more samples before the government sucked up, buried, or otherwise reconfigured the evidence. Loevinger had made it clear he wanted no further part in the thing.

Duval put down his sponge and walked to his supply room. He pulled out a pair of disposable surgical gloves, a disposable mask, and a surgical hat. He walked back to his office, rummaged in a box in a clothes closet, and pulled out a pair of ear plugs he used when swimming. He threw the objects into a nylon backpack and added his camera, a whisk broom, and three padded envelopes that he found in a file cabinet. He secured the pack to his back, picked up his helmet, and headed for his motorcycle.

It was dark by the time he entered Rushville and turned south on State Highway 250. As usual he passed no traffic in either direction and until he spotted the glow on the horizon, the only light available came from the stars overhead and his new headlamp.

The glow first became noticeable about ten miles north of the accident site. A dim aurora bloomed skyward from a light source concealed beyond the ridges of the rolling landscape. It was the kind of night glow a motorist might see on approaching a large settlement from the desert—but there was no settlement ahead, no nothing until the tiny and misnamed hamlet of Lakeside more than thirty miles away. The aurora became brighter as Duval continued south, and, as he crested the last ridge before the crash site, he slowed his bike to a stop. Intuition made him turn off his headlamp.

Below him a half mile away, headlights and yellow flashing Mars lights flickered in the night from an assortment of trucks and construction vehicles working alongside the dry riverbed. Duval shut down his engine and listened to the roar of front-end loaders and the steady "beep-beep-beep" that accompanies heavy equipment moving backward. He also detected a strange, deep-throated whistling noise that sounded like a cross between a small jet engine and a giant vacuum cleaner. Duval found the scene incredible. Here, along a nearly deserted stretch of highway, smack in the middle of one of the most isolated sections of the high plains, a small army of men and equipment was working under artificial light to accomplish some task that couldn't wait until morning. Duval now had no doubt. Sheriff Reiner had been lying. He felt the rage return, rage at Reiner and rage at himself for letting Reiner sucker him.

Duval switched on his light, and accelerated down the ridge toward the gathered vehicles. He pulled to a stop above the dry riverbed, shut down the bike and studied the scene. The men below were so absorbed in their work and their machines were so noisy that Duval believed his arrival hadn't been noticed.

Two flatbed semi-trailer trucks bearing the Ryder Truck Rental logo lined the shoulder on the west side of the highway. They had clearly been used to transport the two front-end loaders and one midget bulldozer working beside the burned-out truck at the bottom of the dry wash. On the east shoulder were two large vehicles that looked like moving vans and a lone dump truck. The top of one van was serving as a platform for several large klieg lights powered by a generator that Duval couldn't see. The second van was distinct only because of a hose, about a foot in diameter, that streamed from its side and down the highway embankment toward the bottom of the dry riverbed. There, two men grasping large handles directed a wide nozzle toward the earth at the back of the wrecked truck. It was the source of the heavy whistling noise. The two vans and the earth-moving equipment were painted in international lime-green and bore the words "Rocky Mountain Toxic Disposal/Denver" in bold orange letters outlined in black. Above the letters, in a style that reminded Duval of Mr. Zip Code, a logo showed a bulldozer picking up a barrel labeled with a skull and crossbones. Oddly, there was no telephone number written anywhere. Duval removed his knapsack and pulled out his camera. With the lens wide open and the flash off, he focused on the logo and snapped off a shot.

He was focusing again when he felt a tap on his shoulder. He was so startled that he lost his footing and fell over with his motorcycle.

Alexander Onega watched Duval pick up his Kawasaki and then spoke.

"Who are you, buddy?"

Duval decided to play dumb.

"Me? I'm a local. I was on my way down toward Big Hill when I saw you guys here and just stopped."

"Big Hill, huh?" answered Onega, pronouncing Hill like heel. "Wouldn't Nebraska 27 have been a better road?"

Duval was trying to determine the man's accent. Polish, he thought, but he couldn't be sure.

"Yeah, but this highway is much prettier."

"At *night?*" asked the man.

Duval had a strong impression that he knew the man from somewhere, but he couldn't be certain. A vertical scar creased the man's forehead, running from the hairline to the top of the left eye, then continuing again from the bottom of the eye down the cheek to the chin. An odd place for Captain Ahab, thought Duval, a couple of thousand miles from the nearest ocean.

"You worry about scenery at night?" Onega scoffed.

"I'm running late," answered Duval, hearing how lame he sounded even to himself.

"Why are you taking pictures?" Onega asked in a threatening tone.

Duval decided to take the offensive. "What are you guys doing here?" he demanded.

"None of your business," snapped Onega, pronouncing business "bee-zee-ness." It struck Duval as a very un-American answer. He was about to protest when he spotted two men struggling up the dry wash toward them. One was a tall, slim blond and the other a stocky Hispanic. From the way his interrogator backed off, Duval figured one of the approaching men was the boss.

The blond man eyed Duval with a faint hint of surprise or recognition.

"Perez and I thought there might be a problem," said Georgi Rovno, indicating his Latino companion. He turned to the man with the scar. "What's up, Onega?"

"This man has been snooping around, Georgi, taking pictures."

Georgi? Duval almost laughed, hearing the name as Georgie. It didn't fit its owner.

Georgi Rovno turned back to Duval. "May I help you?" he asked in perfect and business-like English.

"Nope, I was just passing by. I just wanted to know what you men were doing out here."

Rovno smiled and removing his hard hat, brushed his sleeve against a sweaty brow. "To be perfectly honest, we're cleaning up a toxic spill after a highway accident."

"That's all I wanted to know," replied Duval putting his camera back. "What kind of toxic spill?"

Rovno smiled again. "Oh, just a bunch of chemicals that you've probably never heard of, but that shouldn't be left out here to damage the ground water."

Duval again got the impression that the man knew him or at least knew his face. "You mean like chlorine, stuff like that?"

"Exactly. It took us two days to get our stuff up here from Denver, that's why we're working at night."

The answer was almost plausible, thought Duval, knowing it was a lie. "Well, I'll just be going then," he said as he turned his front wheel to the left.

Onega began to protest. "But Georgi, he was taking pictures—" The man began to reach toward a bulging pocket, and Duval thought he looked like someone reaching for a gun.

Rovno put his hand over the arm of his subordinate and smiled at Duval. "Sometimes Onega, here, gets a little concerned for security. The people who contract us don't usually like a whole lot of publicity as you might guess."

I bet the fuck not, thought Duval. Rovno was smiling again, but Duval was sure he saw malevolence behind the superficially friendly face. Duval started his Kawasaki, flicked on his headlamp, and drove off. He was two miles away before he realized he was heading back toward Rushville and not south toward Big Hill. Screw it, he thought. They know I was lying, and they know I know they were lying too. For the second time since the accident, he wondered if he might be in danger.

Sunday, September 12

North of Chita, Ushta awoke from his long and deep sleep and stomped outside the shed into a spectacularly blue Sunday afternoon. He checked his watch and realized he had slept nearly eighteen hours. He searched in the pockets of his greatcoat and found a half-empty pack of Russian cigarettes and a box of matches. He rarely smoked, especially domestic tobacco, but as he lit the cigarette and inhaled deeply, he felt a certain calm returning to him that he had not known since his encounter with the two soldiers.

He contemplated his options, his back-up strategy, his story, and his goal and, believing he had planned as well as he could, tossed the cigarette aside. He returned to the shed, started the jeep, and backed out into the sunlight. He opened the bag on the seat beside him, took out a thermos, and poured several ounces of water into a large can that until the day before contained stewed tomatos. He turned the motor on, then walked to the front of the jeep, opened the hood, placed the can on the exhaust manifold, and waited. As the water heated, he listened again to the conversation on the jeep's radio. So far that morning, there had been no attempts to contact anyone who hadn't answered. As far as Ushta knew, the flattened sergeant and his venal corporal were not officially missing.

Ushta checked the water with his finger, decided it was hot enough, and using an old bar of soap, a rag, and an uncomfortably dull straight razor, shaved himself in the jeep's left hand, exterior mirror. He found the process painful but visually satisfying. His reflection showed his tired eyes, but once he ran his fingers through his hair, straightened his collar, and put on the corporal's cap, he thought he looked very much like a Red Army noncom. Out here in the boondocks, he thought, they weren't exactly known for their spit and polish anyway. He checked his pockets again, making sure that his ID was in place, and one final time rehearsed the vital statistics: name, rank, serial number, date of birth, and place of birth. Confident that he had the information firmly in mind, he put the jeep in gear and began rolling toward the house.

When he pulled into the slushy front yard, he realized that he was parked before an agricultural outpost. The house was rundown, its unpainted wooden planking split and rotted at the corners, its windows filthy. Across the yard, he saw an ancient, rusting Belarus tractor behind the half-opened doors of a small barn. To the left of the barn were two wire-mesh corncribs in a similar state of disrepair. The place was undoubtedly part of some gigantic state farm or cooperative whose headquarters was probably in the vicinity. Ushta shut down the jeep, walked to the rickety front door, and knocked. Inside, he could hear a crying infant and the sound of scraping chairs, but no one answered. He tried two more times and was turning away when the door creaked open a few inches. A woman who looked fifty but could have been thirty-five peeked through the narrow opening. "What do you want? We don't like strangers here, go away."

Warm, thought Ushta. He remembered his uniform and tried to sound military. "I want to see the man in charge. Where is he?"

The woman said nothing, but pointing with her finger toward the fields beyond the cribs jabbed at the air and then slammed the door.

Ushta walked to the cribs and studying the fields beyond saw a lone man on a tractor approaching the compound on a deeply rutted, snow-covered farm path. Ushta walked back to his jeep, lit another cigarette, and waited.

When the tractor rounded the cribs and pulled into the yard, Ushta saw that it was pulling some kind of implement supporting rows of silvered disks that apparently could be lowered to the earth. Ushta had no idea what it was or why the man would be using it after a snowfall. Since his knowledge of farming came almost exclusively from old propaganda films showing heroic workers bringing in the harvest, he wasn't surprised by his ignorance. Ushta waved at the driver but got no response. The man stopped and shut down the tractor, disconnected the disk implement, and wiped his hands on his jacket before acknowledging Ushta's presence. Ushta offered him a cigarette, which he took.

"Who are you, and what do you want?" he asked.

Friendly people, aren't they? That was Ushta's first thought. "I'm Corporal Tartikoff and I need directions."

"You lost?"

"You might say that," answered Ushta. "I need to get back to Chita, and I can't find the road."

The farmer seemed to think that was funny. "You city boys," he said with a smile. "Couldn't find your cock from your collarbone without a map." A suspicious look then came over the man's face. "How did you get out here, then, if you're lost?"

Ushta tried to sound just a little angry. "Look, I've been up there since three this morning," he said, pointing to the forested hillsides from which he had come. "We got a jeep and two men up there missing, and we're all trying to locate them before they freeze to death. Problem is this jeep here isn't doing too well. I've got to get it back to Chita. So where's the main road?"

Again there was no answer, but Ushta saw that the man was staring beneath the jeep's canvas canopy at something on the back seat. Ushta smiled to himself, turned around, and retrieved the bulldozer's tool kit. He crouched down and unfastened the lid, showing a top tray overflowing with well-maintained closed- and open-ended wrenches, a ratchet set with an extender, and a plug puller, which Ushta didn't think had much use on a diesel. He lifted the tray and revealed various screw drivers, a soldering gun, a voltmeter, an electric drill with a bit set, two plastic funnels, and assorted additional tools. There were more supplies in the tray below that. The man's eyes gleamed.

"How much for that?" asked the man.

Ushta was delighted by his luck. Neither the sergeant nor the corporal had been carrying any money, and Ushta knew he would need cash to lay low in Chita and stock up for beyond. He named a price. The man offered one fourth what Ushta asked. Ushta suggested a compromise. "And, I'll tell you what," he continued. "I can bring you another set for the same price a week from today."

"You can get me more of these sets?" asked the man, showing genuine enthusiasm for the first time.

"No problem. And you know you can sell them on the black market for ten times what I'm asking. You can go into Chita and sell them to, what's his name? Zeya." The corporal he had killed may have been a larcenous cutthroat, thought Ushta, but at least he'd revealed the name of the local black market boss before he died.

"So, you know Zeya, huh?"

"Doesn't everybody?"

"Why not sell to him directly, then?" asked the man.

"Are we talking about the same Zeya?" asked Ushta, "the Zeya working behind the old church?"

"Zeya doesn't work near any church. He's at the railroad station, where he's always been," snapped the man.

"Just checking," retorted Ushta. "I guess you really do know Zeya. If so, you should also know Zeya doesn't like dealing directly with soldiers. He always thinks it's a trap. This way, though, you make money, I make money."

The man considered, and without a word he disappeared into the house. Five minutes later he emerged with a handful of ruble notes, which he carefully counted in a loud voice as he placed them in Ushta's hand. He then gave Ushta a crude pencil drawing of the roads between the outpost and the main highway leading to Chita.

"How far?" asked Ushta.

"Thirty-five, forty miles," said the man, taking possession of his new tool kit. "You can make it in two hours if the roads aren't too snowy."

"And in Chita, if I don't want to stay at the barracks tonight?"

"I thought you came from Chita," answered the man.

"Let's say I'm very new to the area."

The man pointed to the map. "You can stop here, on the edge of town, about three miles outside downtown Chita. He pointed to an intersection marked with the name of a street. Ask for Miss Nina. She'll give you a place to stay. It will cost you though, especially if you're looking for privacy." The man smiled.

Ushta's expression was cold.

"I need some black paint."

"What for?"

"That's my business. I only want a few ounces worth."

"I don't have any black paint," said the man. "You'll have to settle for black rust preventer."

Ushta gestured that rust preventer would be fine and waited for the man as he went to the small barn and returned minutes later with a small glass container of black liquid. Ushta took the container, waved at the stranger, and restarted the jeep.

A mile down the road, out of sight of the farmhouse, Ushta took a rag, dipped it in the black rust preventer, and began daubing at the white numbers on the black military plate. Since the plate was merely painted and not stamped, it wasn't hard for him to change BP 061 FL23 to P 06

L2. It looked a little odd, he thought, but not much cruder than many of the badly made number plates attached to military vehicles. Satisfied, he tossed the paint and rag away and continued down the road.

The hand drawn map was crude but good. It took Ushta only an hour to find the main road to Chita, and the road was well-paved and maintained. Fifteen miles from his destination, however, traffic began to slow and eventually halt. Farm wagons and other vehicles were closely packed as far ahead as Ushta could see. The traffic would inch forward every few seconds, but something ahead was snarling the roadway.

Two hours and a mile later, Ushta felt a shiver in his back and a rolling in his stomach when he first caught sight of a police roadblock. He turned on the radio and listened for ten minutes, but there was still no reference to the missing soldiers. There was, however, at long last, discussion of an escapee from Pechora. Ushta rehearsed his lines. He worried only about the corporal's unit. Nothing on his ID said where the man was based or gave the name of his company or division. Questions about that could be fatal. If pressed, Ushta could say he was from the 341st Engineering Brigade at Pechora. If they checked he would die, but at least it was a real unit.

As he approached the blockade he became increasingly worried by the intensity of the police search. They checked everything and everybody. Identification documents were flashed, grabbed, and checked on radios. Some vehicles were allowed to pass, others were pulled to the shoulder for more detailed searches. A bus carrying farm workers had been emptied and the forlorn-looking men were going through their tattered bags and possessions piece by piece before the eyes of armed police troops.

Ushta pulled the corporal's ID from his pocket and held it open in his left hand as the jeep approached the three officers in charge of the checkpoint. The first officer squinted at him, briefly eyed the outstretched ID, and then with a *V* for victory sign, smiled and waved him by. Ushta sloppily saluted with the hand holding the ID and passed through into normal traffic. His eyes stung from the salty sweat pouring down his forehead.

Eleven miles farther, he came to the intersection where Nina did business. Ushta pulled to a curb and quickly determined which of the nearly identical three-story brick houses at each of the four corners of the intersection was hers. He lit his final cigarette and studied. The layout was clear, even in the gray, fading afternoon light. When he was certain he understood it all, he pulled a screwdriver from his bag and, with some trouble, managed to remove the military radio. He slung his rifle over his shoulder, grabbed the radio, and walked to the house's side entrance, which opened on a narrow pedestrian alley. He knocked.

An attractive woman of about twenty, dressed in a black frock and wearing a white apron opened the door. She looked at Ushta. "We don't want any soldiers here."

Ushta tried again to sound official. "I'm not here to avail myself of your usual services. I've got a message for Miss Nina."

The door closed and Ushta waited, thinking that as suburban whorehouses in provincial capitals went, Madame Nina's didn't look too bad. When the door reopened, a handsome woman in her early fifties, well-dressed in a kind of evening gown, answered. "You want to speak with me?"

"I want a place to stay and clean up for the night. I don't want any of your girls."

"Why don't you stay at the barracks?"

"Let's say I would be more comfortable here."

"I hear they have troubles back there," she said, pointing to the northwest. "A man is missing from a camp, and now I hear on the grapevine that maybe two soldiers are missing as well. Maybe they deserted? Maybe you are one of them?"

Ushta felt doubly lucky to be through the roadblock. If Madame Nina knew that two soldiers were overdue, he was astonished that the police hadn't heard. "I know nothing about deserters," he said, "except that I am not one." He looked her sternly in the eye. "I swear on my children's heads that I have not deserted the Army." Except for the lie about the children he didn't have, Ushta was telling the truth and apparently it showed.

She motioned for him to enter the house, and Ushta was immediately struck by its cleanliness and good state of repair.

"Sorry about that, Corporal. One cannot be too careful. That news about the missing soldiers may be nothing. Just a bit of conversation one of my girls picked up from a colonel earlier this afternoon. Probably nothing, the police don't seem to know anything about it yet. Now to business. Do you have any hard currency?"

"No, but I have something better," said Ushta. He handed her his AK47 and the military radio. "Zeya will pay you well for these, I'm sure. The AK speaks for itself. The radio has many good uses, especially for scanning military and police frequencies. I think Zeya or even you might find that worthwhile."

Madame Nina seemed doubtful.

"Look," said Ushta, "I'm in town to do some business with Zeya. I don't think it would be wise for me to stay in the barracks or in a state hotel. I have something Zeya can use, and I'm sure he'll be appreciative if you help me this evening. In the meantime, I expect to be back next Sunday and the Sunday after that, and, if there's anything you need that perhaps I can help you with, I have some useful military connections. Think about it."

The name Zeya seemed to encourage her. "Okay. I'll keep your rifle and radio. Was that your jeep out there?"

He nodded.

"I'll have my man bring it around to the rear garden. Now, Corporal, why don't I show you a room and help you get cleaned up?" She paused. "By the way, Corporal, are you from Moscow? You sound like someone from Moscow. I've always wanted to go there. Could you tell me about it?"

Ushta burst out laughing. He didn't know if it was from relief or emotional exhaustion.

Anthony Torrelli did not like working Sundays, but it was not because he was a religious man. If asked, he would identify himself as a Roman Catholic, but he was not particularly devout, and missing mass was not something that weighed heavily on him.

Torrelli thought Sunday was properly devoted to family, and family meant more than his wife and three children. Family meant three and four generations of Torrellis gathered at his house for a feast of pasta, for gossip and for ballgames in the backyard.

Sunday was not a time to be at the Baltimore docks. Torrelli liked his work and accepted that losing an occasional Sunday was a price a customs officer sometimes had to pay. He just wished it could be a different Sunday. His oldest son, Paul, didn't get home from college that much, and Torrelli was anxious to spend more time with him.

When Torrelli arrived at the docks shortly after noon, the motor vessel *Cherkassy* was already securely moored to the concrete pier. The ship was out of Odessa with intermediate stops at Barcelona and St. John's, Newfoundland, and had taken twenty-two days to complete the westward voyage to Baltimore. It was a small, diesel-powered, break-bulk cargo ship, one of the few Torrelli saw anymore that actually carried freight in fore and aft holds, and required the services of gangs of stevedores. It would take three days to empty *Cherkassy* of its cargo, when loaded to capacity, while big container vessels carrying three times the load could be emptied by a few men in four hours. *Cherkassy* was never fully loaded. Torrelli sometimes had wondered how the ship could make any money, and he ultimately reasoned that it probably didn't.

He had seen *Cherkassy* several times before. To the extent that any ships from the old Soviet bloc could keep to a schedule, *Cherkassy* was making Baltimore a regular stop about once every six months. He knew the itinerary: Odessa, Barcelona, St. John's, Baltimore, then home again with stops at Cadiz and Piraeus, before the run up the Dardanelles and the Bosporus to the Black Sea and Ukraine. Besides its obvious shortcomings as a commercial carrier, two things about the *Cherkassy* always bothered Torrelli. First, no matter how hard he concentrated, he couldn't help referring to the vessel's home country as *the* Ukraine. He could think of Burma as Myanmar, and had long adjusted to Zimbabwe for Rhodesia, but just plain Ukraine was impossible. In Torrelli's mind, saying you were from Ukraine was like saying you were visiting Rocky Mountains or that Chicago was on Great Lakes. Ukraine needed a *the*. His second concern was a professional discomfort with *Cherkassy*'s odd cargo.

In the last year Torrelli had personally inspected *Cherkassy* two times. It carried the usual vodka, furs, and caviar, but often included a shipment of industrial boilers, a product Torrelli had never seen imported into the United States. For an industrial superpower, America imported an astounding variety and quantity of industrial equipment. It received printing presses from Germany, jet engines from France, baking ovens from Italy, machine tools from Holland. Torrelli had seen them all.

Boilers, however, were unusual. Indeed, industrial equipment of any kind from Russia was exceedingly rare. Torrelli wouldn't have thought more about it except for David McGannon's phone call three days before. Torrelli and McGannon had worked together as young customs officers in New York before moving on to their present assignments in the early 1980s. They had kept in touch on both personal and professional matters, so the call from Boston was not unusual. McGannon had told Torrelli about the fire on the Moran docks and about the odd boiler he'd been inspecting when the explosion hit. He had asked Torrelli to keep his eye out for any boiler shipments to Baltimore, as a professional courtesy. Torrelli had agreed to be alert. He rechecked the vessel's manifest and confirmed again that it was carrying two 2,800-pound boilers.

They were described as light, oil and gas fired, packaged firetube boilers, and Torrelli knew from two previous inspections that they were about seven feet long and three feet in diameter and looked like relics from Victorian England. They were manufactured, according to their Russian and English nameplates, by a company called Sukhona Boiler Works, in the city of Yaroslavl. Each nameplate specified electric power requirements; steam pressure in kilopascals; temperature outputs in degrees celsius; and various serial numbers, manufacturing codes, and special warnings. Neither of the two previous inspections had turned up anything unusual. He had discovered that the machines were extremely difficult to search in any detail—gaining full access to their cores could be achieved only by destructive means. At a minimum, after removing the entire boiler face, which would have required pneumatic wrenches and heavy lift machinery, welders using acetylene torches would have been needed to remove the huge steel disk supporting the ends of thirty-five or forty tubes which ran horizontally from the front of the boiler to its rear. Torrelli had searched as best he could by shining a flashlight through an access plate and by opening and partially disassembling a door supporting a burner and a blower, but he had seen nothing unusual. A dog had not helped.

On his second search, just to satisfy his curiosity, Torrelli had borrowed a German shepherd specially trained to sniff out minute traces of cocaine. He had not been surprised when the animal detected no drugs. Considering the boiler's massive, welded construction, Torrelli figured dealers would have found it too much bother to hide drugs inside or retrieve them later. They had far simpler ways to do that. Still, for reasons he could not quite understand, the boilers bothered not only him, but his old friend David McGannon.

Today, Torrelli finished inspecting the cargo before it was unloaded. The paperwork on the two boilers looked good, and a cursory examination of the machines revealed nothing, as usual. He made a mental note to call McGannon and was walking back to his office by the pier when a shipping agent who identified himself as Stefan Dobrany came up beside him.

"Is everything going to be released, officer?" he asked.

"I don't think there will be any problems," answered Torrelli. "What are you picking up?"

"I'm waiting for two boilers going to St. Louis and Tulsa. I've got a flatbed truck on the clock and burning up my money right now, and I just wanted to make sure there weren't going to be any delays."

Torrelli jumped at the opening. "What's the hurry?" he asked. "You couldn't have held off the truck until tomorrow?"

Dobrany hesitated briefly, and then answered in halting, heavily accented English. "The customer in St. Louis has asked for priority delivery, and he has paid extra for it. We figured that *Cherkassy* couldn't be carrying much and probably could finish off-loading in just a few hours. We decided to save time by standing by."

Torrelli wanted to know more. "Want a cup of coffee, Stefan? It's going to be at least an hour or two before those boilers come off. Hey, you're lucky. If *Cherkassy* had been loaded, you wouldn't be out of here until Tuesday."

Dobrany accepted the offer and followed Torrelli into the customs office. Torrelli poured the agent some coffee and asked him a question. "What do you know about these boilers, Stefan?"

"Me?" Dobrany seemed surprised by the question. "I don't know anything about them. It's like this, Mr. Torrelli. My brother and I immigrated from Czechoslovakia back in nineteen eighty-nine. We both speak Russian and had a cousin who worked for one of the Russian state shipping agencies. When Russia started changing and loosened some of their political control over businesses, my brother and I figured we could start a small American shipping agency and get our cousin to steer some business our way. We're not real big time, but we're starting to make some money. The boiler account is one of our largest, so far. But tell me, why are you so curious about the boilers? I noticed that twice before you inspected them very thoroughly. Is something wrong?"

"Nothing I can put my finger on," replied Torrelli. "It's just that when you work at this as long as I have you notice things that don't seem quite right. The Russians sure are shipping a lot of boilers through Baltimore. Just seems odd, since they never shipped anything like that before."

"Hmmm," said Dobrany. "Well, it's a changing world. They've got to sell something to keep their heads above water."

Torrelli had to concede to himself that the man had a point. The Russians could export only so much vodka.

Eventually, they'd have to start selling industrial products. Boilers were probably as good a place to start as any. Torrelli pointed to a coffee pot. "Care for some more coffee?" he asked. Dobrany accepted another cup and watched Torrelli as he returned to his desk and pulled a copy of the *Baltimore Yellow Pages* out of a drawer.

"Mind sticking around a bit while I make a phone call or two?" he asked.

Dobrany shook his head to indicate that he had no objection, took a copy of the *Baltimore Sun* out of his jacket's side pocket, and began reading.

Torrelli flipped through several pages in the phone book until he came to a listing for "Boilers." He was astounded by the number of entries. There were boiler manufacturers, boiler maintenance and repair companies, boiler installers and cleaners, boiler-chemicals manufacturers, and boiler distributors. He laughed at his own ignorance. Who would have thought it? Who thinks about boilers at all? He looked for the biggest display ad on the page—a boiler sales and service outfit advertising all sorts of services he had never even heard of and a twenty-four-hour number. He dialed and was moderately startled when it answered on the first ring. Good service for a Sunday, he thought.

"I need to talk to someone about boilers."

"Your boiler got a problem?" a man asked.

Torrelli identified himself as a U.S. Customs Service officer and asked if the man could spare a few minutes to answer some questions. The man, who said his name was Raymond Trimble, seemed amenable.

"Are there a lot of boilermakers in the United States?" asked Torrelli.

"Depends on what you mean," replied Trimble. "There are only a handful of big guys. Cleaver-Brooks, American Standard, Babcock and Wilcox, and a few others. There are all sorts of little guys and customizers, but none of them has any real presence nationwide. They're local outfits, more or less."

"How's your foreign competition?"

Trimble laughed. "There ain't any."

"You don't have competitors from Japan or Germany or someplace?"

"Not really. Boilers are big, heavy, and expensive to ship—even small ones. And the technology hasn't really changed that much over the years. It's not like somebody is going to make some huge technological breakthrough and blow everybody else out of business. The boiler industry in America is big, profitable, and mature. The big guys know their stuff as well as anybody else and haven't allowed any foreigners to get a hold of our market."

"Have you ever heard of a manufacturer called, wait a second—" Torrelli looked at a notepad and continued. "Ever heard of a company called Sukhona Boiler Works?"

Trimble paused to consider. "Sukhona? No, can't say I have. What is it, Swedish or Finnish or something?"

"Actually, it's Russian."

"Russian? I've never heard of a Russian boiler company. But then, I can't say I know much about Russia."

"Well," said Torrelli, "I just watched a cargo ship off-load two boilers made by this Sukhona company. I can think of six, maybe seven Sukhona boilers coming into Baltimore alone in the last couple years or so."

"Really?" said Trimble, sounding genuinely surprised. "Funny I've never heard of them. Are they big?"

Torrelli outlined the boilers' dimensions.

"Oh, small ones. Well, that's a lot of boilers coming into the country at one port, big or small. Tell you what, though. If you really need some info you should call one of our industry reps in Washington." Trimble gave Torrelli a name of a Washington PR firm that Torrelli recognized and a number. "It's really a public relations firm and a lobbying outfit, but they do some work for the industry and keep track of things like foreign competition. They can probably tell you about the company, whatever its name is."

"Thanks," said Torrelli. "Just one last question. You think that you would know of a company like this if it was doing a good business?"

"I think so. Look, the company I work for represents a couple of boilermakers. We're not particular. We sell and maintain them all. If there was a new guy in town he would normally come to a company like ours and try to get us to handle his product. We'd be flooded with brochures, get an invite to their factory to see their products, that kind of thing. No Russian company has come to us or anybody else I know of in the business."

Torrelli thanked Trimble and hung up. He checked the document again and called a number in Chicago that belonged to a company called Scriba-Illinois Corporation, located on South Keokuk Street. There was no answer.

Torrelli looked at his watch, then dialed a number at the U.S. Customs Service headquarters in Washington, D.C. It took him five minutes to get the computer center. "I need to check something, Mr. DeVinney," he began.

"Shoot," said John DeVinney, an officer at the agency.

"Can you do some kind of computer run that will tell me how many boilers have entered the United States in the last six months?"

"You mean like hot water boilers?"

"No, I mean industrial boilers. They may be called packaged boilers or firetube boilers or maybe industrial steam generators. I've got two on a ship here that are manifested as boilers, but I've seen some before and their nameplates call them a 'firetube steam generator.'"

"Well, I can take a look. For the whole United States?"

"Yes. But listen, this doesn't have to be perfect. I'm just trying to get a rough idea of how many of these things come into the country."

"Well, I guess I can take a look using the info you've given. But it will take a while. This computer system is not brilliantly cross-indexed. It's a piece of crap if you want to know the truth. It will take some pretty good computer detective work to come up with good numbers. When do you need this?"

"I'm not in a big hurry," said Torrelli. "Late today? Tomorrow afternoon? Tuesday even. Whenever you can come up with some round numbers at your convenience."

"Well, I'm not exactly overloaded today," said DeVinney. "Sounds like a bit of a challenge. I'll get back to you later today or tomorrow by noon, if that's okay."

Torrelli said that would be fine, thanked him, and hung up. He asked Dobrany a few more questions, told him there was nothing to worry about, just an old customs inspector's curiosity, and let him go. Torrelli thought he saw a distinct look of hostility in Dobrany's face as the shipping agent left the room. He wondered about it briefly and dismissed the idea. Must be my imagination, he thought. He started to call McGannon in Boston, realized it was Sunday, and hung up before making a connection. Why bother him on a Sunday? Tomorrow would be soon enough.

The images were vivid. George Duval was sitting with Michelle on a sun splashed balcony overlooking a large swimming pool several floors below. Beyond it was a flat aquamarine sea speckled by white sails.

They were dining at midday, enjoying the smooth hand movements of a young Spanish waiter as he removed a pewter lid covering a tureen of creamy soup and lit the wick beneath a steaming iron pan of soft, yellow paella. Duval was startled when the waiter's head began to sink slowly downward into his collar until his eyes and then his forehead disappeared, leaving visible only the long wavy black hairs of his scalp. Michelle thought it was funny and started pointing and laughing hysterically when the hairs thickened to the size of a garden hose and then stretched upward a foot or more and began waving in unison like some crazed black anemone, angling back and forth from the neck opening of the waiter's jacket, as if washed by a turbulent current.

Duval also watched several geckos, their tiny lizard-like bodies translucent in the powerful sunlight, race from inside the jacket, over the collar, and around the waiter's shoulders before ducking inside the jacket again and scrambling downward to the base of the waving tentacles. A phone began to ring, and the merriment in Michelle's face was soon replaced by a distressed flush and the irregular pattern of blood-swollen veins. A man in a bellman's uniform, his face crushed, with a steering wheel around his neck, handed Duval the phone, but it didn't work. Duval could hear his father just fine, but his father couldn't hear him.

Michelle now began to scream as if in agonizing pain, and Duval watched as the deep blush that suffused her face spread down her neck and concentrated in her chest, now burning so brightly that he could see the glow coming through her white blouse. Flames burst forth from Michelle's throat, and, on the telephone, Duval's father told him she was burning up inside and must be cooled off. Duval lifted her over his head and threw her from the balcony toward the pool below. When she fell short, there was no thudding sound, but rather a series of pops as her body broke into crystal-shaped chunks, as if she had been an immense block of ice. Children, all of them with black anemone tentacles where their heads should have been, ran toward her and were about to pounce on her splintered pieces. Duval was again distracted by the ringing of a phone. Mr. Steering-Wheel Head handed it to him and Duval heard the distant voice of Juanita Muñoz.

"Señor Doctor! Señor Doctor! Wake up. It's me, Juanita. Wake up, Doctor."

It took Duval a half minute to recognize the bedside phone in his hand, to realize he'd been dreaming. He became conscious of the harsh Sunday morning light pouring through the windows. He squinted tightly as his eyes adjusted, and he finally responded to his housekeeper.

"Juanita, I'm awake, awake. Sorry, but I was in a very deep sleep."

"Señor Doctor," the housekeeper continued, in an accent almost as thick as the day she left Mexico fifty years before, "you must come to the clinic, she has been robbed."

Duval was still trying to clear his head. He glanced at the clock-radio behind the phone and was surprised that it was already past nine-thirty in the morning. He was normally not a late sleeper. "What do you mean robbed? The clinic in Whiteclay?"

"Yes, Señor. I come in this morning from my brother's house in Oglala. The back door is broken in. Inside, everything is a mess. All the papers are on the floor, and all the medicines is on the floor too. Many things is broken. I call the sheriff now, no?"

"No," said Duval. No need to call Reiner, he thought. Reiner was probably responsible or at least would cover for those who were. "Leave everything as it is. Don't clean up, Juanita. I'm coming. I'll be there in an hour or so."

Duval threw on a pair of jeans and a denim shirt, pulled on his boots, and walked to the kitchen. He poured himself a glass of orange juice and tried to shake off the dream. Duval didn't have many dreams, and, when he did, he had no interest in analyzing them. He had never particularly enjoyed symbolism, not in literature, painting, music, or conversation. In his mind, symbols were either too obvious, in which case there was no reason to employ them—or too obscure, in which case a work of art was reduced to a puzzle, often an infuriating puzzle with no correct answer. The burning in Michelle's chest was so obviously connected to her inhalation of the alpha particles and the potential for lung cancer that Duval couldn't believe his unconscious mind had made the effort to symbolize it at all. Why not just dream of Michelle getting cancer? The burned man with the steering wheel needed no explanation, and the hydra-headed waiter required more interpretive effort than he was willing to endure. His father's voice was a little odd, he thought, but lately, as he grew older, he thought of his father more frequently. He dropped the dream, finished his orange juice, and walked to the detached garage behind his house.

Against the back wall, sitting several feet above the floor on concrete blocks, sat a polished wooden box about five feet long and a foot wide, chained to a corner post. Duval felt beneath a paint can on a shelf, found a small ring holding two keys, and used one key to unchain the box and the other to unlock it. The Remington pump-action 12 gauge had been given to him by his father on his thirteenth birthday. It was a remarkably well-made weapon, and its cherry stock and pump still shined after years of inactivity.

Duval, like just about everyone in Nebraska, had learned to hunt quail and pheasant before he was ten. By thirteen he was a superb shot and by fifteen he was considered one of the best hunters in the whole Pine Ridge area. By sixteen he had quit hunting forever.

It all began on an autumn Saturday. They had been crossing a brush-covered ridge line shortly after sunrise, looking for a blind they had constructed from twigs and prairie grass two days before.

Tommy Friedlander had been a few paces ahead, telling stories about what he hoped to do with Sally Mayfield if he ever got a date with her, when two shotgun blasts had ripped through the still morning air, tearing him nearly in half.

The two drunken hunters who fired weren't local men. They had come up from Denver to take advantage of the enormous pheasant population attracted to the wildlife refuges scattered north of the Platte River. Investigators said they were so intoxicated they would have fired at a dump truck if it had been moving in the brush. That knowledge didn't comfort Duval, who felt personally responsible for Friedlander's death. It had been Duval's idea to go hunting that morning, and he had selected the trail. Nobody else blamed him; not the authorities, not his parents, not his buddy's mom and dad. But Duval's guilt refused to ebb, and only by locking up his shotgun and renouncing guns forever had he finally come to terms with his conscience. Duval had kept the gun clean and oiled, but otherwise he hadn't looked at it for sixteen years.

He spent several minutes refamiliarizing himself with the shotgun's mechanisms. He placed it in a canvas bag and found that with a little trouble he could fasten it to his motorcycle beneath his left thigh, much like a cavalryman might. He fired up the Kawasaki and took off for White-clay. Just west of Chadron, at a store that sold gas and hunting supplies, he bought six boxes of ammunition. He fired off one box on a skeet range behind the store and decided he was rusty but still pretty good. He loaded five rounds in the Remington, repacked it in the canvas bag, and then took off for Whiteclay.

Juanita Muñoz was waiting at the front door when he arrived. She looked worried, as if she had somehow failed in her duty and Duval would be angry with her. Just what did a sixty-eight-year-old, ninety-six-pound woman think she was supposed to do to protect the clinic from a ran-sacking? Duval couldn't guess. He reassured her with a hug and some gentle pats on the back and followed her inside.

The waiting room was trashed. A couch and several chairs were over-turned, and a number of cushions had been slashed open by a knife or razor. His consultation room was worse. His desk had been thoroughly rifled and the papers in his file drawers unceremoniously dumped on the floor. A number of medical reference books and a stack of periodi-cals had been thrown from a bookcase and—judging from their condi-tion—had been individually searched. Duval walked toward the small sur-gical suite and confronted the same destruction. The glass doors to several medicine cabinets had been smashed, and the antibiotics, and disinfectants, and other pharmaceuticals had been swept from the shelves. Duval couldn't make a complete inventory, but, judging from what he found on the counters and floors, he decided that no drugs had been taken.

It was becoming clear that whoever had invaded the clinic, he, or they, were not intent on theft. They were looking for something.

Duval played a hunch. He looked in the small x-ray bin where he kept unexposed plates and as he expected, discovered that it was empty.

His supply had been low, which was why he was carrying new plates to the clinic on Wednesday, but he distinctly remembered that a handful of plates was still in the bin when he finished his work the week before. He walked back to his office and went through the files dumped on the carpet. Among the various papers there should have been five or six de-veloped x-rays that Duval occasionally used to explain the bone healing process to patients. As he anticipated, they were gone. He looked at his housekeeper. "And your room, Juanita?"

"It is just the same, Señor. They take nothing, but wreck everything. Why to do that?"

"It's a long story, Juanita. But here's what I want you to do." He took out his wallet and found three $100 dollar bills. "Take this money and go stay with your brother for a while. Do not come back here until I tell you. The people who were here may come back again, and they are dangerous. Do you understand?"

"Si, Doctor. But are you mad with Juanita?"

"No, Juanita. You have done just fine. The money is to help you live until we get this settled and get your room fixed up again. Don't worry. The clinic will reopen, and you're still the chief cook and bottle washer."

"The what?"

"You still have a home here. But you must go now. Call your brother and have him pick you up. And Juanita, don't talk to anyone about what happened here. If you have to tell your brother, ask him to be discreet."

"To be what?"

"Ask him to keep his mouth shut." Duval hugged her again, walked out the front door, and remounted the Kawasaki. He had only one thought. If they would hit Whiteclay, his office in Chadron would be next, and Sunday was the perfect time to strike. He accelerated southward and let his mind roll with the passing mileposts. No sense calling Reiner, he reasoned. Reiner had to be the one who tipped off the feds to the photos and the x-rays in the first place.

As the morning sun warmed the tarmac, the heat rising from the highway seemed to flow through Duval's boots, up his legs and torso, and into his brain. Soon his rage was back, crowding out all concentration.

If only Reiner had trusted him. If only the goddamned feds weren't so paranoid, Michelle's lungs would be clear, his office in one piece, and no real harm done. Instead they wanted to play games, lethal games involving innocent lives, and all in the name of protecting American democracy. Why protect a democracy where the government trampled on citizens like a buffalo trampled grass? Duval swerved sharply to avoid the back of a slow-moving tractor that he had not noticed was in front of him, and the scare refocused his mind on the highway. When he again found open road, he tried to keep his thoughts on his driving, but his mind invariably drifted back to the events of the last five days. He couldn't yet see how to expose the government, how to avenge its lies and its blatant disregard for Michelle's life. Reiner was right. If he went to the newspapers now, they would think he was a crackpot, the kind who would stand on a street corner wearing aluminum foil on his head to block the signals from Mars. The pictures and x-rays by themselves would mean nothing. Once they had been soaked in developer and fixer, and then washed with water, the negatives would be unlikely to retain any of the radioactive dust that had marred them. They would just be defective pictures.

Duval decided that if he couldn't yet devise a plan to expose the events he was witnessing, he could at least defend his own property. No American agency had the right to smash up a doctor's office, and no Nebraska jury would convict a man of anything for defending his property from invaders. He decided that if he had to he would use his shotgun to make a stand. That would definitely cause a stir and might even help him bring light to the accident and its aftermath. He would love to show the jury his photograph of the Rocky Mountain Toxic Waste logo. He could hear his attorney's questions.

"Just what were these vehicles doing off State Road 250 at nine o'clock at night? What kind of waste was being cleaned up? Your honor, we request an independent inspection of the site by a reputable company." He would enjoy watching the government take on that.

As he entered Chadron and turned toward his office, Duval became cautious. He parked at the corner gas station where he bought his Pepsis and placed a call to his office. After three rings, he got the recording he was expecting. If there was anyone there, he thought, they were smart enough not to turn off the answering machine or pick up the phone. He restarted his bike, drove slowly by his office's front entrance, and noted nothing unusual. There were no suspicious vehicles parked on his street; in fact, it being Sunday, there were no vehicles at all. He cruised slowly around the block, and, while he could get only a partial view of the rear of his building, he was satisfied that from the outside at least his offices seemed secure. Inside was another matter.

His office was the worst. Hundreds of folders of medical records and insurance forms had been ripped from the sliding drawers of a wall-length steel cabinet and strewn across the floor. The locks on his desk drawers had been jimmied and the drawers emptied of their contents. Someone had ripped open the lining of a raincoat in his private closet and taken the time to dump out the soil supporting two large plants. The lab had undergone the same treatment. As in Whiteclay, the unexposed plates from the x-ray storage bin had been taken, and for good measure two x-ray film cassettes had been smashed open with a hammer or some other heavy object. Except for the plates, Duval again could find nothing missing. No drugs or other medical supplies had been stolen, and no equipment was gone or, so far as he could tell, damaged.

He picked up the phone and dialed Michelle in Denver. As usual, her mother answered. Alice Falk wanted Duval to know how happy she and her husband Mike were to have him as a prospective son-in-law. She wanted him to know how happy Michelle had been since the evening before, how her mood kept swinging from laughter to tears. And no, Michelle wasn't in, but she had said that she would definitely be on the late commuter flight from Denver which arrived in Chadron at 8:45 that night. No, Michelle hadn't said anything today about any film or x-ray plates. She had mentioned that she was going to have an old colleague at the Associated Press photo lab in Denver take a look at some negatives, but that had been before Duval's last call, last night. Today, she had just gone to visit friends. She would tell Michelle that Duval had called and that he would be waiting for her in Chadron. Again, she was so happy for the two of them.

It was only after he hung up that Duval began to wonder if his phone was tapped.

No, he said to himself, that's only in the movies. Then, just to be sure, he decided to check anyway.

He could find no attachments on any of the phones in his office. When he went out the back door to look at his phone line, he saw that the lock on the door had been broken, ripped apart perhaps by a crowbar. To his disappointment, however, he found nothing that looked like a telephone tap. Duval had to admit to himself that he didn't know what a phone tap looked like, that he wouldn't recognize a frigging tap if it had a blinking neon arrow attached to it proclaiming "Tap Here!" Still, he felt better after looking. At least he was trying to be thorough.

He thought about calling the Dawes County Sheriff, but assumed that whatever Reiner knew, Sheriff Hargrove would know also. He decided it was time to confront Reiner himself and not with a friendly little chat at his house. He called Reiner's home, but got no answer and no message machine. He dialed Reiner's office and heard the telephone automatically switch him to an extension. After identifying himself to a Sheridan County Sheriff's Office dispatcher, Duval was told there was a message for him. Sheriff Reiner had called in from his house about an hour ago. He told the dispatcher that if Dr. Duval called, he wanted Duval to know that he had tried to call him earlier to cancel their afternoon meeting, but that no one had answered Duval's phone. Reiner's excuse was that "something had come up." Reiner would be in touch.

It was the last time anybody ever reported talking to Sheriff Dan Reiner on the telephone.

Viktor Papko was approaching seventy-three but looked fifty; an ageless wonder in a town with a lot of old men. The Russian had argued with President John Kennedy during the Cuban missile crisis and had drunk bourbon with Lyndon Johnson. He'd offered condolences to Richard Nixon at the end of his presidency and had twice beaten George Bush at horseshoes. As everyone in town knew, Papko was a Washington "player," and had been one for nearly thirty-seven years. There were no signs that he was considering retirement. He had known every president since Dwight Eisenhower, and every politician, ambassador, and journalist worth knowing since Quemoy and Matsu had been a debate topic.

At times Papko had been called brilliant, energetic, hard-working, and statesmanlike; and at other times, dull, arrogant, lazy, and mendacious. He viewed himself as all those things, but if pressed, would have described himself as a survivor. From Khrushchev to Turgenev, from detente to Glasnost, there had been few constants in Russian diplomacy, but Victor Papko had been one of them.

Like an old tire buried in a landfill, Papko just kept floating to the surface. Every new government in Moscow had tried to get rid of him before discovering that he was indispensable. His value was not connected with his politics. If Papko had any political beliefs, no one knew them. If he were motivated by any ideals, he kept them to himself. What he did have was an intimate knowledge of Washington, D.C., and a record of unswerving loyalty to whomever was in charge at home. If the Soviet empire was expanding into Afghanistan, Papko was for it. If Yeltsin were dissolving the empire and pulling troops from Eastern Europe, he was for that too. American observers concluded that Papko would have made a terrific trial lawyer. He could sue purveyors of kiddie porn and defend child molesters with equal ease. It depended only on who was footing the bill. Party hacks or theoreticians, reactionaries or reformers, it didn't matter who was in charge in Moscow. If they were top dog in the Kremlin, Papko was there to serve. If he had never been made ambassador, that was all right too. Ambassadors came and went, their careers rising and falling with the fortunes of their allies in

Moscow. But as the Embassy's perennial First Secretary for Political Affairs, Papko stuck around.

If an American president wanted to talk turkey with the Russians, Papko was the man to call.

Papko's discreet black Chevrolet pulled into West Executive Drive between the White House and the Old Executive Office Building forty minutes after sunset and was seen only by Secret Service guards. When he entered the Oval Office, he noted with no surprise that Rubio Pinzon and Admiral Greenwood were with the president. The presence of Secretary of State Emily Price was unexpected. No one offered their hands, but President Frank Moran gestured with his hand for Papko to take a seat.

Papko tried an opening thrust.

"This is highly unusual, Mr. President. It is interfering with my normal Sunday dinner plans."

"Viktor," answered the president, "if you're hungry I can get you a sandwich from the White House mess. If you want to talk about the unusual, what about this?" Moran handed Papko a series of photos that had been altered so they wouldn't show just how good the KH17A Super Keyhole spy satellite was.

Papko put on his glasses and pretended to study the pictures. "And what is the meaning of these?" he asked in perfect English with an American accent.

"That's what we want to know, Viktor," said Pinzon. "Why are you deactivating a couple of hundred SS-18s and scuttling some of your newest missile submarines?"

If Papko was startled by the directness of Pinzon's question, it didn't show.

"Rubio," he replied, "President Turgenev has formally requested a meeting with President Moran when he's in New York for the opening of the General Assembly. I can tell you that he wanted to discuss the very question you have raised. But what is your response? You put him on hold. In view of your apparent lack of interest, I hardly think you should now pull me away from dinner to complain about our activities."

"Viktor, that's a bunch of crap." Papko wasn't the only one surprised by the voice of Emily Price. "Our two nations have managed to keep from destroying each other over the last fifteen or twenty years, because on nuclear issues we've played pretty straight. The unwritten rule is: no nuclear surprises. You're breaking the rule." She was a tall, slim woman, admired by many for her patrician good looks and her elegance. Her medium-length blonde hair still caught men's attention, even if she was now a grandmother. People who didn't know her were frequently fooled by her appearance. She was experienced, tough, and direct.

Papko removed his glasses and slowly placed them in a breast pocket. His response was unexpected. "Mr. President, I'll take that sandwich."

The president was tempted to bellow at Papko's evasion but restrained himself. He pushed a button on his desk and asked the duty steward to get Papko a roast beef sandwich. "Lettuce and mayo okay, Viktor?"

"Yes, thank you, Mr. President."

"Now, Viktor," continued the president, "as to Secretary Price's question."

"Gentlemen. Secretary Price. I am not at liberty to discuss much of this matter. I hope you can appreciate that I am a diplomat, not a policy maker. I'm under some tight restrictions here. But I can say this. We have made no attempt to hide what we are doing. Your satellites have clearly observed our actions, so I hardly think we are pulling a surprise or doing something dangerous behind your back. I can confirm what you already know. We are continuing nuclear weapons reductions beyond what is required by the START Treaties. I should think that would please all of you."

"How far are you cutting back?" asked Admiral Greenwood.

"That would not be for me to say even if I knew the number and I don't. I do know the cuts will be very significant."

The president was having trouble hiding his impatience. "Look, I'm just a Kansas farm boy," he said in an exasperated voice. "Please explain to me just why you haven't told us about your reductions."

Papko smirked. "Sir, you're a farm boy with a Harvard law degree, two terms in the House, and three in the Senate."

"Still, why didn't you say anything?"

Papko bristled with what appeared to be genuine indignation. "Why should we? What difference would it make?"

"It might help us build more trust if you were to keep us informed of what you're doing instead of being so mysterious. And that could help get the arms control process going again," said Rubio. "You remember what President Reagan said, 'Trust, but verify.' We can't very much trust a country that is secretly altering its strategic posture."

Papko raised his voice. "We don't need any help with arms control! You're the ones with the problem."

No one responded, so Papko continued. "Look at the record since the late eighties. We announce a moratorium on nuclear testing, and you announce that your testing will continue no matter what we do. We stop, you don't."

"We stopped eventually," said Secretary Price.

"You didn't stop. You didn't ban tests. You just said the United States wouldn't test first," said Papko.

"So what's that got to do with this?" asked Greenwood.

"It's part of a pattern. As I said, look at the record. When we pulled our troops out of Eastern Europe, you cut your forces by less than thirty percent. When we dissolved the Warsaw Pact, you strengthened NATO. Remember, when we agreed to the reunification of Germany, you insisted that *all* of Germany, even the old East Germany, remain in NATO?"

"So?" said Pinzon.

"As I said, it's a pattern. We agreed to a treaty limiting anti-ballistic missile deployment, and you said Star Wars was exempt. That took some gall, let me tell you. Then we cut back our strategic bomber forces, and you built the B1 and the B2. You get my point?"

"That was before my time," Moran said. Neither the president nor Pinzon had ever seen Papko so emotional. If they hadn't known him better, they almost would have believed he honestly meant what he was saying. Greenwood and the Secretary of State were convinced of his sincerity.

"Viktor," said Moran at last, "I support more arms reductions, but I'm not the government. I have a Congress to deal with."

Papko seemed to calm at the president's words. "Mr. President, I believe you. But you can understand, I hope, how we feel. We opted out of the arms race years ago; we couldn't afford it. The United States either hasn't figured that out or has decided to become the *sine qua non* of Superpowers—the only cop on the beat. Either way, it makes no difference to us. We're not going to play anymore. Go ahead, break your backs on dreams of world hegemony. We don't think you can achieve it no matter how much you spend on arms. What are all those rockets and nuclear warheads going to do for you? Did they help you any in Vietnam? Are they going to help you cut your trade deficit with Japan?"

When Papko stopped talking, the office became absolutely silent. No one had heard him or any other Russian official speak so frankly.

Rubio Pinzon finally broke the silence.

"Are you trying to tell us, Viktor, that Russia is going to get rid of *all* its nuclear weapons?"

"Of course not, Rubio, much as we might like to. It's just that we don't need the thousands we've got now and neither do you."

"When did you come to that conclusion?" asked the president, not expecting an answer.

"I can tell you exactly," said Papko. "When President Turgenev took office a year ago, he ordered a top-to-bottom review of our entire strategic posture. Most of the work was carried out by the State Bureau for Advanced Strategic Research."

"Saratov's group?" asked Admiral Greenwood, suddenly looking interested.

"Yes. The bureau looked at everything and concluded that the only good way to protect Russia from nuclear war was to reduce the size of the world's nuclear arsenals, starting with our own. It makes us a less inviting target. Also, the fewer weapons we have, the easier they are to keep track of. Do you know how many people have tried to smuggle nuclear material out of Russia recently?"

A buzzer sounded on the president's desk. He pushed a button and seconds later a white-jacketed steward entered the office bearing a silver tray with a roast beef sandwich and a glass of Coca-Cola. The president pointed to Papko, and the tray was placed on a table next to him. Papko waited for the steward to leave.

"That's really excellent, Mr. President," said Papko. "What did that take, three minutes?" Papko bit into his sandwich.

"Aren't you afraid of us?" asked Admiral Greenwood.

Papko spoke while chewing. "We'll keep enough warheads, Admiral, to make you think twice about striking us."

"What if we went ahead and deployed Star Wars," said Pinzon, "what would your generals think then?"

To everyone's astonishment, Papko started laughing. It started as a giggle and in a few seconds developed into a belly shaking, eye-streaming howl. Everybody stared at him in slack-jawed disbelief. At last, when he could bring himself to something like calm, Papko pulled out a handkerchief, wiped the tears from his eyes, and blew his nose.

"Pardon me," he said, "but your American belief in technology is truly touching. Go ahead. Deploy. You've got thousands of nut cases walking the streets homeless, you've got the worst public schools in the world, and you're going to spend your money on Star Wars while we're cutting our strategic missiles. The Japanese will love it."

Greenwood didn't seem persuaded, and his face reflected disdain.

Papko took a sip of his soda and continued. "Yeah, I love technology. I was really impressed by the billion dollar Aegis radar system on the USS

Vincennes. Couldn't tell an Airbus from an F-14 at twelve miles. And don't forget the Space Shuttle, the 'most complicated piece of machinery ever built by man,' they used to call it. Too complicated, I'd say. How many missions did it fly before it got blown to pieces? Twenty-five?"

"You're dropping your objections to Star Wars?" asked Pinzon.

"Rubio, we don't give a hoot what you do. That's over for us. Go ahead, be the new Roman Empire. We aren't going down that path anymore. We know where that leads."

"Viktor," said the president, "thank you for coming by."

Pinzon and the other officials looked startled. The meeting was being brought to an early and unceremonious close.

"You want to take that sandwich with you, Viktor?" asked the president.

When Papko nodded, the president leaned toward the speaker on his desk. "I'll get you a doggie bag, Viktor."

"No problem, Mr. President. I'll just take it as is." Papko wrapped the sandwich in a napkin and stuck it in the pocket of his overcoat. He shook hands with the president and his advisors and was escorted to his car by a Secret Service agent.

"What do you all think?" asked the president.

"In the words of Napoleon, I believe," said Pinzon, "he's 'a silk stocking full of shit.'"

"Maybe," said the president. "Unfortunately, a lot of what he says makes sense to me and I think to the rest of you. Still, it's hard to square with Russian history."

"What's harder for me to believe," said Greenwood, "is that this all started with General Saratov, their director of Advanced Strategic Research. Put simply, sir, it's totally out of character."

United States Customs officer John DeVinney logged off his computer, made some final notes on a pad of yellow legal paper, and took a swig of a stale soda from a can. He wiped his lips with his shirt sleeve and looked up Torrelli's number in Baltimore, wondering if he would still be at the pier. DeVinney's computer search had been less difficult than he had anticipated, but the answers had surprised him. As far as he could tell with only a cursory search, more than sixty industrial boilers, listed as "steam generators" on the computer, had been imported into the United States in the last couple years. The number was probably on the low side, thought DeVinney. A more detailed search might easily reveal more of the things.

If the number was a surprise, the boilers' points of origin were almost as astonishing. About two-thirds of the machines came from a plant in Yaroslavl in Russia. The bulk of the rest were shipped from a place called the Dzhambul Machinery Works in Alma-Ata in the Republic of Kazakhstan, formerly part of the Soviet Union. A handful of machines came from Germany, Belgium, and the United Kingdom, and two apiece (which appeared to be part of larger industrial systems) had come from France and Japan. But overwhelmingly, foreign-manufactured boilers entering the United States were coming from Russia and one of its closest allies. DeVinney knew nothing about the boiler industry but found the numbers strange. He dialed Baltimore Customs and asked for Torrelli.

"Who's this?" came an official sounding voice.

DeVinney identified himself.

"Was he a friend of yours?" asked the voice.

"No. But what do you mean 'was'? Who's this?"

"This is special agent Walters, FBI. Torrelli is dead."

DeVinney almost choked on his soft drink. "Dead! But I just talked to him earlier today. Dead how?"

"Murdered. A couple walking home from the movies found him in the back seat of his car off Reisterstown Road in northwest Baltimore shortly after six o'clock. Give me your name and number again, so a Washington agent can interview you tonight."

"Tonight? It's almost nine o'clock."

"I know, but sometimes it's best to act quickly, while the memory is still fresh."

DeVinney agreed to a time and place and hung up the phone in shock. He had never known anyone who had been murdered.

Agent Todd Walters had been called in by the Baltimore Police as soon as they learned that Torrelli was a federal officer. Walters had seen plenty of homicide scenes and this one looked like a classic drug gang rub-out.

Torrelli had been shot three times in the head at close range by a small caliber weapon, most likely a 9mm automatic. There were no signs of a struggle, no one heard any shots, and no one could remember seeing Torrelli's car park on the quiet side street where it was found. In the trunk, beneath the spare tire, Baltimore officers found a kilo of high quality cocaine wrapped in a black plastic bag bound by ordinary brown twine. In Torrelli's wallet was a folded piece of white paper with two long numbers hand written across it. One turned out to be the main number of the Bank Verein in Zurich, and the other an account number.

People who knew Torrelli were invariably shocked as much by the news of the cocaine and the bank account as by his murder. Colleagues thought of him as an impeccably honest and honorable father, husband, public servant, and friend. He had never been known to live above his means and putting a few bucks on the state lottery once or twice a week was his only known vice, if it could be called that.

In Torrelli's right trouser's pocket, police also found a folded page from the *Baltimore Yellow Pages*. It was unmarked, but carried entries from "Boat Dealers" to "Boilers - New & Used." "Maybe he was planning to buy a yacht," suggested one detective. Nobody could think of a better idea.

The interview with DeVinney at his home outside Washington didn't help. Nobody told the FBI agent doing the questioning that he should inquire about boilers, and DeVinney never mentioned the word. Asked what Torrelli had wanted on the telephone, DeVinney replied that he had made an informal request for a computer search, that he was running down some information on industrial steam generators. Most of the FBI agent's questions had to do with drugs and the purchase of a yacht, something DeVinney assured him he knew nothing about. The agent, who had been called from a sickbed where he was nursing a cold, soon determined that DeVinney had no useful information regarding Torrelli's murder and reported as much to his superiors.

After a day or two, the torn-out page from the *Yellow Pages,* along with other pieces of evidence, was slipped into a padded envelope and placed in a file drawer, soon to be forgotten.

Duval returned the last of the medical records to a wall-sized filing cabinet and surveyed the room. It had taken several hours to bring some order back to his office, but the job was now nearly done. Satisfied with his progress, Duval sat at his desk and dialed the home of his old friend, Mark Loevinger, in Lincoln. Laura Loevinger answered. "Laura, it's George Duval."

Duval heard a low sigh at the other end. "George, I'm glad it's you. I'm worried about Mark."

It wasn't what he wanted to hear about the professor. "Worried about what?"

"He's been in an absolute tizzy since yesterday afternoon. He was a nervous wreck last night. I don't think he got five minutes sleep. He said it was some experiment at the lab, something to do with you. Come on George, what's up?"

"Does that mean Mark's not home, Laura?"

"George, what's happening? He went to the lab about seven this morning. That's thirteen hours ago, and I haven't heard a thing from him since. I called the lab and got no answer at his office or the main number. It's Sunday, I know. But, still, George."

Laura Loevinger couldn't disguise her fear. "George, there's something wrong, isn't there?"

"Laura," said Duval, trying to sound calm, "I have no reason to think there is anything wrong with Mark. He's probably got his head buried in some experiment or something and has lost track of the time. I'm sure everything's fine." Duval was afraid his own fears were showing. "Tell you what. I'll call back in an hour or so. And if Mark should call in the meantime, tell him I need to talk to him, okay?"

Duval hung up and considered again whether his phone had been tapped. If so, a listener would have had no trouble tracking down Professor Mark Loevinger at the university in Lincoln. For the first time, it occurred to him that he and Loevinger and anyone else involved in

118

the case might be in some danger. Would the government actually harm him?

Duval tried Sheriff Reiner's home a second time and again got no answer. The image of a telephone ringing in Reiner's empty house suddenly hit Duval like a thunderbolt. He slammed down the receiver. Damn! A couple of goons could be tearing apart his own home right now. He checked his watch. If he drove hard he could be home in twenty minutes. That would give him more than an hour to check on things and still give him time to get to the Chadron airport to pick up Michelle. He loaded his medical bag and his shotgun on his motorcycle and roared off.

Duval's house was a long and angular construction of cedar timbers, plate glass, and stone masonry, nestled in a dense copse of quaking aspen and Engelmann spruce. While locals found it strikingly original, Duval had actually ordered it from a brochure published by a company in New England. At ridiculous expense, they had shipped the precut parts, and a local company had assembled them on Duval's wooded lot from a set of standardized blueprints.

The lamps in Duval's house were on timers and normally after dark, as he approached his home from the east, he could pick out lights twinkling through the trees. The first sign that all was not right was the total dark that enveloped his property. He slowed the Kawasaki to a stop about a quarter mile from his driveway. He squinted at the dark trees that marked his lot line, trying to make out any light at all, but could see none. He considered. Power failure? Blown circuit breakers? Paranoia? He turned off the road to the left and parked his bike among trees and dense brush where it couldn't be seen from the highway. He slung the medical bag's carrying strap over his head and pulled his shotgun from its canvas bag and approached the side of the house. He checked the load and then, like some GI walking point in Go Cong province, began moving gingerly toward the side of his house.

He could feel his nerves tighten when he saw the car. It was a silver-gray Ford Taurus, parked behind the house to the left. Whoever drove the vehicle had taken care to conceal it. He could not recall having seen the car before and couldn't imagine why it would be parked behind his house. Not sure what to do, Duval settled to his knees behind thick brush, unlocked the safety on his Remington, and decided to wait.

Fifteen silent minutes passed by slowly. Duval could detect no sounds or other signs of movement from the house and saw no one outside. He was getting to his feet when he heard the crunching sound of footsteps on gravel. He eased back to his knees and saw the faint flickers of a flashlight poking through the darkness as the footsteps came closer.

A figure then emerged into plain view, walking slowly up the driveway toward the house. The mysterious man was wearing fatigue pants and a hunting jacket and had a short-barreled automatic rifle slung across his back. As he passed Duval's position, he switched off the flashlight, pocketed it, walked to the front door, and knocked softly. It opened moments later and a second mysterious man stepped onto the flagstone pavement that marked the entryway. They spoke in low tones, and, try as he might, Duval could not make out their conversation. The man from inside the house held what appeared to be a book in his right hand, and was leafing through the pages. It was only when he fished out a small penlight and pointed it at the pages that Duval thought he recognized his address book. He was contemplating the meaning of that when the reflected glow from the penlight illuminated the face of the man with the rifle.

Duval was so startled he almost cried out. It was Captain Ahab, the prickly fellow from the Toxic Waste outfit. In the dim light, his long white scar showed clearly, running from the hairline and down the cheek. Duval felt a momentary exhilaration, a feeling of triumph. He wasn't a raving lunatic after all. Toxic waste my ass, he thought. How would Sheriff Reiner explain this nasty little development?

Duval tried to remember the man's name. It was like a city in New York. Ojeda or Oneida. Onega! That was it!

Duval felt a tingling of triumph again, but it was quickly replaced by fear. Duval was not a moral or physical coward, but neither was he someone who regularly confronted armed men. He was not a cop or a soldier; he was a doctor. Worse, he could not be certain of the intent of the men he was watching. He believed the government was often guilty of arrogance, incompetence, deceit, and waste, but he didn't think it was evil enough to kill ordinary citizens—even those who knew too much. Burglary, a little unauthorized search and seizure, sure. But murder? He just couldn't accept it; he didn't want to accept it. He decided to face the men invading his home.

"Looking for something?" he called out as he emerged from the brush into the driveway. "Me, perhaps?"

The next few hyperkinetic seconds passed at quantum speeds, but Duval recorded every detail with startling clarity. The man with the penlight ducked back inside the house, while Onega frantically and almost comically worked to unsling his rifle. Duval stepped back into the brush and dropped to his knees.

"Don't shoot!" he yelled, surprising himself at how quickly and easily he uttered one of the greatest clichés of American movies.

Duval heard three loud and rapid pops and the singing sound of bullets flying a foot above his head. He dropped to his stomach and lowered his eyes. A few heartbeats later, he looked up toward the house. The flagstone entryway was now empty, and Duval felt momentarily confused. The thumping sound of running footsteps alerted him to the figure charging directly at his hiding place in the bushes. Duval tried again.

"Stop shooting, I've got a gun!" Onega was brought up short by Duval's words. He stopped and looked toward the sound of Duval's voice, but instead of raising his weapon skyward, he lowered it in the direction of Duval's head and squeezed the trigger.

Onega was a milli-second too late. The enormous boom from Duval's Remington roared across the driveway, as 12-gauge buckshot tore into Onega's torso. He was blown backward to the ground, as if swatted by some giant, unseen club, and lay writhing in an expanding pool of blood with his rifle resting a few inches from his outstretched right arm. Duval felt a surge of revulsion and panic. Where Onega lay squirming, Duval saw the body of little Tommy Friedlander, slain nearly sixteen years before, not many miles away. Duval felt an involuntary touch of sympathy as he looked at the dying man. He overcame it.

"I told you I had a gun, you mother-fucker." He was turning back to the bushes to grab his medical bag when he was called by a deep male voice from some window in the darkened house.

"Drop the gun, Duval, or Michelle is dead." Duval froze.

It wasn't possible, he said to himself. Michelle was on a plane from Denver and wouldn't even arrive in Chadron for another hour. Still, the mere fact that they knew her name was enough to make his skin crawl. He ducked out of sight in the bushes and answered. "Michelle's not here. You're bluffing." He waited in vain for a response and tried another tack.

"If I don't give some medical attention to your friend, he'll be dead in five minutes." Probably dead already, he thought.

"George, George. Run away, run—"

The sound of Michelle's voice sent ice down Duval's back. He thought of breaking from his cover, but stopped himself.

"Come out, Duval," said the male voice, "or I'll kill her, I mean it."

Duval repeated the sentence in his mind, hoping that the man had given himself away with the words "I'll kill her." Did that really mean he was alone?

"If I come out," replied Duval, "you'll shoot me and kill her anyway."

"Actually, I want to talk. But if you want Michelle to live another five seconds, you've got to show yourself now. Five, four, three—"

"Okay, I'm coming. I've coming without the shotgun. I want to see Michelle, and your friend here ain't gonna make it much longer without my help." He emerged from the bushes with his hands up, expecting to be hit by rifle bullets at any second. As he stood in the open and the seconds ticked by without shots, he wondered if he might not live another few minutes after all.

The man emerged cautiously from the front door, and Duval recognized him immediately as "Georgie," the boss from the toxic clean-up crew the night before. He was holding Michelle tightly in the crook of his right arm and pointing a pistol at her left temple. Left-hander, thought Duval, wondering if the knowledge might be of any use. With Michelle alive but in mortal danger, his fears about himself evaporated. They were replaced by rage.

"How bad is he?" asked Georgi Rovno, indicating his companion on the ground.

"He's got a chance if I can stabilize him," lied Duval. "I've got to get some things in my medical bag." He pointed to the bag at his feet.

Rovno moved closer, keeping the gun at Michelle's temple. He reached into his pocket with his right hand, pulled out the penlight and threw it in Duval's direction. "Turn on the light, open the bag slowly, and tilt the bag toward me before you reach inside. I want a good look."

Duval did as he was told, showing Rovno that there was no weapon inside his bag. "I need someone to hold the light for me to work," said Duval. "I can't move him inside, it would kill him."

"She can hold the light," said Rovno.

"I need her to help me with your buddy," said Duval. "I need her two hands. She's my nurse."

"Okay," agreed Rovno, turning Michelle loose. "But no funny business or she gets it in the back of the head."

Michelle kneeled over Onega to Duval's left, while Rovno stood behind them.

Duval was mildly surprised that Rovno gave a damn about his dead companion. He never figured professional assassins to be the sentimental type, and he could not have known that the two men were step-brothers. He pulled a stethoscope from his bag, and with Rovno shining his pen light on Onega's chest, listened for a heart beat. There was none. Poor dumb Onega, Captain Ahab of the Prairies, was deader than a roadkill on a Texas state highway.

"He's going to need an injection of adrenaline, quick," lied Duval. He searched in his bag, found a prefilled syringe containing ten milligrams of morphine, and removed the plastic sheath protecting the needle. Michelle watched in silence, wondering for only a few seconds why her lover, tending to a man whose heart had stopped, had just selected a potent tranquilizer. Duval handed her the syringe.

"Hold on to this and use it when I tell you," he ordered. Michelle nodded. "First, I've got to get this shirt open," continued Duval, reaching into his bag. He clasped his right hand around a Miltex scalpel with a #10 blade, and looked closely at the dead man before him. "I need more light, I can't see what I'm doing."

Rovno bent forward, shining the penlight over Duval's right shoulder.

"Thanks," said Duval, simultaneously removing the scalpel from his bag and slashing backward and upward in a wide arc with all the speed and strength he could muster. He was aiming at Rovno's outstretched throat, but instead caught his right cheek just below the eye, ripping open a gash across the bridge of the nose and the opposite cheek.

Rovno screamed with surprise and brought both hands to his sliced face. Duval slashed again, this time inflicting a deep gash in the muscle tissue at the back of the right thigh, bending Rovno over in a paroxysm of searing pain. Duval grabbed Rovno's right ankle and yanked it violently forward, sending him to his back. He jumped on the bleeding man's chest, and struggled to pin his arms.

"Now, Michelle! Now!" he yelled. Michelle grabbed Rovno by his hair and with her left hand, plunged the syringe into his exposed and engorged external jugular. Despite his injuries, Rovno had amazing resources of energy, and Duval had to struggle fiercely for twenty seconds before the powerful tranquilizer began to take hold.

As he calmed, Rovno made an effort to speak. He was starting to slur, but Duval could make out something that sounded like "Oneg. Tack list lium."

"What?"

"Contact lium."

"What's happening?" said Michelle.

"He's incoherent. I think he thinks I'm Onega, the dead one over there." He indicated the other body. Rovno could not get his words out. In desperation, he pointed at Duval's pocket with a shaking finger. Duval looked and realized the man wanted a pen. Duval slipped it into Rovno's left hand, and tearing a flap of cardboard from a box in his medical bag, held it out so he could write.

Rovno was having difficulty now. His hand was shaking, and he was apparently having trouble seeing. He crudely scratched out some numbers and letters on the flap: 00 1A 0A W . . . then passed out. Duval recognized the beginning of the sequence on the back of the card he had found in Paul Gabrovo's wallet.

Duval took Michelle in his arms, hugging her as she began sobbing with relief. "We got him, honey, we got him. It's okay."

Michelle's sobs soon subsided, but the tears continued. "George, what's happening? Who are these people? George, what are we going to do? Shall we call the sheriff?"

"Michelle, this is somebody the sheriff knows about."

"What?"

"Michelle, I'll try to explain everything later. But first, tell me something. What are you doing here?"

"I took an earlier flight. I wanted to surprise you. I took a taxi home, and, as soon as it pulled out of the driveway, these two were on me. The house is a mess. They've been tearing everything apart. What are they looking for?"

"The film. The screwed-up film and the bad x-ray plates. I'm almost certain of it. You have 'em?"

"Yeah. They're in my suitcase in the house. They didn't have time to search me before you got here."

"Thank God," said Duval. They walked into the house together and found her suitcase on the trashed living room floor. The film strips and x-ray plates were still inside.

"Call me paranoid, but I'm glad I asked you to have your friends in Denver look at them when you left yesterday."

"But my photography friends never took—"

"It doesn't matter. When I talked to Mark Loevinger yesterday and then started getting the runaround from Sheriff Reiner, it all started to fit together. I know what caused the film—"

"Why did you call Mark Loevinger? And what do the x-rays really mean? And why—"

"Shhhhh," interrupted Duval, placing his finger to his lips. "Not so many questions. I think the x-rays and the film can be tied to a nuclear accident and a government cover-up. And I think these guys are with the government." He waved at the two figures on the ground.

"You mean to say the government sent these two guys to kill us?"

"Look, Michelle, I know it sounds crazy, but something terrible is going on. Reiner has made himself scarce. My offices and now my house have been ransacked. Laura Loevinger is worried sick about Mark, and now someone has tried to kill us."

Michelle shook her head. "Do you really honestly think that Dan Reiner would do anything to hurt you or let anyone else do it? I just don't believe it."

"I told you, honey, none of this makes much sense." He made his face as serious as he could. "Honey, the film isn't the only thing they're after."

"Meaning what?" she asked.

Duval made his face as serious as he could. "Isn't it obvious? They're after us. We've got to get out of here and figure out some answers. Here, help me search these two guys."

The wounded man was carrying no money and no wallet. The dead man had a wallet containing a driver's license, valid credit cards, and about $200 in cash. They took the wallet, got into the Ford, and headed west on U.S. 20 toward Sioux County and the Wyoming border. They both thought Rovno would bleed to death.

Monday, September 13

Ushta was awakened by three short raps on his door in the Russian whorehouse. Before he could answer, a pretty young woman entered the room, crossed to the window on the far side, and, with both hands, unceremoniously yanked open a set of short drapes. Gray light filtered through astonishingly clean window panes, showing the fresh-cut flowers on the table at the foot of the bed. Ushta hadn't seen such luxury since his Moscow days, and even then had experienced it only rarely.

He glanced at his watch and was shocked to discover that it was mid-morning. When he had entered the room the night before, he had kicked off his dirty corporal's uniform and crashed into bed without so much as washing his hands. He was filthy.

The girl left the room and returned a moment later with a porcelain pitcher of water and a drinking glass. She set them on a desk and eyed Ushta without expression.

"There is a bathroom down the hall. Miss Nina has left clothes there for you. You are to clean yourself up, get dressed, and meet her downstairs in thirty minutes." She walked from the room without waiting for an answer and closed the door behind her. Ushta noted that the uniform he'd left crumpled at the foot of the bed was gone.

Ushta soaked in the hot tub for fifteen minutes, watching the filth of the camp in Pechora float away in the steaming water. He shaved, combed his overly long hair as best he could, pulled on a clean set of underwear, and slipped into a civilian shirt and trousers that appeared brand new. A stiff pair of shiny black loafers made from real leather fit his feet perfectly. Ushta had no time to wonder about or fear his special treatment. When he was finished dressing, he was due downstairs.

Madame Nina greeted him in a small sitting room that doubled as her office. Like the girl, she had no expression on her face and gave no hint of her intentions. The formal gown of the night before had given way to a businesslike skirt and sweater. "I trust you slept well, Corporal?"

"Yes, Miss Nina. Very well. You have a wonderful house."

"Yes, I think so. Now, on to business. If you're straight with Zeya and really have something he can use, perhaps you will enjoy our accommodations again. If you play badly with him, then the rest of your life, what little there will be of it, will most assuredly be unpleasant." Madame Nina spoke with no obvious malice. She was simply telling the truth as she saw it.

"I understand. Shall I go see him now?"

Madame Nina shook her head softly. "No, Corporal. You will first have some breakfast and then one of my men will take you over to the Station Prospekt for your appointment."

The breakfast was as good as the bedroom. For the first time since his sentencing, Ushta ate fresh fruit, drank good tea, and enjoyed the civility of porcelain plates and a full set of utensils. If he was about to die, he thought, at least he was going on a full stomach and a good night's rest.

He was driven through the streets of Chita to the large square that fronted the railroad station. There, he entered a nondescript, three-story brick building facing the station's huge center entrance arches, and walked up two flights to a suite of offices guarded by two tough-looking men, dressed in leather jackets.

Zeya was standing when Ushta was escorted into a large, private office. He was a small man, about fifty, with a ruddy complexion and Russian features. He wore a well-tailored, double-breasted, wool suit and combed his light-blond hair straight forward across his high forehead. He pointed to a chair and told Ushta to sit. "Cigarette, Corporal?" he asked, opening a silver box on his desk, which contained an assortment of Western cigarette brands. When Ushta politely declined, Zeya snapped the box shut with a sharp metallic "clink," and sat in the leather chair behind his desk.

"So," he continued, "did you kill the two soldiers?"

Ushta remembered Madame Nina's advice. "Yes," he said. "but they tried to kill me first. It was self-defense."

"Oh, I'm sure that is true, Professor Ushta. However, I'm afraid the authorities will not find that an acceptable plea for an escapee from Pechora. Don't you agree?" Zeya offered what appeared to be a sympathetic smile.

"Yes, I agree."

"So, the question is, what do we do with you?"

Ushta knew the decision had already been made. "Before you decide my disposition, Mr. Zeya, would you tell me how you have already learned so much about me?"

"Of course, professor. You see, information is my business. Oh, I buy and sell a few items here and there. I have interests in a few shops, a couple of clubs where busy gentlemen can relax from time to time. But my real income is derived from processing information."

Ushta nodded as if he understood.

Zeya continued. "You were carrying the papers of one of the missing soldiers. The license plate on your jeep had obviously been altered and when I got hold of the real number, it wasn't difficult to see how you altered it. So, you see, it wasn't that hard."

"Why not just turn me into the police?"

"Well, maybe I will. But I don't really like the police very much or the military either for that matter. They're so cheap. A few rubles here, a couple of bottles of vodka there, and you own these people. How can you respect that?"

"I see your point."

"You, on the other hand, show some real courage and ingenuity. Did you know that you're the first man to escape from Pechora? Nobody has gotten out of there in the last year, except you. A remarkable achievement."

Ushta didn't know how he was supposed to respond. He pointed to the cigarette box. "May I after all?" he asked.

"Certainly, certainly, help yourself," said Zeya, opening the box and extending it in Ushta's direction.

Ushta took a Camel filter and lit it with a brass lighter sitting on a corner of the desk. The cigarette was fresh. Ushta was impressed. He slowly exhaled his first puff and looked directly into Zeya's eyes.

"Is there some information I might be able to provide you?"

Zeya laughed. "Oh, Ushta, you are a very smart man. Here's my problem. As a man who deals in information, I have to know anything significant that is taking place in and around Chita. Pechora is a vast project. We know its name, and we have a good idea how many prisoners are working there and how many military men. We know the project has been underway for at least twelve months, maybe longer. We have some idea of the materials that have been brought to various sites. What we don't know is what the Pechora Project really is. Our usual sources have no information. Enlisted men at the Pechora Camp and its many subcamps rarely come into contact with the public, and those who do don't know what they're working on."

"Yes," agreed Ushta, "security is the toughest I've seen since being in the camps."

"Exactly," said Zeya. "Officers who in the past could be relied upon to get drunk and spill the beans to their favorite girls are tight-lipped about what's going on at Pechora, or themselves have no idea what the project really is. I've never in all my years in this business seen anything like it. Obviously, whatever they're doing is important and would be worth a lot of money to the right people. You've been at Pechora for many months. You're an educated man and, as we know, a thoughtful man. Maybe you can help us understand what is happening across that god-forsaken wilderness."

"And what do I get in return?" asked Ushta.

"What do you want?"

Ushta paused to formulate his answer. He didn't want to sound greedy. "I want papers, some cash, and a chance to get out of this country. I've been thinking that Mongolia might be nice this time of year."

Zeya laughed again and selected a cigarette for himself from his silver box. "Mongolia? Nice? Mongolia's a shithole. A bunch of yak yankers living in yurts. Still, there's no accounting for taste. You want Mongolia? You got it. That is, of course, if your information is useful."

Ushta squirmed in his seat. "How do I know I can trust you?"

"You don't. But anyway, it's not something you have to worry about, because you've got no choice. You either go along with us on this, or you're dead. Listen, Ushta, I'm not a cruel man—a greedy man, a thieving man, a selfish man, yes. But not cruel or especially murderous. Help me and I'll help you."

"Where will my information go?"

"Ushta, for a man in your position you sure are particular." Zeya laughed again, his happy eyes twinkling with satisfaction. "I'm in a generous mood today, so I'll tell you. Three years ago I took a vacation to Paris. Nice city, Paris. Ever been there?"

Ushta admitted he hadn't by shaking his head.

"The French are pricks, but they've got a nice country. Anyway, I made some contacts there and sure enough, one day, a certain gentleman from a certain government agency came to visit me. A French gentleman, from a French agency. Anyway, we struck up a business relationship. In exchange for certain information, he puts money in a Swiss account in French francs. Now the French, being the cheap shits they are, despite all their wealth, like to haggle about every dime. Soon I realized that the only way to get any money out of these fellows was to dribble out any information I have in installments. If Pechora is as important as I guess it is, I figure to string the frogs along for a month or two, maybe longer."

"But if you let me go, aren't you afraid I'll give the information to someone and undercut its value to you."

"Not really. First, I expect you'll be staying with us for at least a couple of weeks. In fact, I can guarantee it. I'll have gotten a couple of big payments by then and have the frogs gasping for more. Second, if you do go to Mongolia, there's at least a fifty-fifty chance the locals will kill you for your wristwatch. If you escape them, I figure the government locks you up in solitary for a year, just for starters. The only question they'll ask you is what other Russian spies have entered the country lately. They won't have the patience to listen to any hot air about a secret project and your desire to flee your homeland."

Ushta could see the logic of Zeya's reasoning. He didn't know if the man was trustworthy, but, as Zeya had correctly pointed out, it didn't matter.

Zeya stubbed out his cigarette in an ashtray and rubbed his hands over his cheeks, as if he were trying to smooth away wrinkles.

"Finally, Ushta, what if you do make contact with some intelligence agency? What are your bona fides? Who the hell are you? You start telling

them about Pechora and they'll think you've got a screw loose. Eventually, you might persuade them you have some hot info, but by that time
the Frenchies will have put a couple hundred thousand in Banc Agricole
in Zurich and my retirement villa will have been paid for. See?"

Ushta began talking. He described the dimensions of the project and
the vast and expanding road network needed to connect the central Pechora Camp to outlying construction sites. He sketched in details of the
trench lines and the immense grid pattern they stitched across the
rolling, forested landscape. He described the enormous spools of copper cable, the nearly finished power plant with its associated fuel tanks,
the heavy security, and the baffling reliance on human labor for work
that could be done faster and more efficiently by machines. Zeya took it
all down, scratching detailed notes on a pad of lined paper as fast as he
could write. From time to time he would ask questions and Ushta would
answer as honestly as he could. In the end there remained the biggest
question of all. What was it all for? What was the purpose of this enormous project? Ushta reminded Zeya that he was a geographer and cartographer, not an electrical engineer, and that his conclusions about the
meaning of Pechora were surmises and speculations.

Zeya showed impatience. "Come on man, what do you think? What is
it? It must be military."

"Oh, it's military all right," answered Ushta. When he told Zeya what
he thought it all added up to, Zeya was astonished. He'd never heard of
anything like it in his entire life, and Zeya was not ignorant.

"But why would they need such a facility?" he asked. "It seems like a
spectacular waste of effort. I mean, there are other ways, cheaper ways
certainly?"

"I agree with you, Zeya. It's quite a mystery."

Zeya ordered a carafe of thick Turkish coffee. Ushta was so delighted
with his first good coffee in years that he decided to return his host's hos-
pitality with a gift of his own. "I know where you can pick up a good bulldozer and maybe a couple hundred gallons of first-class diesel fuel.
'Course, you might want to wait a couple of days until things cool down."

Zeya listened with interest as Ushta described where he'd hidden the
bulldozer and the fuel buffalo. "Thank you, my good friend Ushta. Very
generous of you. More coffee?" He poured Ushta another steaming cup.

The two men sat in silence a few minutes, enjoying their coffee and
thinking their private thoughts. Zeya broke the silence. "I still can't figure why the military would invest so much time and effort up there."

"Maybe your friends in Paris will have some answers," suggested Ushta.

"I don't know if they will, Ushta. But I'm sure they'll pay well for this information. Or, at least I think they will." His face displayed an expression of uncertainty. "Won't they?"

Ushta shrugged his shoulders. "Beats me. You know them better than I do."

A loud knock interrupted Saratov's morning briefing. When Kachuga rose from the table and opened the conference room door, a young and extremely agitated captain entered the room and saluted stiffly. He had a message board in his right hand.

"Well, Captain?" said Kachuga.

"I have a Flash message from Washington," he answered. He started to hand the message board to Kachuga, but Saratov, standing next to the doorway at the head of the conference table, grabbed it from the captain's extended hand. As the captain left the room, Saratov adjusted his reading glasses and, remaining on his feet, scanned the message quickly. Saratov was fair skinned, and any distress he experienced was immediately reflected in a reddening complexion. Kachuga, Bransk, Belovo, and the others saw the color deepen in Saratov's cheeks and then spread across his forehead and down his throat. Saratov said nothing at first. He simply handed the message board to Bransk and removed his reading glasses. He turned to Belovo and slowly spoke in cold tones.

"Admiral, it is becoming clear to me that the people you have chosen to direct our operations in America are incapable of doing the job."

Belovo had no idea what Saratov was talking about and made no attempt at answering. Bransk handed him the message board so he could read the bad news for himself.

Saratov addressed the others. "The targets in Nebraska have escaped. The doctor and the girl. One of Belovo's men is dead, the other severely injured."

Everyone noted that Saratov had referred to the agents as "Belovo's men."

Saratov took the pointer he had been using and slapped it viciously against the tabletop. Kachuga was convinced the pointer would splinter like a dried twig with another blow. He looked at Belovo and roared. "Are your people *so fucking incompetent,* Admiral, that they cannot handle a country doctor and his sniveling nurse?"

Belovo had to say something. "They got the Sheriff, General. He's at the bottom of a well behind his house. And they got the professor at the university. And the customs man in Baltimore is done. They'll get the doctor and the girl, I assure you."

"And the pictures they've taken?"

"That, too."

Saratov wasn't mollified. This time he spoke with contempt. "Let me see if I've got this clearly, Admiral. You send *two* trained and experienced agents to a bumpkin's farmhouse in the boondocks. They lie in wait for an unsuspecting doctor and a woman, and one agent ends up with his guts spilling out and the other has his face slit like a sack of flour?"

Admiral Belovo tried to sound calm. "These things can happen, General. Special operations is not an exact science." He wanted to tell Saratov that many Americans, especially rural Americans, owned rifles and knew how to use them. He wanted to explain that in remote regions of the United States people were used to depending on themselves for their security and were suspicious of outsiders. He wanted to tell Saratov to shut up. But, in the end he said nothing.

Saratov whipped his pointer down hard on the tabletop a second time, making ashtrays jump. Everyone flinched, but Saratov wasn't finished. "And now we learn that the doctor and his nurse stole our agents' IDs, money, and credit cards and are running around the country, God only knows where?"

Kachuga had never seen Saratov display such fury, but except for Belovo, who was starting to perspire, the others at the table sat stone-faced.

General Bransk, whose mission was to coordinate elements of the National Police, the Militia, and other internal security groups when the coup began, looked at his fingernails as if bored. Bransk was not a man easily rattled. Zhitnik and Salavat, both sat impassively and silent as always. They were both in charge of nationwide military units.

Belovo couldn't afford to remain quiet.

"We will get them, General. We will. It's only a matter of time."

Saratov took his seat and, trying to control himself, managed to speak in a conversational voice. "Not good enough. They are time bombs, Admiral. They know too much. How long before they get the word to someone who can start putting the pieces together? A day? Two days? A week?"

Kachuga gathered up his courage. "General, if I may?"

Saratov seemed surprised that Kachuga wanted to speak. "Yes, Colonel?"

"I believe our recordings of various phone conversations make it pretty clear that the doctor is a long way from figuring out what he's stumbled into." Kachuga rummaged in a file folder where he kept recent information that might be needed during the daily morning briefing. He removed copies of recorded telephone transcripts and passed them to the center of the desk. "I believe you've all seen these already. The original English versions are available if anyone wants to see them."

No one reached for the transcripts, so Kachuga continued. "This doctor, it should become clear, thinks he's up against the American government. He won't be running *to* authorities. He'll be running *from* them. That should help us."

For the first time in several minutes, Saratov had heard something positive and his interest showed on his face.

"His government is, in fact, looking for him," continued Kachuga, "or will be shortly. Gentlemen, as you know, various crimes against people and property have been committed. The doctor's fingerprints are all over those crimes. Literally. Especially in the case of the sheriff."

They began to understand. The words "interesting," and "of course" could be heard above a low murmuring.

Kachuga continued. "That gives us some time to find him and to cover our tracks more thoroughly. Of course, with luck, he may die at the hands of the FBI."

"The what?" asked Bransk.

"The federal police in America."

Saratov interrupted. "I don't care who gets them," he said, getting to his feet again. "The doctor and the girl must go. No excuses this time. Call me when the job is done and *not* before." Saratov whipped the pointer against the tabletop three times rapidly, splitting it in half. He threw the two pieces over the head of a general at the side of the table and watched them ricochet off the far wall. Without further comment, he wheeled left and stomped out of the room.

Kachuga wondered if the pressure was getting to his boss.

Tuesday, September 14

"How much is left?" Duval guessed she would know to the penny.

"Ninety-seven dollars and change," Michelle said. "We spent about thirty-five on gas and maybe sixty on food and supplies." She poured him a second cup of coffee and, taking him by his free hand, led him to the front porch of her father's cabin. They watched in silence for several minutes as the Tuesday morning sun peaked above the wooded slopes of the Gros Ventre Range to the east.

Duval set his coffee on the porch railing and blew on his chilly hands. "That's not going to last us long, especially since we need a car."

Michelle didn't understand. "What's wrong with the Taurus?"

"It belongs to Hertz, that's what. And it's missing."

Michelle looked hurt. "Sorry, George. I've never been on the lam before."

He put his arms around her and gave her a kiss on the neck.

"I'm sorry, honey. I didn't mean it that way." He kissed her lightly on the lips and rubbed her back with his right hand. She seemed to forgive him. "It seems to me," he said, indicating with his thumb the Ford parked behind the cabin, "that we can't use that car much longer, that's all. We're going to have to get a car, unless you want to run from the cops on a bus."

She seemed unconvinced. "George, you have many talents, but you couldn't steal a car with a pocket full of slim-jims and the keys in the ignition."

"True," he said, smiling. "But stealing isn't the solution. A stolen car would be just as hot as the one we're driving now. We've got to buy a car, somehow. And we can't stay here much longer either. It won't take them forever to figure out your dad has this little vacation retreat."

Michelle brightened at that. "It's not in his name. It's in my mom's maiden name. Don't ask me why."

Duval thought that was a bit of unexpected good news. "Still, how long do you think it will take the feds to put that together. A day? Two days? We roll tonight."

"I guess you're right." She looked unsure. They had driven all Sunday night and most of Monday morning, traversing the three hundred and eight miles from Chadron to Bondurant in ten hours. It was good time considering the mountainous terrain and two-lane roads, but it had exhausted them. They had slept most of Monday afternoon and evening and, after cooking themselves a late dinner, had slept again. They were rested now, and calmer, but neither had much experience eluding authorities. Both were aware of their ignorance.

"Where do you go for help when the police are trying to kill you?" asked Michelle. She said it calmly.

"I guess your family in Denver, or my mother in Scottsdale would be the first choice. But I'm sure they're being watched. And we can't call them, either."

"Why?"

"Because if they tapped the phones and hooked up 'caller ID' they'd trace us in a second. Besides, the phone here is out of order. I've checked. The TV is broken, too, as you know."

"What about a pay phone?"

"They'd still trace the call to this area. This is not exactly New York City. Strangers get noticed in places like this."

Michelle frowned. "I see your point. So, we've got no car, no money, no one to call, and we can't stay here. Kind of up a creek, aren't we?"

Duval studied the thick pines climbing up the slopes of the Gros Ventre. Gros Ventre and Grand Tetons, he thought. The Big Stomach and the Big Tits. It wasn't hard to surmise that the first French explorers to wander into the region had been away from civilization a long time.

"What about our credit cards?" asked Michelle.

"My guess is they've got our credit card numbers and will trace them just like phone calls. You know how it is most places nowadays. They slide your credit card into a little machine hooked to the phone and get instant verification. If our numbers come up, alarm bells will go off, and the local cops will be on our backs in a second. No good."

"How about the dead guy's cards?"

The dead man, Alexander Onega, had a typically American billfold, replete with driver's license, a VISA credit card, and a bank ATM card. Except for the name, the information on the driver's license was accurate, and the credit cards were good.

"You have the wallet?" asked Duval.

Michelle walked back into the house and emerged a minute later with an apple in one hand and a wallet in the other.

Duval took a bite from the apple when Michelle extended it to his lips, and examined the credit cards. "Same problem as before," he said finally. "They can trace these cards."

"George, I told you we should have gotten money cards. At least we could have pulled out a couple of hundred dollars from some bank machine when we left home Sunday night."

"Michelle, if I had an ATM card I'd be going to the machine every five minutes. And I hate being charged a dollar every time I take my own money out of my own bank account. Besides, I'm always afraid I'm going to go up to a bank machine some night and a guy is going to put a gun to my head."

"In Chadron, Nebraska?"

Duval surprised himself by actually laughing. Not much funny had happened to him in the last thirty-six hours.

He sipped his coffee and scratched Michelle's back.

"Okay, I see your point. If we ever get out of this alive, we'll get ATM cards."

Michelle's eyes suddenly widened. "Hey, how about *his* ATM cards?" She pointed to the wallet.

Duval looked at the ATM cards, which carried the name of a nation-wide system.

"Same problem, Michelle. It can be traced."

"Maybe not," she replied. "Let me see the wallet." She studied the contents of the wallet for a few seconds. "Look, George. This VISA card is a corporate card. See? It says so right on it."

Duval looked, and saw the words *Corporate Card* and *Ilium Corporation* stamped on the square of plastic. "So?" he said at last. He wrinkled his brow. "And why would federal agents have credit cards with the name of a private corporation on them?"

"Part of their cover, I guess," Michelle replied. "But listen, George. Did you ever hear of a corporation issuing its employees an ATM card? A corporate credit card, sure, but an ATM card?"

"Well . . . no, I haven't."

"This ATM card is personal. Do you think there's a chance that no one knows about this card, except the guy who owned it?"

"You mean that maybe they haven't yet been cancelled, or that no one has been alerted to trace them?"

"Yeah, that's what I mean. Why would they worry about an ATM card anyway, even if they did know. You can't use them without a PIN number."

"What's that?"

"A personal identification number."

"Oh. Well, I suppose it's possible that they don't know about the ATM card. But it's only a matter of time before they figure that out too."

"True, but in the meantime, say today and tomorrow, maybe, we can use them. After that we'll be long gone."

"Fine. But how are we going to use them without a the PIN number you were talking about?"

"Let's go into Jackson Hole and I'll show you."

"Done. But first, I've got one or two chores to do." He walked back into the cabin, grabbed his leather jacke,t and returned to the porch. "What time you figure that little hardware store opens on the other side of Bondurant?"

"Early. This is ranching country."

"Good. It will take me at least ninety minutes to walk there. While I'm gone, keep the car off the road."

"Don't be such a worrywart. I'll keep it at the back of the cabin. But why are you going to the hardware store."

"Tell you when I get back. Okay? But for now, I have a question. Think hard, Michelle. What's the number of your license plate on your car back in Chadron, the one I took to Tom Colgan's repair shop Saturday morning?"

"My license plate?" she asked. "Why?"

"Just answer if you can. What's the number?"

"Let's see. I know there's a four. And there's a three or a two." She thought again. "I don't know, George. I never bothered to learn it."

"Good. Just what I thought. Now, come help me get the license plates off the car."

Even walking at a brisk pace it took Duval nearly two hours to get to the north side of the settlement of Bondurant. Twice motorists stopped and offered him a lift, but both times Duval persuaded them he was out for his morning power walk. The motorists shook their heads in derision and moved along without argument. When he reached Sorensen's Hardware, it had already been open for an hour and a half and was doing a brisk business. Duval bought a gallon of matte gray paint and several brushes. He purchased a supply of heavy duty, wet-and-dry sandpaper and two large containers of auto paint primer and body filler. He paid for his purchases in cash, which left him just $41, and bought Monday's regional edition of the *Denver Post* from a newspaper machine outside the door. Without looking at it, he stuck it in a bag with the rest of his purchases and walked a half mile to the parking lot at the side of a café locally renowned for its breakfast service. There, he removed his brushes and other items, and pretended to be preparing for some kind of work.

He carefully examined every car and driver that arrived. He ignored two teenaged boys who pulled up in a pick-up truck. Boys were too interested in cars. He dismissed a middle-aged man dressed in jeans and a checked shirt, who pulled off the highway at forty miles an hour. He was too reckless, too likely to be stopped by the sheriff or state police. A woman of about fifty, well-dressed in a simple pair of slacks, blouse, and white cardigan sweater appealed to him. Her car was neither too old nor too new, neither expensive nor bargain basement, neither garish nor unusual. She drove carefully but not like someone who was afraid of automobiles. She struck Duval as sensible, moderate, and utterly without interest in wheels. When she entered the restaurant, Duval moved to the rear of her car, removed the license plate and replaced it with one he had taken from his Hertz Ford Taurus. He was briefly startled by two high school girls who left the restaurant and walked to a parked Toyota; but they paid him no attention, and when they pulled away, he replaced the front plate. He put the two stolen plates in the bag with his hardware store items, and in less than two hours was back at the cabin. Michelle was waiting by the front porch.

"What did you get for me, honey?"

He showed her his purchases. "Don't say I never think about you."

"Sandpaper." she said. "Just what I always wanted, and it's not even my birthday."

"Honey, will you go grab that electric sander your dad keeps in the tool shed?"

For the next three hours Duval worked diligently to destroy the finish of the rental car. He sanded off paint, dulled grillwork, dented the side door and quarter panels, applied filler, and crudely rolled on matte-gray paint where appropriate. He broke off the radio antenna and replaced it with a wire hangar. He smashed the passenger side exterior mirror, and bent the metal flap covering the gas tank filler tube. He finished by removing the Hertz sticker and the Taurus logos. Then he bolted on the stolen license plates.

Michelle thought it was a masterpiece. "A new car, and all for under one hundred bucks," she laughed.

"A real bomber, don't you think?" asked Duval proudly. "This thing would look right at home on the streets of Mogadishu."

They cleaned themselves off with a garden hose, and Duval offered to make them both a late lunch. "There's a *Denver Post* in the bag," he said. "Maybe there will be some news."

Duval was attempting to shred a head of lettuce in the kitchen and had nearly sliced off a thumb when Michelle startled him with a loud cry from the front porch. He darted for the front of the house and met her just as she entered the living room. Tears streamed down her cheeks, and the newspaper was clenched firmly in her right hand.

"Oh God, George! Oh God! Dan Reiner's dead!" She collapsed in his arms.

"What? What are you talking about?"

"It's here, here in the paper. Oh, God, George. What's happening?" She began sobbing uncontrollably.

He held her tightly for a minute, trying to soothe her shaking body, then released her just enough to take the paper in his left hand. The headline was below the fold, in the right hand corner of the front page. "Nebraska County Sheriff Murdered." It was accompanied by an official-looking black and white photo of Reiner, and read:

> Rushville, Nebr. (AP) Sheridan County Sheriff Daniel R. Reiner was found bludgeoned to death at his home late Sunday night by sheriff's deputies. Reiner, 55, was discovered shortly after 9:00 PM in the bottom of a well behind his ranch house, eight miles east of Rushville, the Sheridan County seat. Deputies went to Reiner's house after he missed several appointments on Sunday and could not be contacted by radio or telephone.
>
> "It just wasn't like him to be out of touch like that," said Helen Mirrett, a long-time Sheriff's Department employee. Reiner's home was ransacked, but Deputy Sheriff Tom Reynolds said nothing valuable appeared to be missing, and that at present investigators had established no motive for the crime. He added that there were, as yet, no suspects in the case.

Duval dropped the newspaper to the floor and held Michelle tightly in his arms. Dan Reiner murdered? He could make no sense of it. Reiner was part of the cover-up, a man who had made it absolutely clear that there would be no serious investigation of the accident, the bodies, the photos, and the x-rays. It was Reiner who told Duval to stop imagining things, to stop worrying about events he could not control.

Reiner had to know what was going on; he had to be part of it. Why would they kill him?

"George," said Michelle through her tears, "I've known Dan Reiner all of my life. I can't believe he's been murdered. Who would do such a thing?" She looked at him for a possible answer, but he had none.

Duval racked his mind for an answer that seemed logical. Maybe it was burglars, he thought, or a jealous husband. God knows there could be any number of them. But bludgeoned to death? Dan Reiner, who was strong as a bull and twice as wary? No, he couldn't imagine a man like Dan Reiner being beaten to death by an ordinary criminal. No, it wasn't possible. It must have been federal agents. It had to be them. Didn't it?

In Towson, Maryland, just outside Baltimore, Raymond Trimble was scanning the pages of a day-old *Baltimore Sun* in the waiting room of his wife's obstetrician. Trimble, had been through the pregnancy routine once before when his wife, Susan, was carrying their son, Scott, but he had forgotten the paucity of reading material in Dr. Gautier's waiting room. He was reading the *Sun* by default. Few articles in *Modern Maternity* magazine interested him, and the *Journal of Obstetrics and Gynecology* was even worse. The copy of *People* magazine was three months old, and he didn't care about Madonna anyway, so the Monday *Sun* was his best bet, even if he had already read the sports page the day before.

On page five of the first section, Trimble came upon an item he had missed in his first reading of the paper. It concerned the murder of a man named Anthony Torrelli, a customs inspector who was apparently involved in some kind of drug dealing. Trimble couldn't shake the feeling that he had heard the victim's name somewhere. Trimble had just finished the article's second sentence, which identified Torrelli as a customs officer, when his wife returned to the waiting room, ready to go. "Everything all right, Sue?" he asked.

"No problems, you'll be glad to hear. We're getting a good heartbeat on the sonogram now."

He kissed her on the cheek and helped her with her raincoat. "Did you see this in the paper yesterday?" he asked, showing her the article.

She studied the newspaper briefly, then shook her head that she hadn't.

"I think I talked to this guy Sunday on the phone," he said. "In fact, I'm almost sure of it."

Susan looked at the article again, reading it more thoroughly this time. "Really?"

"Yeah, I remember now. He was asking all sorts of questions about boilers. I remember his name because of that Italian restaurant we used to go to out in Hagerstown. It was called Torrelli's, remember?"

"Sure, I do. But it was Tonnelli's."

"Oh, that's right. Anyway, close enough. That's how I remember this guy, and anyway I've never been called by a customs inspector before so it stuck in my mind."

"Maybe you should call the police."

He considered the idea briefly, then dismissed it. "And tell them what, that the guy had a boiler question? I can't imagine that that would have much to do with a drug murder."

"Yeah. You're probably right," she said.

It was late afternoon when Carolyn Richards turned into her driveway. She hadn't realized that her license plates had been changed. Karl, her sixteen-year-old son, was waiting for her.

"Hey, Mom. Can I borrow the car tonight?"

"A big date on a Tuesday?"

"Yeah, well, kinda."

"Sure, you can have it."

Karl gave his mother a kiss and walked in the house to get a container of car wash detergent, a bucket of water, and a sponge. For the next thirty minutes, he went over every inch of the car, soaping down and hosing off every speck of dirt, grease, and grime he could find. He was finishing the headlights when something about the front license plate caught his eye. He stopped his sponging, stood up, and stepped back for a better look. He couldn't quite put his finger on what was wrong. He turned his head away from the car briefly and then turned back for a fresh look. "Ha!" he said to no one in particular. "Hey, Mom."

"Yes, Karl," she answered through the open kitchen window.

"When did you change your license plates?"

"What are you talking about? I didn't change my license plates."

"That's funny, because the ones you got on here now are sure as shootin' not yours."

The jagged peaks of the Grand Tetons loomed intermittently through a mist of blowing snow, a harbinger of the winter that soon would descend from the mountaintops to the forest lands below. Duval lowered his gaze from the icy crags to the late-summer highway before him and tried to recall the last time he had visited Jackson. It had been almost a year.

Michelle reached over from the passenger seat and patted his leg. "I like your hair short."

"You do?" Duval took his eyes from the road and looked at himself briefly in the rearview mirror. He stroked the back of his neck, feeling skin where his ponytail once fell and faked a spasm of chill. "Feels kind of naked back there to me."

"You'll get used to it," said Michelle. "And it makes you look more mature." It was a word Duval disliked, a word that in his experience was used almost exclusively by women. Men didn't want to be *mature* and wouldn't demand it of anyone they liked. A father might tell a son to "grow up" or "act his age" or "be a man" but would be unlikely to demand that junior be *mature* about something. He turned to Michelle. "What does hair have to do with maturity?"

"In the abstract, nothing. But in the real world, a physician ought to radiate seriousness and wisdom. A ponytail doesn't do that."

"You mean that a ponytail on a man is frivolous?"

"Yes, that's what I mean."

It struck Duval as a superficial and even sexist judgment. "How about high-heeled shoes, lipstick, earrings, women's things? Aren't they a little frivolous? I don't hear you complaining about women not being serious if they put on a pair of stilettos, so they can break their ankle when they trip on the office carpet."

"That's different."

There was no answer to that and Duval didn't attempt one. It meant: No argument you make will change my mind. And Duval had learned long ago that continuing the discussion would be pointless. He turned to a new topic. "You really think I'm less recognizable?"

"Yes, I do. With no ponytail, no beard, and those drugstore reading glasses, your appearance has been dramatically altered."

Duval wasn't certain she was serious.

"If you had a pin-striped suit, you could pass for a banker."

"Great. Just what I always wanted."

They drove along in silence for several minutes, lost in their own thoughts and overwhelmed by the scenery. Duval passed a mile marker and checked his watch. They'd be in Jackson by four o'clock.

Michelle broke the silence. "I think we should turn ourselves in." She spoke without emotion.

"You what?"

"I think we should go to the local police or sheriff in Jackson and turn ourselves in."

Duval couldn't believe what he was hearing. "You can't be serious. I thought we talked this out."

Michelle reached in a brown paper bag at her feet and retrieved an orange. She began peeling it slowly and, when she was finished, handed Duval a slice before biting into the tangy fruit. She sucked in silence for a few seconds and removed a seed from her mouth. "Running is a dead end. Eventually we'll get caught and considering our experience in these matters, I doubt it will take long. Anyway, we haven't done anything wrong."

Duval heard her out in silence, registering no facial expression and keeping his eyes trained on the curving roadway. "Michelle, in case you forget two men tried to kill us Sunday night. Dan Reiner *has* been killed. Murdered. So how can we turn ourselves in?"

"But you don't know the government is doing the killing. The more I think about it, the more far-fetched it all seems. Nuclear weapons, suspicious toxic waste companies, government agents—it all seems wrong."

"And I suppose I'm making up the guys Sunday night and whoever tore apart my offices and whoever killed Reiner?"

She bit into the orange a second time. "No, I know that's all happening, that it's real. I just think maybe we've got the wrong slant on things. Maybe it's not the government doing all this. Those guys at the house Sunday didn't have anything on them to connect them with the government. They didn't have FBI IDs."

Duval couldn't answer immediately, because for some time he'd been wondering the same thing. Who did those men work for?

"George, try to reason it out. If you stumbled onto a nuclear accident, don't you think the government might first come to you and ask you to be quiet about it if they wanted it kept under wraps?" She paused to choose her words carefully. "Wouldn't it be easier to appeal to your patriotism or threaten you with legal action than to bust up your offices and murder you and your girlfriend. Isn't that more logical?"

"Maybe."

"There have been nuclear accidents before, accidents involving bombs. Loevinger told you that, himself." She tried to see if anything she was saying was sinking in, but Duval's face remained passive. "And he also told you that the government didn't attempt to keep quiet about it. God almighty, George, when that missile exploded in Arkansas a few years back and dumped an atomic bomb on some field nearby, the Air Force announced it immediately and opened the site to TV cameras."

That got Duval's attention. "You remember that accident?"

"I remember it, because I was just a kid at the time, and, when I saw something about it on TV, I didn't know what an atomic bomb was. I had to ask my dad about it."

"It was a hydrogen bomb."

"Whatever it was, the Air Force didn't deny there had been an accident. So why would they be so silent about this accident? And, anyway, you're no nuclear physicist. You don't really know for certain what you stumbled on back home. You're just jumping to conclusions based on a single conversation with Mark Loevinger."

"And I suppose I'm imagining the two thugs lying in our driveway?"

Michelle thought they were starting to go in circles. "They're there, all right. It's just that you don't know who sent them after us. You don't know that they're government types."

"Okay, I'm not absolutely sure. I am sure, however, that the cops are after us. If nothing else, they're certainly going to want to know what two corpses are doing on our property."

"When they find them." Michelle wondered if they should have attempted to hide the two men, but dismissed the thought. On Sunday night the only thing she and Duval wanted to do was get away from the house in case the two men had accomplices nearby. "It could be days before anyone visits our house."

Not likely, thought Duval, driving on in silence.

Michelle tried another angle. "Let's start at the top."

"You mean, back to the day of the accident?"

"No. I mean the top of the U.S. government. Do you think President Franklin Moran is a murderer or that he would condone what's being done to us?"

Duval smiled. "Do you think Abraham Lincoln is the type of man to suspend habeas corpus? Do you think Ronald Reagan is the type of man to send arms to the Ayatollah Khomeini?"

"That's different."

Sure, thought Duval. Like high heels and lipstick. "Michelle, I don't know what to think. Maybe you're right. But I do know that someone tried to kill us, and I'm not turning myself or you in to anybody official until I get a much better handle on what's really going on."

"How long will that take?"

"A couple of days, maybe."

"And then we go to the authorities?"

"If we can be certain they're not the ones chasing us. But I want to be sure."

They entered Jackson and began searching for an automatic teller machine that would accept the bank card they had taken from Onega Sunday night. When they found one at the side of a small office building on a quiet side street, they waited in the car until an elderly man finished a transaction and then approached the machine warily on foot.

"Okay, now what?" asked Duval.

"Give me the guy's wallet," Michelle demanded. She took a wallet from Duval's hand, removed the bank card and driver's license belonging to Onega, and placed them on the narrow sill below the ATM machine. She studied both items briefly, then picked up the bank card, tapped it against her teeth three times, and finally inserted it forcefully into the ATM slot. After a few clicks and a high-pitched grinding sound, the ATM's small screen produced a message: "Please Enter Your Personal Identification Number." Michelle looked again at Onega's driver's license and entered four digits. The screen's white lettering remained unchanged for a moment, then read: "Incorrect Personal Identification Number. Try Again?"

"Shit!" said Michelle. She punched the "Yes" button, and looking at the driver's license again tapped in four new numbers. Seconds later she slapped her thigh in disgust as the machine again rejected her entry. "Try Again?" it asked. She punched in "No" and removed the card.

"Why didn't you try again?" asked Duval.

"Because most machines are programed so that if you miss the PIN three times, it eats your card."

"So?"

"So, I've eliminated two possible numbers for this card, meaning that we'll have better odds the next time we try it. We can't try at all without the card."

"Great, you've eliminated two possibilities. By my reckoning that means we have one chance out of 9,998 to hit the jackpot next time."

Michelle was not amused. "Let's try another machine."

They drove in random circles on the streets of downtown Jackson until they found a second machine on a quiet block.

Duval watched as Michelle repeated the procedure she had just attempted with the first card. This time when she entered the four digits, the bank machine made the familiar clicking and grinding sounds and the message on the screen changed. It now read: "Type of Transaction?"

Duval was stunned. "How did you do that?"

"I didn't work two summers in a bank for nothing, Georgie boy. Now, how much do we want?"

"Try a thousand."

"Too high. Let's try five hundred." She pushed the buttons to obtain $500, but the machine refused to give it. She tried $250 and was rewarded with four $50s, two $20s, and two $5s. She removed the cash and the card and almost skipped back to the car. "Let's eat, I'm starved," she said.

"Sure. But first, how did you do that?"

"Easiest thing in the world. I punched in his birthday. Here, look at his license. He was born on November fifteenth, nineteen forty-one. I punched it in."

Duval considered. "You punched in eleven-fifteen-forty-one?"

"No, dummy. I punched fifteen eleven. If that didn't work, I'd have tried nineteen-forty-one. No luck there? Then eleven fifteen. George, it's amazing how many people use some version of their birthday for their personal identification number. People don't remember numbers well— or don't like to make the effort to remember."

"I'll be damned."

"You said Scarface or Ahab or what's his name spoke with an accent. Probably European, right?"

"Yeah, his name was Onega, or at least that's what the other guy called him."

"Well, doctor, Europeans reverse their days and months."

"Huh?"

"His birthday, according to his license, is November fifteenth. In the States we write that as eleven-fifteen. In Europe, they write it as fifteen-eleven—the fifteenth day of the eleventh month. It worked."

"I'm impressed."

"You ought to be. Now let's get dinner, I'm starved." She smiled broadly, savoring her triumph over the machine.

They filled up the car's tank, checked the oil, and found a quiet restaurant connected to a resort hotel. They ate a full and leisurely dinner and luxuriated in the anonymity of the crowd. Afterwards, Duval purchased the regional edition of the *Rocky Mountain News* from a vending machine near a bank of pay phones, and pretended to read it while watching people punch in phone numbers. When he was certain he had gotten two good telephone credit card numbers, he folded the newspaper and joined Michelle in the car. "Wanna make a credit card call to Angola?" he asked. He explained what he had been doing. "We're ready to rock and roll now, honey," he said, kissing her on the cheek."

"Hooray for us," said Michelle.

"Now, let's find a place to stay for the night."

"What's wrong with this place?"

"Nothing, except it's booked solid. Let's try some of the resorts up by the lake. In the meantime, you can scan this and see if there's anything new." He handed her the paper.

They were five miles south of Jackson Lake Lodge when Michelle let out a sharp yelp. "God, look at this!"

Duval pulled to the side of the two-lane highway, set his flashers, and squinted at the Tuesday morning regional addition of the *Rocky Mountain News*. The headline Michelle was pointing to was at the top of page five. "Regional Manhunt for Nebraska Couple."

Chadron, Nebr. (AP) Nebraska state police have launched a regional manhunt for a Chadron physician and his assistant, wanted in connection with the deaths of two men and the disappearance of a third.

Duval looked up from the paper. "Who disappeared?" he wondered out loud. He returned his gaze to the paper.

Authorities say they want to question Dr. George Duval, 32, and his assistant Michelle Falk, 24, in connection with the murder Sunday of Sheridan County Sheriff Daniel R. Reiner, 55, and the suspicious death of an unidentified man found fatally shot Sunday night in the driveway of the home the couple shared near Fort Robinson.

"What the hell?" Duval slapped at the newspaper with his hand. "They suspect us of killing Reiner?"

"That's crazy. Everybody knows you and Reiner have been friends for years. What I want to know is what happened to the guy we pumped full of morphine? They only talk about one body at the house."

"Maybe he somehow woke up and got away."

"Or stumbled off into the bushes and croaked out of sight. Let's see the rest of the story."

Duval was last seen in public Sunday afternoon when he visited a medical clinic he operates in the settlement of Whiteclay. Falk has not been seen since Sunday evening when she was dropped off by a taxi at the contemporary home she shares with Duval near Fort Robinson. Authorities say that for now, neither Duval nor Falk have been officially charged with any crime, but they add that could change pending further police investigation.

Duval and Falk are reported by local townspeople to be a highly respected and well-liked couple, unlikely to be involved in a crime of any kind. Sheridan County Sheriff's deputies say, however, that Duval and Sheriff Reiner were known to be feuding about a traffic accident and speculate that their disagreement may have degenerated into violence.

Duval dropped the paper to his lap without finishing the article. "This is even grimmer than I thought. I told you they'd be looking for us."

"You'd be looking for us too, considering the circumstances. And we haven't even been charged yet. It doesn't sound like they're preparing to blow us off the highway, à la Bonnie and Clyde. But what about the missing person? Is there anything on that? Read some more."

Duval returned to the paper.

Authorities in Lincoln say they would also like to talk to the couple about the disappearance Sunday of University of Nebraska Materials Science Professor Mark K. Loevinger.

"Oh, no!" Duval threw the paper aside and covered his face with his hands. "No! No! No!" he barked, before wrapping both hands around the steering wheel and shaking it with all his might.

"What's wrong?"

"It's Mark. Look at this." He picked up the newspaper and pointed to the paragraph. They read together in silence.

Loevinger, 31, has not been seen since Sunday morning when he left his home in northwest Lincoln to work at his laboratory on the University of Nebraska main campus.

Security guards found the lab wrecked late Sunday afternoon after Loevinger's wife called to say she hadn't heard from her husband and wanted someone to see if he was working late. There was no trace of Professor Loevinger, although he was signed into the building by security guards Sunday morning. Duval and Loevinger were college roommates and long-time friends, and Laura Loevinger said her husband had been very upset ever since talking to Duval on the telephone last Saturday afternoon.

"Jesus Christ! Now Mark Loevinger's missing?" Duval felt sweat begin to break out on his back as the story sunk in. "Michelle, they're going to kill us both."

Michelle said nothing at first. She took a deep breath, then calmly removed the paper from Duval's hands, folded it in half, and tossed it on the rear seat. She grabbed the back of Duval's neck and pulled his head toward hers until their faces practically touched. She spoke softly. "I think you're getting hysterical."

"I'm getting hysterical?"

"Yes. You're not thinking clearly. You're a surgeon, George. You're supposed to be able to handle emergencies, keep your cool, think clearly. You're not doing that."

"And you are, I suppose?"

"Better than you." She let go of Duval's neck. "George, think about it. If there were some kind of government conspiracy to get rid of anyone who knew anything about this accident you were in—this nuclear thing—do you think the government would go out of its way to tie everyone in it together publicly?"

"I don't follow." He took his hands from the wheel and leaned back in his seat.

"The State Police just publicly connected you with Loevinger. Why do that? It raises all sorts of difficult questions. They also tied you and Reiner together with the accident you had out on Highway 250. Why do that? If they wanted to get rid of people, they'd just do it, right? Why get everybody else involved—the local police and the press? Why bring attention to everything and raise all sorts of difficult questions?"

"What are you saying?"

"What I said before. Maybe the cops aren't part of all this. Maybe the federal government and the military aren't either. You don't know anything at all really, but you're reacting like somebody who's got it all figured out."

Duval's head was spinning. He was having trouble keeping his thoughts straight. "And just what do you propose we do?"

"I'm not sure, just yet. I do know that sometime, somehow, you're going to have to trust somebody if we're going to get out of this mess."

Duval tapped his fingers on the steering wheel, as if the rhythmic noise would clear his mind. "I'm still not ready to face the police. I will call Howard Silber."

"The guy you know at the *Denver Post?*"

"Yeah."

"What can he do?"

"Maybe nothing. But I trust him. And something else. His dad used to be a big mucky-muck with the DIA."

"The who?"

"The Defense Intelligence Agency. He might still be there. Maybe he can help."

"And maybe he can turn us in," said Michelle, with a hint of doubt.

"Maybe. But as you said we're going to have to trust somebody. I trust Howard more than some FBI agent."

Duval killed the flashers, pulled the Taurus back onto the highway, and resumed the drive north toward Jackson Lake.

A bank employee named Peter Hall walked out of the Richmond, Virginia, office building and crossed the street to a pay phone on the far corner. He reached inside his pants pocket and pulled out a business card with a phone number scribbled on the back. He studied the card and dialed the number collect.

"Hello," came a deep male voice at the other end.

"I have a collect call for Mr. Bishop from Mr. Rook," said the operator. "Will you accept the charge?"

There was a pause. "We'll accept the charges."

The operator hung up, and Hall tried the phrase written on the back of the business card. "I have a money order for Mr. Bishop."

"Yes."

"He can pick it up at the Cudahay State Bank outlet on Ninth Street in Jackson, Wyoming."

"Excellent. He will thank you in person at seven tonight at the bar of the Keystone Hotel." The man with the deep voice hung up.

Hall returned the business card to his pocket and clapped his hands together sharply.

"Yes!" he shouted. In fifteen years as an electronic data specialist with the Universal Bank of Virginia, his annual salary had never exceeded $25,000. As the bank grew from Richmond to outlying cities in the state and then into D.C. and the Maryland suburbs, its deposits and profits expanded twenty-fold, but Peter Hall barely kept ahead of inflation. Now he had just made $2,000 for five minutes work.

It had been so simple, too. All he had to do was program his computer to tell him when and where cash was withdrawn from an ATM card. Examining the ATM and VISA card transactions of Universal Bank customers was the kind of thing he did every day. No one would ever notice anything unusual or suspect him of any wrongdoing. If the Washington-based private detective he'd met the day before needed a little inside info once in a while to pursue a divorce case or other matter on the Q-T, it was all right by him. Why shouldn't he pick up a little cash for it? And fuck the bank anyway.

Wednesday, September 15

In a private garage on North Halstead Street in Chicago, a Russian agent named Gavril Apraxin sat on an aluminum and nylon lawn chair and read a Louis L'Amour novel. Apraxin was consumed by the American frontier. Starting with the hunters and trappers of James Fenimore Cooper's colonial New England, his reading had migrated across the Mississippi and the Great Plains to the outlaws and rustlers of L'Amour's "Wild West." Apraxin couldn't get enough of the stuff, and, now that he had seen the West for himself, he was more hooked than ever.

A series of steady, high-pitched beeps from the computers to his left interrupted his reading. Apraxin grudgingly put down his paperback and turned to the work at hand. He checked his watch against the electronic clocks above the computer screens and rapped his fingers rhythmically on the table top in satisfaction. They were right on time. Ilium leaders would be pleased.

The clicks and whirs from the cipher boxes began a minute later. To Apraxin, they sounded a lot like the mechanical noises made by a printer tapping out a spreadsheet, but he knew the comparison was superficial. Cipher boxes were right out of Edison, he thought, while a laser printer was a product of the computer age. He touched the cipher boxes lightly, confirming with the vibrations that wheels and disks were turning in all three boxes as they were supposed to. He adjusted the contrast on the center computer screen and watched. The top half of the screen consisted of row upon row of constantly changing letters and numbers. It hurt his eyes to watch them spin and dance to the tune of the standby transmission, but he kept his eyes glued on them anyway. When the first decoded letter popped into the lower half of the screen seconds later, Apraxin snapped his fingers.

"Correct," he said out loud, as he looked at the oversized "C" on the screen and saw that it matched the printed cipher sheet on his lap. Over the next two minutes, ten more letters and numbers appeared on the screen, and each was as it was supposed to be. At the end of the sequence, a message appeared in English:

Tranmission test 01. Sequence Qualifier. Sequence Check. Reset baud rate if parameters exceeded.

Apraxin double-checked the number-letter sequence one more time, and then typed instructions on a keyboard. Forty-five seconds later, the computer screens went blue, and, moments after that, an ever-changing geometric pattern started twisting and folding where the numbers had been. Apraxin looked at an electronic device attached to the drain in the center of the garage and read the number from it. The reception was even better than expected.

He put his paperback book into his back pocket and, folding his chair up against a wall, let himself out of the garage into the rainy, predawn darkness. He had good news for Ilium. He also had four other locations to check that day, and the nearest was ninety miles north in Milwaukee.

Oh well, he thought, it beats roughing up dissidents in Gorki.

"How wonderful to see you looking so well, Professor Ushta. A walk in the evening air has done you a world of good. Cigarette?" Zeya opened his silver cigarette box and extended it to Ushta on the other side of the desk.

"No, thank you."

"Mind if I do?"

"Certainly not, Zeya, it's your office."

"That it is, sir." Zeya examined his box, selected a Dunhill, and lit it ceremoniously with an ancient but well-preserved Ronson lighter. He blew a stream of smoke toward the ceiling and leaned back in his chair.

"Ushta, there has been a change of plans. You won't be staying with us as long as I had anticipated."

"What happened?"

"You're just a little too hot. They still haven't found the two soldiers you so unfortunately met, and they may not find them until spring, if then. They are certain, however, that you had something to do with their disappearance. They've been snooping around some of the remote agricultural stations below the mountains."

Ushta felt his pulse quicken. "They're snooping in the right place."

"Yes. Well anyway, what to do? I suppose I could just turn you in. Or I could dispose of you." Zeya spoke without obvious malice.

"Yes, you could easily do either." In an odd way, Ushta almost didn't care.

"I must say, however, that you have been an excellent guest. We found the tractor and the fuel carrier just where you said. When it cools down a bit, we'll retrieve the fuel for ourselves and then report the tractor to the authorities. Too bad we can't keep it." Zeya stubbed out his cigarette and picked a piece of tobacco from his tongue. "I've smoked too much today. Anyway, to business. I'll be visiting France again shortly. If the information you gave me is as good as I think, I will make some very handsome profits. In view of all that, I'm going to let you go."

"Thank you, Zeya." All things considered, Ushta thought, Zeya was actually one of the more honorable men he had met. No doubt he was a thief (and if need be worse), but he appeared to be a man of his word, and Ushta didn't know many men he could say that about. "When do I go and where?"

"Ordinarily, I'd be able to get you safely to a Western country with little difficulty. Unfortunately, as I said before, you're a very hot property at this moment. I can't afford to take many chances. Therefore, while I'm going to give you some help, a lot will depend on your own abilities."

Ushta listened without expression and said nothing.

Zeya continued. "You go tonight on the nine o'clock train for Harbin." Zeya looked at his Movado watch. "That's in fifty minutes."

"China? I don't want to go to China."

"Of course not. You have a ticket for Harbin. But you leave the train at Borzya. From there you travel straight south, forty or fifty miles. Follow the southbound railroad tracks if you dare. When you come to the Wall of Genghis Khan, you are out of Russia, smack on the China-Mongolia border. Go southwest and you can be sure you're in Mongolia."

"There are no border markings?"

"In northeast Mongolia?" Zeya couldn't stifle a grin. "Ushta, you amaze me. You, a professor of cartography, a geographer, speaking such nonsense. Ushta, you're going into 'Indian Country.'"

Ushta didn't understand. "It's an expression, Ushta. I heard it in a John Wayne movie. It means you are going into a dangerous and uncivilized territory where you clearly don't belong."

Ushta felt both sheepish and defensive. "The American Indians had a civilization."

"Professor, it's just an expression. The point is that northeast Mongolia is not the Bois de Boulogne. Once there, survival is up to you. You can march southwest toward Ulan Bator, the alleged capital of that godforsaken land, or go anywhere else you want. It's your call."

Ushta crossed his arms over his chest and stared at the silver cigarette box, thinking. He looked at Zeya. "I've always wanted to see the Wall of Genghis Khan."

"Good." Zeya reached into a desk drawer and brought out a train ticket and a doctored passport. "I think you will find this passport acceptable. It's the best I could do on short notice. One of my men will walk you across the street to the station. He'll give you a bedroll, some light provisions, and a small sum of cash."

"I thank you again, Zeya. You needn't be so generous."

"My parting gift to a condemned man."

"You think I won't make it?"

"I think you'll reach Mongolia. After that, who knows? They're a rude and uncivilized lot in my view, Ushta. They are liable to kill you for your socks. Still, you speak Mongolian, correct?"

"Yes."

"And you are the only man who has ever escaped Pechora—an impressive feat. Maybe you can talk those barbaric yak drivers into sparing your life. I doubt it, though."

"And if I do?"

"Then you'll eventually have to face the Mongolian authorities, a corrupt and unseemly lot. They are always looking for a way to get in bed with their former Russian masters. I expect they will send you back to the Russian border police for a couple bottles of vodka. If they learn how important you are, they may demand a case." Zeya laughed, shook Ushta's hand, and ushered him toward the door. "Good luck, my friend. You'll need it."

The Tuesday night train to Harbin was packed. More than half the passengers were soldiers, most of them headed for dreary border outposts along the Argun River. There, over the coming winter months, they would do battle with perpetual boredom by getting drunk as often as possible and screaming insults in bad Mandarin to the equally insensible Chinese conscripts on the far bank.

Most of the remaining passengers were single men; they were petty smugglers who crossed into China, stuffed suitcases with toothpaste, ra-zor blades, shampoo, and other western toiletries available on the Chi-nese market and returned to Russia to sell them for hard currency at a 600 percent mark-up.

Border police looked the other way in exchange for a few bars of soap, a bottle or two of cheap cologne, or, if they were lucky and hard-nosed, a half-carton of Marlboros. A handful of western tourists, most of them university students, rounded out the passenger list. All in all, Ushta thought that the smugglers were a pretty desperate-looking lot.

As the four-car train rumbled east toward the Chinese border, Ushta wondered if Zeya's description of Mongolia and its people came any-where close to reality. For a man with a Mongolian mother, Ushta con-sidered himself embarrassingly uninformed about the immense land sep-arating China and Siberia. He knew its geography and geology, of course, and, because of his mother, he could speak the language with some fa-cility, but he had never visited the country and had no direct experience with the daily life and culture. Still, he had doubts about Zeya's charac-terizations. Ethnic Russians were a notoriously xenophobic and bigoted people, especially those residing near their country's frontiers. Their as-sessments of neighboring peoples were as likely to be based on profound ignorance and ancient prejudice as on any first-hand knowledge, and were therefore highly suspect. Mongolia was a remote, rugged, and sparsely populated land, but it was also home to an ancient culture that had known its moments of glory.

Ushta's rumination naturally turned to his mother, a woman he had known for only ten years. He remembered her as a slim woman with long, straight, jet-black hair who often hummed quietly to herself as she moved about the family's small apartment near the Moscow River. As a child, Ushta had concluded that his mother was a genuinely happy woman; and while he now recognized that a child's understanding of his parents' marriage is often superficial, he still firmly believed that his mother and father had deeply loved one another. That made the end more difficult. On her thirty-first birthday, Ludmila Altay Ushta was pricked in the neck with a single horsehair from a decorative cushion she had received as a gift from a friend. The cushion had been purchased at a flea-market specializing in smuggled goods from Kirgizia, and its horsehair stuffing was loaded with anthrax bacillus. She had contracted the disease and died three days later before doctors could determine what she was suffering from.

The train jolted sideways as it passed over a switch, and Ushta was brought back to the reality of the crowded and stuffy coach. He watched a young soldier as he tried to strike up a conversation in rudimentary German with a young, female tourist, and casually observed two of the semi-professional smugglers onboard as they played a game of chess on the side of a suitcase. It was a game Ushta never particularly enjoyed, although his mother had taught him and encouraged him to play.

Ushta smiled to himself. If Mongolians were primitive, his mother was certainly atypical. She loved to tell him stories about her people, including the conquests of Genghis and Kublai Khan. She spoke of the skillful riders and herdsmen who had wrenched a living from some of the most inhospitable land on earth. She told him how a yurt was made, and how flowers changed the landscape in the spring, and how children passed their time with elaborate games when their chores were done. Often, she sang him Mongolian songs, songs so different from the sharp and regular notes of Russian folk music that they might have come from another planet.

The more he reminisced, the more confident Ushta became that Zeya was wrong. Mongolians were poor. They were not barbarians.

It was nearly eleven o'clock when the slow-moving train pulled into the quiet station at Borzya. Except for a handful of soldiers waiting for a westbound local, the platform was deserted. Ushta walked into the small station to wait for the soldiers to depart and was struck by the sight of six police officers standing near an open ticket window. He turned on his heels and retraced his steps to the platform, hoping they didn't notice his abrupt about-face. He paced the platform nervously, trying to stay out of the weak light cast by overhead lamps, but he needn't have worried. The policemen remained inside.

Ten minutes later, Ushta watched the soldiers board the westbound train. He moved to the end of the platform and, when the red trailing light of the last coach rocked by, stepped down onto the tracks and began heading east. Five hundred yards farther, a single track branched off the main line and turned south. Ushta looked at his watch and calculated that if he kept his pace up, he could make twenty-five miles by dawn. That would put him within a day's walk of the border, maybe closer. He hunched his shoulders to make his backpack fit more comfortably and stepped off toward his mother's homeland. The temperatures had risen significantly in the last two days and the warmth cheered him.

* * *

Colonel-General Uri Saratov stood at the head of the table and offered a toast.

"Gentlemen, I regret the very late hour. It took us many hours to confirm the Pechora results because, as you know, we're keeping the number of operators in America to a bare minimum for reasons of security. Still, the news is good. Pechora fired almost perfectly today. With the exception of some minor computer problems in location two in Los Angeles and a few other minor glitches, it couldn't have gone much better. We got sixty-three confirmed kills out of a possible sixty-six. On the first try! Gentlemen, we are almost halfway home. A toast to Pechora and to Ilium." He raised his glass of Moët-Chandon and sipped gingerly. The others did the same, and then without speaking began to softly applaud.

"Gentlemen," said General Bransk raising his glass, "I propose a toast, a salute to Colonel-General Uri Saratov who has made this all possible." Bransk and the others drank and applauded once again, and putting down their glasses, they began filing out the door.

Saratov motioned to Kachuga to stay behind. When they were alone, Saratov poured his aide another glass of champagne, refilled his own glass, and walked to the window overlooking the operations center. He spoke with his back turned. "Andrei, you know why I value your opinions?"

Kachuga, seated at the table's far corner, looked down at his champagne glass. "No, I'm not certain why, General."

"Because in addition to your intelligence and obvious talents, you are younger and for the most part better educated than the rest of us. How many languages do you speak?"

"Five, sir."

"And how much time have you spent in the West?"

"About six years I guess. Most of it was in Germany, however."

Saratov took his customary seat at the head of the table. "Yes, of course. But you are from a different generation than me and the other generals, Andrei. I like to get diverse opinions on things, and in this group you're about the only one who might have a fresh insight on something."

"Thank you, General."

Saratov took a sip of champagne and swished it around his mouth before swallowing. He decided he preferred vodka. "You think the coup will be as smooth as planned, Andrei?"

Kachuga considered his response carefully. "I think it will work reasonably well, sir. General Bransk is a very good officer and he has guts. His forces are professional and loyal . . . loyal to him. We've still got three months to hone the operation, and by then I believe we can take control of the larger cities without too much trouble."

"But there will be resistance?"

"Yes."

Saratov looked absent-mindedly at the ceiling. "How bad?"

Kachuga fingered his glass before responding. "Nothing that can't be put down quickly with the proper force, and Bransk's men will use force."

Saratov still had concerns.

"Will any units in the army resist?"

"The professionals will stay with us, we're certain. Conscripts may be a problem, but nothing we can't deal with pretty quickly."

Saratov pushed back from his chair and walked to Kachuga's side. He lightly patted his aide's shoulder. "You know that Turgenev plans to speak to the nation in a few minutes, and that the subject is disarmament?"

"Yes. But considering the late hour, I expect his speech is really intended for America."

"It is."

"I thought he was going to make his big splash at the United Nations."

Saratov pointed to a stack of intelligence reports on a clipboard at the center of the table. "Apparently the Americans are starting to ask questions. Turgenev figures there's no sense in waiting any longer."

Kachuga said nothing.

Saratov tightened his arm around Kachuga's neck. "Soon Andrei, it won't make any difference what they think in America." Saratov released his aide and returned to his chair. "Our weapons in America will outweigh any nuclear force they can muster."

Kachuga nodded but chose not to speak.

"Andrei, nuclear strategy in Washington is based on having enough time to detect a Russian launch and then respond. Even if we launched our ICBMs without warning, they'd have twenty-five or thirty minutes to fire back. We both lose in that scenario. But this is different. If we had to, we could eliminate them nearly instantaneously with the push of a button. You see?"

"I think so."

"We push a button here, and Washington, D.C., is gone. No White House, no Pentagon, no nothing. Los Angeles is gone, Chicago—all their major cities and military bases. And the best part? Their satellites wouldn't detect any Russian missile launches, because there wouldn't be any."

"And their nuclear subs?"

"Who will give them orders, and how? There will not be many leaders left, and there will be no transmission facilities left standing. And why would they fire at us anyway? No missiles will have been fired from Russia. They won't know what hit them. Better than that, they won't know who hit them."

"Why, then, the disarmament charade?"

"As I said before, Andrei. Just an extra precaution. They can't launch what they don't have."

"True."

"But all this is theoretical anyway, Andrei. It is not our intention to use the weapons, as you know. It's not what we want."

Kachuga was beginning to wonder about intentions, but he didn't push it.

"We can never again allow the Americans to dominate us as they have. In a few months, with Ilium complete, we will be their equals in every way. Superior, in fact." Saratov sounded happy.

Kachuga again wondered how the Americans could be buffaloed by a weapon they didn't know the Russians possessed, but it was clear that his discussion with Saratov was over. Kachuga got to his feet and saluted.

"Thank you for your confidence in me, sir." He started to leave, then turned toward his superior. "General, if you wouldn't mind? Can you tell me how deep Turgenev's arms cuts will be?"

"Down to two hundred warheads. All land based. All ballistic missile submarines disarmed, and eventually scuttled."

Kachuga let out a low whistle. "That's deep. That will cause some rumblings in America." He considered a moment and asked a final question. "And how, General, did you get Turgenev to proceed with this fantastic disarmament proposition?"

"Easy, Andrei. He thinks it's his own idea. It came to him after a little study we did for him. He thinks he's going to win the Nobel Prize. The idiot."

The phone at the *Denver Post* rang four times before reporter Howard Silber answered. The connection was bad, but Duval didn't want to dial again. "Howard?"

"Yes. Who's this?"

"Duval."

"Is that really you, George?"

"Yes."

"Where the hell are you? Are you all right?"

"Yeah, I'm all right for now."

Duval felt a tugging on his sleeve. He looked at Michelle and covered the mouthpiece. "What?" he whispered to her.

"Are you sure you can trust this guy?"

"Honey, I've known him since Chicago, when he was at the *Trib*. I trust him."

"George, you there?"

"Yes, Howard."

"What in God's name is going on? They've got every police department from here to Chicago looking for you and your girlfriend. You may make the FBI's ten most wanted."

"They just want to ask me some questions."

Silber was agitated. He spoke rapidly, phrasing in staccato. "Wrongo, George! You're wanted for murder. Killing a sheriff. They found your prints all over some wallet that the sheriff had in his hand when he was found."

It took a few seconds for Duval to put two and two together. Finally, he recalled the wallet he had taken from the dead men at the accident site and sent to Sheriff Reiner. "I didn't kill him, Howard."

"I believe you. But what about the guy they found at your house?"

"Self-defense." Duval felt the tugging again. This time Michelle was pointing at something. He squinted his eyes and saw a Sweetwater County Sheriff's car turn into the parking lot of the convenience store they were calling from. His stomach felt queasy.

"George?"

Duval gathered his courage. "Is this really front page in Denver?"

"No. It's more like second section. But in my job you read all of the paper every day, and, when a friend is being chased around the countryside for murder, you tend to pay attention."

Duval watched a deputy get out of the sheriff's car and begin walking toward the beaten-up Ford Taurus. The deputy walked to the side of the car, then bent down to look at something underneath. Duval hunched closer to the pay phone, hoping he would be inconspicuous. Michelle tightened her grip on his arm.

"I need your help, Howard," Duval softly continued.

"I'll give you some advice," said Silber, "turn yourself in and explain everything."

"I can't. Not just yet, anyway." Duval went directly to the point. "Tell me, does your father still work for the Defense Intelligence Agency?"

"No. He retired about two years ago. Why?" Silber was obviously surprised by the question.

"I need to find out something. Maybe he can help."

"Shoot."

"Can he find out if there has been a nuclear accident in the past week?"

Silber wasn't sure he'd understood the question correctly. "You mean like Three Mile Island, a power plant?"

"No. An accident involving a nuclear weapon."

Silber didn't answer for a moment. "I think we would have heard of that. Broken Arrows are usually reported nowadays, especially if they're in the States. Why do you need to know?"

"Because I think I stumbled onto a nuclear accident and the people responsible for it are trying to kill me."

"George, the U.S. government isn't trying to kill you."

"Yeah? Well, somebody is. They've killed Sheriff Reiner and a friend of mine, a certain professor at the University of Nebraska is missing. I'm the one who got him mixed up in this."

"That guy Lerninger?"

"Mark Loevinger. Please find out if there's been a nuclear accident. My life may depend on it—Michelle's too."

Silber was having difficulty swallowing Duval's story, but he could hear the fear in his friend's voice.

"Okay, I'll do what I can. Where was this accident supposed to have happened?"

Duval wasn't sure he wanted to answer. "Why do you need to know?"

"Because if you did stumble onto something nuclear and our government isn't responsible, they'll sure as hell want to investigate, don't you think?"

Duval thought there was some sense in that. "But Howard, if it's not our government it can only be someone up to no good. I'm talking about a nuclear weapon here, a hydrogen bomb."

"Hydrogen bomb?" Silber couldn't hide his dismay.

"Yes."

"George, you sure you don't want to give yourself up and get a good lawyer?"

Michelle's grip tightened again, and Duval looked for the sheriff's deputy. He was standing at the front of the Taurus, running his hands across the dents and fresh filler. He was clearly intrigued.

"George, turn yourself in and you can straighten it out. Right now if they find you, they're liable to shoot first and you know what later. They think you're a cop-killer, George."

"I'm not and I hope you know it."

"I believe you George, but I don't count."

"Find out about the accident. It may be the biggest story you'll ever get."

"Okay, I'll do my best. But first, where did this happen?"

Duval explained where the carcass of the burned-out truck could be found and added a warning. "Howard, if this wasn't done by the government, if it's terrorists or something, they could be watching the site. A government investigation would tip them off."

Silber didn't know the clinical definition of paranoia, but he had seen it before and thought Duval had now demonstrated enough symptoms to be measured for a straight-jacket. He decided to test his diagnosis with some amateur psychiatry. "How do I get a hold of you?"

"I'll call you back tomorrow."

It was not the answer of a trusting friend. One check in the "yes" column for paranoia, thought Silber. He continued his examination. "Where are you now?"

"Rock Springs, Wyoming."

Silber looked at the caller ID indicator and saw the Wyoming area code. "Just a second," he said, pulling a Wyoming phone directory from his desk drawer. He ran his finger down a list of exchanges until he found the one Duval was calling from. To his surprise it was assigned to Rock Springs. He cleared his throat. "Great town, Rock Springs. Call me back tomorrow afternoon or evening. I expect my dad can get an answer by then."

"It may be my life, Howard."

"I'll remember, George. And one other thing."

"Yes?"

"Be careful. Please be careful."

Duval hung up. Michelle excepted, it was the first time in days that anyone had said anything kind to him. He was turning from the phone when the sheriff's deputy began walking directly toward him. Duval felt his legs shaking.

"That your car over there, buddy?" asked the deputy, pointing back to the Taurus and looking Duval directly in the eye.

Duval's first instinct was to make a run for it. He controlled himself. "Yes, officer, it is."

The deputy looked Duval over closely. "You're parked in a handicapped space. It's marked on the pavement right beneath your vehicle. You got ten seconds to get it out of there."

"Yes, sir!" said Duval as he half-trotted with Michelle through the front door to the parking lot. They got into the car and pulled away. Duval watched in the mirror as the deputy walked into the adjacent café and pointed to a fresh tray of donuts.

Raymond Trimble had never been fond of authority. He didn't like the IRS, the strictures of his Catholic Church, or major league umpires—and he never would. Trimble's wife thought this facet of her husband's personality was probably the result of some latent resentment of the stern upbringing he had received at the hands of a loving but difficult father. Whatever the cause, Trimble was not the kind of man to voluntarily associate himself with officialdom of any kind. Still, he was a decent, honest, and hardworking man, and he had a strong sense of right and wrong. He couldn't stomach the idea of murder in any circumstance, and the thought that he had information that could lead to the arrest of a killer gnawed at him.

Trimble finished his lunch, got in his car, and drove to a commercial block in northwest Baltimore not far from Memorial Stadium. He found a public phone in front of a dry cleaner's, and grasping the handset with a paper napkin, dialed the FBI field office in Baltimore.

"Special agent Walters," said a man with a strong southern accent.

"I have some information on the Torrelli murder."

"The customs inspector?"

"Yes."

"Well, tell me. Who is this?"

"None of your business. I talked to Torrelli the day he died."

Walters pushed a button on his desk to record the call and flipped a lever to determine the phone it was coming from. "Yeah, where did you see him?"

"I'm not saying. But here's the scoop. He wanted to know about boilers."

Walters wasn't sure he understood. "Broilers? Like chickens?"

"No, boilers. Like hot water boilers, steam boilers. He wanted to know about industrial boilers." Trimble decided now was a good time for a little white lie. "Why he wanted to talk to me I'll never know. I don't know dip about boilers."

"I see. What did he want to know?"

"Just about big boilers. Who made them. What they are used for. That kind of thing. I couldn't help him, but maybe it can help you."

"Why are you so reluctant—?" Agent Walters heard the line disconnect at the other end. He yelled across the office to a secretary. "Luanne, can you get me the Torrelli file?"

He opened the file, pulled out a large manila envelope, and emptied the contents on his desk. There was not much there, but he found what he was looking for. It was a single leaf torn from the *Baltimore Yellow Pages*. He examined the entries. The top left-hand corner was headed by "Boat - Renting & Leasing." There followed "Boat Repairing," "Boat Storage," and "Boating Instruction." Beneath that heading in dark capital letters was an entry he'd given no thought: "Boilers - New & Used." He shook his head. Boilers? What the hell did Torrelli want with boilers?

Thursday, September 16

Ushta slept fitfully and intermittently, unable despite his weariness to blot out the harsh afternoon sun or the growing exhilaration that accompanied his progress to Mongolia. Now, as he awoke again beside a boulder within sight of the Wall of Genghis Khan, Ushta could contain the intoxicating joy no longer. He rose to his feet, filled his lungs with dry desert air, and, with all the power he could gather, bellowed out a thunderous roar of triumph. Spreading his arms wide and prancing in tight little circles, he allowed himself to revel at last in the victory of escape. The Wall of Genghis Khan told his eyes what his heart was afraid to believe: He had succeeded in getting out of Russia.

The train had helped. Two hours out of Borzya, Ushta had heard the rumblings of a decrepit, five-car freight train moving south along the single track he was following to Mongolia. He had hidden at the side of the roadbed to let the train pass by, but it was moving so slowly that he managed to run alongside and pull himself through the open door of an empty boxcar. Sometime after three in the morning, although Ushta didn't recognize it, the train rolled across the Mongolian border near the frontier town of Ereen Cav. The train had not stopped. There had been no border posts, no guards with dogs and machine guns, no barbed wire fences to tell Ushta that he was safely out of Russia. South of Borzya, the Russia-Mongolia border was as unprotected as the frontier between England and Wales. Not until sunrise, when he spotted the Wall of Genghis Khan, had Ushta been convinced that he was at last in another country. He had jumped from the train and slept for seven hours.

As the late afternoon light began to weaken and the Wall cast longer and dimmer shadows, Ushta's self-satisfaction was gradually replaced by a growing uneasiness. What, he wondered, was his next step? For all his meticulous preparation, for all the months he had spent rehearsing the most trivial details of his flight from Pechora, Ushta had never given much serious thought to the possibility of success. Questions roiled his mind. Was Mongolia now truly independent, or were Mongolian authorities still fronting for a cadre of Russians who held the real reins of power? Would a Russian who had escaped from a labor camp be regarded as a victim of persecution, or would he be seen as a trouble-making provocateur? Would his accented Mongolian speech make him more or less welcome by people known to revere their ancient oral traditions? Who should he contact first, ordinary people or some official?

He watched the sun as it dipped below the horizon and decided his best chance would be to reach a small village. The people there were likely to be more receptive, he reasoned.

With the mountains and forests well behind him, he was now in a rolling, treeless plain where, except for an occasional boulder or shallow depression, there were few places to hide. An hour after sunset, when he was confident his silhouette would blend into the surrounding darkness, Ushta took a final swig of water, hitched up his backpack, and walked south through a gap in the Wall cut for the railroad line.

He walked at a steady but unhurried pace for two hours, stopping only briefly to remove his backpack and relieve his shoulders or to drink from his canteen. He was getting ready to stop again when his first Mongol encampment came into view.

At a distance of a quarter mile in the late evening light, the tent village blended into the shadowy landscape. He could easily have passed by without seeing it, but the sour odor floating by from a herd of yaks alerted him to the nomad settlement. Ushta sat on the side of the roadbed and, lifting a pair of binoculars to his eyes, studied the portable village. He could see no human movement and detect no fires, but wisps of smoke wafted skyward from several of the yurts. In addition to the yaks, he made out at least a dozen unsaddled horses, some of them tethered on long lines but most free to roam and graze as they wished. There was also a dark, boxy structure at the edge of the compound, but he couldn't determine what it was. Ushta observed for a quarter of an hour, then decided to push on along the railroad track. He thought a bigger settlement would be better..

He was rounding a bend where the track cut through a low rise when he came upon a herder watering a horse in a shallow rivulet, thirty feet in front of him. Even in the poor light, Ushta could see that the man was young, sixteen or seventeen at best, and armed with a rifle. Ushta's sudden appearance clearly surprised him.

"Stop! Who are you?" said the herder, trying to pull his rifle from his shoulder.

Ushta reacted instantaneously, charging the boy and knocking him to the ground before he could lower his weapon. He yanked the rifle from the surprised youth's hands, but in doing so accidentally squeezed the trigger. The countryside echoed with the loud crack of a rifle shot. The boy was so frightened that he didn't attempt to resist but instead sprang to his feet and began running back toward his village. Ushta aimed the rifle squarely at the teenager's back and then lifted the barrel toward the sky. He's just an innocent boy, he thought, turning to the south and beginning a double-time trot.

Ushta was still fresh, and the adrenaline now flowing through his veins gave him speed and endurance that he had not expected. No man can long outrun a horse, however, and when he heard the hoofbeats behind him, Ushta guessed the game was lost. He looked over his shoulder and spotted seven or eight armed riders closing in. Behind them was a whining all-terrain vehicle bouncing violently across the rutted landscape, its headlights jiggling up and down like lanterns oscillating on short bungee cords. The vehicle was an English model, thought Ushta, probably the boxy object he had been unable to identify when he surveyed the village through his binoculars. He was contemplating the oddity of a Land Rover trailing behind galloping Mongolian nomads when he heard the riders' voices.

They were yelling at him to stop, to give himself up. A crack from a rifle so startled him that he almost tripped over his own feet. He considered turning on them and firing, but quickly decided against it. He would not kill innocent men in Mongolia, and, even if he succeeded in holding them at bay for a while, they would eventually overpower him. He turned to face the horsemen who were now almost upon him, but he acted too late. The horses were moving at full gallop and Ushta's sudden wheel gave them no time to react. The lead horse hit him nearly square, knocking him backward several feet, and the hoof of a second horse caught him above his left brow.

The blow cracked his skull, sending a series of hairline fractures outward from the point of impact like a mirror shattered by a BB gun. The skin above opened in a long and smoothly curved slit, dripping with blood.

When he regained consciousness, Ushta was in the back seat of the Land Rover bumping roughly toward the village. Above loomed the face of a middle-aged Caucasian man who was attempting some kind of medical evaluation. Ushta spoke in Russian.

"Kill me." There was no response, but Ushta was determined never to go back to Pechora or to Russian military justice so he tried again. "Kill me."

"What'd he say?" The white man spoke in English.

The driver of the vehicle was a Mongolian. "I don't know. I don't speak Russian."

Ushta tried again, this time in Mongolian. "Kill me now please."

The driver heard him clearly. "That I understood. He wants you to kill him, he says."

"Kill him? Why?"

The Mongolian spoke to Ushta in Mongol. "Why do you want to be killed?"

"Better to die than to go back to Russia," said Ushta.

The driver considered a moment and then laughed. "He thinks you're a Russian, and you are taking him back to Russia."

The white man smiled. "Tell him not to worry."

The driver looked over his shoulder at Ushta. "He's not a Russian, my friend, and he's not a policeman either."

Ushta tried to digest the information through the pounding pain and at last understood. "Who are you?" he asked, pointing a finger at the white man's chest.

The white man's name was Bill Kimberlet, and he was employed by the Federal Election Commission in Washington, D.C. Kimberlet's job was to teach the nuts and bolts of democracy. While others lectured on democratic theory, Kimberlet was sent from country to country to teach the mechanics. Exactly how are elections held? How does one determine who runs for an office, and who's eligible to vote? By his own reckoning,

Bill Kimberlet had worked in more than thirty countries which were, for the first time, considering the novelty of electing their governments. Kimberlet liked to work at the provincial and even village level, teaching democracy from the bottom up. He had been working in remote Mongolian settlements for the last two weeks. Slowly and as distinctly as he could, Kimberlet stared at Ushta and uttered the only Mongolian phrase he knew: "My name is Bill. Have you registered to vote yet?"

It was the oddest question Ushta had ever heard.

The six-vehicle convoy was led by a Nebraska State Police cruiser and moved at low speed over the rolling plains south of Rushville. Behind the cruiser were two flatbed trucks, one transporting a bulldozer and the other a large backhoe. They were followed by a dump truck, a truck outfitted with a large mechanical auger for digging postholes, and a third flatbed semi carrying thick wooden posts and spools of inch-thick steel cable. When they reached the accident site, the police cruiser signalled the convoy to stop and then went ahead to place warning signs indicating that highway construction was underway.

In took nearly an hour to unload the bulldozer and backhoe and set up the other equipment necessary to repair the broken cables and sheared posts that guarded the east side of the highway. The men worked at an unhurried pace. One group concentrated on removing the damaged section of guardrail, the men detaching the old cable by hand while the backhoe dug out the shattered stumps of the old posts. The bulldozer worked on the embankment, periodically dipping down to the bed of the dry wash to scoop up the new earth necessary to shore up the roadbed.

When the damaged guardrail had been removed and new holes dug, a crew of four men inserted the thick, creosoted pine posts that would secure the new cables. That finished, the auger and the backhoe tracked down to the dry wash to help stabilize the earth around a culvert that carried the occasional waters of the dry wash beneath the highway. Several holes were drilled in the riverbed about halfway between the culvert and the burned-out frame of an old truck. Posts were dutifully inserted into the holes and then secured by cables to pins that had been fastened to the culvert's corrugated steel lining.

A civil engineer would have found such work in the dry wash puzzling in its absolute uselessness, but a casual observer wouldn't have noticed. Work was in fact being accomplished, but it had nothing to do with highway repair. The bulldozer and the backhoe each carried a pair of sensors, one sensor designed to record alpha particles and the other to measure gamma rays. When the devices recorded positive readings, the work crews redoubled their efforts to selectively retrieve soil samples from "hot" spots and shovel them into lead-lined containers. The men working the soil wore jumpsuits that completely covered their bodies and heavy gloves and boots. Those working near the dry wash covered their faces with masks to protect themselves from the prairie dust.

When the chief FBI agent was satisfied that they had gotten the samples they came for, he signalled to the others that it was time to pack up. An hour later, the convoy was moving back toward Rushville. Neither the chief agent nor the lookouts in the Nebraska State Police cruiser or the dump truck had spotted anyone observing the work. Four cars had passed by in the three hours it took to survey the site, but all were occupied by people who were recognized by a local deputy assigned to the survey.

The soil samples were taken by private jet from Chadron to Denver, and then by an unmarked FBI van to Rocky Flats, east of the city. It took very little time for the rough analysis to be completed, and when the results were examined, there could be little doubt. The trace materials found at the crash site included various isotopes of uranium, plutonium oxide, beryllium, lithium-6 deuteride, and polystyrene. To the weapons experts at Rocky Flats, the combination of elements added up to only one thing: a hydrogen bomb. There was no other logical explanation.

The chief FBI agent listened to the experts' conclusions without expression, then excused himself and in a private office placed a call on a secure telephone to a superior in Washington. The next step of the investigation seemed obvious enough to both men. They had to get ahold of George Duval.

Laurie Huddleston finished work at the diner and drove home. She pulled a business card from a junk drawer next to her kitchen sink and dialed the number scribbled on the back. She read a phrase that was handwritten beneath the number and was instructed by a voice on the other end to speak. "They were working at the site this afternoon," she said.

"What kind of work?"

"A state highway crew was repairing the guardrail. The cables on the guardrail were wrecked in an accident."

"What were they wearing?"

"The workers?" She paused briefly. "They were wearing jumpsuits and orange vests. The usual outfit."

"Were there any markings on their vehicles?"

"Yeah, I looked for that. I had to slow down to look real good, but I don't think anyone noticed. The trucks had the state seal on their doors and above that they had writing that said Nebraska State Highway Department. They were just your regular repair trucks."

"Did they actually fix the guardrail?"

"Of course, what else would they be doing out there? The rail was just about finished when I drove by the first time. I went back later, and they were all done and gone."

"Was the burned-out truck still there?"

"Yup. Still there."

"Thank you then. You will receive a cash payment by mail in two or three days. Keep your eye out. Your government is depending on you."

Laurie Huddleston hung up, clapped her hands, and jumped up and down twice. She had now made $500 for half a day's work. The money would come in very handy, and it was all in a good cause. Laurie was a patriotic citizen, and, when government authorities needed a favor, she was happy to help. She could keep her mouth shut too, just like they asked.

What she didn't know was how persuasive she had been. The Ilium watch officer in Washington didn't even file a report.

"You found parts of a thermo what?" The president didn't appear to understand. Frank Moran knew farming, and history, but science was not his strong suit. He scanned the faces of the others in the Oval Office, hoping for clarification.

Rubio Pinzon tried again. "A thermonuclear weapon, Mr. President. In layman's terms, a hydrogen bomb." As always in front of others, Pinzon addressed Moran formally.

The president studied Pinzon's face briefly, then turned calmly to CIA Director Owen Caulfield. There was no agitation in his voice. "So what are parts of a hydrogen bomb doing in a field in Nebraska? How did we accomplish that?"

Caulfield was surprised that Moran was having such difficulty putting two and two together. "We didn't accomplish it, Mr. President," said Caulfield in a clear and firm voice. "We are not missing any nuclear weapons. We have not had any Broken Arrows."

The president removed his reading glasses, turned his palms upward, and shrugged his shoulders in obvious belwilderment. "What *are* you talking about, Owen?"

"What he means is there have been no recent accidents involving U.S. nuclear weapons," Pinzon said.

Caulfield decided to lay it out straight. "Mr. President, to put it simply, there are chemical and nuclear residues and certain other materials scattered across a quarter acre of prairie in Nebraska that could only have come from a hydrogen bomb. It is not our bomb. Therefore, it belongs to someone else."

Moran finally got the picture. For a moment he held himself motionless. Only the color visibly draining from his face betrayed his comprehension. When he finally spoke, he shook his head from side to side as if the truth could be overcome by denial.

"God, you can't be serious, Owen. You can't be serious!" He pushed back his chair and rose to his feet. Gripping the edge of his desk as if to steady himself on a rolling deck, he extended his arms stiffly like a man doing bad push-ups. He spoke slowly.

"Jesus H. Christ . . . you mean it has finally happened?" He paused, searching his vocabulary in vain. "It has finally goddamned happened? Nuclear terrorists have brought a goddamned atomic bomb into the country?"

Neither Pinzon nor Caulfield answered immediately. Moran may have grown up on a Kansas farm, but his language was rarely barnyard, even in private, and the president's two advisors were briefly taken aback. Pinzon finally took the initiative. "Not quite, sir."

"Well, what then, Rubio?"

Pinzon raised his voice slightly, like a tourist in a foreign land hoping that higher volume will increase intelligibility. "It's not an atomic bomb, it's an H-bomb, a hydrogen bomb. We don't think terrorists, or at least not your average terrorists, could build a hydrogen bomb. That kind of work is almost certainly beyond the needs or capacities of terrorists. Except for a handful of countries, it's beyond the capacity of most nations."

Moran seemed briefly stunned, like a boxer who's taken two quick and hard jabs and hasn't quite registered it. He shook off the punches. "Oh for Christ's sake, that's even worse! Isn't there some other explanation?"

Both Caulfield and Pinzon shook their heads "no."

The president fidgeted nervously with his glasses, and then, pulling a clean handkerchief from his breast pocket, began cleaning the lenses. When he had removed the invisible smudges, he returned the glasses to his face and sat back down in his chair. He doodled with a pen on a green blotter, and then looked at his two aides.

"Well," he began, in a tone equal parts anger and exasperation, "who the hell *is* responsible, and how did this weapon wind up in pieces?"

"It had to be built by a government, sir," said Caulfield softly.

"A government?" said the president incredulously. He had difficulty accepting the idea. "God, a government? What government?"

"It could only be the British, the French, the Chinese, or the Russians. We don't know of any other countries that have the technical skill or resources to put an H-bomb together."

"Somehow I don't see the British or the French bringing one of these things into the country," said the president, his voice drenched with sarcasm.

"Nor do we," said Pinzon. "And quite frankly, we can't see the Chinese doing it either. Which leaves us with a problem. If it's a Russian weapon, was it brought here by the Russian government, or was it some weapon they've lost?"

The president's mouth fell open. "Lost? In Nebraska?" To Moran, it was sounding crazier by the second.

"Yes, Mr. President," said Caulfield. "Since the breakup of the old Soviet Union, the Russians' command and control of their nuclear weapons has been a problem, as we all know." The Director of the CIA pulled a sheaf of papers from a briefcase on his lap and studied the first two pages briefly. "Given how many weapons the U.S.S.R. had and where they were situated, it's entirely possible that some rogue element in the army of Russia, Ukraine, Belarus, or Kazakhstan could have gotten its hands on one of these devices without anyone being the wiser."

"But what would they be doing with it over here?" Moran asked.

No one had any idea, and no one was anxious to offer a guess. Pinzon finally spoke. "Believe me, we've been asking the same question." He sighed. "FBI Director Novello has an intelligence team war-gaming possible motivations and scenarios right now. He should have some ideas for us when he gets back from Los Angeles in about an hour. Owen's got a team at CIA working on the same problem, and DIA is also studying it."

"Great," said the president with some irony, once again removing his glasses and reaching for his handkerchief. "Why would any government bring a weapon here?"

"Why are the Russians deep-sixing nuclear submarines?" asked Pinzon.

The president sounded irritated, as if tiring of having his questions answered with questions. "You think there's a connection?"

"Maybe,"Pinzon wavered. He had not until that moment actually considered it. He stopped momentarily, as if trying to explain something so preposterous that he couldn't find the vocabulary. "Sir, we've been sitting here for more than a week now, asking what the hell is going on in Russia. Now this happens. Maybe there is some connection."

"Whoever brought the weapon in is highly organized," said Caulfield. "The survey crew in Nebraska reports that an effort was made to clean up the site. A sophisticated effort."

President Moran changed the subject. "What's the latest on Duval, the guy who tipped us off."

"Actually it was a reporter at the *Denver Post*, a friend of this Duval character," said Pinzon. "They're doing everything they can to find him, but he's pretty elusive. He's wanted in connection with some murders."

"He's a murderer?" Moran bellowed, unable to contain his disbelief. "Maybe," answered Pinzon.

President Moran tried to speak logically. "This guy, this suspected killer, just calls up a friend and says he's found a nuclear weapon? Why did anyone take him seriously?"

"Because his friend with the *Denver Post* is the son of a recently retired big wheel at DIA. A very big wheel who still has lots of contacts. That was enough to get things rolling."

Moran picked up his telephone and told an aide to connect him with the head of the FBI. That done, he turned back to Pinzon and Caulfield as they shuffled papers on their laps. "I want Novello to join us in person when he arrives in D.C. later."

Both men nodded, and Caulfield spoke. "Mr. President, we've got Rocky Flats studying the debris from Nebraska. It's just possible they may be able to tell exactly where that weapon was made. Every weapon type has individual characteristics. Signatures, so to speak."

Moran mouthed the word *good*, without pronouncing it, then turned in his chair to glimpse the White House south lawn and parts of the Ellipse beyond. While the view was obscured by heavy foliage, he could make out the small crowd that had gathered on the Ellipse shortly after noon and remained as the day wore on. Where a month before hordes of tourists had strolled, knots of protesters now walked back and forth, waving placards, stretching out banners, and chanting slogans in the direction of the White House. Moran couldn't hear them through the thick bulletproof windows of the Oval Office, but he could guess what they were saying. They were calling him an imperialist, a militarist, and a tool of defense contractors and tri-lateralists and even the Masons. He was certain that most of those present were permanent members of the protesting fraternity, adherents of the Socialist Workers Party, followers of Lyndon LaRouche, and others well out of the American mainstream. But he also knew that the vast political middle of the country would soon begin to stir in reaction to the remarkable speech Russian President Turgenev had made to the nation on television the day before. Moran had issued a statement welcoming Turgenev's moves, and confirming that the White House was studying the speech carefully. But he had offered nothing concrete. It was a holding action, at best, and soon he'd have to say more.

But politics wasn't Moran's concern now. Like every president since Harry Truman, Moran was conscious that he had at his fingertips the ability to kill millions, even end life on the planet. In fact, most of those presidents, including Moran himself, hadn't considered it that much of a burden. The liklihood of somebody actually starting a nuclear war seemed happily remote. Sure, people had talked about nuclear terror for years, thought Moran, but what president ever thought he might actually face it? Intellectually he had considered the possibility, but, in his gut, he had never prepared himself to confront it. Moran was not a man of little confidence. Still, for the first time since his election, he wondered to himself if he was up to the job.

Howard Silber sat in his office at the *Denver Post* and listened to his phone ring three times before the FBI agent beside him gestured that he could answer. He watched the agent write down a number that appeared on the caller ID machine, and then spoke. "Hello?"

It was Duval. "Anybody there with you, Howard?"

Silber hated lying. "No, George. Just me." He shook his head at the agent who was now listening on an extension.

"I don't believe you, Howard. But it makes no difference. I won't be at this phone in another minute, and they won't get here before then. So, did you do what I asked?"

"I did, George, and you were right. They found the nuclear stuff you were talking about. They say it's not ours, that it wasn't something done by the U.S. government."

Duval laughed bitterly. "They would say that, wouldn't they, Howard?"

Silber begged. "They say they need your help. They say the country could be in danger."

There were a few seconds of silence at the other end, and for a moment Silber thought his old friend had hung up.

"Did they really find something, Howard?"

"Yes, George. They did. You were right. You've stumbled onto something big and dangerous, but they aren't exactly sure what and can't find out without your help."

"What do they need?"

"They need to talk to you, to get more details."

Duval didn't like it. "I'm not ready to trust 'em yet. How do I know they're telling the truth?"

"Please, George. Turn yourself in. You can clear this all up. They know you're not a murderer."

Duval tried to gather his thoughts. "Look, Howard. In the last few days I've been run off the road, almost blown to pieces, and had my home and office ransacked. I've disembowled a man with a shotgun and slashed the face of another with a scalpel. A sheriff I've known my whole life is dead, and a college friend is missing. This ain't good, Howard. This ain't normal."

Silber tried to sound calm. "George, Professor Loevinger is dead. The state police fished him out of the Platte River near Ashland about three hours ago. It's all over the wires. I'm sorry, George."

Silber waited for a reply, but there was none. He wondered briefly if Duval had hung up, but decided the line was still open. Silber raised his voice, sounding almost angry, "George, you've got to trust me! Turn yourself in."

Duval spoke softly, his voice tinged with a tired resignation. "So they got Mark Loevinger, too. God, Howard, do you believe all this? Can you believe this is really happening?"

"Trust me, George. Come in, George."

Duval's tone suddenly seemed almost chipper. "I do trust you, Howard. It's the big mug next to you that I'm worried about. I need time to think, Howard."

"It's time to come home, George."

"Maybe. Look, it's time for me to go. I'll send you some material by courier and some notes I've made. I'll send it tonight, but I'm going to hold some stuff back. If I see any sign that anyone is trying to arrest me or Michelle, I'll get lost forever. They'll never see the evidence I've got. The cop with you got that straight?"

The FBI agent nodded, and Silber relayed the message. "The FBI says they understand. They'll do nothing for now, pending the delivery of your package."

"Bye, Howard. Thank your dad for me. I'll be in touch tomorrow." Duval hung up his telephone.

The FBI agent looked at the number he'd scratched on a pad. "Well, he's in Denver. Somewhere out by the new airport judging from this exchange." He showed Silber the three digit prefix from the caller ID machine.

"What are you going to do now?" asked the reporter.

"Sit and wait for his delivery. No sense in sending out the police to this telephone. He'll be long gone by the time they figure out where it is."

Ninety minutes later a taxi driver entered Silber's office, accompanied by a *Denver Post* security guard working in the paper's front lobby. He dropped a large manila envelope on Silber's desk and refused payment, saying the man who gave him the envelope had already tipped him more than was necessary.

Inside, Silber and FBI special agent Cal Ritter found two yellow legal pages of handwritten notes signed by George Duval. They were accompanied by three eight-by-ten black and white photographs. The first two photos were obscured by fire and smoke. Ritter and Silber squinted at them, trying to make out anything useful. "What do you think?" asked Silber.

"Hard to tell," replied Ritter. "Looks like some kind of huge cylinder maybe?"

Silber nodded. Both men then examined the third photo, which was clear. It showed the logo of some company. The two men then read Duval's notes.

"What's that say?" asked the FBI agent, pointing to the photo showing the logo. "I forgot my glasses."

Silber squinted. "It says Rocky Mountain Tonic something. Tonic water maybe?"

"You got a magnifying glass?"

Silber did. He pulled it from his desk drawer and the two men squinted at the image together. "Looks like Rocky Mountain Toxic Waste, Denver," said the agent.

Silber pulled a *Denver Yellow Pages* from a small bookcase and scanned the listings for "Waste Removal," and "Toxic Waste." "Not listed here," he said.

"Is that a current directory?"

"Brand new."

"Hmmm."

"What do you think this thing is?" asked Silber, pointing to the obscured cylindrical object featured in two of the photographs.

"Duval's notes say that that was the thing that blew up," said Ritter.

"You mean that's the bomb?"

"Apparently so."

"It's certainly big enough."

"Too big if you ask me," said Ritter. "Looks like something from 1945. Our guys will try to enhance these pictures and get a better look."

"It looks to me like some kind of industrial strength hot water heater," said Silber.

"Or maybe a boiler of some kind."

"More or less the same thing, don't you think?"

"Yeah, more or less. Anyway, I've got to get these to the lab boys in Washington. There's some kind of label on the tank. See?"

Silber saw a small black square on the cylinder face. "That?"

"Yeah. Probably a manufacturer's label. Maybe the guys at the lab can somehow read it." He glanced at Silber. "You can go home now, Howard. Another agent will relieve me in a couple of minutes, just in case Duval calls back tonight. Remember now, you're still sworn to absolute secrecy, and we're still on your home phone."

Silber nodded that he understood. He put on his suit jacket and walked to the front lobby, feeling very guilty that he had lied to Duval, even if Duval knew why he was lying.

Ritter placed a call to a makeshift operations center at the FBI regional headquarters in Denver. "This is Cal Ritter," he said, "you guys get all that?"

"Yeah, we did," said an agent named Al Harris, "and we got more."

"What?"

"Wednesday morning a lady up in northwestern Wyoming reported that somebody had switched the plates on her car the night before. It took until this morning for anyone to make a connection."

"What connection?"

"The plates came from a Hertz Ford Taurus rented in Cheyenne by two men, who said they planned to drop off the vehicle in Chadron, Nebraska, on Monday. The Ford never showed up."

"So?" said Ritter, letting his impatience show.

"Hertz put out a description of the car and of the two men who rented it. One just happens to have a very prominent facial scar, a long white streak. That piqued the interest of the Dawes County Sheriff in Chadron, a guy named Hargrove. Just playing a hunch, he sent a photo of the stiff found in Duval's driveway Sunday to the Hertz office in Cheyenne. A clerk there positively IDs the guy. Voilà!"

Ritter was starting to feel stupid. "And?"

"Think about it," said Harris. "A guy rents a car, drives to Chadron, and winds up dead at Duval's house. The license plates from his rental car then show up in Boondock, Wyoming. Guess who has a cabin there?"

"Who?"

"Duval's girlfriend's father."

"Yeah?"

"We figured that out going over the phone bills of her folks from their house here in Denver. Wyoming State Police just checked the cabin. No one there, of course, but the place has been used in the last few days. There was fresh milk in the fridge."

Ritter finally understood. "Duval killed the guy, stole his Hertz car, and then switched plates."

"Now you're cooking," said Harris.

"Find a Taurus with the Wyoming lady's missing licence plates, and you'll find Duval."

"Yep. And since we know that Duval was on the east side of Denver ninety minutes ago, we may have a pretty good chance of finding him. If he's still using the Ford."

"Let's have the locals start checking any Ford with Wyoming plates. Concentrate on hotels and motels. They have to sleep somewhere. But if they spot him, tell 'em not to make an arrest."

"Why not?"

"You heard him. He's scared. He thinks we may be the guys trying to kill him. If we try to arrest him, he could do something crazy and get himself or one of us killed. We need him alive."

"Okay, boss."

"If you find him, let me know immediately. But just keep an eye on him, nothing more for now."

"Done."

"Incidentally, who was the dead guy in Duval's driveway."

"Mr. John Doe Shotgun Blast?"

"Yes."

"We don't know. The driver's license and other info he gave to Hertz in Cheyenne was bogus."

"Well, it serves him right, then."

Al Harris agreed.

Duval and Michelle drove randomly in the vicinity of the old Stapleton Airport, trying to decide which of the now half-empty hotels would best suit their need to remain inconspicuous. They finally selected a nondescript motor lodge that once belonged to a major national chain, but had long since changed ownership. From the outside, the two-story brick and glass rectangle was identical to hundreds of others across the country, and the only thing that distinguished the small lobby was a jagged tear in the wallpaper to the right of the reception desk. What was once a vibrant hotel district had been reduced to a quiet and somewhat shabby commercial strip by the construction of the new Denver airport to the east. Even the motor lodge had seen better days.

"I'd like a double for this evening and tomorrow," said Duval to the nineteen-year-old girl behind the reception counter.

She pushed some buttons on a computer keyboard and acted genuinely surprised that the motel just happened to have a vacancy for two nights. "Please fill out this registration card," she said, "and I'll need an impression of your credit card."

Duval hated the expression. It was pompous and affected and vulgar at the same time. He raised his hands directly above his head, like a referee signaling a touchdown.

"Sir?" said the receptionist.

"This is my impression of my credit card," said Duval. "I'm sorry but it's hard for me to make myself look rectangular. I'm better at balloon impressions."

The girl had no idea what he was talking about, but smiled as people do when talking to someone whose behavior is incomprehensible. "I'll need your credit card, sir."

"I want to pay cash."

"That would be fine, but I'll still need your credit card. Company policy."

"Well, my credit card is a little over-used right now, you know how that can happen. I'd rather pay cash. I sure don't want to put anything more on the old card."

The girl smiled. "Don't worry, sir. I'll just get an impression of your credit card. Nothing will be added to your credit card. When you check out in two days and settle your bill with cash, you'll get the credit card form back, or I'll rip it up in front of you."

Duval considered the dangers, and then reluctantly handed over the VISA of the man he'd killed on Sunday. The girl placed it in an electrically operated machine that printed the card's raised numbers on a triplicate form. She seemed relieved to have won over her difficult customer, and let out a big sigh as she returned the card to Duval.

As they left the office and began walking back to the van, Michelle gave Duval a puzzled look. "What's the big deal as long as we pay in cash?"

"I can't think of any problem right now, but it bothers me to hand anyone that card, even if it's not going to be used. I don't want to end up as dead as its owner."

As Duval and Michelle searched for their room, a clerk in an office behind the reception desk adhered to another company policy. He ran Duval's VISA through their automated validation system. Seconds later an authorization number came back. The card was good, even if the guest had indicated he intended to pay cash. Can't be too careful in the motel business, thought the clerk.

At an FBI computer center outside Washington, a different kind of clerk also worked throughout the night. Among other things, he prepared to run a series of word searches at the request of the FBI's Denver office. The clerk looked at the message from Denver, and tapped into his computer screen:

    A/ Word Search/
The computer responded:
    File(s) type?
He typed in the appropriate identifier:
    Case files/
    Case file(s) name(s)?
    All/
    Year(s) or date parameters?
    Last two years/
    Word or word group?
    Group/
    Bad command.
"Piece of fucking shit," said the clerk out loud. He retyped his entry.
    Word Group:
    Indicate word group.
    Rocky mountain toxic waste/
    You have entered 'Rocky mountain toxic waste.' Is that correct?
    Yes/
    Bad command.
    Correct/
    Search begun.

Despite the blazing speed of the Cray III Super Computer, it took nearly five minutes to search all FBI case files compiled over the last two years. "Rocky Mountain Toxic Waste" appeared in no file.

The clerk repeated the procedure, this time looking for the word group *water heater.* There were two entries. The body of a U.S. Forest Service ranger had been found lying beside a hot water heater at a Forest Service office in Portland, Oregon. He had died of natural causes. There was also a reference to a hot water heater in a case involving the scalding of a kidnapped child. The case had been closed. The clerk printed out both case files and put them aside.

He began his third and final search by typing in the word boiler(s). This time the computer screen came alive instantly, listing three cases in which the word boiler(s) appeared. Two cases involved a Cuban tramp freighter that had broken down in the Gulf of Mexico and drifted into U.S. territorial waters. A third case involved a fatal boiler accident at a NASA research facility. None of the cases seemed particularly interesting to the clerk, but the computer's ability to find them instantly piqued his interest. The cases had to have been searched and compiled recently and stored in the computer's sixty-day quick reference memory. He tapped his keyboard:

Search history ||| {boiler(s)}/
Bad Command.

He swore aloud again and retrieved a thick program manual from the shelf above the monitor. He scanned a page briefly and tried again.

Search history ||| {boiler(s)}
Word 'boiler(s)' searched 9/15 by Special Agent
Todd Walters, Baltimore Office

The clerk composed a brief E-mail message indicating the results of his word search, and dispatched it to agent Cal Ritter in Denver. It was all in a night's work.

In Richmond, Virginia, Peter Hall took a sip of hot coffee from a styrofoam cup, and began searching the VISA card transaction files on the computer screen before him. When the bank employee saw the authorization for a motel in Denver, he nearly spit the coffee on his shirt. He wrote the name of the motel on a pad of paper and checked it against a master list of authorized VISA merchants in central Colorado. When he had the particulars he needed, he left his office building and walked across the street to the pay phone he had used before. He used a telephone credit card to dial a number in Washington and, when a man with a deep voice answered, went through a now familiar ritual that he found both silly and melodramatic. "Hello, this is Mr. Bishop and I have a message for Mr. Rook."

"Yes."

"The party you are looking for is at, or was at, the Stapleton Bon Vivant Inn, in Denver, Colorado.

"Excellent, Mr. Bishop. And can you tell me what name our colleague is using?"

He's using a new name, one he picked up in Nebraska last Sunday. A name belonging to a dear, departed colleague. He's not using his old name."

"Superb, Mr. Bishop. You will find us very generous in this matter. The usual arrangements apply. Thank you and good day."

Peter Hall smiled at the thought of what he could do with the extra money.

Friday, September 17

"Why does he want to talk to me?" Bill Kimberlet could not imagine a single thing he could offer to an armed Russian who had been run down by a horse while fleeing tribesman in northeastern Mongolia. Kimberlet, after all, was an American government employee working overseas.

"He won't tell us," said the Mongolian security official at his side. "We don't know a thing about him and can't get anything from him. He says he'll talk to us if he can talk to the American first. You're the American."

The security official was a young man, in his late twenties guessed Kimberlet, and unlike most Mongolian government employees spoke excellent English. As far as Kimberlet could tell, the man was an investigator for some agency that combined border security, counter-espionage, and intelligence gathering under one roof; a sort of FBI cum CIA combo with a little Immigration Service thrown in for good measure. Kimberlet couldn't imagine how a country that had barely any roads could spend any resources on investigative police work, but there were a lot of things about Mongolia that were beyond him.

"What are you going to ask him?" said the young Mongolian as he parked the car in front of a dilapidated three-story clinic in the provincial city of Cojbalsen.

"I haven't got a clue."

"A what?"

"I don't know what to ask him. He's the one who wants to speak to an American, right? Anyway, why are you giving him such special treatment?"

"We just want to know who he is, and how in the world he got to where we found him. He's a Russian, that's for sure, but what was he doing trekking across the plains near the Wall of Genghis Khan? He's not very interested in speaking with us. Maybe if we let him talk to you, we can find out."

When they entered the ward on the third floor, Ushta was sitting up in bed, his head swathed in white bandages. He was smoking a local brand of cigarette, which, much to Kimberlet's surprise, didn't seem to bother any of the score of other patients sharing the ward. Mongolians were only just entering the age of smokable cigarettes, and Kimberlet guessed it would be another generation before they contemplated giving up their new vice.

The young security official spoke to Ushta in Mongolian, then switched in mid-sentence to Russian. To Kimberlet's untrained ears, they appeared to be exchanging sharp words, but whatever hostility existed was soon replaced by softer tones and mutual nodding. The official helped Ushta get out of bed, and Ushta, gingerly at first, and then with more confidence, followed the agent as he left the ward and headed to a small office at the end of a dimly lit corridor. Kimberlet fell in behind the two men, wondering how a Federal Election official had gotten messed up with a Mongolian security officer and a Russian border jumper. Once inside the office, the agent remained standing while Kimberlet and Ushta took seats in two dirty and threadbare easy chairs.

"What is your name?" asked the officer in Russian.

"My name is Leonid Ushta, and I am a professional cartographer and geologist. Formerly, I was a lecturer and researcher at Moscow State University."

The expression on the security agent's face showed disbelief. "What are the mountains in the eastern United States called?" he asked.

Ushta smiled. "They are called many things. They are the Adirondacks, the Great Smoky Mountains, the Blue Ridge. Those are the local groups. They are all part of the Appalachians, which were created by the Appalachian geosyncline, a kind of immense upheaval millions of years ago."

The agent couldn't be certain about the details, but he recognized the word *Appalachian* and was impressed. He told Kimberlet what had been said and looked at Ushta again. "And so what is a professor at Moscow State University doing on foot in northeastern Mongolia with a rifle?"

Ushta lit another smelly Mongolian cigarette. "I am an escapee from a Russian military labor camp northeast of Lake Baikal."

"The Russian military doesn't run slave labor camps anymore."

"Is that what you think?" asked Ushta. "You're quite wrong, you know. I worked for several months at the Pechora Camp."

The young security agent wasn't buying that. "Pechora is in northwestern Russia, it's a river."

"True," said Ushta, "but the camp northeast of Baikal is called Pechora nonetheless. We were working on a secret military project. Get me out of Mongolia and I'll tell you what it was."

The agent smirked. "And just how did you get from this Pechora Camp to Mongolia?"

Ushta smiled. "I walked."

The young officer found that preposterous. He wondered if the prisoner was mocking him but couldn't be sure. "You just walked a couple of hundred miles through mountains and forest, with the Russian police chasing you."

"I walked from the Russian border. Before that I rode a bulldozer and a train."

The security agent leaned over Ushta, his face a few inches from the Russian's, and slapped his palms on the arms of Ushta's chair. "This is absurd. Who are you and what do you want with an American?"

If Ushta was rattled it didn't show. He calmly stubbed out his cigarette and sat upright in his chair, his expression suddenly stern. "I am who I say I am. I have information that would be very valuable to the Americans, information that would reflect well on Mongolia in American eyes. Help me get that information to them."

The agent frowned, turned his back, and walked to a window. "Maybe I'll just turn you in to the Russian border police."

Ushta was ready for that. "Of course, you could do that. But what would that get you? Russia is in a mess, and you know it. They can't afford to give Mongolia any economic aid, and outside of weapons they haven't got anything to sell or give you that your country needs. Besides, you hate the Russians. Fuck Russia."

"What's he saying?" asked Kimberlet.

The agent shook his head in exasperation. "He says he's got Russian military secrets that would be very important to the United States. He says he'll reveal them to American authorities if they give him asylum in the States."

Kimberlet cupped his hands behind his head. "Tell him it's not my decision who gets to enter the United States, and I couldn't tell the difference between an M1 Garand and an M1 Abrams tank."

"What?"

"I don't know anything about military or any other kind of intelligence."

The agent translated for Ushta, listened to his answer, and turned back to Kimberlet. "He says you could get his information to people who can help. Of course, he's right about that."

"He is?"

"Sure, you could talk to Steve Wannamaker, at the U.S. embassy in Ulan Bator."

"Wannamaker? The chargé d'affaires?"

"Same guy. He's also the CIA station chief."

"He is?"

"Of course. It's not a big secret, believe me." The agent smiled. Kimberlet couldn't tell if it was from amusement at his ignorance or just professional hauteur.

"Well," said the American, "tell him I'll do my best. What does he have for us?"

Ushta was reluctant to talk in front of the Mongolian, but realized soon enough that he had no choice. He asked for a piece of paper and a pen. With it, he began drawing a grid pattern. In Cyrillic letters he marked one square of the grid with the notation "1 kilometer." When that was finished, he added an arrow and a letter to denote north, then penned in a rough outline of some kind of compound which he labeled "power plant/administration." He handed the drawing to his two inquisitors.

Both men studied the document briefly, but neither understood what it represented. "What's this?" asked Kimberlet.

"What you have here," said Ushta in Russian, "is a grid of high voltage copper cable buried a few feet below the surface over an area of several thousand square kilometers. Miles if you prefer. The power plant supplies electricity to the grid."

The young Mongolian agent and Kimberlet looked at each other with incomprehension.

"Interesting, don't you think?" said Ushta, smiling.

"What is it?" asked the Mongolian.

"Just what I said," answered Ushta.

"What's it for?" asked the security agent.

"I am not an electrical engineer," said Ushta, "but I have an idea what it is. Think about it. What would happen if you ran high voltage electricity through this grid?" He pointed to the crude drawings he had made. "What would you get?"

Neither one had any idea.

"Well, for one thing," continued Ushta in Russian, "you'd get a lot of electromagnetic radiation. Some would spread through the air, but most of it would hug the surface of the earth and the first few feet of topsoil."

The agent translated, and then turned back to Ushta. "So?"

"I believe the Pechora Camp is a gigantic radio transmitter," said Ushta with a certain look of pride, "an immensely powerful transmitter that can send radio messages to any spot on earth, and it can't be jammed. If I'm right, it's the most powerful, the most awesome machine ever built to transmit a message, and it's almost invisible from the air. No spy satellites would pick it up unless they were looking for it."

"How do you know that?" asked the agent.

"Believe me, in my profession you see a lot of satellite and aerial imagery. The Pechora Project was built by manual labor—prisoners using picks and shovels. I think that was a deliberate effort to hide what was being built."

The agent still seemed unimpressed. "But why would they build it? Why not just build a radio tower if you want a strong transmitter."

Ushta began sounding like a college lecturer. "Because radio waves traveling through the air are subject to all sorts of limitations. Ground waves aren't."

"But why would they need that?" asked the agent.

"That is for American intelligence to fathom," said Ushta. "I'm sure it has a military application, but I don't know more than that."

The agent told Kimberlet Ushta's theory.

"It sounds pretty bizarre to me," said the American, "but, hey, I think recording the human voice on ribbons of plastic tape is bizarre." Kimberlet looked at Ushta and felt some sympathy for him. He turned to the government official. "I guess we ought to tell Wannamaker in Ulan Bator. Or you better tell your government. Or we do both."

The agent nodded his agreement.

In suburban Baltimore, FBI special agent Todd Walters was fighting a bad cold. His head was stuffed and his throat was sore, and he was in no mood to conduct business when his bedside phone rang shortly before seven in the morning.

"Walters here," he answered in a scratchy voice.

"Special Agent Walters, FBI Baltimore?"

"The same."

"Todd, this is Special Agent Cal Ritter, FBI Denver. Sorry to bother you so early on a Friday morning, but I've got a problem."

Walters threw his feet over the edge of the bed and sat up. Out of habit, he reached for his glasses on the bedside table, and in doing so knocked over a glass of water his wife had set there the night before. Damn, he thought to himself. "Go ahead, what's the problem?"

"I'm involved in a national security case out here, and yesterday, last night actually, I requested a routine word search of recent FBI case files. I was searching the word *boiler* when your search request popped up. There's probably no connection, but can you tell me what you were working on?"

"How do I know you're really Agent Ritter of the Denver Field Office?"

Ritter did not respond for several seconds. "You ever work at headquarters in Washington?" asked Ritter at last.

"Yeah."

"Ask me the name of anybody who's been there more than a few years."

Walters thought a second. "I got a better idea. You at your office now?"

"Yeah."

"I'll call you right back. Ritter in Denver, right?"

"Yes."

Walters retrieved an internal FBI phone directory from a drawer in a bedside table and called an unpublished number at the Denver office. Ritter answered the phone.

"This is Walters. I recognize your voice, Agent Ritter."

"Good. Now, as to the boilers?"

Walters tried to clear his sore throat. "I've got a murder investigation going on here. A U.S. Customs officer, a federal agent that is to say, got himself murdered a couple of days back. It looked like some kind of drug deal gone sour, but this guy is as clean as a whistle as far as I can tell. Anyway, the evidence that this guy was killed in some kind of drug dispute is *too* clean. It looks planted. I got suspicious. You still there?"

"Sure, go ahead."

"In his pocket, this customs inspector had a single page torn from the *Yellow Pages*. It had these listings for 'Boats,' and 'Boat-Builders.' That led us astray. Then a few days ago I got an anonymous tip from somebody who said the inspector called him on the day of his death to ask about boilers. I went back and looked at the *Yellow Pages*, and sure enough there were listings for 'Boilers,' and 'Boiler Repair'—that kind of thing." Walters cleared his throat again. "Still with me?"

"Yes."

"Having no better ideas, I decided to run a word search on *boiler* in the FBI case files, but it didn't turn up much."

"Yeah," said Ritter, "I ran the same thing last night and got just about nothing."

"Exactly. But listen. I had better luck with the Customs Service."

"Really?" Cal Ritter sounded intrigued.

"Uh-huh. My murder victim was a customs officer, right? Having no other leads, I asked Customs Service to run a search for the word *boiler* on their import/export databank. Bingo."

"What?"

"Well first, it turns out this dead inspector had also requested a search on *boilers*. Actually they're called 'industrial steam generators.' Anyway, the jerk who did the search at Customs Service headquarters in Washington didn't mention that fact to us when we first interviewed him following the inspector's murder."

"Why not?"

"We didn't ask him. We knew he had talked to the victim the day he died, but since we didn't ask him about a word search, or anything about boilers, the idiot didn't think it was important enough to mention. Remember, we were interested in boats."

"Well, what did you find?"

"We found that the United States is getting a lot of boilers from overseas nowadays."

"Really?"

"Really. And you wouldn't believe where most of 'em are coming from."

"Try me."

"Russia. Yaroslavl to be precise. A lot are also coming from Alma-Ata, in Kazakhstan. Amazing, huh? We're buying industrial boilers from the basket cases of the industrialized world. But we still can't figure out why our victim was so interested in boilers, or what, if anything, it has to do with his death."

Ritter didn't hear the last sentence. He felt a shiver spread across his back, but his mind was fixed on Russia. He fell silent.

"Agent Ritter?" said Walters.

"Yes, Ritter here. Sorry about that. Listen, do you have a description of these boilers?"

"I have a schematic drawing and a written description but no photos."

"Can you describe one?"

"Sure, just a second." Walters crossed to a dresser against the far wall of his bedroom, rummaged in a briefcase, and returned to the phone with a file folder in his hand. "Here it is. They're described as industrial steam generators. According to the drawings, they're mostly a big tank, a cylindrical tank, sort of what you'd expect. They have some wires and tubes coming out of some kind of circular door at one end. They're sitting on some runners or skids."

"How big are they?"

Walters hadn't thought about that. "Their size is described in meters, but I'd guess they are about six or seven feet long and maybe three or three-and-a-half feet wide. They're heavy . . . more than one thousand kilos. That's about two thousand five hundred pounds I'd guess. That's about it."

Ritter couldn't hide his growing interest. "Hey, can you fax me a copy of the import records, including the schematic?"

"Sure."

"And Walters. Do you know how many of these Russian boilers have come into the country?" asked Ritter, afraid to hear the answer.

"Just a second, I've got a note here somewhere about that." Walters returned to his dresser and fumbled in his briefcase until he found a small notebook. He scanned some pages and returned to the phone. "Ritter?"

"Go ahead."

"Best I can figure, about sixty or sixty-five of these things have come into the country in the last couple years.

"Sixty-five did you say?"

"Yes. Give or take a few."

"Have any of them ever been inspected by customs officers?"

"I don't know. I do know that two arrived in Baltimore the day my man was murdered. He was the officer who cleared the shipment. That's as far as I've gotten in the matter."

There was no response on the other end.

"Ritter?"

"I'm here. Just thinking. Listen, Walters. This could be a very big national security issue. Could be. Those boilers may be the key to something we're looking into, something critical to U.S. security. I can't be sure right now, but I am sure that we don't want anybody tipped off that we have any interest in those things, the boilers I mean. Look, I'll get you something quick from the very highest levels, but in the meantime don't do anything that would raise any suspicions that we're interested in boilers coming into the country. Take my word for it that it's absolutely critical."

"Sure, sure. No problem. For me, it's just a murder investigation. I'll sit tight. But get me some orders on paper, will you? And you better tell the Customs Service too."

"I will. And Walters, you've been very helpful. Very, very helpful. Thanks."

Todd Walters hung up his phone and prepared to face a long day.

Moran paced back and forth on a circular carpet bearing the presidential seal. The sun had risen above the ancient oak trees separating the Treasury from the White House and was casting sharp shadows on the Oval Office walls, but no one was thinking about the beautiful September morning. President Moran kept his back turned as he spoke. "Let's start with an overview, just to make sure we're all on the same page. Rubio, a summary, please."

Rubio Pinzon looked haggard. The usually impeccable Spaniard wore a rumpled suit, and the shine on his shoes was dull. He waited for Moran to seat himself and began.

"In the last twenty-four hours we've had the experts racking their brains to come up with an alternative explanation for the trace products found in Nebraska, but they can't find one. The materials all point to a hydrogen bomb." Pinzon looked up from his pad briefly, but, seeing no change in anyone's expression, took a sip of water. His throat was remarkably dry, his tongue, thick and sticky. "The composition of the chemical explosive used to trigger the device points to the Russians."

It was a statement no one in the room wanted to hear or believe.

"It could come from one of the former Soviet Republics that still has nuclear weapons on its soil," said Owen Caulfield. He knew he was whistling in the dark.

"I don't think so, Owen," said FBI Director Carlos Novello. As always, the second-generation Mexican-American spoke softly in a voice that contrasted sharply to his huge and muscular frame. Novello had briefed the president and Pinzon on the telephone only twenty minutes before, but the others were hearing the information for the first time. The director adjusted the frames of his gold-rimmed glasses, unsnapped the flap of a leather briefcase with his brown left hand, and removed three black and white photographs.

"Look at these, please. All of you." He passed the pictures to Moran, who studied them and distributed them down the line, one at a time to Pinzon, Emily Price, Admiral Greenwood, and Caulfield. "These photos were taken last week by the physician in Nebraska who started this whole thing. I believe you all know his story by now."

"The guy we still can't find?" asked Moran.

"The same," Novello replied. "That is the weapon or what we believe to be the weapon that spread nuclear material all over the prairie. One of our agents in Denver, through some very good footwork, managed to connect the object in these pictures with another case we're working on." Novello retrieved a thin file from his briefcase, opened the blue cover and glanced briefly at several pages.

"The other case involves the U.S. Customs Service, and that case has led to some very startling news." Novello looked up from his file to make sure that he had everyone's close attention.

"We think about sixty or sixty-five of these things have been brought into the United States in the last year or so. Most came from Russia, the others from Kazakhstan."

There were audible gasps from the Secretary of State and Caulfield, but Novello ignored them. "The object in your pictures is listed on customs forms as an industrial boiler. We have shown the pictures to a customs officer in Boston who confirms that he's actually taken a close look at one of these things."

Admiral Greenwood looked doubtful. "Maybe that's exactly what they are—industrial boilers."

"Maybe, admiral," said Novello, "but there's a problem." Novello lowered his voice, an old college debating trick he had learned to get people to listen carefully. "We can't track any of them down. It shouldn't be too hard. They weigh more than a ton and were all consigned to specific purchasers at specific addresses. We couldn't find a single one."

The Secretary of State looked startled. "Why not?" she asked.

"Every one of the companies these things were being forwarded to has turned out to be phony." Novello closed the folder and dropped it on the floor in front of him. "If these things are boilers, innocent pieces of industrial equipment, why have they all disappeared? A customs invoice can be wrong. A shipping agent can make a mistake. But *sixty* mistakes?"

There was shocked silence in the room.

"But why in God's name would the Russians be bringing hydrogen bombs into the United States?" asked the president. "What's the advantage?"

Greenwood, who knew more about nuclear strategy and weapons than anyone in the room, spoke. "If they could put those things all over the country and blow them all at once, without warning, we'd be destroyed. They could flatten us as a viable country in a second, and we wouldn't even know what hit us."

"But what about U.S. retaliation?" asked Secretary of State Emily Price.

Greenwood's face was solemn. "There might not be any," he said. "One second everything would be normal. The next second everything that was America would be gone. There's every chance we would never hit back."

Moran walked around to the rear of his desk and eased down into the high-backed leather chair. He chewed on the end of a pen, thoughtfully. "I think Turgenev's disarmament moves are now understandable," he said. "It's a sucker play."

That made no sense to the Emily Price. "But they have to know that if we ever found out what they were doing, it would be an act of war, an act that could well drive us to a first strike."

"Sure. But if they can set these weapons off by remote control, they'd have plenty of warning and plenty of time to blow them while our missiles were in flight," retorted Admiral Greenwood.

"But they'd still lose," said the president. "That would be Mutually Assured Destruction." He tapped the pen against his teeth. "And that means, if they have any suspicion that we're on to them, they're very likely to set the things off before we decide to attack."

Caulfield was still looking for a ray of hope. "Maybe they don't actually intend to use the weapons," said Caulfield, "except as a threat or as an insurance policy against a U.S. missile defense system."

Moran slapped his palm down hard on his desktop. "Anyway you look at it, Owen, it's still insane." He again got to his feet and strolled to the window to peer at the south lawn. "Which is why nothing being discussed here today is to leave this room, under any circumstances. Not even the NSC is to be told about this yet, except for the Defense Secretary and Watson at the National Security Agency. I guess he's going to have to know."

The Secretary of State shook her head rapidly from side to side, a habit indicating she was about to ask a question that might sound naive. "But if the Russians did bring these things in, and still are, can't we somehow track them?"

Novello nodded vigorously. "Yes, and that's what we intend to do.

There's a boiler scheduled to arrive in Norfolk this afternoon, and we'll be there."

"And then what?" she asked.

"And then nothing for now," said the president, turning back toward his aides. "We need more information and we need some options." He looked at a notebook sitting on the green blotter on his desk. He leaned over it, and, after making a few strokes with a felt tip pen, examined what he had written. He looked first at Greenwood. "All U.S. strategic forces are to remain at their present condition. There will be no increase in readiness, nothing to raise suspicions."

"Aye, sir," said Greenwood, like a helmsman responding to an order from the officer of the deck.

"Director Novello and Director Caulfield, continue as you have planned. Find out if the boiler is a weapon, who put it here, where the others are, and how they're controlled."

He looked at the Secretary of State. "Secretary Price, I want you on the next plane across the Atlantic. Prepare to speak personally with the prime minister of the United Kingdom and the president of France. One-on-one, no aides."

"Are you sure you want London and Paris in on this? Doesn't that increase the possibility of a leak?"

"It's a chance we may have to take. Just get over there and stand by." She nodded.

He turned to Pinzon. "Rubio, I want you to work with Admiral Greenwood on military options. Pick the best brains you can without letting this cat out of the bag. Come up with something. Somehow I don't think diplomacy is going to do much for us on this one."

Patrolman Jerry Sarkis had an upset stomach, and it was putting him in a bad mood. The thought of ruining someone else's day cheered him up a little, and he considered the best way to do it.

Working traffic gave him plenty of possibilities, but there wasn't much gratification in handing out a speeding ticket to someone who really deserved it. Nailing somebody for parking too close to a crosswalk, or not close enough to a curb, was always good. It invariably made drivers furious. Sarkis felt his stomach growl as he pulled out of the McDonald's parking lot and decided he would get as low-down and mean as he could. It was one of the compensations for the lousy working hours and plentiful abuse he endured.

Sarkis pulled to a halt at a stoplight in front of the Bon Vivant Inn and surveyed the motel's parking lot. It was only half-full, but there were enough cars there to keep a really imaginative officer busy all morning. The fact that some of the cars would be from out-of-state was an extra incentive. Tourists get really pissed at traffic tickets.

Sarkis pulled into the lot and slowly drove behind the line of vehicles, parked front-first against a low wall.

A beat-up Taurus immediately caught his attention. It was the worst looking piece of shit he'd seen in a long time. Migrant workers, he thought. Probably cost 'em a hundred bucks!

He got out of his car and began examining the wire coat hangar that was being used as a radio antenna. What a bomber, he thought, strolling back toward the trunk to hand out a ticket for every violation he could think of. He wrote on a ticket, "broken passenger side mirror." It might not stick in court, he thought, but it was good enough to write up and wonderfully petty besides.

His stomach was starting to feel better. He bent down to copy the license plate, and for the first time he realized it was a Wyoming tag. Something stirred in his memory. He thought for a second and returned to his car to look at a number he'd written down at the morning roll call. He looked back at the tag on the Taurus and said: "Holy shit!"

It took the FBI just five minutes to get there. The agents had been cruising the neighborhood themselves.

Duval wondered about the car door. He distinctly remembered locking the driver's side door when he parked the Taurus the night before at the motel, but now it was unlocked. He considered the possibility of burglary, but the car showed no signs of forced entry. On the other hand, he thought, a good man with a slim-jim could enter a car in a few seconds without so much as a scuff. Duval considered the situation and ultimately decided he didn't really care that much. It wasn't his car, and there was nothing in it worth stealing. He just wanted it to start.

His second warning was the cologne. When Duval slid into the driver's seat and Michelle stepped into the passenger's seat next to him, they both noticed the heavy lilac odor. They looked at each other momentarily, Duval scrunching up his nose and squinting his eyes as if to say, "Boy, do you smell that?"

Michelle smiled and let out a short chortle. "Now that's *cheap* cologne!"

Despite the warning signs, neither was prepared when an arm emerged from the rear seat and placed the barrel of a revolver at the back of Michelle's head. "Do what I say or I'll blow your girlfriend's brains out," said a young man with a heavy Bronx accent, as he raised his head into view. The man couldn't have been more than twenty-five, thought Duval, and with his coat and tie and clean appearance, he hardly fit the stereotype of a mugger or a strung-out, drug-starved doper. Duval wanted to say something, anything, to keep the man from pulling the trigger, but he was distracted by the second man. The accomplice became visible in the rearview mirror as he sat upright to the gunman's left. The second man was older, mid-forties thought Duval, and somehow did not look American. Was it the style of his haircut? The strange cologne? "She's my fiancée," said Duval calmly.

"Listen buddy, who gives a fuck?" said the younger man. "Wife, girl-friend, Sister Mary Rose, whatever she is, if you don't listen up and do what I say, she's gonna be missing some gray matter. Now pull out of this friggin' parking lot and drive south on that main road there." He indicated the boulevard in front of the motel.

For reasons he would never fully comprehend, Duval was absolutely calm. Maybe he was getting used to it, or maybe he was suffering battle fatigue and there just wasn't any emotional energy left. After the initial surprise, his heart rate had quickly returned to normal, and the adrenaline had ceased pumping through his veins.

"Listen, fuckface," he said to the young man, "aren't you a bit young to be giving orders? What about grandpa here?" He twisted his head backward to indicate the older man behind him.

The young man swatted at the back of Michelle's head with the barrel of his revolver, cutting a gash just above and behind her right ear. Michelle screamed out in pain, and Duval stepped down hard on the brakes and slowed the car to a stop. "Touch her again, and this car ain't going nowhere, pimplehead."

The young man yelled. "I'm taking you out right now, Jack, and it will be a pleasure to—"

"Stop it Tom!" said the older man behind Duval. He pulled a handkerchief from his breast pocket and extended it over the seat to Michelle, who was trying to ease her pain by shaking her head. "Here, try this to stop the bleeding," he said, with a clear accent indicating he was from the Midwest. He turned to his partner. "Tom, keep your mouth shut. Duval, start driving."

Duval didn't know what surprised him most. Was it the fact that the man was so obviously American, or that he knew his name? This was no ordinary mugging, he thought. He stepped on the accelerator and continued driving south. "Where to, boss?"

The older man instructed Duval to intercept Interstate 25 South and head toward Colorado Springs.

"What's all this about?" asked Duval when the man said nothing more. "I haven't got much money, but you can have it. Just let us go."

The man waved his finger toward the windshield, indicating that Duval should just keep driving straight ahead.

Duval turned to Michelle. "You going to be all right, honey?" Michelle shook her head up and down in the affirmative and put her left hand on Duval's knee. Reassured, Duval turned his attention to his captors again. "So, this is the FBI in action, huh? I'm really impressed."

The younger man couldn't contain a guffaw. "The FBI? Christ almighty, are you fucked up," he said.

"I told you to shut up, Tom," said the older man in a loud voice. "Duval, just keep driving if you want your fiancée to survive."

Survive, my ass, thought Duval. Survive for maybe thirty minutes, an hour? Survive until they were ordered to turn off Interstate 25 and climb up some back road toward the Front Range where there would be no incidental traffic or the prying eyes of witnesses? He was certain that he and Michelle were on a one-way trip.

As he left the Denver suburbs behind and the morning inbound commuter traffic on I-25 thinned, Duval saw his best opportunity for survival slipping past. Once they left the highway, there would be little he could do. His only chance lay in taking action now.

Duval glanced out of the corner of his eye at the man behind Michelle. His revolver was no longer against her skull, but resting against the top of the seat back, pointed out the passenger side window. As far as he could tell, the older man behind him had no weapon in his hand. Neither one had a seat belt shoulder harness on. Duval knew of people who wore lap belts, but refused to use a shoulder harnesses, but they were relatively rare. He checked his own belt and harness, glanced briefly to ensure Michelle was properly secured, and scanned the road.

Ahead about thirty yards distant was an eighteen-wheeler with a mud-splattered trailer. The name embossed on the back of the trailer was not familiar, and Duval figured the driver was probably an independent. He knew that many independent truckers carried guns, that most had cellular telephones, and that they all had CB radios. Maybe that would give him slightly better odds. Gently, Duval eased to the left lane and pulled in front of the giant rig. When he moved back into the right lane about a hundred yards in front, Duval put his left hand outside his window and waved.

"Knock it off, Duval," said the older man, "roll up your window."

"Did you say roll?" The last syllable was accompanied by a loud grunt. Duval, using both hands, jerked the steering wheel left as fast and far as he could, while simultaneously slamming down on the brakes with all his strength. Both men in the rear seat were violently thrown forward against the locked front seats, and then sideways to the right. The scream of screeching tires, the deafening pop of a gunshot, and the blaring roar of a truck horn sounded simultaneously, but Duval didn't register them consciously. His mind was riveted on the road twisting off to his right, and on the Taurus's remarkable stability. Until he crossed the shoulder, and flew down into the grassy, V-shaped ditch that served as the median strip, Duval wondered if the car would ever overturn. When it finally did, it rolled with energy. Duval counted as best he could while wedged between his seat and the suddenly inflated airbag. He thought he felt one, two, three rolls, and then a fourth half-roll, which stopped the car on its roof, twisted perpendicularly to the highway.

Duval hung suspended from his seat belt, the top of his head resting against the partially crushed roof. When the airbag deflated, he looked quickly to his right. Michelle was hanging in the same position, her hair draped over the roof liner, her collapsed airbag suspended from the dashboard like a punctured bubble of chewing gum from the mouth of a little leaguer. He heard her groan, and saw her head weave.

She was alive!

He looked over his shoulder and saw no one in the back seat. The right rear door was sprung open, and Duval guessed that the brutish younger man had involuntarily exited during one of the rolls. He was turning to find the older man when the barrel of a gun was stuck literally between his eyes by a bloody hand. The older man had lacerations across the bridge of his nose and forehead, and some kind of puncture wound in his right cheek. One eye was half-closed against the blood dripping from his wounds, and the man's nose was also running red, but he was apparently conscious and lucid.

"You're gonna die now," he said, pulling back the hammer on his pistol.

A loud shot roared through the car, followed by a second and a third in rapid succession. Duval felt no impact. He opened his eyes and saw his assailant slumped across the roof liner, absolutely still.

"Duval, you alive?" came a man's voice from outside the car.

"Yeah, I'm here, who wants to know?"

"Special agent Cal Ritter, FBI. How are you? Are you badly hurt?"

At the mention of FBI, Duval felt a jolt in his stomach. He just couldn't shake them. God knows he'd tried. He attempted to concentrate on his injuries. "I hurt a lot everywhere, but I seem to be in one piece. Check Michelle."

"She's not too bad off, all things considered," came another voice from the other side of the car. Maybe a concussion, but she's half-way conscious, and I can't see any external injuries. She's moving her feet, that's good."

"Okay Al," said Ritter. "Hang on, Duval, we'll roll this thing upright and get you two out of here. Sorry we couldn't help earlier, but those two turkeys must have crawled into your car before we started watching it. We were as surprised as you were when they popped out of the back seat. They must have been hiding under this," said Ritter, pointing to a dirty blanket.

Duval wasn't sure he understood. He could think of no answer and sat mute while the two FBI agents, helped by the trucker they had passed on the roadway and two other bystanders, rolled the car upright. Even then, neither he nor Michelle could be extricated. They were forced to wait another fifteen minutes until a Fire and Rescue team equipped with a large pair of powered, metal shears cut open the roof of the car like a housewife with a can of tuna.

"Let's get you guys to a hospital," said agent Ritter.

"Would that be a federal prison hospital?" said Duval with a smirk.

Ritter looked exasperated. "George Duval, let's get one thing straight right now. The U.S. government ain't out to get you, Georgie boy. No way. We've been desperately trying to *save* your life."

Duval was not persuaded, but he was in too much pain to argue. "What about the two guys who tried to kill us?"

"Both dead. The young guy got thrown out of the car and it rolled over on him. They'll need a spatula to remove him from the median strip."

Duval couldn't say he was sorry to hear it. He watched Ritter walk to a car and talk to someone for a few minutes on a cellular phone.

Two hours later, on the fourth floor of Roseland Hospital in the Denver suburb of Littleton, Duval and Michelle sat upright in their beds waiting for the results of their last round of lab tests. Both were sporting various bandages and patches, and Michelle's lower right arm was in a cast. She was also missing a swatch of hair above and just behind her right ear. Duval had a blackened left eye and a severely puffed-up lower lip. While they were both on painkillers, their heads were clear. If the lab tests and MRIs showed no internal bleeding, they could be hospitalized overnight for observation, then released.

Ritter knocked on their door and quietly entered, extending each of them the afternoon edition of the *Rocky Mountain News*. On the front page was a large black and white photo of their crumpled Ford, standing upright on the median strip of I-25.

"I think you'll find this interesting reading," said Ritter. "And don't worry, we've already told your parents you're alive."

The headline read: "Fugitive Doctor and Fiancée Killed in Car Accident."

"Huh? What's this?" asked Duval. He read on.

Larkspur, Co. (Special to the *Rocky Mountain News*) Fugitive Nebraska physician George Duval, his girlfriend and two unidentified men were killed early this morning in a single car accident on Colorado Interstate 25 near Larkspur.

Colorado State Police said that the car the four were riding in apparently went out of control at high speed after passing a tractor-trailer truck, ran down into the median strip, and rolled over several times. The two unidentified passengers were killed instantly, while Duval, 32, and Michelle Falk, 24, died of their injuries at Roseland Hospital in Littleton.

The story went on to explain that Duval was wanted in connection with two murders in Nebraska and had been the subject of a manhunt in four states.

"Don't look so concerned," said Ritter with a smile. "When this is all over, you two will be brought back to life. Just like Lazarus. Better. Somebody will pay you big bucks just to get your story. You'll be on *Geraldo* and all the others. You'll love it." Ritter laughed.

"Can't wait," said Duval.

FBI special agent Todd Walters stood beside a new, four-door Chevrolet Caprice, a bathtub of a car—as ordinary as the Norfolk field office could find on three hours notice. From his vantage point at the northern tip of Ocean View Drive, Walters trained his field glasses on the rust-stained hull of the SS *Tilsit*, an ancient 10,000-ton Liberty ship now groaning away its final days in the service of a third-rate Ukrainian steamship company. *Tilsit* dipped its flag to a Burke-class Aegis destroyer en route to the Mediterranean, passed into Hampton Roads, and turned to port at Sewell's Point. Ninety minutes later when it began unloading at the Norfolk International Terminal, Walters watched from the Chevy, 200 yards down the pier.

"Where's this shipment supposed to be going?" asked Steve Hughes, one of the two FBI agents accompanying him.

"The manifest says it's going to the Rebel Heating and Air Conditioning Company in Spartanburg, South Carolina. Of course, the company's a phony. We have no idea where it's going."

"If the transporter makes a run for Los Angeles, we're going to be very tired puppies," said Hughes. "Not to mention it gives him three thousand miles to make us."

"Hey, Walters," piped up agent Martin Hureaux from the rear seat, "why didn't we just put an electronic tag under his rear bumper and let the satellites track him?" The agent pointed upward with his finger.

"We can't take any chance on his finding the tag. But look, we're going to get some help from an overhead spotter. We've got a King Air loitering at about ten thousand feet with big cameras and all the other junk they can think of. Once we ID the truck and it gets out of town onto some kind of highway, they can watch him from time to time, and we can drop back a little. At any rate, if this guy goes beyond twenty-four hours we'll get relieved somehow, or so I've been told."

Hughes shook his head in disbelief. "That's going to be fun to see. How are they going to relieve us when they don't even know where we're going?"

Walters put his field glasses on his lap and shrugged his shoulders. "I've been kind of wondering the same thing, Hughes. But I don't think it would have been real wise to ask the brass about it."

The cellular phone on the cradle between the front seats beeped. Walters picked it up, identified himself, and listened for less than ten seconds. He recradled the phone. "That's it, guys," he said to his two companions while pointing through the windshield. "That piece of shit flatbed up there is our baby. I'm sort of pleased now that I see it."

"Why's that?" asked Hughes.

"Frankly, Hughes, because I don't think that decrepit assemblage of belching iron can run more than an hour before breaking down."

Colonel-General Uri Saratov stared at a faxed copy of the front page of the Friday late edition of the *Rocky Mountain News*. General Bransk, Admiral Belovo, and the two other officers seated in the conference room overlooking Ilium Control were feeling the effects of a long day now verging on early morning, but they stifled any temptation to yawn or close their eyes. Despite the day's news, Saratov had so far maintained a quiet and outwardly calm demeanor, and none of the conspirators wanted to do anything to awaken his legendary wrath.

Lieutenant Colonel Kachuga stood behind Saratov and slightly to his right, ready to help his superior with translation. Saratov's English was not good, but he had no difficulty understanding the *News* article. When he finished reading it for the second time, he removed his glasses and calmly folded his hands on the table before him. "So, gentlemen," he began in a surprisingly resigned tone, "do we believe this? Are the doctor and his girlfriend really dead?"

No one ventured an answer, so Saratov continued. "It seems to me, just thinking out loud mind you, that this 'accident' is awfully convenient. *Too* convenient. If my suspicions are correct, it is the worst possible news. It means the Americans are on to us or soon will be."

General Bransk didn't believe it. "General Saratov, I see no reason to suspect that the newspaper story is anything but true. Our agents grabbed the doctor and his girlfriend and were taking them out of town, someplace remote, where they could be eliminated without difficulty. Something happened en route." Bransk used his hands to explain his theory, grabbing at the air as if he were steering a car. "There was a struggle perhaps, and the doctor lost control of the car. Or maybe it's even simpler. Maybe it was just an ordinary auto accident. They were traveling on a highway at high speed and rolled over. Everyone died. It's not that unusual." Bransk's face registered a certain satisfaction.

"And there is the confirmation from the phone taps, sir," said Admiral Belovo. "The doctor's mother and the girl's parents were both called by the state police and told about the accident—told that it was fatal."

Saratov looked again at the *Rocky Mountain News* headline, then began studying his fingernails as if his collegues' comments bored him. "Has anyone actually seen the bodies?" he asked.

The assembled officers lowered their eyes or fidgeted with notepads.

"Do we have any proof-positive that the Americans actually died from their injuries? I think it's just a little suspicious that both the doctor and his girlfriend expired behind closed doors in some hospital while our two agents were both killed at the scene. At least that's what it says here, doesn't it?" He slapped the faxed copy of the *News* with the back of his right hand and glanced behind him at Kachuga. Kachuga nodded.

Admiral Belovo tried to sound reassuring. "General Saratov, my agents are combing all of Denver to verify the story. We will know soon enough if this is some elaborate charade."

Saratov remained calm, but his voice was cold. "I think your agents are incompetent bunglers, Admiral! If this newspaper story is correct, you have now lost five of them in the last two weeks, while a sixth is disabled for life." Saratov shook his head from side to side in apparent dismay.

"Accidents are unavoidable, General," said Belovo. "Sometimes people *do* get hit by lightning. We can't prepare for car accidents."

"All I know, Admiral, is that ever since this doctor turned up, we've been losing a lot of men. This is not '007' we're talking about here." Saratov stood and walked to the glass window overlooking Ilium Control. "We must decide soon what to do if this doctor is alive. If he is, or for that matter if Admiral Belovo's agents are alive and in American hands, we must assume that the Americans have figured out what we're doing or soon will." Saratov returned to the head of the table and paused. "In that case, gentlemen, we must strike!" Saratov slammed his right fist into his left palm with a loud pop, startling everyone.

General Bransk recovered first. "I do not agree, General. If Ilium is ever compromised, and that's a big if, I say we stick by the plan. The options have been meticulously researched, and we all know them."

"Yes," said Belovo. "If compromised, we tell the Americans what they're facing, and let them make the first move."

Saratov didn't try to hide his contempt. "That *only* applies when the Americans have been de-fanged, when they've cut back to a few hundred weapons. They are still *fully* armed, my friends!" He turned to Belovo. "Admiral, what if the Americans' first move is to launch a massive first strike?" He looked at Bransk. "What then, Nikolai?"

Bransk had lost none of his confidence. "General, that would be stupid of them. Suicidal."

Saratov resumed sitting at the head of the table.

"The Americans are not suicidal. But they can be gamblers if they feel threatened. If they discover the full extent of Operation Ilium, they will not sit tight. They might believe they can destroy us before we can react and detonate the weapons we've planted. It would be a huge gamble on their part, but it's a gamble they might feel compelled to take." Saratov lifted a glass of water, sipped, and then swished the ice cubes in the glass with his finger. "Put yourself in their position, Nikolai. Do you think they would just sit there and trust us not to pull the trigger? Would you in their place?"

"This is all premature, Uri," answered Bransk, the only member of the group who ever addressed Saratov by his first name.

As usual, Generals Zhitnik and Salavat said nothing.

Each participant was considering privately the arguments being advanced; each weighing the logic, the dangers, the consequences of what they heard.

"I agree the Americans can be dangerous,"continued Bransk. They are, of course, still fully armed. If the time comes that we suspect our plans are coming to light, I would consider destroying them. That is better than waiting to be destroyed ourselves. But the time has not yet come. We have no indications we are compromised. The opposite if anything."

Admiral Belovo agreed. "President Moran released a statement saying that he welcomed Turgenev's arms initiative. U.S. forces are *not* on heightened alert. Why are we talking about striking?"

Saratov could see he didn't have the votes to even contemplate a first strike. "We do nothing for now, then," he said. "But consider what I've said this evening."

Kachuga was considering it. He was certain, now. Saratov had planned to destroy the Americans from the beginning.

"Let's go over it all one more time," said agent Cal Ritter. He looked at the grimace on Duval's face and almost felt sorry for him. "You want something to eat or drink? Cup of coffee, a soda?"

The doctor shook his head, and it increased the pounding in his temples. "No, I'm okay. But I've told you everything I can." He looked at the articles on the desk one more time. There was a VISA card, an ATM card, a driver's license, and a receipt from a dry cleaner's in Minneapolis. There were also three $20s, a $5, and some singles. "I've told you everything I can about this stuff, Cal. I took it off the guy with the shotgun who attacked me. Onega, he was called. That's all there was."

Ritter couldn't decide if Duval was tired, naturally testy, or a little bit of both. Ritter, himself, was getting fed up with the small hospital examination room, and he wasn't even banged up. The agent was about to pour himself another cup of coffee when the door opened, and a second FBI agent entered the room.

"We got the negatives and the x-ray plates from the motel room, and they're en route to Washington as we speak," the second agent said. "I don't know what they're going to do for us."

Before Ritter could respond, Michelle returned to the room, accompanied by a nurse. She eased slowly into a chair beside Duval, looking exhausted. "When can we get some rest?" she asked of no one in particular.

"Soon, honey," said Ritter. "Just a few more questions."

Duval decided to ask a question himself. "What did the credit card tell you, Ritter?"

"This VISA?" asked Ritter, pointing to the card on the table. "Not much. The card is good, the bill gets paid every month, but the name on the card is pretty certainly an alias. Bad address, bad phone number. Same with the driver's license."

"That's reassuring," said Duval.

Ritter tried again. "One more time, George. Is there anything about the stuff spread out before you here that you haven't told us?"

Duval looked at the items for the hundredth time, trying to see anything significant. He was about to admit defeat, when it suddenly occurred to him. He smiled, as if he had just achieved some kind of minor victory over an irritating Monopoly opponent. "Just one thing," he said, pointing to the table. "You haven't got everything I took."

"What?" Ritter didn't seem to understand.

"You're missing my hairdressers's card," said Duval, "or the hairdresser I would call if I'm ever in Washington."

"George, what *are* you talking about?"

Duval considered stringing Ritter along, but decided against it. He was too tired to play more games. "It's in my own wallet. I got it from one of the bodies at the accident site. I'd forgotten about it."

Ritter found Duval's personal wallet and handed it to him. He watched as Duval rummaged in a pocket and extracted a business card bearing the name and phone number of a hairdresser on Wisconsin Avenue in Washington, D.C. The name on the front was scratched out, as Duval remembered, but the handwritten number on the back was still legible. "Now, you really do have everything. Case is solved, right?"

Ritter examined the card. The number-letter sequence on the back was odd: 00 1A 0A WM M PA 1 V* 00. He looked at it carefully. "This number mean anything, George?"

Duval thought back to his house. "I can't say. I can say, though, that the guy at my house, the one who didn't die—" Duval closed his eyes to concentrate and started from the top. "I found that card on one of the dead men at the accident site in Nebraska. His name was Gabrovo, right?"

Ritter nodded his approval.

"I forgot to give it to Sheriff Reiner. The number on the back is weird. I remember wondering about it. Anyway, I heard that number again, or part of it, the night Michelle and I were attacked at my house. The guy who didn't die, the one you didn't find, was trying to tell me this number. He was so full of morphine, that he didn't know who he was talking to. But I remember he was calling out these numbers, and I remembered at the time having seen those numbers before. Must be something important. Eh?"

Ritter shrugged his shoulders and handed the card to his fellow agent. "See what you can make of this, Al, but don't call anyone directly. Not yet, anyway."

* * *

At CIA headquarters in Langley, Virginia, analyst Ezekial "Zeke" Matsui looked at a transcription of a coded message received several hours earlier from the station chief in Mongolia. Not a lot came from Ulan Bator, or at least, not a lot came marked "Urgent," and it pricked the analyst's interest. He looked over the message a second time, then punched some keys on a desktop computer in front of him and watched a map of the eastern part of central Asia appear on the screen. He jotted down the rough coordinates of an area east of Lake Baikal, and punched in a number on a telephone.

When the phone answered, Zeke Matsui asked for the watch officer and got a sleepy sounding John Lindquist on the line.

"John? Zeke Matsui. I've got a question."

"Shoot."

"Do we have a bird passing anywhere near—" He paused to look at his notepad and read off the latitude and longitude he had written down.

"Just a sec," came the reply. Matsui could hear some tapping on a computer keyboard and Lindquist's deep breathing on the other end of the line. Lindquist was clearly cradling the phone in his neck as he typed. "Zeke, we got a pass near there tomorrow morning at about seven o'clock our time."

"Can I make a request for a look-see."

"Sure, you can request it. But Harlow will have to approve."

"I know. Put it through channels, will you? I'll talk to Harlow directly on this."

"Sure, now what are we looking for? And how exact is our position?"

"Our position is not very exact. You'll need to take this very wide. We're looking for something that resembles a power plant or an industrial compound of some kind. And we're looking for patterns in the forest surrounding it."

"Patterns? Like what?"

"Like a grid, with the squares of the grid a kilometer or two on a side. The grid might be indicated by disturbed soil—like someone has been digging trenches miles long in the middle of the forest, without cutting down any trees, and then covering them up again."

"That could be tough."

"I know."

"Tell you what though. We'll run some infrared and some false color, and that may show us if the trees have been disturbed. Sometimes if you dig near their roots, the leaves look just a little different at different wave-lengths. And we'll do a radar run. If we use really short wavelengths, it might show where soil has been dug up and is not as compacted as the soil around it. Might work, might not. What's this for, anyway?"

"It's probably nothing. But it could be the world's largest radio trans-mitter. The question is, why would anybody be building something like that in the middle of absolutely nowhere?"

Saturday, September 18

The sweet, metallic odor of burnt iron ore wafted gently through the air conditioning vents, silently displacing the aroma of virgin plastic and fresh paint that came with every new car. To Steve Hughes and Martin Hureaux, the smell of cooked ferrites was merely pleasant and unusual, a curiosity to be silently contemplated, stored for future reference, and dismissed. But for FBI Special Agent Todd Walters, the heavy scent was like an invisible time machine, effortlessly transparting him to the early 1960s and his youth on Lake Michigan's southern shores.

The giant mills that stretched along the curving waterline were by any measure horrifically ugly: mile after mile of immense, squat, industrial buildings, their sides stained a dark ochre by the dust deposits that for decades billowed from coke ovens and blast furnaces and spread like warm fog across the flat, dreary northern Indian landscape.

No doubt about it, Todd Walters said to himself as the mills by the Great Lakes finally came into view, this place is just as fucking ugly as I've always remembered it.

As if reading Walters's thoughts, Steve Hughes turned his eyes from the road ahead to catch the expression of his fellow agent. "So you really grew up here, Todd?" Hughes asked, both hands on the steering wheel.

"Yeah, beautiful ain't it?"

"About as beautiful as a strip mine," Hughes grunted, now scanning the highway ahead. He spotted the truck they had been following for the last sixteen hours about a quarter mile in front.

"Anybody see the second truck?" Walters asked Hughes and a third agent. He looked in the rear view mirror.

"It's back there somewhere," said Hughes, at least that's what our friend upstairs says." He pointed at the roof liner.

The airborne spotter warned them of the second flatbed truck about three hours out of Norfolk. It was transporting a medium-sized forklift, and while it typically stayed four or five minutes behind, it exactly duplicated the route of the flatbed they'd been following from Norfolk. Walters and his colleagues felt lucky. They knew that without the airplane overhead, they would never have "made" the second truck.

"What did your family do here, Todd?" asked Hughes, picking up where he'd left off.

"Same as everybody else's. Made steel. Made money. Raised kids. Survived," replied Walters.

Hughes asked no more about Todd Walter's youth. He turned to business. "So, what do you think, Todd? Is this it? Is he stopping in 'Chi-town'?" Hughes pointed in the direction of the lead truck in front.

"Could be. But coming up from Virginia he could be going on north or northwest too. Up to Minneapolis or out to the coast. If he's dropping that package in Chicago, though, we'll know soon enough." Walters looked at his watch absentmindedly. "We'll be at the Chicago Skyway in a couple of minutes, and after that it's a straight shot up the Dan Ryan to the Loop, if that's where he's headed."

The three FBI agents rode in silence for twenty minutes, following the truck as it passed to the west of the Loop on I-94, and then signalled it was exiting the freeway on Chicago's northwest side.

Walters sat upright in his seat. "Look alive, guys, this may be it." Walters looked over his shoulder to see if the backup car with the three agents they had picked up on the outskirts of Chicago was still with them. It was.

The truck turned east and headed toward the lakefront with Walters, Hughes, and Martin Hureaux following a block behind, happy that the morning traffic made their being detected unlikely. At Halstead Street, the truck turned south and traveled three blocks before stopping at the curb in front of a gray, stuccowork bungalow. Hughes pulled in behind a parked mini-van a block beyond, and the backup eased to curbside thirty yards south.

The agents waited for the second truck. It arrived five minutes later, stopped momentarily beside the first truck, and then drove off, with the FBI backup car following at a discrete distance behind.

"Must not need the forklift anymore," said Hughes.

Walters raised a pair of field glasses to his eyes and watched a man wearing a red baseball cap emerge from the truck's passenger seat. He walked up a driveway separating the bungalow from a frame clapboard house beside, then disappeared from view. "I'm going on foot, friends.

Follow the truck if it leaves while I'm gone. Check with the Chicago office if you get something."

Walters ducked into a driveway and followed it to an alley. From there he walked north, paralleling Halstead, until he came within sight of the rear of the gray bungalow. He scrambled over a low, chain-link fence, and shielded himself behind a thick hedge and several large, plastic garbage cans in the neighboring yard. A set of rickety wooden steps led from the back of the bungalow to a tiny unkempt yard, bordered on one side by a narrow driveway leading to a one-car, detached garage. The only sign of life was a robin picking at something in the overgrown lawn, thick with weeds. Walters was contemplating where the man in the red cap might have gone when he heard the creaking of hinges and watched the heavy double-doors of the garage swing open. The man from the truck emerged into the weak morning sunlight, pushing a three-foot square wooden crate mounted on a dolly. Shielding his eyes from the sun, Walters tried to get a look inside the garage, but before his eyes could adjust, the man closed the doors. He then turned a large steel handle, which appeared to engage some kind of reinforced lock, and tapped in a sequence on a set of numbered buttons on a pad below the handle. The man grabbed the dolly's handlebar and rolled the wooden box down the driveway and out of view.

Walters remained crouched behind the garbage cans until he heard the truck start up, shift into low gear, and pull away. He then sat quietly, looking for any sign of activity, any sight or sound at all that might indicate that someone was in the garage or watching nearby. He got tired of waiting in less than a minute. Hell, he thought, the guy locked the thing. Walters climbed over the hedges into the driveway and faced the garage.

"Hey you, what are you doing?" came a voice from behind him.

Walters turned to see an elderly man, a pistol in his right hand, standing on the bungalow's back steps. "I'm looking for someone," said Walters, not very convincingly.

"Get your hands up, buddy," ordered the old man, stepping down three stairs and approaching Walters with his gun raised. "Who yuh lookin' for?"

"I was looking for two of my friends. They were supposed to have been here by now."

"You with the research project?" asked the man in a suspicious tone.

Walters found it a curious question but tried not to show it. "Yeah, they were supposed to meet me here. I . . . I'm supposed to check on a problem they've got, but I can't get in there unless they're here. I don't have the combination to the door." He pointed to the number pad.

"Got any ID?"

The man came closer, and Walters, even without his contacts, could see that the frail old coot was at least eighty. Walters was certain he could disarm the octogenarian without much danger but, after studying the oldtimer's face further, decided honesty might work best. The man certainly didn't look like anybody's idea of a Russian agent. "Yeah, I got this," said Walters, opening his wallet and displaying his FBI identification. He held it up to the man's face.

"FBI?"

"Yeah, and who are you?"

"Me?" said the old man. "I'm Koziak. Leon Koziak."

"Well listen, Leon. I want in there *now*." Walters pointed to the garage.

"I'd be glad to oblige if you're really the FBI, but I can't get in there either. Not without setting off a million alarms." The man suddenly looked suspicious. "You really FBI? Why yuh snooping around here?"

Walters ignored the question. "Put that goddamn gun down before I break your neck." To Walters relief, the old man actually did as he was told. Walters relaxed his voice. "The alarms make a lot of noise do they?"

"Don't think so. I believe they're what you call silent alarms. Leastwise, I've never heard them go off, even when they were installed. They're connected to some security outfit downtown."

"Yeah, which one?"

"Southfield Security."

"How do you know?"

"Because I get the bill every month, mailed right here to my house. They pay for it, though. The researchers, I mean."

"You ever see what they're working on?"

"I just got a peek once. It's a big machine, kind of like one of them oil tanks people used to have on the side of their houses. It's hooked up to computers or something."

Steve Marley had been an FBI research assistant for only three months and still felt uncomfortable around the veterans. His uncanny feel for the *New York Times* Sunday Crossword Puzzle had earned him a reputation for brains, and none of his superiors doubted his insight into numbers. But Marley didn't yet know that, and no one was about to tell him. He would learn of his value soon enough, the veterans thought. When

Marley knocked on Guy LeClaire's door, he did so with some trepidation. Marley was certain he was right, but would LeClaire, a special assistant to Director Novello, be pleased with his work or wonder why it had taken him two hours to figure it out and follow it through?

LeClaire seemed friendly enough when he asked Marley to take a seat. "So, Steve, what have you got?"

"I think I've got an answer on the number."

LeClaire looked surprised. "Really? The one I gave you two hours ago? Let me look at it again." He shuffled through some papers on his desk until he found the page he was looking for. On it was a cryptic number and letter notation: 00 1A 0A WM M PA 1 V* 00. It was something the doctor in Nebraska had gotten from one of the two men who had been killed in the truck in Nebraska. "Does it belong to a safe?"

"No, but we wasted time finding out. We checked with Mosler and the other safe makers, and none of them manufactures an alpha-numeric combination lock in that form."

LeClaire had expected as much. "Well, whatever it is, if you've got it you beat the crypto boys over at NSA in Maryland. They said it's too short to work with." LeClaire smirked. "Hell, if they can't run something on their eight zillion gigaflop computers, they can't tie their own shoes. No imagination. What is it then?"

"I think it's a Washington, D.C., phone number."

"Wh-a-t?"

"A D.C. phone number. The thing really had me stumped. I didn't have a clue. I started by eliminating the first and last set of double zeros."

"Why?"

"Because they looked like parameters. You know, start-points and stop-points that don't mean anything by themselves. They are zeros, after all."

LeClaire had no idea what he was talking about.

"Then what?" he asked.

"I was picking up my office phone to dial Nancy and tell her I might be late coming home tonight. While I was phoning and looking at the numbers, a silly thought occurred to me. Businesses are always using the letters on the telephone dial to remind people of phone numbers. You know, dial 1-800-Car-Wash, that kind of thing. Just for laughs, I compared the letters in our little problem to an ordinary, standard U.S. telephone. 1A 0A WM M PA 1 V* comes out to 12 02 96 6 72 1 8*. That's (1) 202 966-7218."

"What about the asterisk at the end?"

"Some people think pushing the asterisk sign helps speed the connection on a long distance call. It does for some overseas calls. That's all."

LeClaire started to laugh. "Here we have some of the greatest mathematical minds in the world available to us, and a wet-behind-the-ears kid six months out of college puts us all to shame. Good work! Is it a working number?"

"Yes. I tried it and got a recording."

"You put in a trace request?"

"No. I've come to you first. How do I get authorization for a trace request to see if this number makes any sense or if I'm wrong."

"Well, normally you ask me, and I go through all the legal hassles, including getting a warrant to search records if I need one." LeClaire stopped talking and wrote something on an index card. "Call this man at this number," he said to Marley, showing him the card. "He's a friend at C & P Telephone and he'll give you what you need without a lot of BS."

Marley took the card.

It took nearly thirty minutes to get two FBI agents to the headquarters of Southfield Security. It took the agents forty minutes longer to persuade Southfield to disable the alarms at the garage on North Halstead Street and telephone Todd Walters that all was clear. Walters left the old man named Leon Koziak in his living room, and walked down the front steps to confer with the four other agents watching the house in two unmarked cars across the street. If the two men from the truck or any of their companions decided to return to the garage unexpectedly, there would be no time to clean up and secure the scene. They would have to be captured, preferably alive.

Walters finished his instructions and walked back up the driveway to the garage. A twenty-two-year-old graduate student in electronic engineering was standing in front of the door. Technically, Josh Scribbner was a contract FBI consultant. In fact, Scribbner did occasional consulting work to stay out of prison on charges of illegally tapping into the FBI's ongoing criminal investigation files, a felony he had committed in answer to a challenge from a fellow student. Scribbner was more or less a genius at anything to do with computers or electronic devices.

"I see you didn't have much trouble with the electronic lock," said Walters.

"No, it was real chicken-shit stuff. Off the shelf junk."

Walters opened the doors wide and surveyed the cramped space. A large, cylindrical tank, lying on its side, sat in the center of the garage, one end pointing forward toward the door. Various wires connected the tank to a bank of three personal computers and other electronic hardware nestled on a table nearby. The computers were on-line, their blue screens displaying an ever-changing pattern of geometric shapes. Another series of cables ran from the computers to two large boxes that to Walters's untrained eye looked like radio receivers. A rack of automobile batteries, two portable gasoline-powered electrical generators, and an assortment of tools, crates, and other equipment stacked against the back wall completed the picture. "Bingo!" he said in a low voice.

"What *is* this stuff?" said Scribbner.

It was the first time Walters had ever heard Scribbner express any ig-norance of anything. "Can't say for sure," said Walters. "I just hope the fucking thing doesn't go off."

"Did you say off? Like kaboom?"

"Don't worry. It's highly unlikely."

The electronics wizard didn't seem very reassured. "Hey, Walters, I'm no explosives expert."

Todd Walters took his eyes off the cylinder and turned to the young man. "Listen Josh, you don't have to touch that thing at all. In fact, don't touch it. We cut the alarm protecting the garage itself, as you know." He pointed to the boiler. "But that, and everything else in here, may be alarmed separately. Your first job is to find out."

"Wonderful."

"Listen up. After you check that, I want you to give me some kind of inventory of what all this stuff is and some preliminary ideas on how it's all wired to the outside world." He touched the top of one of the computer monitors. "These desktop computers are clearly wired to the boiler there."

"Is that what it is, a boiler?"

"Supposedly. But look here. How are these computers and the boiler and the other stuff in this room connected to one another and to the outside world?"

"Who says there are any connections?"

"Look, Josh. There may not be. But until we get some other experts in here to look at this stuff, I'm depending on you." Walters left the garage to check in with the agents out front.

Josh Scribbner set to work. For twenty minutes he traced cables, read labels, and played with the computer keyboards. Twice he stepped out-side, once walking to the back of the garage and a second time looking at the rear of the house. When he was satisfied, he turned to Walters. "Okay, Todd. What do you want to know?"

Walters couldn't tell a transistor from a toothbrush and wasn't afraid to admit it. "I'm not smart enough to even ask a question. You tell me, boy genius. What is all this crap?" He spread out both hands to indicate everything in the room.

Like many experts in a particular field, Josh Scribbner had a certain arrogance, an arrogance that carried over into other fields where he was less informed. "Tell you what, Walters. I'll fill you in on this 'crap' as you call it, if you fill me in on the boiler. Trade you even-up."

Walters detected condescension in Scribbner's voice, and, except for the fact that he needed him, wouldn't have minded popping the smart ass in the jaw. Instead, he spoke with a certain pleasure. "I think it's a hydrogen bomb. It may well be armed. It's not one of ours."

Scribbner's face went white. He tried to stammer some words, then stopped to regain his composure. "You . . . you mean it's a weapon of some terrorists?"

"Something like that. Anyway, I expect it's remotely controlled, don't you? Seriously, Josh, would you want to be within thirty fucking miles of this thing when it goes off?" Walters actually laughed. "So, smart ass, how's it controlled?"

Scribbner calmed himself down and began explaining. "It's controlled by the computers." He pointed to three shoe box–sized containers next to the computers. "Those are cryptograph machines, you know, decoders. A message comes in, they decode it and send it to the computers. The computers run through some program to trigger the bomb, if that's what it is."

"Christ, Josh, even I can see that. How do they get the message?"

"By phone."

"*Phone?* You mean somebody dials up a number here, plugs in a code, and boom?" Walters got a mental image of a bank of telephone operators in babushkas speed-dialing the telephone numbers of sixty-odd nuclear warheads as fast as their little fingers could whirl a Russian dial telephone. It didn't seem right. "That's it?"

"There's another way. See these boxes here? They're radio receivers. They're connected to an antenna outside the garage." He pointed to the cables leading to the garage wall.

"I didn't see any antenna outside the garage."

"It's a ground antenna. At first I thought it was a lightning rod or a simple electrical ground. But it isn't. It's an antenna for picking up ground waves." He pointed to a drain on the floor attached to a cable. "That's an antenna too."

Walters looked confused. "Ground waves?"

"Sure enough." Scribbner's arrogance had returned. "That's a radio wave that travels just above and into the first few feet of the earth. It's not a very efficient method of sending radio signals, but it's very reliable."

Walters put his hands on his hips. "Okay, good work. Now, what's all this other shit?" He pointed at the batteries.

"All this other stuff is just to guarantee electrical power."

"Including all those boxes and things against the back wall?" Walters pointed to his left.

Scribbner shook his head. "Naw. That stuff's not hooked up. It's spare parts. Looks like whoever set all this up was using this place as a warehouse too."

"That explains why the truckers stopped here this morning. One of them took something out on a dolly."

Walters paused, then pointed.

"Is this stuff here, the working equipment, alarmed?"

"I don't think so. There are no obvious alarms. Anyway, the only way to get a distress signal out of here is by telephone. The telephone line hooking all this stuff up to the outside world runs from the garage back to the house, where it's connected to the home phone, I'd guess. Disconnect the home phone, just take it off the hook, and for sure no alarm is getting out of here."

Walters told Scribbner to stay put, then walked to one of the FBI cars staking out the house. He placed a call on a secure phone to FBI headquarters in Washington and was connected to Guy LeClaire who was coordinating FBI efforts around the country.

"Telephone?" asked LeClaire.

"That's what Scribbner thinks. And radio too. Something called a ground wave receiver."

When Walters finished he trotted back to the garage and patted Scribbner on the back. "The agency thanks you, son."

"So what now?" asked Scribbner.

"In an hour or so, a team of technicians and their equipment are going to be arriving from Fermilab out in Batavia. They can tell an H-bomb from a hemorrhoid."

"What?"

"Never mind." Walters scanned the garage. "Agent Nelson should be here shortly with a duplicate computer. When he gets here, switch it with one of the computers on the table, and get back to your lab at the University of Chicago. You'll have some help there. We want to know everything there is about this computer and its program. Okay?"

"Why replace it with a duplicate?"

"Because when we're done, we want this place to look untouched, in case somebody comes snooping around."

"But the duplicate won't have the same program."

"The duplicate will be out of commission. It will look like it had a short or something."

"If someone comes snooping, why not just arrest him?"

"That wouldn't be very smart, Josh. Might tip off the competition." Walters smiled. "And one more thing, Josh. If that thing blows, it was nice knowin' you."

Scribbner gave Walters the "finger."

At FBI headquarters in Washington, LeClaire first called Director Novello, then dialed his inhouse FBI communications experts. They knew of no ground wave transmission facilities in the United States outside the control of the Pentagon. They recommended he contact the FCC, and if that didn't work, the NSA and CIA. The FCC had nothing. The National Security Agency had picked up some errant ground wave transmissions in the last week, but could make nothing of them. The CIA had better news. As a matter of fact, the CIA did have some new information about a possible ground wave transmitter. It had just come in the day before via HUMINT, human intelligence . . . a source on the ground. When LeClaire explained why he was asking, he was put directly through to CIA Director Owen Caulfield.

Roseland Hospital in Littleton, Colorado, had been open only six weeks, and in the words of its administrator, was still in its shake-down phase. While Roseland's public relations department boasted of the hospital's magnificently equipped trauma center and its plethora of the newest and most expensive medical whizbangery, the fact was that Roseland's staff was not yet up to the quality of the fancy new gizmos it had to play with. The doctors and nurses were well vetted and qualified, but the administrative and support services were still understaffed, and many of the positions that were filled were occupied by low paid workers with little motivation and less experience. It was a problem familiar to many of the "for profit" hospitals and clinics that had begun springing up across the country during the Reagan-Bush years.

It was no surprise, then, that a custodian whose name tag identified him as J. Perez went about his duties undisturbed. If no one had seen him before, it made little impression. There were new faces popping up at Roseland every day. Even security found his presence unremarkable. In addition to his hospital-issue name tag, Perez had a special security badge in a plastic jacket pinned on his left shirt pocket. It displayed his photo, his hospital employee number and other pertinent information, and was identical to the scores of others issued to hospital staff.

For more than an hour, Perez busied himself in the lobby area, emptying trash cans, polishing door handles, cleaning windows, and generally doing the dozens of unremarkable things that custodians do. When he finished with the main floor, he took his trash cart to the second floor, and repeated his chores, carefully noting the activity on each floor and when possible, glancing at the patient list posted at the central nursing station. For nearly two hours, Perez continued his humdrum routine, finishing a floor, and then lugging his cart to the service elevator for the ride up to the next level. Shortly before 9:00 A.M., Perez punched in 4 on the elevator panel and climbed slowly to Roseland's top floor. When the door opened, Perez immediately saw the difference. Two athletic-looking men in their late twenties, both dressed in suits, were standing at the nurses station chatting with an attractive young blonde RN, and two other similarly dressed men stood outside a patient's door about ten yards down the hallway. Perez began to push his cart onto the floor, when the men talking to the nurse heard him and wheeled in his direction. "Hey you!" said one in a stern voice, pointing at Perez, "you can't come here."

Perez pointed his thumbs at his chest and arched his eyebrows as if asking, "Who, me?" as the two men walked quickly toward him.

"Didn't your supervisor tell you this floor is off-limits, buddy?"

Perez shook his head. "No, nobody told me nothin'. I'm just here to clean up."

The second man reached for Perez's ID card, and putting on a pair of reading glasses, scanned it. "Look here, Mr. J. Perez. You're not supposed to be up here. Now get your little ass back in that elevator and off this floor, or you won't be working at Roseland much longer. Scram." Perez bowed and nodded and weaved backward, mumbling "Sorry, sorry, Señor," as he did so, but kept his eyes pinned on the young woman with the cast on her arm being wheeled by a nurse from a room down the hall. Perez didn't get a long look at her, and the bandage over her right cheekbone hid some of her features. Still he had seen enough to be sure. It was her all right. He liked her name: Michelle Rebecca Falk. Perez didn't get a good view of the man standing near the water cooler to the left of the nurse's station and might not have recognized him anyway. The fact was, Duval looked remarkably different without a beard. Duval, however, did get a good look at Perez. Duval was certain he knew the custodian, but he couldn't remember from where.

Perez liked the pay phones at the 7-11 on Silver Creek Road, two blocks north of Roseland. He had used one that very morning to call Washington, and the line was good. Even better, there were three phones in place, and he expected one would be available. When he arrived, however, all three were occupied. Perez waited impatiently for two minutes, trying to show that he was in a hurry, but no one responded. Finally, and, with his customary bad temper, Perez grabbed the arm of a teenaged girl on one phone and demanded she give it over.

The girl refused, and Perez pulled her roughly aside and tossed her to the pavement. A termite inspector calling his office from the phone to the right, pulled out his heavy-duty flashlight and brought it down forcefully on the back of Perez's head, rendering him unconscious.

Perez was taken by ambulance to the emergency room at Roseland. For two hours he lay oblivious as he was x-rayed, shaved, and sutured, all within a few feet of a working telephone. It may as well have been miles. His call would be delayed.

Steve Marley knocked sharply on LeClaire's open office door at FBI head-quarters in Washington.

"Got something, Steve?" asked LeClaire.

"Yes. Your contact at C & P Telephone was very helpful." Marley opened a notebook and quickly studied the first three pages. "The phone number I came up with belongs to a private residence, one of those mansions in the Kalorama section above Rock Creek Park. It's owned by something called 'Concessimus Partners, Ltd.,' based in the Cayman Islands. Whatever 'Concessimus Partners' is, they've leased the place to a diplomat and his family from Uzbekistan, of all places. They apparently live there."

LeClaire showed no expression. "Go on, Steve."

"Here's where it gets interesting. The billing records at C & P Telephone show that the number in question is fairly active," Marley explained. "Maybe ten or twenty long distance calls are placed on it every day. But here's the kicker. The house has more than a hundred separate telephone lines."

"What?"

"It's wired up just like some business, a big law firm, or maybe a newspaper. You could place a hundred calls at once if you had the manpower."

"Or a computer driven automatic-dialer," said LeClaire. "You would need only one person, and he wouldn't even have to be at the house. He could place a call to the house from anywhere in the world, and the automatic dialers would take over."

Marley couldn't understand why LeClaire was so interested in how the house's phone lines could be employed.

LeClaire tapped his fingers nervously on his desk. "Are a lot of calls made on those extra lines?"

"Not normally. But get this. About once every two weeks, all the lines get active at once. Anywhere from fifty to sixty-five calls go out at the same time or nearly the same time." He fumbled in an inside jacket pocket for several full-sized sheets of typing paper. "Look at this, it's a xerox of the billing records for July, August, and September."

LeClaire looked at the records, seeing nothing at first.

Marley pointed at a column showing the time and date various calls were made. "Look at the first one hundred calls or so. About half were made on the sixteenth of July. To be precise, fifty-one calls were made over fifty-one separate telephone lines, from six minutes after eleven AM to eight minutes past eleven AM. All of the calls lasted about twenty seconds. Then, no calls were made from any of those numbers until about two weeks later on August second, when the routine was repeated. The same numbers were called, but there were three or four additional numbers. Same thing on August eighteenth. Weird huh?"

LeClaire shook his head. "I'll say," he responded, trying to contain his excitement. "Any calls made to Chicago, area code three-one-two?"

"I don't know, let's look."

They ran down the billing sheets. A number in Chicago had been called in early June, and re-called at roughly two-week intervals ever since. LeClaire circled the number. "Trace this immediately. Use the phone over there. Is our friend at the phone company still cooperating?"

"Yes, sir."

LeClaire looked at the other numbers on the bill, trying to discern more patterns. About the only thing he could see was that calls went all over the country.

Marley had an ID on the number in under two minutes.

"Yes?" said LeClaire.

"The number belongs to a house on the north side of Chicago."

LeClaire practically jumped from his seat. "North Halstead Street."

"Yup. Some guy named Koziak."

"Damnation!" shouted LeClaire. He picked up his phone and dialed the direct line to FBI director Novello's office. Putting his hand over the mouthpiece, he winked at Marley. "Steve, this is truly excellent work. *Thank you!* And shut the door when you leave, please."

Marley knew better than to ask what it was all about.

LeClaire reached Novello on a secure cellular phone. The director was in a car en route to the White House.

The machine sat in the back of an ordinary utility van, the kind of vehicle used by plumbers and electricians and termite exterminators. Agent Todd Walters had no idea what it was, but it was obviously heavy.

It required four burly men to ease it down a ramp from the van's rear doors and push it toward the garage. Once inside, the lead technician asked Walters to leave. Walters refused, and the technician showing his irritation handed Walters a heavy vest and ordered him to put it on. It weighed more than twenty pounds and to Walters felt very much like a military flak jacket.

It took the lead technician and an assistant ten minutes to set up the machine and connect it to an electrical socket. When ready, they gruffly ordered Walters to stand back. Over the next fifteen minutes they busied themselves positioning the machine at different angles to the large boiler. They would roll their machine to the right rear of the boiler, align it with some kind of sighting device, push a series of buttons, and then repeat the procedure from the left rear. Walters thought they looked slightly ridiculous, but was relieved when they completed their work, took off their heavy jackets, and told him he could do the same. They then proceeded to open a panel on the side of the machine that revealed what appeared to be a television screen. The senior technician switched on the screen and asked Walters to turn off the lights.

At first, Walters could make no sense of the images. They were green and white and ghostlike and appeared to an untrained eye as little more than surrealistic lines and angles intersecting with no particular regularity. Walters was not enlightened by the technicians' jargon. "Beryllium latticework here, it looks like," said one, pointing a pen at something that looked like a plastic egg box, and "Pretty good image of the lens from this angle," said the other. The lead technician worked various switches to change images, blow up frames, and increase or decrease contrast, all the time pointing at various points on the screen and saying "Lookee here," to his colleague. Finally, he shook his head and stood up. "I've seen enough, Bruce. How about you?"

"Yes. There's no doubt about it. Let's open her up. There's an access plate." The technician named Bruce pointed to a hatch above a circular door at the front of the boiler.

Walters again was asked to leave, and again he refused. This time he was handed a white, plasticized suit designed to cover his entire body, including his shoes, hands, and head. In addition, he was given a pair of goggles and a face mask hooked up to some kind of breathing apparatus, which could be hooked to a belt.

"Suit up," said Bruce, pulling on a garment himself. Walters discovered quickly that the suit was airtight. No one could be expected to stay in the thing more than a few minutes without suffering heat prostration.

The boiler's access plate came off easily, each of its hexagonal bolts turning counter-clockwise without resistance under the force of a powered socket-wrench. The senior technician shined a flashlight through the opening, scanning the boiler's innards with a trained eye. "It's good work," he said to no one in particular. "From here, it looks absolutely like a normal industrial boiler, firetubes and all. I wonder if it really works."

Walters couldn't be sure if he meant as a boiler or a bomb.

"Okay, hand me the detector."

The detector was a long, thin tube, attached via cable to some kind of control box the second technician had slung over his shoulder.

The technician stared at a gauge on the box. "Just a sec," he said, while simultaneously pulling on a pair of earphones attached to his control unit. "I'm getting steady gamma . . . it's low but very steady."

"What about now, Bruce?" asked his colleague standing at the access plate.

"Less."

"Now?"

"Steady again, same rad count."

The technician stepped from the side of the boiler and removed his mask. "There's no danger, it's very well shielded." He waited for the others to remove their masks. "I'm satisfied. Let's button this thing back up. Agent Walters, we've got a thermonuclear weapon on our hands. A big one."

FBI director Novello was sweating profusely when he and Owen Caulfield were shown into the Oval Office. The president, Rubio Pinzon, and Admiral Greenwood watched him wipe his face with a blue handkerchief. Except for the gentle hum of the air-conditioning system, the room was absolutely quiet.

"The latest, gentlemen?" asked the president.

Caulfield deferred to Novello who remained standing.

"I've just heard from Chicago," Novello said. It's a hydrogen bomb. A very big one. One megaton, maybe a little more. That's five or six times the size of one of our typical warheads, maybe fifty times the size of the bomb we dropped on Hiroshima."

Greenwood whistled, and Pinzon uttered a low "damn," but Moran was silent. No one seemed anxious to speak. Moran ran his hands backward through his silver-gray hair and tilted his head toward the ceiling as if searching for a crack in the plaster. "Is there any doubt at all?"

"Apparently not," said Novello. They got good shots of its construction from a portable x-ray machine of some kind. And they got a gamma ray detector inside the thing. It's a bomb."

Novello walked slowly to a chair to the right of the president's desk, sat down, and casually crossed his legs, as if such an ordinary gesture might somehow lessen the shock of his news.

"What about 'command and control'?" Moran asked.

"It's remotely controlled. It can be detonated either by radio or telephone. We believe we have found the Russian telephone control center. It's right here in Washington—not ten blocks from us."

Pinzon practically squawked. "Here—in *Washington?*"

Novello pulled a notepad from an inside pocket and studied it. "We've traced calls from the telephone center here in Washington to the weapon in Chicago. We also believe those billing records will lead us to other weapons."

"Then we can track them down and neutralize them," said Pinzon.

Novello looked at his feet and shook his head slowly. "It's not so simple, Rubio."

"Why not?"

"Because the phone line going from the phone center to Chicago doesn't go directly to the weapon. It goes to a phone in a house, and then goes over a jury-rigged phone line to the weapon."

"Jury-rigged?" asked Pinzon.

"He means they've strung a kind of unauthorized extension cord from the house to the bomb," said Caulfield.

"So?" said Pinzon. "We trace the calls from Washington, to wherever they go, and then eyeball the extension lines to the weapons."

"Exactly, Rubio," said Novello. "But that will take time and a lot of visible manpower. What if they've run an extension line a couple hundred yards? It's not difficult. What if one is run into a five-story apartment building? If we're spotted tracing a phone line, or, if we set off an alarm, the Russians will have time to blow their weapons while we're searching."

"Are you telling me the Russians just make a call and a bomb goes off?" Moran asked.

"Or transmit a radio message. Ground wave radio is first choice, telephone is backup. Either way, a transmission is routed into a bank of three ordinary desktop PCs. We've removed one from the Chicago site, and experts at the University of Chicago are studying it."

"What does that tell us?" said the president.

Novello wiped his forehead again and restudied his notes. "One computer detonates the weapon, and the other two are emergency backups. A message comes in from the outside world, is decrypted by an old-fashioned electro-mechanical crypto system, and is sent to the computers. They arm the weapon."

"What's that mean?" asked the president.

"The weapon is on a kind of standby mode, for safety. A coded message takes the bomb off standby and arms it, sort of like shoving a round into a rifle chamber."

"Yes."

"A second coded message, followed a few seconds later by a confirmation message—what's called an Authenticator—triggers it."

Moran squirmed in his chair. "So the weapon is armed by a signal, then two additional signals are sent back-to-back and Chicago is instantaneously turned into rubble?"

No, no, Novello gestured. "Not quite. It looks as if there's a delay. It appears right now that the last signal, the Authenticator, carries a time hack. It tells the weapon to detonate at a very specific time. My guess is between two and three minutes after the Authenticator message is received—it varies from weapon to weapon."

"Why's that?" asked Pinzon.

"Our best theory right now is that the delay, the time hack, is to make sure that every weapon in the country goes off at precisely the same time."

"I don't follow," said the president.

Novello slowed his speech, ensuring that every word came out clearly. "Mr. President," said Novello, "even a good phone system like ours is not perfect. Sometimes long distance circuits are slow and calls get delayed. If the Russians intend to detonate their weapons by telephone, they have to make sure all the weapons get a detonation signal before one goes off in Omaha, or some other important switching center, and destroys long distance service across the country. The other weapons wouldn't get a signal. Ground wave radio signals are also comparatively slow. They could conceivably arrive at some weapons ahead of others. If one weapon goes off prematurely, the electromagnetic radiation could screw up the radio signal to the other weapons."

Pinzon wasn't finished. "Can't we take out the phone center?"

"Sure, Rubio. But my guess is that there is a backup phone center here, or in Canada, or someplace else with good phones. And it wouldn't solve the problem of a radio transmission."

Moran thought a solution was obvious. "Can't we jam the radio transmissions?" he asked.

"Probably not. A powerful ground wave would probably get through. It turns out the Russians have just finished the largest ground wave radio transmitter ever built. That's your department, Owen."

Caulfield got to his feet. "We just heard about this transmitter, yesterday. The information just fell into our hands, plain dumb luck, in other words." Caulfield passed around color xeroxes of satellite imagery of Pechora. President Moran studied his pictures.

Caulfield continued. "Last night we scheduled a satellite pass over this ground wave *transmitting* facility we'd been tipped off about, but we didn't really connect it to anything until this morning. That's when one of Novello's men in Chicago figured out that he was looking at a ground wave *receiving* antenna."

"What do these show?" asked the president.

"It's confirmation," said Caulfield. "These pictures are about an hour old. Picture number one shows the central complex of an immense facility located east of Lake Baikal in Russia. If you look at picture number two, you can see a false-color view of the land around the central complex. You see the grid pattern? That's made by hundreds of miles of copper wire buried in the soil. They form a huge ground wave transmitting antenna."

"Why go to all this trouble?" Moran asked. "Why not just transmit from regular radio towers or from satellites?"

"Because ground wave transmissions are surer. They aren't so affected by trees, weather, or buildings. As for satellites? Satellites break down, go into the wrong orbit, and don't last very long—at least Russian satellites. They're also highly visible and always suspicious. Believe me, Mr. President. My experts have gone over this and so have Kermit Watson's over at NSA, and we agree the Russians are going to control these weapons with ground wave radio transmissions from this site called Pechora and use telephones as a backup."

"And if we take out this Pechora site with ICBMs?" said the president.

"They pick up the launch and destroy us while our missiles are en route."

"Thought so. In that case—"

The phone rang on the president's desk. Moran picked it up, listened, and handed it to Novello. As the FBI director listened, his face showed no emotion. Novello turned toward Moran when he hung up.

"Yes, Carlos?" Moran asked.

"Chicago confirms a second weapon. It was delivered on the truck we followed from Norfolk yesterday. It's now located at a private warehouse on Chicago's south side."

Moran stood and put his hands behind his back. His face showed a hint of anger. "Gentlemen, I think that pretty much settles it." He took a deep breath and let it out through pursed lips. "We can now assume that every so-called boiler shipped from any location in the old U.S.S.R. is in fact a nuclear weapon. God save us."

The air-conditioning system shut down, and the Oval Office became absolutely still.

The president didn't know where to proceed, and he admitted it. "Well, if anybody's got any ideas, now's not the time to keep them to yourselves."

"I've got a couple of thoughts," said Admiral Greenwood, "but I need some time to put them together."

Moran looked at his watch. "Gentlemen, it's just about eleven AM. Think your best thoughts and be back here with them in one hour. I know it's not much time, but it's the most I can give you for now."

5:00 PM Greenwich Mean Time (GMT) (Noon Washington, D.C.)
In the White House situation room, President Moran finished the last page and closed the file folder. His expression was grave. "Is this the only option?" He felt a burning in his stomach as he waited for an answer.

"It's the only one we think has a real chance of success," answered Admiral Greenwood.

Moran looked at Pinzon, Novello, and Caulfield. "Gentlemen, are we perhaps being too hasty? The Admiral has had just an hour to flesh out this operation. It's not much time for reflection. Do you all agree that this is the correct approach? What about diplomacy? Why not just confront President Turgenev. I can't believe he's part of this? It's not like him."

"I agree, sir," answered Greenwood, "this is not like him. A thousand to one he doesn't know anything about this. But what if we're wrong?"

"If we're wrong, we're dead, Mr. President." The words came from Pinzon. "If Turgenev *is* involved, then confronting him could lead to instant Armageddon. And even if he isn't, Turgenev couldn't take action without alerting whoever is responsible for this madness. One leak to the wrong person, and it's button-pushing time."

The president looked at Novello. "It's out of my league, Mr. President," said the FBI director. "But I can think of no other plan. It's better than an all-out American first strike. They'd retaliate for sure when our missiles left their silos. It's like what Churchill said about democracy. It's the worst plan there is except for all the others."

"Can't we just wait a while?" Moran asked.

"Every hour we wait, Mr. President, gives them more time to learn that we're on to 'em," said Caulfield. "What they're doing is a reckless act of war, and, if they find out that we've caught on, I don't think they'll wait around quietly to find out our response. They've got to be on a hair trigger already."

"Concur," said Pinzon.

"When, then?" Moran asked.

"The sooner the better is our judgment, Mr. President," said Pinzon. "If this is our course of action, there is no advantage in waiting."

"'T were best 't were done quickly."

"Yes, sir."

The president briefly studied his fingernails. In all his years in government, in life, he had never been confronted with a decision remotely connected to the one he was being asked to make now. No amount of education, experience, or professional preparation could ready a man to deal with the kind of security crisis he was facing. Moran would have to apply his intelligence, his experience, and his instincts to a problem no politician, no man, in fact, had ever faced before. The president silently prayed for wisdom and looked back at his advisors. "And how quickly could we be ready, Admiral Greenwood, if we decided to go ahead?"

"We're more or less in position right now."

"Should we leave Washington and coordinate from elsewhere?" asked Pinzon.

"No," said the president, "We've got—"

The president was interrupted by a lieutenant colonel trotting toward them from the main communications desk. "Director Novello is wanted on the phone, sirs."

Novello stepped to a desk to his right and picked up the phone. The others could not make out Novello's responses to the caller at the other end. They did see his face grow steadily darker, and watched as he began wiping bubbles of perspiration from his face with his soggy handkerchief.

"That was Colorado," he said as he returned to the group. "Dr. Duval claims that he, or his girlfriend, I should say, has been spotted by a Russian agent." Novello slumped into a swivel chair and twisted his form sideways in agitation. At first, no one seemed to comprehend his words.

Pinzon finally understood. "At the hospital?" he asked in disbelief. "How's it possible that Duval or his girlfriend could be spotted at the hospital when the two of them are on a guarded floor, surrounded by FBI agents?"

Novello looked embarrassed, as if the security breach was a personal failure. "The Russian agent came on Duval's floor this morning disguised as a hospital custodian. It's taken Duval this long to remember who the guy was. Duval remembers him from the clean-up crew at the accident site."

Pinzon understood the implications immediately. "Christ, you know what the Russians are going to do when they hear about this?" he asked. "Do you know how they'll react when they realize Duval is alive, and we're hiding him?"

"Well, it seems to me—" began Greenwood.

"Gentlemen," interrupted the president. "I approve option 'Low Blow.'"

All conversation stopped. Moran looked at his watch. "Admiral, it's twelve-ten PM right now. When can we commence?"

"Everything can be go in an hour or so, one-fifteen, one-thirty at the latest, sir."

"Then do it. It's now 'Operation Low Blow,' and it starts as soon as possible. Rubio, have Secretary Price inform the French and British leaders now. We also must get word to the Chinese."

"Yes, Mr. President."

"And get word to the congressional leadership immediately. Fill them in as best you can, and tell the House and Senate Majority and Minority leaders that they are welcome to join us here immediately, if they wish. It is not a demand."

"Yes, Mr. President."

"Ambassador Given is ready in Moscow?"

"He's standing by," said Pinzon. "Turgenev is in Moscow, and he's agreed to see us on short notice if we ask."

The president again looked at his watch. "This is going to be the longest few hours of our lives, gentlemen. May God have mercy on us."

6:26 PM GMT (10:26 PM Magnitogorsk)

Colonel-General Uri Saratov was approached by a white-jacketed waiter as he was about to sample the caviar at the Flag Officers' Club near Katusov Prospekt in central Magnitogorsk. Katusov was the name of a young student killed in Magnitogorsk while demonstrating in support of Gorbachev during the bungled coup attempt against the Soviet leader. Saratov had promised himself that the first thing he would do when he achieved real power, was rip down Katusov's name and replace it with that of a colleague killed in Afghanistan.

The waiter cleared his throat to get Saratov's attention and handed the general a sealed envelope. Saratov opened it, read it, and immediately excused himself from the others at the table. It took him nearly twenty minutes to fight his way through traffic and reach the conference room overlooking Ilium Control.

Kachuga was waiting for him. "The others have been called, General, and they should be arriving shortly."

Saratov had no time for small talk. He removed his hat and threw his overcoat on the table.

"Let me see the dispatch, Andrei." Kachuga handed him a message attached to a clipboard. It took only a few seconds to read and when he was done, Saratov took off his glasses and turned to look down at the officers seated at their consoles in Ilium Control below. "Are we absolutely certain it is her?" he asked.

Kachuga nodded. "Yes, sir. Admiral Belovo's man knows the woman well and says there can be no mistake. He got a very good look at her."

"But still no news of the doctor?"

"No."

As they spoke, Admiral Belovo and General Bransk entered the conference room, one behind the other, and read the message. General Zhitnik and Marshal Salavat arrived a minute later and repeated the procedure.

When the five officers seated themselves around the conference table, their faces were uniformly grim.

"Gentlemen," began Saratov, "I think we can agree that this is the worst possible news."

The assembled conspirators nodded their agreement.

"We can only assume that the man, the doctor, is alive and well. And even if he isn't, the girl certainly knows enough to injure us. The fact that the Americans have lied about the girl indicates to me that they are at the very least knowledgeable about the weapon accident in Nebraska. I can't imagine that it will take them long to discover more. Perhaps they already have. In view of that and our previous discussion, I believe the time has come to strike."

Admiral Belovo jumped from his chair. "Just like that? Just blow them to pieces? Two hundred fifty million victims?" Belovo was severely agitated.

Saratov felt a distinct pleasure at Belovo's distress. He had long suspected that Admiral Belovo lacked guts. If he hadn't needed his international security operation, he would never have enlisted the assistance of such an indecisive and sniveling officer. He spoke softly, trying not to reveal his contempt.

"Admiral, I don't believe now is the time to worry about American victims or bourgeois morality. We have to worry about our nation first. The Americans will strike if they know what is happening. We must cripple them and decapitate them before they launch."

General Bransk would be the swing vote, and everyone knew it. Bransk was not a man easily bullied, and, while he recognized Saratov as first among equals, he wasn't intimidated by his fellow officer.

"General Saratov, I agree with your overall analysis. But I believe we can wait a while longer before striking. As we concluded before, it's one thing for the Americans to discover a nuclear weapon and quite another for them to confirm that it is ours and that there are others." Bransk paused, lit an enormous Cuban cigar with a flip-top lighter, and exhaled the spent smoke across the table. "I suggest we upgrade Operation Ilium to War Alert and stand by."

Belovo was aghast. "Go to War Alert? Transmit the Arm Order? This is premature. This is—"

"Listen to yourself, Belovo," said Saratov. "You're losing control, you sound like a housewife."

General Bransk again tried the middle ground. "We should be prudent, not hasty. Obviously we have to be ready to strike instantly, given the circumstances. Let's arm and stand by."

The debate continued for more than ten minutes, but no minds were changed. Saratov could count. Belovo would vote against any action, Bransk was for something in between, and the two others would go with whichever way the wind was blowing. He could not prevail.

"I can support General Bransk's option," said Saratov. "We arm the weapons and prepare to instantly respond to any danger. Do we agree?"

Bransk raised his hand. Zhitnik and Salavat glanced around the table, and then together quietly raised their hands. Only Belovo was not in favor.

"That's it then. Kachuga, sound general quarters, order the operations center to War Alert and prepare the arming order for my signature."

Saratov waved at General Bransk's cigar smoke with his left hand, indicating that it bothered him. When Bransk made no effort to douse his cigar, Saratov gave up and returned to the decision that had just been made. "All of us will now reside here at Ilium Control. At the slightest American provocation, we strike. Agreed?"

Except for Belovo, whose hands were shaking, and Kachuga who had no say, the men in the room nodded in agreement.

7:15 PM GMT (3:15 AM Pechora)

Colonel Valery Shurtin sniffed the early morning air outside the Pechora complex. Based on the smell and the declining temperatures,

Shurtin guessed he would see the first wisps of snow in less than fifteen minutes and a heavy downfall within the hour. He stubbed out his cigarette with the toe of his custom-made military boot and, cupping his hands over his mouth, warmed them with his breath.

"You're wanted inside, Colonel."

Shurtin turned to see the young face of an army corporal. The man was pointing back toward the command center, a single-story prefabricated building situated a hundred yards from the power plant. Shurtin nodded his understanding and, scanning the skies one last time, pulled up the collar of his greatcoat before turning toward the center.

Inside, Shurtin was greeted by an agitated army officer holding a message board in his hand. "This just came in a minute ago, Colonel, while you were taking your smoke break," said the major.

Shurtin read the single line dispatch. He squinted his eyes and frowned. "No test message?"

"We've double-checked, sir. It's not a test."

Shurtin momentarily felt queasy, then forced himself to overcome it. "Very well, Major. Sound General Quarters immediately." Shurtin hurried to a position at a central computer console facing fifteen other computer workstations and watched men scrambling into position as the alarm for General Quarters pounded out a steady and ear-splitting "clang, clang, clang" throughout the buildings and grounds of the central Pechora complex. He checked the electronic clock on his screen and put on a headset. He spoke to the major without looking at him. "Status, Major?"

"Condition Alpha, War Alert in ten seconds, Colonel."

As the second hand of his watch brushed twelve, Shurtin heard the General Quarters alarm go silent, and listened to a disembodied voice over his headset. "Pechora Control is at Condition Alpha, War Alert."

Shurtin looked at his screen and responded. "This is Colonel Shurtin, senior duty watch officer, Pechora Control. I have Command, the major is second." Shurtin took a deep breath. "This is not a test. Commence pretransmission checks for an Operational Arm Order," he said into his microphone.

The major began the process. "Power?" he said into his headset.

"Five million, nominal," answered a technician.

"Oscillators?"

"One, three, and four synchronized, two gaining," answered a second voice.

"Carrier?"

"Nominal."

"Modulation?"

"Nominal."

"Crypto?"

"Crypto is on standby; code status checked and verified, pins checked."

In less than two minutes, the pretransmission checks were complete. Shurtin's computer screen showed green checkmarks from top to bottom. Shurtin had been through the routine on test runs many times before and had every item on the checklist memorized, much as an airline pilot does. He knew exactly which systems often gave trouble and which were trouble free. Two times before, in test runs, he had gone to War Alert and actually transmitted a test signal. Each test had gone better than the one before, and Shurtin was confident he could reach 99 percent of the weapons in the United States on his first real try.

Still, he felt nervous. He wondered if this perhaps wasn't a test too, a test of his loyalty or ability to react quickly. Shurtin felt a nervous rumble in his stomach. Whatever was going on, he thought to himself, he was ready and so were his men.

Ten minutes later, Shurtin saw the Arm Order from Ilium Control in Magnitogorsk spring to blinking life in large white letters on his computer screen. The agitated major spun in his chair to look Shurtin in the eye. His expression was startled and fearful.

Shurtin nodded to indicate that what the major was seeing was no illusion. He pushed a button on his console and spoke into his headset.

"This is senior duty watch officer, Pechora Control, and we have Arm Order 'Sierra' from Ilium Control. Prepare to Transmit Arm Order 'Sierra' on my mark."

"On mark," said several voices.

Shurtin realized that his heart was beating as if he were in a foot race, and he paused to catch his breath. "Stand by to transmit," he huffed into his headset.

"Standing by," came the disembodied voices again.

Shurtin paused briefly, then spoke. "Ready."

Except for the hum of computer cooling fans, Pechora Control was absolutely silent. Shurtin could hear his own breathing in his headset, and it sounded almost like panting. One more time he tried to catch his breath, and when he succeeded he gave the final order. "Execute!"

The lights in Pechora Control dimmed briefly as power suddenly drained from the power plant into hundreds of miles of copper cable. "Arm Order 'Sierra' away," said a voice on the intercom. "Sequence nominal, transmission nominal."

"Magnitogorsk confirms," said another voice.

Shurtin began to relax as he watched the numbers and letters of the Arm Order, slowly, one by one, materialize on his screen. He estimated a Full Arm all across America in two minutes.

7:25 PM GMT (1:25 PM Chicago)

"Todd! Todd! Wake up. The machines are coming on-line!"

Todd Walters was dreaming, and it took him several seconds to realize that he wasn't being jostled back and forth by a rocking subway. Instead, he felt the hand of Josh Scribbner shaking him. "What'd you say, Josh?"

"The computers. In the garage. They're receiving a message, a transmission! They're decoding some kind of message. Jesus, Todd, this may be it!"

Walters bolted upright in the front seat of the van and instinctively checked his watch. He'd been snoozing only a few minutes. He threw open the door and, with Scribbner at his side, double-timed down the driveway past the frail old man named Leon Koziak and into the garage at the back of the house. Koziak was smiling. Two other men, one an FBI agent and the second a computer expert from the University of Chicago, were leaning over the bank of three computers. Walters edged between them and looked at the screens. The middle computer, the one he had swapped, was blank. The other two were alive with dancing electronic imagery. The top half of each screen was filled with row upon row of rapidly changing letters and digits. The characters changed too quickly for the human eye to follow, reminding Walters of the arrival and departure boards at European airports when they list again the day's flights. The bottom half of both screens was calmer. Two large white letters, *D* and *P*, stood out in bold, quiet peace on the left side of the screen. As Walters watched in wonder, a third letter, *M*, suddenly joined the two already present. It didn't take an electronics whiz to see that the computer was receiving a complex incoming message and decoding it to a handful of letters. When complete, those letters would order the weapon to do something. Walters looked at the boiler to confirm to himself that it was no longer attached to the computer bank.

"What do you think?" he asked the expert from the University of Chicago.

240

"I think this is pretty clearly an Arming Order. When this sequence is complete in about a minute, that bomb will be armed and ready to fire." The man corrected himself. "Well, it would be if it were still plugged in."

The computer expert had only confirmed what Walters already knew. He picked up a cellular telephone and began dialing a number in Washington. Although raised Roman Catholic, Walters was not a particularly religious man. As he waited for the phone connection to be made and watched another large letter solidify on the screen, he surprised himself by silently reciting a prayer.

7:30 PM GMT (2:30 PM Washington D.C.)

In the White House situation room, the phones seemed to come alive in unison. From Walters in Chicago and a National Security Agency listening post in Fauquier County, Virginia, and at NSA headquarters outside Washington, the message was the same. The Russians were transmitting an Arming Order, and in less than a minute more than sixty hydrogen bombs secreted across America would be ready to fire.

President Moran paced back and forth in front of a situation screen, continually referring to his watch and listening to shouted messages from various military personnel. "Anything from *Aurora*?" he asked of no one in particular, knowing the answer.

"Nothing, sir," said an Air Force major sitting at a console with a headset on. "ETA is seventy minutes, sir."

The president looked at his watch again, then turned to Rubio Pinzon. "Maybe we should pull them, Rubio."

"Pull the phones? Now? But that will tip off the Russians that we're on to them. I thought the plan called for us to wait until impact was—"

"But if they're arming, why wait?" The president searched the eyes of his advisors. It was clear to him that no one was certain of the proper move.

"I'll give you all five minutes to think about it," Moran said. "In my view, we ought to shut down the system now, but I'll wait five minutes for a credible objection." He looked at his watch. It was accurate to within three seconds and read 2:37 PM.

7:40 PM GMT (1:40 PM Chicago)

Leon Koziak had the face and physique of a curmudgeon. To agent Todd Walters, the frail old man could easily have walked straight off a Vermont dairy farm, the kind of farm where people don't talk much to strangers and keep their words, even among themselves, to a bare minimum.

It was understandable, then, that even an experienced and skeptical agent like Walters would not suspect that beneath his Robert Frost exterior, Leon Koziak did not adhere to the New England virtues of hard work, self-reliance, frugality, honesty, or reticence. He had, in fact, a criminal record longer than most of the residents of San Quentin and had spent a good portion of his life in and out of one jail or another for everything from check-bouncing to printing his own food stamps. Koziak's background would have been easy enough to check, but in his haste to examine the garage, Walters had temporarily let the matter slide.

As the two agents in his living room sipped coffee and watched the afternoon soap operas, Koziak excused himself to take a shower and clean up for a late lunch, which he planned to make for himself. Once upstairs, he hurried to the telephone beside his bed, and picking up the handset was surprised and delighted to hear the sound of a working line.

"Jerks," he said to himself, thinking of the agents downstairs.

He had despised the police, everyone from the Cook County Sheriff to the head of the FBI for as long as he could remember, and anything he could do, anytime, to make their life more miserable was a godsend, a little bit of something to bring joy to the humdrum routine of his declining years.

He opened an address book, and moving his bony index finger through the pages, found the number he was looking for. It was a 202 area code, which he knew was a Washington, D.C., number. Long distance, he thought. It could be expensive. He paused briefly, but dialed anyway. 1-202-555-7218. When a man's voice answered at the other end, Koziak identified himself and spoke plainly:

"Hey, buddy. This is Leon Koziak in Chicago. That's right, Koziak. You know that the FBI is crawling all over my garage? There must be ten of 'em here. They're having a wonderful time with your machine, taking pictures, cutting wires, opening it up. See ya now."

Koziak hung up the phone without waiting for a response. He chuckled to himself and headed for his shower.

"Fucking FBI," he said.

7:43 PM GMT (2:43 PM Washington D.C.)
"Okay, gentlemen," said the President. "Any objections?"
No one could think of any.

"Pull them now, then," ordered President Moran.

In a huge, three-floor complex in Manhattan, at seaside terminals in Maine, New Jersey, and Florida, at a satellite receiving station in Colorado, and at other long distance routing centers across America, technicians began snapping switches and typing into electronic terminals. Within fifteen seconds, the entire United States long distance phone system was inoperable.

A man in Detroit talking to his mother in Seattle suddenly heard the phone go dead. A college student in Birmingham trying to call his girlfriend in Shreveport found himself connected to a pet shop in Milwaukee.

Most people attempting long distance calls couldn't even get a line. The recording, "I'm sorry, your call cannot be completed as dialed," was heard by thousands of frustrated callers from Irvine to Ipswich. Except for the independent military phone system, the United States hadn't been so disconnected since before the invention of the telegraph. President Moran watched the situation screen reflect his order and turned to Admiral Greenwood.

"Cat's out of the bag, Admiral."

"Aye, sir," said Greenwood, turning to speak into his headset.

8:16 PM GMT (12:16 AM Magnitogorsk)

Colonel-General Uri Saratov couldn't contain his fury, and the walls of the conference room at Ilium Control barely muffled his booming voice. He picked up the message before him with both hands and shook it.

"Will somebody please fucking explain to me why a fucking message from Chicago took thirty-six fucking minutes to reach us here at Ilium Control? Are we all fucking incompetents?"

No one would look the raging commander in the eye. Even the normally unruffled Bransk looked wary. Kachuga finally spoke.

"Our people in Washington couldn't use normal communications. Something went wrong with the phones. We've been assured it's just a temporary problem at our Washington communications site. They had to radio relay the message they got from Chicago, and it took time to set up."

Saratov wasn't mollified, and he barked at his fellow conspirators while waving Koziak's message in his right hand. "Are you satisfied now, gentlemen? Is this goddamn proof enough for you?"

Bransk affirmed that it was proof enough for him.

"The Americans are now tearing apart one of our weapons," continued Saratov, "and that leaves us absolutely no options. We must now attack. It is kill or be killed."

Belovo was falling apart. His hair was unkempt, his tie askew. He paced nervously near the center of the conference room, continually licking his dry lips like some overgrown, pink reptile. "But the Americans have not gone to Full Alert. There is nothing to indicate they are going to launch. We must wait, Uri!"

Saratov snapped back. "You have lost your nerve, Belovo—and your sense. They are ripping the guts out of one of our weapons as we speak, and you want to wait? For what? To die?"

"But General, the American leadership is in Washington! Moran is not in the airborne command post; the blast doors at NORAD aren't secured. They are *not* doing anything."

Saratov didn't respond. He looked at Bransk, Zhitnik, and Salavat. "A show of hands, please."

"Attack," said Bransk.

"Agree," said the two generals simultaneously.

"That's it then," said Saratov. He looked at Kachuga. "The attack command and the Authenticator are loaded, Andrei?"

"Yes, General." Saratov prepared to leave the conference room for the floor of Ilium Control. "Make an order for General Quarters."

Because it was already on war alert, Ilium Control was fully manned for an attack exercise. Although the duty officers noted with curiosity the unusual presence of General Saratov at the 'Command' computer station, most of them had no idea that they were about to commence a real attack.

"This is Ilium Command," said Saratov into a headset. "Prepare to transmit Fire Command 'Tango' on my mark."

"Standing by," answered a chorus of anonymous voices.

Admiral Belovo reached across Saratov's computer screen and grabbed him by the shoulders. "But Uri, you can't—"

Bransk and one of the generals grabbed Belovo from behind and pulled him away. "Sergeant, arrest this man," said Saratov to a security guard. "Get him out of here, now!"

Belovo did not go quietly. He struggled with the sergeant and the two other enlisted men who came to assist. He let his knees buckle, forcing the men to drag him from the room. "You're mad, Saratov, a lunatic! You will be the death of us all, you will destroy every—"

Belovo's ravings were cut off by the heavy soundproof door that slammed behind him as he was hauled from Ilium Control. Saratov straightened his tunic, as if the act of straightening his uniform would restore discipline to the room. He spoke into his headset. "Firing sequence?"

"Firing sequence loaded and—"

"Anomaly in Program X2B," interrupted another voice. "Checking program lines now."

For eight minutes the technicians at workstations ran through computerized lists to track down the glitch in the automatic firing sequence. When they found it, Saratov took control. "Firing sequence?" he said.

"Firing sequence loaded and locked," answered a voice.

"Excellent," replied Saratov. "Stand by for Fire Command 'Tango.'" He paused for two beats. "Ready. Execute!"

Saratov and two other officers turned the keys on their consoles and fire command 'Tango' flowed eastward.

Two seconds later in Pechora, Colonel Shurtin and two of his colleagues repeated the procedure. The coded order to fire began streaming from Pechora, pushed across the surface of the earth by the power of five million watts.

Exactly one minute later, the Authenticator would follow on the Fire Command's electromagnetic heels.

8:31 PM GMT (2:31 PM Chicago)

In the garage on North Halstead Street in Chicago, the word *ARMED* was flashing in English in two-inch high Roman letters on the two computer screens. The rows of dancing characters and the eleven-character letter-number sequence they had decoded were gone. Agent Walters thought it was the most frightening thing he had ever seen. He turned to speak to Josh Scribbner, taking his eyes off the console. "Josh—"

"Something's happening!" said another man.

Walters turned toward the University of Chicago computer expert who uttered the words. The man's widening eyes were riveted on the computers.

Walters looked. The screen had changed. The word *ARMED* was now gone, replaced again by a half screen of dancing letters and numbers, as the machines began deciphering Pechora's lethal message. A large solitary *A* popped onto the lower left half of the screen, followed seconds later by a *T*.

"My God, my God, this *is* it!" said the computer expert from Chicago.

"The launch order? The order to *fire?*" Walters barked, afraid of his own question.

"Yes! Yes! They're going to fire." The expert pulled a card from his shirt pocket and held it in his shaking right hand. "The next letter will be a *W.* It's all in the program we took apart."

Walters felt his body begin to shake as he watched the letter *W* join the *A* and *T* already on the screen. "Now what? What happens next?"

"Eight more letters and this sequence is complete. Then there will be a five-letter Authenticator, and that's it. Two minutes or so later, the weapons will blow!"

One minute later, Walters watched the eleventh and final letter of the sequence lock in. The computer screen turned red, and four, two-inch-high white letters began pulsating rapidly. Walters thought that for the first time in his life he was going to faint.

In English, the flashing letters spelled *FIRE.*

8:34 PM GMT (6:34 AM Sea of Japan)

On board the USS *Salt Lake City,* a hundred feet or so below the surface of the Sea of Japan, Captain Morris Hackel also studied his watch. The calculations had been carefully made, but estimating flight time can be a tricky business. Like airplanes, cruise missiles are affected by wind speed and direction, air temperature, density, altitude, humidity, and a host of other factors. His best guess was that the first weapon would impact in two to six minutes, but he wouldn't be surprised to be off by a couple of minutes either way.

"Mr. Hoffman," he said into a speaker, "this is the captain. Let's bring her up to periscope depth and see what we can find out."

Captain Hackel was less worried about time than about malfunction. Fourteen hundred miles was a long shot, at the extreme range of the Tomahawk III missile, and a lot could go wrong. The Tomahawk navigated by receiving radio transmissions from a number of Global Positioning Satellites (GPS) in orbit around the earth, and compared their signals to an internal map of the geography it was flying over. GPS was accurate down to a few yards and very reliable. Even civilian GPS receivers, available at any electronic outlet, were accurate to a hundred feet, and the receivers on the Tomahawk III were an order or magnitude better. Still, Hackel worried. Any piece of equipment made by man could and would occasionally fail.

Hackel knew that for all their successes in real combat, cruise missiles could screw up like anything else. That's why he'd fired two.

If the first one worked, the second would be destroyed by the explosion before it could detonate. If the first one failed, the second would back it up. Hackel didn't worry about opposition. The Tomahawk III not only had nearly twice the range of the original Tomahawk but had incorporated the latest in stealth technology. With radar-absorbing skin coatings and other secret design tricks, the missile had the radar cross-section of a hummingbird. Hackel's two missiles would spend most of their flight time traversing remote sections of northeast China, and Hackel doubted the Chinese would even spot the low-flying, terrain-hugging missiles. Even if they did, he figured they were unlikely to find a way to shoot them down. When they crossed the Russian border east of Chita, they would be home free. The Russian military had so deteriorated that Hackel figured that most of the air search radars along the Chinese border were either inoperable or manned by bored and resentful conscripts who could barely keep their eyes open in the wee hours of the morning.

The missiles had now been airborne just over two hours and fifteen minutes. A ballistic missile would have been a lot faster, he thought. Of course, he reminded himself, a ballistic missile was very visible, even on faulty equipment, and would attract a lot of attention and give whomever was being attacked the warning necessary to fire back.

He looked at his watch nervously. One minute to impact. Estimated.

"Bring up the receiving antennas, Mr. Hoffman. We're supposed to be hearing a little static shortly."

8:35 PM GMT (4:35 AM Pechora)

At Pechora, Colonel Shurtin prepared to send the final order. "Stand by to send Authenticator," he barked into his headset.

"Authenticator on standby."

Shurtin put his hand on his firing key, a device similar to an old roller skate key. After receiving the Authenticator command from Magnitogorsk on their computer screens, Shurtin and two other officers would twist their firing keys a quarter turn to the right and the Authenticator would radiate from Pechora to the world.

"Okay, gentlemen," he said into his headset. "Just like this was an exercise. Just like in practice. When the Authenticator command comes from Magnitogorsk Control, we execute on my mark. Everybody clear?"

No one answered.

8:36 PM GMT (4:36 AM Pechora)

The explosion was first spotted by Air Force Major Sergei Yakalov, flying over the Lake Baikal area near Pechora. Yakalov was a first generation American, but his parents' interest in education and his own drive had brought the thirty-eight-year-old man to near the top of his profession. He was cruising his *Aurora* SR92 at 112,000 feet and Mach 3.6 when a brilliant flash to his left snapped him to attention. He looked west over the great expanse of tundra and forest below him and saw the first traces of the immense fireball northeast of Lake Baikal, 175 miles away. He forced his eyes from the sight and scanned his instruments. The electromagnetic radiation had already impressed itself on his aircraft's sensors and their recorders. There could be no doubt about it. The missile had struck. He checked a side-scan, synthetic aperture radar linked to GPS and softly whistled. The Tomahawk was right on target.

8:42 PM GMT (12:42 AM Magnitogorsk)

Colonel-General Uri Saratov stared at the wall-sized map of the United States now filling the status board at Magnitogorsk Control. The nuclear detonations would be picked up by satellites with microwave, infrared, and radiomagnetic detectors. The locations of the explosions would be measured against GPS satellites for position, and signaled via deep space communication satellites to Magnitogorsk. Each explosion would be represented on the status screen by a red circle, with a slash through it.

At precisely one minute after the transmission of the Authenticator, Saratov could feel his heartbeat quicken. Any second now, he said to himself, any second now. Saratov began feeling some anxiety thirty seconds later when no circles appeared on the screen. A minute later he could contain himself no longer. "Status report" he roared into his headset.

"Nothing to report, Comrade Colonel-General," came a voice. "No confirmed detonation, sir."

Saratov scanned the board again. "How about seismic?" he asked. "Anything from seismic?"

"No seismic activity," came a second voice.

"No electromagnetic either," came a third.

"General," said a young officer. "Moscow reports they're still getting CNN, sir. Atlanta still exists, sir."

Another minute went by before Saratov could admit to himself that something had gone horribly wrong. "Activate secondary systems."

No one spoke.

"Activate secondary systems!" yelled Saratov with all his might.

"Sir, we're trying, sir. But we can't raise Pechora, sir," said a young officer at a nearby console.

"What do you mean you can't raise Pechora?"

"All communications with Pechora are dead, sir. Land-line, radio. We can't get them sir."

"Seismic activity!" barked someone over the headset.

The man's voice was shaking, but Saratov felt exhilaration. "At last," he answered. "Where is it?"

"We're getting a huge seismic disturbance near Lake Baikal, sir, near Pechora." Saratov could not understand what that meant. Seismic activity near Pechora? It made no sense. He momentarily panicked. "Have the Americans fired? Anything from central surveillance?"

"Surveillance indicates the Americans are not on alert and have launched no ballistic missiles, sir."

Saratov couldn't reconcile the facts he was hearing, but he had no time for further consideration.

"Any communication with Pechora yet?"

"No, sir."

"Then we activate the secondary system from here. Now." He looked down at his console. "I want an Authenticator order out immediately. All systems ready?"

"Secondary system ready, sir."

"On my mark. Ready. Stand by." He paused to make sure everyone was with him. "Execute." Keys were switched to activate the automatic dialers in Washington and Winnipeg. The room suddenly became quiet. The status board did not change, no voices came over the headset. No orders, no commands, no confirmations.

"Well, what's going on?" yelled Saratov.

"Sir, the Authenticator order is not being received," came a timid voice. "What? Why not?"

"Sir, we can't get any calls connected. We're getting through to Winnipeg, but Winnipeg can't get through to anyplace else. We're not getting Washington at all."

Saratov roared. "What the hell is going on?"

"Winnipeg is getting busy signals or a recording saying our calls cannot go through. We're trying backup numbers and routes, but nothing is happening."

Saratov wouldn't give up. He pushed a button on the console in front of him that connected to the intelligence and analysis desk. "What is our analysis?"

The man at the other end sounded flustered. He stammered twice before uttering a coherent sentence. "We're being blocked at the other end, sir. They are purposely blocking us, sir."

Saratov slumped back into his chair. He continued watching the status board, but a look of resignation, almost boredom, had inscribed itself across his face. He half-consciously monitored the rising confusion and disarray reflected in the voices of the officers and men of Ilium Control as they chattered nervously over their headsets. Soon, all semblance of military order and discipline had broken down.

"We have failed, Comrade Kachuga," said Saratov, as his aide approached.

"No, General. I would say the failure is entirely yours." For a moment Saratov seemed surprised by his aide's impertinence. Then his expression turned to fear. Kachuga pulled a 9mm Baretta from his tunic. Aiming squarely at Saratov's heart, he quickly pulled the trigger. When he was certain that Saratov was dead, Kachuga put the gun to his left temple. He fired again.

8:45 PM GMT (3:45 PM Washington D.C.)

President Frank Moran ordered the nationwide FBI raids to begin the moment the Pechora detonation was confirmed. Seventeen weapons were tracked down in the first minute, others were taking longer as agents eyeballed telephone lines leading to weapons.

At about the same time, the NSA and CIA, using the separate military telephone system, confirmed to the situation room that no further transmissions were being received at the weapons sites in Chicago. They also confirmed that no telephone messages were getting through. Three minutes later, with forty-one weapons tracked and disconnected, the president thought he could wait no longer.

He turned to Viktor Papko, the first Russian to ever sit in the White House situation room.

"Viktor," said Moran, "the call is now going through to President Turgenev. The U.S. ambassador is with him now, explaining what he can. Incidentally, I believe you, Victor. I don't think he had any part in this. You must confirm what our ambassador is telling your president."

To the astonishment of Moran, Pinzon, and others, Papko actually had tears running down his cheeks. "I will do what I can, Mr. President. But the horror, sir. My mother country struck by a nuclear weapon?"

"A very remote part of Siberia, Viktor. I doubt there are five hundred dead. The weapon was small. The target, so far as we can tell, was hit extremely accurately. It could have been worse, Viktor. It could have been an all-out nuclear holocaust."

Papko seemed to brighten a little.

"Stress to your president that we intend no further attacks. Tell him we are not on alert." Moran paused, and then, leaning forward over the seated Russian, put his hands on Papko's shoulders. Papko took a telephone receiver from a Navy officer.

"Hello," he began. "Mr. President. It is Viktor Papko, sir. I am sitting in the White House situation room." He paused briefly. "No sir, there is no nuclear war. Be calm, sir. Please. It is all over."

Monday, October 4

It was odd to see what people really looked like. Duval could recognize almost everyone at the White House, but it was taking imagination to connect the faces before him with the younger, more glamorous images that he was used to from television and the movies. Duval was finding it amusing, and a bit frightening, that America's highest ranking politicians were just as star-struck as their constituents. Senator Kerr couldn't get enough photographs of his meeting with Sharon Stone, and Sylvester Stallone was a big favorite with everyone, even the Frenchies. Duval, himself, was pretty goggle-eyed by Cal Ripken, a star who turned out to be a pleasant, if private, man.

Michelle was surprisingly unfazed by the evening, chatting comfortably with White House chief of staff Rubio Pinzon and with some naval officer named Vandergrift. She, especially, enjoyed her conversation with the president's daughter, which shouldn't have been surprising considering how close they were in age.

Duval had been to the White House before. As part of a high school group, he had been one of the thousands of ordinary citizens who parade through the public rooms of the mansion each day. This evening he was getting a more personal look, guided by the president, himself, through the Oval Office, the Cabinet Room, and a sitting room in the private quarters. If Duval and the president didn't have a lot in common, at least they had come from similar, rural backgrounds. They both had roots in the Great Plains. Small talk was not difficult.

The State dinner itself was more pleasant than either Duval or Michelle could have imagined. The Nebraska doctor and his fiancée were also lucky to be alive. The food was superb, the celebrities fascinating, the entertainment first-rate. Not many people could say they had dined at the table of the presidents of the United States and France. Both leaders were aware of Duval's role in the events of September, but neither mentioned it over dinner.

The fact was that much of the story was still not known by the world's press, although the *New York Times* and a Japanese newspaper were getting close. Duval couldn't understand how a nuclear detonation in Russia could remain a mystery so long, but, for now at least, the world believed that a remote and largely uninhabited part of Siberia had been struck by a small, but devastating, meteor. It had happened once before in this century, and it would take some time before the world learned that the latest meteor left nuclear debris.

For a while, Duval had wondered how the previous month would change his life. In the end, he had decided that it would not change it much. He would stay in northwestern Nebraska, practice medicine, get married to Michelle, and raise a family.

President Moran turned from his daughter and faced Duval and Michelle across the table. "There's a man who should be sitting with you tonight, but he's getting some badly needed rest and recuperation in France." Moran took a sip of water and continued in a low, almost conspiratorial tone. "His name is Ushta. He's an academic, and he will soon be starting a research job at Ponts et Chaussées, an engineering school in Paris. The president of France has taken a special interest in his case." Moran turned his head and nodded in the direction of his french counterpart. "I hope someday you two can meet Ushta in person. You'll have a lot to talk about; I can guarantee it." The president smiled, as if reflecting on some private joke.

Michelle smiled back. "Certainly, Mr. President. If you say so, sir." She stopped, wondering if it would be proper to press forward. She squeezed Duval's hand and decided to be bold. "Mr. President," she began "you asked if there was anything we needed."

"Yes, Michelle?"

"Well, we've got a problem with our x-ray machine."

Moran took a place card, wrote something on it, and handed it to an aide. "Michelle," he said, "I think we can do something about that."